ACCOMPLICE TO MURDER

A British Murder Mystery

MICHAEL CAMPLING

Shadowstone
Books

GET THE SERIES PREQUEL FOR FREE

WHEN YOU JOIN THE AWKWARD SQUAD - THE HOME OF PICKY READERS

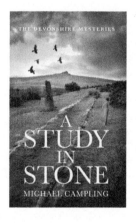

Visit: michaelcampling.com/freebooks

This book is dedicated to Jake and Zach; princes among men.

If you want something very, very badly, let it go free. If it comes back to you, it's yours forever. If it doesn't, it was never yours to begin with.

— JESS LAIR

PROLOGUE

The room is dark, lit only by the blue-white glow from my laptop's screen.

The keyboard clicks beneath the relentless thudding of my too-fast fingers.

It's all there. Every possible course of action plotted out in painstaking detail, every outcome laid out in rows and columns. Facts and figures. Pros and cons. Risks and rewards.

I'm feeling my way, sifting through the data, looking for the one path that will make everything all right. But I'm getting nowhere, lost in a sea of doubt.

Unless…

I stop suddenly, staring at the screen, and my chest tightens. *Oh no.* My mind spins and I force myself to breathe, exhaling in a long, unsteady breath.

"I can't do that," I whisper into the darkness, but the logic remains, the data indisputable; stark black letters stretched across the glaring white background.

A sly question creeps into my mind, unbidden: *What if I could get away with it?*

No. There must be another option, a way out. I wait, my hands curled so tightly into fists that my fingernails nip my skin. I need the pain, need something to tether me to the real world. Because I shouldn't even be thinking of such a terrible thing. It's a bad dream, a fantasy. I can't let it linger in my mind or it will overwhelm me, swallow me up in its madness. I have to beat this, escape its inexorable logic. I cannot admit defeat.

But my fingers find the keyboard, like the hands of a puppet, pulled by fine threads of fate, and words appear on the screen, the skeleton of a plan.

I read the text as it forms in front of me and I can't hold back the moan that creeps from my throat.

But the dark voice inside me grows stronger. *You can do it*, it says. *The dead tell no tales.*

A tremor runs through me, fear mingled with revulsion. In a flash of anger, I slam the laptop shut. I hang my head, covering my face with my hands, fingertips pressing hard against my eyes until I see starbursts of green.

After a while, my mind grows still, the turmoil replaced by a sense of acceptance. I *will* have to do this. I have no choice.

MONDAY

CHAPTER 1

D an Corrigan adjusted his tie without breaking his stride as he advanced on his destination. Tucked away discreetly behind Exeter Cathedral, Southernhay West was stirring into the type of early morning life found in cities all over the world. Smartly dressed people climbed from their cars and bustled toward their places of work. Vans and taxis vied to be the first away from the traffic lights, and colourfully clad cyclists pedalled past, their backpacks bulging. No doubt they'd be carrying a change of clothes for the office, a pair of smart shoes and a laptop too. Dan had his own small backpack slung over his shoulder, although for him the circumstances were reversed; dressed in his best suit, he'd brought along his sports kit in case he fancied a run after work.

A bus trundled by, belching exhaust fumes, and Dan smiled, feeling a certain kinship with his fellow travellers. With every stride, every urgent turn of the pedals, they proclaimed a sense of purpose. They weren't here for the shops or the scenery; they were here to work. An atmosphere of energy and purpose buzzed all around him. Everyone was going somewhere, and none of them wanted to be late.

That includes me, Dan thought. *But I've got plenty of time.* Dan had been in Exeter for quite a while already, although his appointment wasn't for another half an hour. He'd parked down by the quay, and then he'd spent the time walking through the city, limbering up, and while he'd pounded the streets, he'd felt his senses becoming heightened, his mind growing sharper.

It's good to be taking on a proper job, he told himself. *I'm back.* But there was something different about his latest foray into the world of work. He wasn't stepping into his old life. Not quite. There was none of the stress, the underlying anxiety that had driven him to compete until he'd burned himself out.

This time, he felt in control. He was independent, a freelance business intelligence consultant. It had taken him almost a year to get this far: a year of taking on small jobs with firms that could hardly afford to pay him properly; a year of hunkering down in cramped offices, drinking bad coffee, and fighting to keep his head above water; months of returning home tired, only to spend his evenings studying to refresh his skills.

But he'd been determined to carve out a niche for himself and here he was, about to start his first big contract, and he'd been headhunted no less. The company had contacted him out of the blue and he'd seized the opportunity. His new life was about to begin.

Corinthian House was visible from some distance away, its brutal red brick and plate glass construction at odds with its more genteel neighbours. When Dan had told Alan about today's appointment, Alan had called the place a carbuncle and muttered something about it spoiling a row of beautiful Georgian town houses. Dan had told him that it was no use railing against progress, but Alan hadn't been swayed.

"That monstrosity isn't there because of progress," Alan had argued. "It's all down to the Luftwaffe." And Alan had explained, not for the first time, about the so-called Baedeker Blitz: the wartime bombing campaign that had targeted the cities mapped out in considerable detail in the Baedeker guidebooks meant for tourists. A campaign that had left Exeter's city centre pockmarked with craters that would later give rise to a cobbled-together collection of the old and the new, mellow medieval stonework cheek by jowl with fifties modernism.

Dan had endured Alan's lecture without batting an eye. He was going back to work, and at last his financial worries would be over. He'd enjoyed his time away from the pressures of commerce, but he'd grown increasingly concerned about the state of his bank balance. Certainly, he'd learned a great deal while he'd been tackling all those cases with Alan, but that hadn't paid his bills. It was time to step back into the real world. It was time to grow up.

As if reading his mind, Dan's phone emitted a muted beep from the inside pocket of his jacket. Twenty-five minutes to his appointment. If he slowed his pace, he'd breeze in through the front doors of the office with twenty minutes to spare. Perfect.

Or would that be too early? Would it make him seem too eager to please?

Dan slowed to a halt, and someone barged into him from behind. Dan turned around, an apology on his lips, but the middle-aged man simply tutted in disapproval and stomped onward, not even sparing a backward glance.

Rude, Dan thought. *What's the matter with him?* But as Dan resumed his journey he remembered, with a twinge of regret, that when he'd lived in London, he'd always hated it when people dawdled on the pavements, especially during rush hour. *That was the old me*, he told himself. *I'm different now, aren't I?*

Dan straightened his jacket and strode onward, heading

for the steps that led up to the main entrance of Corinthian House.

The plate glass doors, emblazoned with the navy-blue letters CEG, the logo of the Corinthian Enterprise Group, slid aside noiselessly, and Dan stepped into the air-conditioned interior. He'd arrived.

Dan presented himself to the reception desk, which was staffed by an elegantly dressed young woman equipped with a Bluetooth headset and Nordic good looks, her ash-blonde hair and pale complexion emphasising the dazzling blue of her eyes. "Good morning," she said. "I'm Samantha. How may I help you today?"

"Morning. I'm Daniel Corrigan. I have an appointment with Mr Cooper."

Samantha referred to her computer. "Perfect. I'll let Mr Cooper know you're here. Please take a seat, and someone will come down to meet you in a moment."

"Thanks. I'll wait over there, but I prefer to stand. After all, why sit when there's no reason not to stay on your feet?"

Samantha seemed mildly bewildered by this, so Dan blundered on. "They say the chair is the killer, don't they? We're not really designed to sit down all day. It's not good for our muscles." Dan glanced at Samantha's high-backed chair and hurriedly added, "Not that I mean to imply any criticism of people who prefer to sit. Some people have to, of course, for their jobs."

Samantha favoured him with a professional smile, but a slight lowering of her eyebrows revealed a hint of concern. "Would you like a glass of water or anything, Mr Corrigan?"

"No, thank you. I'm fine." Dan knew he should walk away, but he was certain that Samantha had already marked him down as an awkward customer. That was no good. He couldn't start his new role by creating a bad impression the moment he walked through the door. *Take a deep breath*, he told himself. *Start again*. Dan searched for something to say, but beneath Samantha's glacial gaze, his mind was a blank. "It's nice and cool in here," he managed, "but it's getting warm outside. I think it's going to be a nice day."

"Yes, I believe so." Samantha smiled again. "Mr Corrigan, I'm sure someone will come down to collect you in a moment." She raised a hand to her headset. "I'll tell them you're here. Please, have a... I mean, please make yourself comfortable in the seating area." Samantha seemed to be waiting for Dan to move away, so he thanked her for her help and then obliged, stepping over to the cluster of comfortable chairs grouped around a coffee table.

That went well, Dan thought. He cast his eye over the publications arrayed on the table, hoping to catch up with some of the magazines he used to buy, but there were only glossy brochures for CEG, the covers showing nothing more interesting than stock photos of athletic-looking people, all with white-toothed smiles, all with that dead-behind-the-eyes expression that robbed them of any character. Most of them, of course, were wearing branded leisurewear.

CEG owned a raft of smaller companies that manufactured sporting goods in factories all over the world. They had links with supermarkets and online retailers, but that meant their goods were rebranded and sold at low prices. Millions of people around the globe wore shoes and clothes made by CEG, but hardly anyone had heard of the brand. Nike and Adidas had nothing to worry about. But that was all set to change. CEG had big plans, but first they needed to make the group more profitable. They were restructuring their operation, and that's where Dan came in.

Dan glanced back at Samantha and saw that she was reapplying her lip gloss with one hand while holding up her phone with the other, intent on her own image on the screen. She would definitely go by her full name, Dan decided. He thought of Sam, who ran the pub near his home in Embervale. It was hard to imagine ever calling her Samantha, but then the two women could hardly have been more different.

The face that the receptionist showed to the world was a creation: the result of long hours spent reshaping eyebrows and applying expensive beauty products, foregoing all carbohydrates and caffeine in favour of spinach smoothies and the latest superfoods, whereas Sam's beauty was natural. It was in the warmth of her smile and the way her eyes sparkled when she laughed. Dan knew which style he preferred.

Footsteps ringing out on the polished granite floor snapped Dan out of his reverie, and he looked up to see a besuited man heading toward him. Dan hadn't heard the lift arrive, and he noticed that the glass door at one side of the lobby was still swinging shut. *He took the stairs*, Dan thought. *A young man in a hurry.*

"Dan," the man called out as he strode across the lobby. "Good morning."

"Morning." Dan pulled back his shoulders, hoping he looked more relaxed than he felt as he stepped forward to meet the new arrival. They shook hands, and the man's grip was firm.

"I'm Joseph Clayton," the man said. "But call me Joe. We like to keep things friendly around here." Slim and fresh faced, Joe exuded self-confidence and energy. His smile was genuine, and there was something about Joe's manner that made Dan like him right away.

"Nice to meet you, Joe." Dan returned Joe's smile, but he held back from saying more. He couldn't recall anyone mentioning the name Clayton, and Joe hadn't given his job title. He could be an assistant or an intern, despatched to collect the visitor from reception. On the other hand, Joe's suit looked tailor made and very new. Dan had already made one gaffe with the receptionist and he didn't want to make any more hasty assumptions.

"You're probably itching to get started," Joe said. "I know we're all looking forward to working with you. You came highly recommended."

"That's very kind. I've worked with a lot of up-and-coming businesses in the area. I've been lucky."

"Please, no false modesty. That wasn't luck. I know a carefully thought-out strategy when I see one. You've been making waves in the business community, and I dare say you aren't done yet. Am I right?"

"You could be," Dan admitted with a smile. "If you don't mind me asking, Joe, have you spent some time in the States?"

"Yes, I spent a couple years over there, working for Microsoft, but I guess you saw that in my online bio. Nothing wrong with that. It pays to check people out before you meet. We all do it."

Dan hesitated. He had studied the names and backgrounds of CEG's senior management team online, and now that he'd had a moment to think about it, he was sure he hadn't seen any mention of Joe's name. It would hardly be diplomatic to mention the fact, so instead he said, "I have a keen ear for accents, that's all, and I detected a certain transatlantic flair in your speech patterns."

"Oh." Joe's smile slipped, but only for an instant. "My fiancée teases me about that all the time, but never mind. We've got people waiting to meet you, so let's go."

"Great. Are we going to meet Mr Cooper now, or do we need to run through some paperwork first?"

"You signed your contract online, didn't you? And the NDA?"

"Yes," Dan said. "It was all straightforward. Neil Hawthorne took me through it. Will we be meeting with Neil this morning?"

"No. That's not going to happen."

Joe's expression hardened, and Dan was taken aback by

the sudden change in mood. "That's a shame," Dan said. "I was looking forward to meeting Neil in person. We've spoken several times on the phone, and I'm keen to talk to him."

"Dan, you'll be working with me. I'm the new head of online operations."

"I see. Has Neil been promoted? I spoke with him last week, and he didn't mention anything about changing—"

"Neil Hawthorne is no longer with us," Joe interrupted. "That is, he no longer works for CEG. He's taken early retirement."

"I had no idea. I hope he's okay. It wasn't his health or anything, was it?"

"No. Neil's fine. As far as I know, he's on his boat somewhere. Why do you ask?"

"No reason," Dan said, but that wasn't quite true. In his last phone conversation with Neil Hawthorne, he thought he'd detected a note of tension in the man's voice, as though he was under stress, holding something back. But Dan wasn't going to bring that up now. In business, people came and went all the time, often with no advance warning. He should know.

As if sensing some disquiet in Dan's expression, Joe leaned a little closer and said, "You know how it goes, Dan. We're taking the company in a new direction, and that's partly why you're here. We're shaking things up, and Neil wasn't..." Joe tilted his head from side to side as if weighing up his words. "Let's just say he was comfortable with the status quo, but that wasn't going to work. We're moving forward, and it's important for us to be pulling in the same direction. Neil preferred to opt out, so we looked after him. He was well rewarded for his valuable years of service, and he'll be fine, believe me."

"Right." Dan summoned a smile, but he couldn't help thinking of Neil trudging from the building with his possessions in a cardboard box. The image brought back memories from a dreadful day in Dan's past; a day he'd rather forget.

"We're headed up to the fifth floor. Are you okay taking the stairs?" Joe asked. "I like to get ten thousand steps under my belt every day."

"Sure. Lead the way."

"Great." Joe headed back toward the door at the side of the lobby, and Dan followed, deep in thought. It had taken a great deal of effort to work his way back into the corporate world, and now that he was here, he needed to be ready to do battle. He'd got off on the wrong foot, annoying the receptionist and then name-dropping a man who'd either left or been ousted. He had to do better, and he had to hope he hadn't bitten off more than he could chew.

CHAPTER 2

In addition to Dan and Joe Clayton, there were three members of CEG's senior management team in the room. After a round of introductions, they took up positions around a long wooden table and sat down, each person taking a place as if it had been allotted to them. They chatted amicably enough for a few minutes, but then Dan made a remark that caused everyone to stare at him in silent bemusement.

Finally, Doug Petheridge, the company's CEO, laid down the tablet he'd been holding and removed the slim pair of reading glasses that had been perched on his nose. While he did this, his shrewd gaze never left Dan, not even for an instant.

Doug cut an avuncular figure with a markedly upper-class mode of speech, and it seemed to Dan that the others deferred to him at all times. Doug was clearly in charge. He had an air of authority, and with his greying hair and three-piece, pinstriped suit, he put Dan in mind of a long-standing government minister or senior civil servant.

Doug smiled benignly, and in a gentle tone of voice he said, "I think we must be at cross purposes, Dan. We're just getting started, and I think it's important to fill you in with a little company background. Our mission statement sums up what we're all about, but you're saying that you don't want to hear it?"

"That's right," Dan replied. "I find these things get in the way. I've been careful to avoid all your promotional material because I want to judge this company for myself, and I'll base my findings on data, pure and simple."

Doug nodded thoughtfully. "I can see that you're keen to make an impression, Dan. You want to kick our arses from the outset, make us think. That's all very well, but we spent a fortune on rebranding this year. We're rebuilding this company, and our core values are at the heart of everything we do. We happen to think that a shared understanding of those principles is rather important. Don't you agree?"

"I'm afraid not." Dan offered a smile around the group, but it wasn't returned. Doug was right; Dan had wanted to throw down a marker. It had been impulsive, and probably ill advised, but he couldn't back down now. There was nothing for it but to soldier on. "Let me explain. You've hired me as a business intelligence consultant, and I'm here to bring a laser-like focus to the data that drives your decisions. Facts and figures tell their own story, but they can also lead us astray. We're all very good at seeing the world as we want it to be. We like to believe that we aren't easily fooled, but it's extremely hard to be objective. Every decision we take is coloured by our personal interpretation of the evidence as we see it. We like to construct narratives that appear to explain the patterns we've perceived, and we assign a greater degree of significance to data that agrees with our ideas."

Sitting on Doug's right, Melanie Steele, the company's chief financial officer, took a haughty breath, flaring her nostrils. Dan guessed that Melanie was in her early forties, and she was an impressive woman. Her dark auburn hair was short, revealing a strong bone structure that lent her an austere beauty. Her eyes were a striking shade of dark green, and when she turned her gaze on Dan, her stare burned with the cold light of hostility. "Dan, every member of our team is a professional, but you're here in an advisory capacity and you'll work on our terms. I would've hoped that the parameters of your involvement would've been made clear from the outset." As she made this last remark, Melanie looked past Doug, directing her attention to the man seated on Doug's left: Seb Cooper, the chief technical officer.

Seb arched an eyebrow. "Everything was spelled out when we hired Dan, so you needn't worry on that score." Seb flashed Melanie a warm smile. He was a handsome man with deep brown eyes, his dark hair swept back, and he was the only man at the table to be sporting designer stubble. Dan suspected that Seb's smile worked wonders on most women, but if he'd expected Melanie to be won over, he'd clearly overestimated his appeal.

Melanie shook her head, her hairstyle remaining perfectly in place as she did so. "So far, I'm not impressed. In the time we've spent discussing the reasons for not hearing the mission statement, we could've read the damned thing ten times over."

"If I might interject," Joe began, "I think Dan was trying to make a point, so why don't we give him a chance to explain?"

"Fair enough," Doug said. "Mr Corrigan, the floor is yours, but I suggest you give us something to which we can all relate."

"Thank you. I'll do my best." Dan took a moment to look at each of them in turn, then he began: "I'm an outsider, and that helps me to be objective. If I'm brought into the fold, if I become just another voice in your echo chamber, I may as well not be here. It's imperative that I keep my mind free from any kind of bias." He looked to Melanie, knowing that she was the one he'd have to work hardest to win over. "Do you know the popular theory about why it's hard to get a taxi on rainy days?"

"Of course," Melanie replied. "It's an idea in behavioural economics." Glancing at Doug, she added, "A study in New York found that cab drivers focused on making a target amount each day, so when they'd made enough money, they ended their shift early. In effect, they missed out on the opportunities offered on rainy days and they had to work longer shifts on sunny days. It's an example of bad decision-making."

"We used to joke about it when I was in the States," Joe put in. "And I worked in Seattle, so I heard that story *a lot*, usually from some poor sap who was soaked to the skin."

Joe laughed, chuckling softly, and the mood lightened as Doug, Seb and Dan joined in.

"It is a good story, and it chimes with our personal experience," Dan said. "That's why it caught the popular imagination, and it's been doing the rounds since 1997. Unfortunately, it's completely untrue. A later, and much more comprehensive, study showed that taxi drivers are, like most people, maximisers. They work as hard as they can for as long as they can, because they want to put food on the table. But the situation is complex. On rainy days, taxi drivers don't necessarily make more money, because people are more likely to take a taxi for a short journey. All those short rides tie up the taxi, but they aren't very lucrative for the driver. Every pickup and drop-off takes time. The same number of vehicles are there, but they're not as available as usual. A simple narrative seemed to explain the situation, but the data tells a different story."

A silence hung in the air, and then Melanie held up her hands in mock surrender. "Okay, Dan, you've made your point. You want to concentrate on the data. I get it."

"I think we all see where you're coming from," Doug said. "Listen, Dan, if we seemed sceptical, it's because a number of consultants have sat in that chair over the last few months, and they've promised us all manner of miracles. So far, none of them have delivered. Joe's predecessor assured us that you are different. We need someone who isn't afraid to rock the boat if that's what gets results, and it looks like we've found the right person. It's time for us to draw this opening bout to a close, and I'll leave you in Joe's capable hands. He'll show you the ropes, and if you need anything, I'm certain you'll ask."

"Count on it," Dan replied. "I don't make idle promises, Doug. I'll give you the results you need. By the time I've finished, you'll have an actionable plan that you can use to take this company forward."

"And make more money?" Melanie asked.

"In the long term, yes," Dan replied. "I guarantee it."

CHAPTER 3

I t's no good. I thought I was strong enough, but I'm not. I can't do it. I cannot.

There has to be another way. A way that doesn't involve violence.

But...

But if there is another option, it's closed off to me, hidden in the shadows in my mind.

There's a mug of tea beside me. I've no memory of making it, but it's there, so I pick it up and drain it.

It's cold. Stone cold and far too strong, the bitter tannin coating my tongue, setting my teeth on edge.

God, I wish I could think straight. I'm so sick of struggling, fighting against the inevitable. It's all so exhausting.

I close my eyes and breathe deep. I can't pray, not for this, but I wish with all my heart for some kind of epiphany: an open door that will lead me out of this hellish torment.

And maybe it works, because a sense of resolution washes over me.

"I see," I murmur. "I understand."

Life becomes so much simpler when you acknowledge the reality of the path that's been laid out for you. Now I can see that it's not a question of whether I can do this or not.

It's just a matter of when.

CHAPTER 4

After the meeting, Joe offered to show Dan where he'd be working. They walked in silence along a quiet corridor until Joe halted in front of the last door. "This is you," he said, pushing the glass door open. "Okay?"

Dan peered inside. The room was a little shabbier than he'd expected. The other offices they'd passed had been bright and airy, but this place was in need of a lick of paint and a new carpet.

"It's nothing special, I know," Joe went on. "Since we started expanding, we've taken on a lot of new staff and we're up to capacity. Seb's already talking about finding new premises."

"That sounds exciting," Dan said.

"Seb has plans, but we'll see. It's up to Doug, and he likes to take his time. That's fine. It's his company."

"Doug keeps a tight grip on the purse strings?"

"You could say that. It's understandable. His father built CEG from nothing. That's quite a legacy, and you can see how Doug might not want to take too many risks with it."

Dan nodded firmly.

"A word to the wise," Joe went on. "Doug might look like

a man comfortably off and heading toward retirement, but he's not going anywhere soon. This company is very important to him, and he works long hours every day. He puts most of us to shame, and he's a solid guy. He could've taken a back seat and lived off his dividends, but he hasn't. He's got principles and he's earned a lot of respect. So, when you met him, that show you put on..."

"It wasn't very clever," Dan said. "Point taken, Joe. I'll tread more carefully."

"Good. I'll tell you what. I'll give you a chance to redeem yourself. We're having a company get-together on Friday afternoon. Four o'clock. I know that's early, but it's afternoon tea at Batworthy Castle. Have you ever been there?"

"No, but I've heard of it. It's quite posh, isn't it?"

"Very," Joe said. "It's a country house hotel really, not an actual castle, but it's a grand old building. Doug's a regular. He takes people up there to wine and dine them, and there's a golf course too, so that doesn't hurt."

"We won't be expected to play, will we? I'm not a golfer."

"Me neither, but don't worry. This is mainly a social thing. It's just tea and conversation. It'll be bone china, tiny sandwiches and fancy cakes on those little stands. The full 'afternoon tea' experience. What do you say?"

"I'd love to come, and I'll be on my best behaviour. I appreciate the opportunity."

"Glad to hear it, because we've got some people coming over to talk about a merger. It's all part of Seb's expansion plan, so we don't want any feathers ruffled, okay?"

"Understood."

"Excellent. Oh, and partners are invited, so if you have someone to bring along, feel free. There'll be some shop talk, but it's really meant to be a social occasion."

"Thanks, but I'll probably come on my own," Dan said. "I might be able to bring someone, but it's short notice."

"I understand. Teri, that's my fiancée, she's already picked out her ensemble. It's okay for us guys, we just throw on a shirt and tie and we're done, but most women like a little time to get ready, don't they?"

"It's not that. My, er, friend might like to come with me, but I haven't exactly asked her out yet, and I'm not sure if this would be the right time."

"What are you waiting for? Go for it." Joe punched Dan's upper arm. "She'll love the place. It's very romantic. People get married there. It's like something out of a picture book."

"I'll think about it. Thanks for the invitation."

"No problem." Joe looked back along the corridor, and Dan followed his gaze to see a middle-aged man shambling toward them, a much younger woman at his side, a laptop case slung over her shoulder. "Right on time," Joe said. "I asked Celine to come along and get you set up. She's one of our IT support team and she knows her stuff. If there's anything you need to know about the system, she's the one to call."

"Who's that with her?" Dan asked, his heart sinking as he recognised the man who'd barged into him on the pavement.

"That's Tom. Tom Hastings. He's our head of IT, but I don't think you'll be seeing much of him. He's a back room kind of guy, if you know what I mean. He spends most of his time down in network services on the lower ground floor. It's below the lobby, and it's like his private lair down there. If he's come up to say hello, you should be honoured. Seriously."

"That's good to know."

Joe checked his watch. "Okay, I really have to go, but I'll leave you in Celine's capable hands. I'll catch you later, Dan."

"Bye," Dan said, but Joe was already marching away. Joe exchanged a couple of words with Tom and Celine as he passed them by but he didn't slow down, and it was clear that he wasn't much given to chatting with his co-workers. Something in the set of Joe's shoulders and his resolute stride reminded Dan of his own days in the City. He'd stalked many a corridor in his time, always on the lookout for the right gaze to meet, the right hand to shake. But it didn't have to be like that. There was another, kinder way to do business, and though he'd made a couple of missteps already, he'd try to do better.

Dan stayed by the doorway of his new office, watching as his visitors drew closer. Tom wore heavy-framed spectacles and he pushed them back on his nose, all the better to fix Dan with an appraising look. Was he remembering their earlier encounter?

He might not recognise me, Dan thought. *He wasn't wearing his glasses when we bumped into each other.* Deciding to brazen it out, Dan offered a friendly smile. Celine smiled back, and Dan's spirits lifted. Celine was in her twenties, and her smile had a devil-may-care quality that hinted at boundless optimism. It was Celine who stepped forward to shake Dan's hand first.

"I'm Celine, Mr Corrigan. Celine Grayson. It's a pleasure to meet you."

"Likewise," Dan said. "But please, call me Dan." He looked to Tom, and after a moment's pause, Tom offered his hand for a shake.

"Hastings," he said. "IT. I was passing, so I thought I'd come and say hello." He sniffed. "Right, Celine will sort you out with a laptop and your login details. Okay? Good. Fine. I've got a lot on, so…" Tom inclined his head toward the corridor, then he turned and walked away.

"Don't mind him," Celine said. "Tom's a sweetie really, but he doesn't do small talk." She extended her arm toward the office door. "Shall we?"

"Certainly. Be my guest." Dan stepped inside and looked around properly. "I'd offer you a coffee, but I've no idea what we do about that."

"There's a small kitchen along the corridor." Celine paused. "Didn't they show you around?"

"No."

"No induction, no staff handbook, no health and safety briefing?"

"Nothing like that, but then I'm not an employee, so I've been thrown in at the deep end: sink or swim."

"Even so, it's a bit poor. I'd give you a tour, but I really haven't got time, so if the fire alarm goes, the main stairs are halfway along the corridor, next to the lift."

"Thanks. I know where the stairs are. I came up with Joe."

"But, as I was about to say, there's another stairwell much closer. Hardly anyone uses it, but it's right next to your office. Go out of your door and turn right. You can't miss it. It's at the end of the corridor, next to the toilets."

Nice neighbourhood, Dan thought. *The toilets and a fire escape.* But all he said was, "Right."

"The staff kitchen is harder to find, but I'll be passing it on my way back to my desk, so I can show you later if you like, unless you need something now."

"No, I'm good." Dan nodded to the laptop bag hanging from Celine's shoulder. "Is that for me?"

"Yes. It's a nice new one. Lenovo ThinkPad. P series. Okay?"

Dan beamed. "More than okay."

"I knew you'd appreciate it. You've done some tech support yourself, haven't you?"

"Where did you hear that?"

Celine sent him an innocent smile. "Someone must've mentioned it."

"I see. Well, I did try my hand at IT support for a while, but it was just domestic stuff, nothing in a commercial environment. I know my limits."

"You won't be tinkering with the network while you're here?"

"I wouldn't dream of it."

"Okay." Celine slipped the laptop bag's strap from her shoulder. "Take a seat and we'll get this thing fired up."

Celine pulled the laptop from its case and laid it on the desk while Dan pulled out the office's only chair. "You have the chair, Celine. It looks like they've only given me one."

"No, I'm fine. You take it. It's your office."

Dan decided not to argue and he sat down, Celine standing at his side and leaning on the desk while she powered up the laptop. He edged his chair a little further from her, and she cast him an amused glance. "Sorry, Dan, was I invading your personal space?"

"No. I was just trying to respect yours."

"Your medal is in the post." Celine concentrated on the laptop, tapping the keys rapidly. "I would've said something if you were too close. Believe it or not, I can look after myself."

"I'm sure you can." Dan leaned back in his seat, folding his hands in his lap. He watched as Celine typed, the commands appearing on the screen in rapid succession. Celine hit the return key and lines of text scrolled upward, faster than Dan could follow.

She makes me look like an amateur, Dan thought. *Which I suppose I was.*

"I've installed the software you requested," Celine said. "I'll check everything's okay. It was mainly Tableau you wanted, wasn't it?"

"That's right. I'm going to build some dashboards and pull lots of data together, so it's displayed in a meaningful way."

"I know what the software does," Celine said without taking her eyes from the screen. "I'm not an expert by any means, but I've used it a few times, and I can manage the basics."

"That's great. I'll know who to ask if I run into trouble."

"Sure, but I'm pretty busy, so it might be a while before I can come. We have to prioritise."

"Of course. What's keeping you so busy at the moment? Is it to do with the expansion plans?"

"Not exactly. We're short staffed and we've got to keep the place running, but I don't mind being busy. It makes the time pass quickly, and I like what I do. Give me a couple of servers and a bunch of cables and I'm happy. I've never been interested in pushing pennies from one column to another. I leave that to the code junkies."

"Is that what I am?"

"No offence meant. You can't be any more tech obsessed than I am. It's a different flavour, that's all. Some people see functions and variables when they close their eyes; for me, it's flashing lights on a server and a cooling fan running at the wrong speed."

Dan laughed quietly, deciding that he liked Celine. Her honesty was distinctly disarming and her openness was infectious. Casting a critical eye around the room, he said, "I'm not sure about this office. It's very quiet at this end of the corridor."

"Yes. Neil liked it that way."

"This was Neil's office? Neil Hawthorne?"

"Yup." Celine moved back from the desk. "Okay, I've restarted your machine, and as soon as it's booted up, you can log in." She opened a side pocket on the laptop case, pulling out a small, laminated card and sliding it across the desk to Dan. "There are some useful phone numbers on there, and I've written your username on the back. There's a shortcut to the company portal on your desktop, and the first time you use it, you'll be prompted to set your password. It's easy enough, but if you need help, I can stay and talk you through it."

"Thanks, but I'm sure I'll work it out." Dan hesitated. "Celine, how long have you been with the company?"

"A couple of years. Almost three."

"Right. So, you must've worked quite closely with Neil."

"Yeah. Neil was…" Celine's gaze flicked to the doorway. Dan had left the door wide open, and it seemed to hold Celine's attention.

"He was what?" Dan prompted.

"Neil was nice. You know, he was easy to work with. I liked him. As a colleague, I mean. He was a good listener."

"I thought so too. We had some long conversations on the phone, and he seemed very perceptive."

"Yeah." Celine fidgeted, avoiding eye contact and holding her hands tightly together in front of her stomach. "I'd better get back to my desk. Er, did you still want to make a coffee? Because I'm going past the kitchen, and I can show you if you like."

"Thanks, but I can find it myself." Dan waited until Celine met his gaze, then he seized the moment to ask the question that had been bothering him. "What happened to Neil?"

"What do you mean?"

"Why did he leave so suddenly?"

"I don't know," Celine said quickly.

"Really? Only, I was in a meeting with some of the company's directors earlier, and nobody mentioned Neil's name. Not even once. They must've all known he was the one who wanted me brought in, but no one referred to him by name."

"We've all had to move on. Things are changing here. The days are racing past. It feels like ages since Neil left."

"I can imagine, but I can't help wondering—"

"You're overthinking it," Celine interrupted. "Neil made his decision, and as far as I know, he was happy with it."

"Okay." Dan smiled and told himself to let the matter drop. Celine was right; he was reading too much into mundane events, seeing shadows where none existed. It was time to change the subject.

"Joe seems great," he said. "He has a lot of energy and he's done well for himself. A stint with Microsoft and now a top job here; that's good going for someone his age."

"Hm. There's a different way to tell that story, but you won't hear it from me." Celine headed for the door, pausing on the threshold to look back and say, "If I were you, Dan, I wouldn't go around asking questions and digging up the past. You'll have plenty to keep you busy, so why stir up trouble for yourself?" She left without waiting for an answer, but Dan formulated a reply in his mind.

Because it's what I do, he thought. *It's the way I'm made.*

CHAPTER 5

Alan hurried along Magdalen Street. It was almost eleven o'clock and he was going to be late, but he'd struggled to find a parking space in Exeter city centre. He'd spent the last half an hour driving around a car park, waiting for someone to leave. He'd found a space eventually, but it had taken far too long, and his mental timetable for the morning had been left in tatters. *Today of all days*, he thought. *Just when I need to be on time.*

As a writer of children's books, Alan was used to setting his own schedule, but every now and then he was obliged to step away from his keyboard and attend to mundane matters of business. Like today, and this unexpected meeting with his literary agent.

Alan had been represented by Emsworth Literary for a few years, and they'd looked after his interests well. The agency was based in London, and they usually communicated with him by phone or email. But not today.

Katy Emsworth was in Exeter, staying at the Hotel du Chambray, and she'd asked him to join her for coffee.

It must be something important, Alan told himself for the fifteenth time. As head of the agency, Katy Emsworth didn't travel beyond the outskirts of London unless she was jetting off to a high-powered meeting in New York or some other city that could provide her with the requisite degree of luxury. Alan had no idea why she'd ventured so far from her comfort zone, but he was in no doubt that he'd been summoned. He had no option but to attend, and it wouldn't do to keep Katy waiting.

At last, Alan spotted the Gothic towers of the Hotel du Chambray and he slowed a little, pulling a clean tissue from his pocket and dabbing at the perspiration on his brow. Fortunately, he'd chosen the linen jacket from the scant collection in his wardrobe, and it still looked okay. After all, it was supposed to be crumpled, wasn't it? He just had to hope it was within the dress code expected at such an upmarket venue.

The Hotel du Chambray had once been a sanatorium, built for patients recuperating from TB and other long-term illnesses, and it had been constructed on a grand scale. The red brick building had several wings, and almost every corner was adorned with a small tower of one kind or another. The hotel had a good reputation, although it had always seemed to Alan like an odd place for an overnight stay. He had visions of echoing rooms crammed with rows of beds and nurses in starched white uniforms bustling along the hallways carrying gleaming bedpans. But then he'd never been inside.

When his parents had last visited him in Devon, Alan had toyed with the idea of taking them for a meal in the hotel's restaurant, but when he'd viewed the menu online, one look at the prices had been enough to immediately dismiss the plan from his mind. He wasn't made of money, and anyway, he preferred to eat in less formal venues: the kind of places where he could relax and enjoy a pint.

After today, I might change my mind, he thought. *Let's see what I've been missing.* Alan made his way inside and followed the signs to the restaurant, pausing in the doorway to survey the opulent room. He was quietly impressed. The restaurant had been tastefully converted, and there was no trace of its humble origins. The walls had been painted in a sophisticated shade of deep red, and the space was lit by the modern equivalent of chandeliers: the myriad small light bulbs hanging from steel wires, their glow diffused by carefully arranged clusters of glass spheres.

The tables were laid for lunch, dazzling white tablecloths topped with neat arrangements of glasses and precisely positioned cutlery. A waiter strode purposefully toward Alan, but there were few customers in the restaurant, and Alan spotted Katy Emsworth sitting at a table by the window, a dapper young man lounging on the chair beside her.

Alan signalled to the waiter to indicate that he was meeting someone, then he picked his way between the tables.

Katy looked up as Alan approached, a carefully cultivated smile on her lips. Her gaze seemed to take in everything about him, from his ruffled hair right down to the scuffs on his shoes. As always when he met his agent, Alan was glad she was on his side.

"Katy," Alan said. "I do hope I haven't kept you waiting."

"Not at all," Katy replied. "We've only just ordered. I took the liberty of getting you an Americano and an almond croissant. That is what you like, isn't it?"

Alan tried to hide his surprise, but he didn't make a very good job of it. "Perfect. That's exactly what I'd have chosen. Thank you."

"I always remember the details for my best clients, but do sit down, Alan. There's no need to stand on ceremony. You're among friends here." Katy gestured to her companion. "This is Clive Merriwether. He's our new PR guru. Sit next to him. You're going to get on like a house on fire."

"Nice to meet you, Clive," Alan said as he pulled out a chair and sat down. "Always good to know a guru."

While they shook hands, Clive regarded Alan from beneath lowered eyelids. "Happy to be here, Alan. I've been reading up on your career, and I was looking forward to meeting you in the flesh."

"Well, here I am. What you see is what you get. I hope that I don't disappoint."

"Not at all." Clive smiled indulgently, but he shared a look with Katy, some unspoken message passing between them that Alan couldn't quite interpret.

A waiter arrived bearing a tray of drinks and pastries, and while the refreshments were dispensed, Katy made small talk, asking Alan about his plans for the summer.

"Oh, I'll probably take a week or two off and catch up with some gardening," Alan said, taking a sip of his coffee. "And I'll have plenty of days out, either up on the moors or at the coast. That's the beauty of Devon. You don't have to go far to enjoy some of the best scenery in the world. It's right here on our doorstep."

"That sounds perfectly idyllic," Katy replied. "So, you're not planning on getting involved with any mysterious murders then?"

Alan spluttered into his coffee cup and he set his drink down on the table, grabbing a napkin to dab at his mouth. "I beg your pardon?"

"There's no need to be so coy," Katy said. "We live in the Internet age, Alan. News of your exploits has travelled. There's no such thing as privacy anymore. Isn't that right, Clive?"

Clive leaned forward, fixing Alan with a keen gaze. "Come on, Alan. You didn't really expect to get away with it, did you? In certain circles you're a household name. Your books are probably in every school library in the country. There are children who dress up as your characters on World Book Day. People know who you are. Did you really think you could solve a murder and no one would find out?"

"Well…" Alan picked up his cup and gulped down a mouthful of coffee, playing for time while he tried to work out how much Katy and Clive already knew about his adventures with Dan. But Katy and Clive were studying him intently. He had to say something. Clearing his throat, he said, "To be honest, I'd hoped to keep that side of things under wraps. I suppose that was a little optimistic of me."

Clive stared at Alan as though he was a member of some exotic species. "Seriously? You have heard of Google, haven't you, Alan?"

"Of course, but which case are you talking about?"

"The young guy who died on Dartmoor," Clive said. "Back in February. In the snowstorm. It was picked up by the media, and there was some coverage overseas as well."

Alan nodded sadly. "Simon Fowler. It was tragic, but I did what I could to help."

"Back up a minute," Katy said. "Just now you asked which case we were talking about. Are you implying that this kind of thing has happened before?"

"That's right," Alan admitted. "But it wasn't just me. My neighbour does a lot of the heavy lifting, but I assist where I can. I do my bit."

"Okay, okay. Hold on." Clive pressed his fingertips against his temples then flicked his fingers at the air. "My mind has just blown. We thought this murder angle was dynamite, but now you're trying to tell me you've done this kind of thing more than once?"

"Oh yes," Alan said. "Each case was different, but interesting in its own way. As I said, my neighbour tends to take the lead, but I play my part. I'm good at research. Since you've taken an interest, Clive, I'm surprised you haven't unearthed the other cases already. Haven't you heard of Google?"

"Touché." Katy mimed applause. "But you'd better explain, Alan. How many cases have there been?"

"Half a dozen. The first case wasn't technically a murder at all, although you could argue that it should really have been treated as unlawful."

"Half a dozen?" Clive murmured. "Are you telling me that you've been personally involved in six separate crime investigations?"

Alan nodded, then he sent Katy a questioning look. "Am I in trouble, do you think? I suppose it doesn't exactly fit with my image as a writer for children. If these cases become more widely known, and people put two and two together, will it harm my branding or whatever you call it?"

"I'll let Clive answer that," Katy said. "He has a proposition for you. That's why he's here. Although, after what you've just told us, I suspect he's rapidly rethinking his strategy as we speak."

"You're not kidding." Clive sat up straight as if readying himself to make a speech. His earlier incredulity was gone, replaced with an expression of calm poise. "Alan, you've made great strides with your author career, but it's fair to say that, to date, your success has been home grown. Your stories are known and enjoyed all across the UK, but you haven't made your mark on the international market. There are millions of readers out there who would probably love your books, but the truth is they've never heard of you. At Emsworth Literary, we feel that it's time for that to change. But to make an impact on a global scale, you need an angle. As chance would have it, you have given yourself that much-needed edge."

Clive spoke with such conviction that Alan listened with rapt attention, but in the silence that followed, he was forced to suppress a snort of disbelief. "I'm sorry, Clive, but I'm having difficulty following your logic. Surely any hint of crime and criminals in my past will be bad news." He glanced at Katy. "Or are you going to tell me that there's no such thing as bad publicity? Because I won't believe that for a minute."

"Listen to what Clive has to say," Katy replied. "Hear him out."

"All right. Go ahead, Clive. I'm all ears."

"It's a question of alignment," Clive began. "Your books conjure an atmosphere of adventure and excitement. Your character, Uncle Derek, is an oddball. He doesn't abide by the rules of society. He's transgressive. He goes on wild goose chases, setting off at the drop of a hat, and he always takes his young nephew, Jake, with him. That's the stuff of dreams when you're a kid, and that's why your stories speak to your target audience."

"They're not targets to me," Alan said. "They're my readers."

Clive shrugged, spreading his hands wide. "Fine, but those kids, and their parents—"

"And carers," Alan put in.

"Right. Their parents and carers are the people who pay your bills, Alan, but to them you're just a tiny photo on the back of a book. They don't know who you are, and frankly, they don't care."

Alan sat back, folding his arms. "That's putting it a bit strong. I may not be the most outgoing person, but I'm not entirely characterless."

"But your character is Mr Nice Guy," Clive said. "That's all very well, but it's vanilla."

"I rather like vanilla," Alan replied.

"Yes, I bet you do, and therein lies the problem." Clive frowned. "The point is, Alan, you need a change of image, and this is it: Alan Hargreaves, amateur sleuth. By day, he writes exciting tales for kids, and by night, he stalks the wilds of Dartmoor, hot on the trail of real-life villains."

"I don't know," Alan said. "It's a bit over the top, isn't it?"

"In this business, there's no such thing," Katy replied. "You need to make an impact or vanish into obscurity. To put it more succinctly, it's a case of go big or go home."

"I appreciate what you're trying to do, and I'm sure your understanding of the publishing business is much greater than mine, but…" Alan shifted uncomfortably in his seat. "I just don't think I could carry it off. It's not my style. It's not me."

Katy laid her hand on his arm. "Not yet perhaps, but it could be. We can help you get there, Alan."

"It'll take some work, for sure," Clive said. "But we've done some market research, and frankly, it's worth the effort. I can go through the figures with you later if you like, but the upshot is that, with the right kind of campaign, you could crack the American market and make huge inroads all over the world. We're talking global success, Alan. Not quite J K Rowling, but certainly Anthony Horowitz."

"I don't see how that could be possible," Alan protested. "I'm nowhere near as prolific as him."

Clive waved Alan's argument away. "You're missing the point. It's not about the amount of shelf space you take up, it's about market penetration. It's about the perception of you as an author. It's about brand awareness."

"And not to put too fine a point on it, it's about money," Katy said. "With very little outlay, this could give you a degree of financial security that you'd never achieve if you simply kept plodding on as you are."

"I've never really wanted to be rich," Alan replied. "That's not why I write."

"I understand." Katy looked Alan in the eye. "You have values, and we wouldn't want you to compromise your principles in any way. But many great writers have stepped into the limelight to further their careers and it didn't do them any harm. Think of Charles Dickens."

"Dickens worked himself to death," Alan said. "Many people believe it was the stress of performing his work on stage that killed him."

"There's no need to be melodramatic," Clive countered.

"Sure, a few public appearances would be helpful, but we're not talking about a performance at the Albert Hall. Besides, we'll take care of you. We'll even help you find the right clothes."

Alan glanced down at his shirt. It was new, and he'd made a point of ironing it carefully before he came out. As far as he could see, there was nothing wrong with the plain white cotton. It was a classic.

"We could put you in a nice trench coat," Katy said, "and a hat. You've got to have a hat." She clicked her fingers. "A fedora. It has to be a fedora."

"What are you talking about?" Alan spluttered. "I can't go around looking like a cut-price Philip Marlowe. I'd be a laughing stock."

"We'll figure something out," Clive said. "I'm thinking of something a bit more down to earth. Rough and ready. He'll need a haircut, and maybe we could do something about his teeth, but—"

"I am sitting right here, you know," Alan interrupted. "And there's nothing wrong with my teeth. I floss religiously."

Clive made a non-committal noise. "A little whitening wouldn't hurt. Tell me, Alan, have you ever considered growing a beard?"

"No."

"Shame." Clive ran his fingers along his own clean-shaven jawline. "I know what would work. A nice leather jacket. Not black, but something more subtle."

"Suede?" Katy offered, but Clive grimaced.

"No. Nubuck. I've seen something perfect online." Clive produced a large phone and tapped on its screen before turning it around to show Alan. "What do you think?"

"Okay, that's not bad," Alan said. "Quite nice in fact, but I can't see the price. How much does it cost?"

Clive pocketed his phone rapidly. "Never mind about

that. We'll work out a budget. It'll be fine. All we'll need are some measurements."

"I can buy something myself. I like to try things on."

"Do you?" Clive asked, running his gaze over Alan's jacket. "I guess we could see what Exeter has to offer. Are you free for the rest of the day?"

"I'm meeting a friend for lunch," Alan replied, "but that isn't until one o'clock."

"Then we've got our work cut out for us," Katy said. "Finish your coffee, Alan, then we'll hit the street."

CHAPTER 6

D an logged into the company's portal, quietly impressed with the system's slick interface. He flexed his fingers. This was going to be interesting. But before he could begin work, a rumbling roar rose from somewhere outside, rattling the windows. The sound faded rapidly, but Dan was already on his feet. "What the hell was that?"

He went to the window, but all he could see from his office was a narrow alley with a high stone wall beyond. A solitary man strolled through the alley, his head down, shoulders hunched in his long, grey raincoat. The man was in no hurry, and there were no sounds of panic coming from the street, no distant wail of sirens.

Nevertheless, Dan headed into the corridor. There was no one in sight, so Dan marched to the office next to his, peering in through the glass door. The place was empty, the desk bare, and some impulse made Dan push the door open. This office was much larger than his and better furnished, but it looked unused.

There was nothing on the shelves except for a fine layer of dust, and Dan felt certain that if he opened the drawers of the filing cabinet, he'd find them empty. For a second, Dan forgot his sense of urgency. Joe had told him that all the other rooms were taken, and there was no reason for him to lie, was there?

At any rate, Dan would have preferred this office, its large windows lending it a sense of light and space. Even the office chair, modern and mesh backed, looked better than the one they'd given him.

Dan hadn't expected the red carpet treatment, but they'd put him in the pokey room at the end of the corridor and that felt like a slap in the face: the workplace equivalent of being given the bottom bunk. Did they want to keep him out of the way?

Forget about it, Dan thought. *I still don't know what made that noise outside.* He stepped back into the corridor and hurried to the next office, which was on the other side of the corridor. Through the glass door he saw Seb Cooper sitting at his desk, working industriously at a laptop. Dan knocked on the door and entered.

Seb's eyes briefly flitted upward from his laptop, a MacBook Pro, and he continued typing as he spoke. "Dan. What can I do for you?"

"I just wondered about that noise. Did you hear it?"

"Noise?" Seb stopped typing and looked up, his expression tightening in irritation. "What are you talking about?"

"The huge booming noise. Outside."

"I didn't notice anything, but that's hardly surprising. I had them upgrade the soundproofing in here. Triple-glazed windows. It's quiet as the grave. Besides, I've been busy. Working." Seb smirked. "It's what we get paid to do around here."

"Of course. I'll leave you to it." Dan began to back out, but Seb called him back.

"I saw Celine pass by. I expect she was up here to get you started on the system. She wasn't with you for long. Everything okay?"

"Yes, thanks. She was very efficient."

Seb's smirk was back. "That's not all, eh?"

"Sorry?"

"Celine. I'll bet she put a spring in your step."

"She's good at her job, and I respect that," Dan said.

"Oh God. You're one of those, are you?"

"One of what?"

"The woke liberal elite," Seb sneered. "*Me too*. All that."

Dan pulled himself up to his full height. "I believe in equality, if that's what you mean. What's wrong with that?"

"*Equality?* What does that even mean? Look at the people in this building. Are we all equal? Of course we aren't."

"That may be true, but we all have an equal chance of getting on if we—"

"If we work hard enough?" Seb interrupted. "Do me a favour. Some of us have the dice loaded from the start." He looked Dan up and down. "Did you go to public school?"

"Yes, but that didn't get me where I am now."

Seb laughed bitterly. "Do you know where I got my education? Plymouth. A comprehensive school. The roof leaked and the heating broke down every winter. It was a dump."

"I'm sorry to hear that, but you're defeating your own argument. You worked your way up. I might've had a privileged start in life, but I'm just a hired hand. You're on the board of directors."

"That's not the point. There were plenty of kids who worked hard in my school, but they never got anywhere. They're probably still living in the same crappy streets, working zero-hour contracts to pay the rent. That's because there's no such thing as equality, Dan. You need an angle to survive. We're a competitive species. Winners and losers. That's the way it's always been."

"I don't see it that way," Dan said. "Without cooperation, the human race probably wouldn't have survived at all."

"Ah, you're a leftie, Dan. Is that it? Bloody hell. You're in the wrong place, mate."

Dan drew a breath. "Seb, we're getting off on the wrong foot here. I like a good argument, but let's call it quits. We need to work together, and I don't bring my politics into the office. Okay?"

"Whatever." Seb returned his attention to his laptop, and Dan took his cue to leave.

He stomped back to his dingy office, a sour taste in his mouth, and the strange noise from outside all but forgotten. Seb probably resented Dan being there. *I know the type*, Dan thought. *Either he's too arrogant to accept my help, or he's overcompensating for something.* Dan smiled grimly as he retook his seat. He'd show them soon enough. He knew his job, and when he was done at the CEG, they'd know his worth. It was only a matter of time, and the work began now.

The company portal had timed out Dan's session, so he logged back in and got to work, keeping his head down as he went through CEG's record-keeping systems one by one. He had a mountain to climb if he was ever going to make sense of the reams of data available. Each company in the group had its own set of databases, and it soon became clear that no two were directly compatible. The whole set-up was a mess. It was no wonder they'd called in outside help.

Dan began making notes and sketching out a structure diagram in the hope of pulling the disparate datasets together to form a coherent picture, and as he settled to his task, the time passed quickly.

His phone buzzed in his pocket, breaking his concentration. Grabbing his phone, he saw Alan's name on the screen, and he checked the time. *Quarter past one? How did that happen?*

Dan accepted the call. "Hi, Alan. Sorry. I didn't realise the time."

"That's okay," Alan replied. "I'm running a bit late myself.

I'm on my way to the restaurant. I thought you might be there already."

"No, I'm still at work, but I won't be long. I'm starving." Dan closed the lid of his laptop. "I'll be there in five. It's just around the corner."

"Great."

Alan ended the call, and Dan made for the door. It had been an odd morning, but he'd made a good start on his work, and he was about to have a decent lunch with Alan. Things were looking up.

It took Dan six minutes to get to the restaurant.

The Tagine was a Moroccan-themed eatery that Dan had only recently discovered. Close to the cathedral and housed in a narrow, half-timbered building, the restaurant was easily overlooked from the outside, but the interior was a different matter. Dan stepped inside, and it was as if he'd entered an Aladdin's cave of colours and reflections. If there was a patch of wall unadorned with brightly patterned fabrics or glittering brass ornaments, he couldn't find it. Even the tabletops were made from gleaming sheets of beaten copper and the chairs were decorated with rows of polished brass studs.

At the back of the dimly lit restaurant, a vaguely familiar figure rose a hand in greeting, and it took Dan a moment to realise it was Alan. What on earth was he wearing?

Dan made his way to Alan's table and sat down, trying very hard not to stare at Alan's new outfit.

"Hi," Alan said. "What kept you?"

"I took one minute longer than I promised, Alan, that's all. Anyway, I was busy at work. We can't all spend our time on retail therapy, you know."

Alan smoothed the sleeve of his leather jacket. "Oh this? It's just a little something I picked up."

"I'll bet the price tag wasn't so little. That looks like nubuck to me. Good quality, too, but it's an odd choice for this time of year. Aren't you roasting in that thing?"

"I'm fine, and there's no need to sound so dismissive. You're always telling me to get some new clothes. I thought you'd approve."

"Hm."

"Well, I like it," Alan said. "Anyway, my agent insisted. It's my new look."

"Ah, I see. You're trying to copy your fictional character and pass yourself off as an international explorer, are you?"

"Not really. It's something a bit closer to home. It's a question of image, apparently."

"What effect are you aiming for? The rugged, hard-bitten writer? A sort of home-grown Hemingway?"

Alan shook his head.

"What is it that you're not saying?" Dan went on. "Come on. You're hiding something."

"If you must know, my agent heard about my success with the Blackingstone Rock case, and she thought—"

"Your success? You mean *our* success, don't you? From what I remember, it was me that put it together."

Alan folded his arms. "I was the one who did all the legwork, asked all the right questions. Anyway, I tried to tell my agent how we work, but she wants to play up my involvement and emphasise that aspect of my… activities."

"She wants to paint you as some kind of amateur detective, is that it?"

There was a pause before Alan nodded. "It's something like that, but as I said, it's just an image. It's a matter of presentation, for publicity photos and such."

"Well, well. Who'd have thought?"

"It's not such an outrageous idea. Why shouldn't I do something to raise my profile? You have your new job, and I've started a new phase in my career. It's about time I did something to step things up a bit. You don't begrudge me that, do you?"

"Of course not." Dan offered a reconciliatory smile. "I shouldn't have poked fun at you. You're right to pursue your career, and I wish you every success. You deserve it."

"Thank you."

"Let's get some lunch. We'll see what's on offer, shall we?" Dan picked up a couple of menus from the table, passing one to Alan, and after the briefest hesitation, Alan took it.

"Thanks."

They studied their menus in companionable silence, but Dan still had something on his mind. "Actually, Alan, I'd be grateful if you would downplay my part in our investigations. You have your new image, and I have mine. It would be best if you left my name out of it entirely. You can arrange that, can't you?"

Alan concentrated on his menu. "Definitely."

A waiter appeared, and they ordered their food, Dan choosing falafel and salad while Alan opted for spiced chicken with couscous. Dan ran his eye over the drinks list, his gaze lingering on the bottled beers, but he ordered a sparkling mineral water, and Alan asked for the same.

The ordering complete, Alan asked Dan about his new job.

"It's early days," Dan said. "I think it's going to be a challenge to get everyone onside, but I haven't really got to know everyone yet."

"They'll come around."

"I hope so. They've invited me to a social event on Friday, so that ought to help. Afternoon tea at Batworthy Castle."

"Very swish. I've only been once and it was great. I'm sure you'll enjoy it."

Their drinks arrived, closely followed by their food, and

as they began tucking in, Dan said, "Did you hear a loud noise this morning?"

Busily attacking a piece of chicken, Alan absently shook his head.

"You must've heard it," Dan insisted. "It sounded like an explosion. Was something being demolished?"

Realisation dawned on Alan's features. "Oh, that was just the bomb. Nothing to worry about."

"A *bomb?* Alan, in what context is a bomb *nothing to worry about?*"

"When it's been dealt with. I'm surprised you haven't heard about it. It was on the news. They found an unexploded bomb over by Belmont Road. They knocked down a block of flats, one of those concrete monstrosities they built in the fifties. They're planning to build houses on the land, but when they started to dig out the foundations, they found the bomb. A thousand kilos of high explosive, so they say. I knew the army experts were going to carry out a controlled detonation, but I wasn't expecting it to be so loud. People must've heard it for miles." Alan frowned. "I hope everyone was okay."

"They'll have evacuated everyone to a safe distance," Dan said. "Nothing will have been left to chance."

"You're probably right."

"I'm relieved to finally find out what it was. I asked the guy in the next office, and he claimed not to have heard it. I was starting to wonder if I'd imagined the whole thing."

"Now you know," Alan said. "Problem solved."

"Another successful case for Hargreaves, super sleuth."

"You're not going to go around calling me that, are you?"

"I wouldn't dream of it," Dan replied. "The thought hadn't crossed my mind."

CHAPTER 7

Sitting at her workstation, Celine Grayson leaned forward, intent on the rows of animated charts displayed across her three monitors. The other technicians, Justin and Rob, had left for the day, citing an early start the following morning as their excuse for going home half an hour before the allotted time. That was fine with Celine. She worked best when the place was quiet, and she had plenty to do; plenty that she preferred to keep to herself.

A reflection flitted across the screen, and she sensed someone standing behind her. Closing her screens with a click of her mouse, she turned in her seat. "Tom. I didn't hear you come in."

"No. So it would seem." Tom Hastings looked down at her, his hands in his pockets and an odd, lopsided grin on his face.

Celine waited for Tom to say more, but he just stood there, his gaze fixed on her. *He's in one of his moods*, Celine decided. *A bee in his bonnet*. What would it be this time? Was he going to moan about the Wi-Fi on the top floor again? Or was he about to launch into some long-winded whine about the company in general? *Please, don't let it be about the IT budget,* Celine thought. *Anything but that.*

Aloud, she said, "Can I help you with something?"

"Such as what?"

"I don't know. Is there a problem with the network? Because if not, I'm busy." Celine indicated her monitors. "We're getting some errors when we deploy the latest update for—"

"That's not what you were working on just now," Tom interrupted. "What was that? What were you doing?"

"Nothing."

Tom's eyes widened, the thick lenses of his heavy-framed spectacles making his stare uncomfortably severe. "I'll ask you again, Ms Grayson. What were you working on?"

"All right. I was checking on the servers again, making sure all the scheduled tasks are running. I know you told me to leave them alone, but I'm worried. I'm concerned about the backup system. It isn't up to the job."

Tom took a step toward her, and lowering his voice, he said, "Is that so?"

"Yes." Celine fought the urge to push her chair away from her boss. Normally, she could handle him, but today there was something very strange in his manner. What the hell was wrong with him? Was he ill? He certainly didn't look well. His complexion was even more pallid than usual, and there was a sheen of sweat on his brow.

"Tom," she began, "are you all—"

"That's Mr Hastings to you."

Celine held up her hands. "Fine. I was just going to ask if you're feeling all right. You look like you might be going down with a cold or something, so I was trying to offer you a glass of water, *Mr Hastings.* Okay?"

"Oh. That's very…" Tom looked away, taking a shuffling step back, and when he faced her again, he seemed to deflate.

His cheeks twitched as though he wanted to smile but couldn't quite recall how to do it. "Erm, thanks for your concern, but I'm fine. I'm under a lot of pressure at the moment. The budget. You know things have been tight. It's difficult. We're under a lot of pressure, all of us, so it's very important that we all stay on-task." Back on familiar territory, Tom cleared his throat and his voice grew stronger. He glanced meaningfully at Celine's blank monitor and added, "We can't be seen to be wasting time."

"I wasn't wasting time," Celine said. "I was checking the servers. If one of them fails again, we'll be in trouble. It won't be easy to restore the system with the backups we have."

"We've always managed in the past. We have our own ways of working. When you've been here for a few more years, Celine, you'll understand."

"Don't bank on it."

Tom's face fell. "You're not thinking of leaving us, are you?"

"I've been considering my options, looking around, seeing what's out there."

"But you can't go yet. The expansion... if it goes ahead, we'll be incredibly busy down here. I'll need someone who knows the network."

"I'm sorry, Tom, but you might have to manage without me." Celine stood. "It's nearly four o'clock. I want to catch Dan before he goes home."

"Who?"

"Dan Corrigan. The new guy. The consultant."

"Oh *him*. I wouldn't be surprised if he'd left ages ago." Tom's lips curled into a scowl. "I don't know why they insisted on bringing in an outsider. We could've handled everything in-house. *Business intelligence*. What a load of nonsense. It's a complete waste of time and money."

"The CEO doesn't seem to think so."

"It's nothing to do with Doug," Tom protested. "All these buzzwords and mission statements are down to Joe. Okay, he's been to the States. So what? We do things differently here. Always have done. But he doesn't understand that, and we all know why Doug listens to him."

"I don't get involved in all that, but listen, Tom, I need to go if I'm going to catch Dan."

"All right, but what's so important? Why can't the high-and-mighty consultant wait until tomorrow?"

Celine clasped her hands in front of her waist. "I forgot to run through a couple of things with him."

"That's not like you. What didn't you do?"

"It's his laptop. I didn't encrypt the drive. Somehow it slipped my mind, and I haven't had time to get back to him, but it'll be fine, so long as I make sure he doesn't take it home with him."

"Are you telling me you forgot to—"

"Yes," Celine interrupted. "I'm sorry, Tom. It's been on my to-do list all day, but I've been slammed. I'll encrypt it first thing in the morning, and so long as it doesn't leave the building, there's no harm done."

"I'll be the judge of that. Call him, tell him to wait."

"I can't. There's no phone in his office. Neil refused to have a landline, remember? And I don't have Dan's mobile number."

"Then you'd better get your skates on," Tom said. "Make sure you catch him, and make sure that laptop doesn't get beyond the front door, because if he takes it out and loses it, there'll be hell to pay. I'll make damned sure you never work in IT again."

"Come on, Tom. That's not fair."

"I said *go*," Tom growled.

"That's exactly what I was trying to do, so if you'll excuse me…" Celine stormed from the room to the stairwell at the end of the corridor, taking the stairs two at a time, but when she reached the ground floor, she changed her mind. She hated using the lift, but it would be quicker, so she headed into the lobby, not slowing until she reached the lift door. She pressed the call button and waited, chewing on her fingernail.

It would be okay. It was only five to four, and Dan wouldn't leave early, especially on his first day. On the other hand, Dan had struck her as the sporty type, like Joe Clayton, so he might take the stairs, and then they'd pass each other.

"Come on, come on," Celine muttered, staring at the lift door, willing it to open.

Behind her, someone giggled and Celine glanced over her shoulder. Of course, it was Samantha, laughing and fawning over a man who was leaning carelessly against her desk, his back to Celine. Who was she flirting with now? Seb Cooper, probably. No surprise there. At every opportunity, Samantha was all over him. *Yes, Mr Cooper. No, Mr Cooper. Can I fetch you an expresso, Mr Cooper?* The silly woman didn't even know the word was *espresso*, but nobody corrected her. Every man in the building could do nothing but beam at Samantha as if she was something special, ignoring the fact that she didn't have two brain cells to rub together.

The lift door opened and Celine stepped into the small compartment, her stomach tightening in response to the sense of confinement, but at least she would soon be spared the sound of Samantha's sycophantic cooing. *I shouldn't let her get to me*, Celine told herself. *But she brings out the worst in me.*

Samantha had a way of looking down her nose at her female colleagues. Every day, when Celine arrived at work, she had to endure Samantha's disapproving gaze: a cold stare that swept from Celine's shoes to her hair. Afterward, there was always the same sad little smile. A smile that seemed to say, "Oh, you poor thing. You tried, but you just can't pull it off, can you?"

Celine jabbed at the button for the fifth floor. There were still two minutes until four o'clock. She could make it, so long as nothing held her up.

The lift door slid closed, but a hand was thrust into the gap, the door juddering open again. *What now?*

Celine stood back and as the door opened fully, Seb Cooper stepped inside.

"Celine, hi. Going up?"

Celine nodded. "Fifth floor."

"Me too. Left something on my desk." Seb flashed her a smile, and Celine found herself smiling back.

"Allow me." Seb reached across, pressing the button to close the door. The movement took him closer to her, and she caught a hint of his aftershave. It smelled good. Expensive.

Seb stood beside her so they were both facing the door. Their arms were almost touching, and Celine imagined she could feel the warmth radiating from his body. She didn't like Seb. Really, she didn't. He was smarmy. Self-satisfied. But when he'd smiled at her, her heart had skipped a beat. Maybe it was his perfect teeth. Or his eyes. Seb had lovely deep brown eyes, and he was always so well dressed: effortlessly stylish.

"Are you nearly finished for the day?" Seb asked.

"Me?"

"Who else?" Seb laughed, but it was warm, genuine laughter. He wasn't teasing her or trying to make her feel stupid. He was sharing a joke with her, making her feel included.

"Yes. Of course, you meant me," Celine said. "I don't know why I said that."

"You've had a busy day."

"Yes. Yes, I have, and the answer to your other question is also yes. I'm almost finished."

"Back home to the boyfriend, eh? Patrick, isn't it?"

"Erm, yes, but Patrick won't be home yet. He works late most days, so I'll have the flat to myself for a while."

Celine paused. Her last remark had sounded like an invitation, hadn't it? That hadn't been her intention, but she'd made her voice soft, lowered her lashes. *Oh hell!* Speaking quickly, she added, "Actually, I don't mind being on my own. It gives me a bit of time to myself."

If Seb had thought she was flirting with him, he didn't let it show. "I know what you mean," he said. "It's important to have some space to decompress. Personally, I go to the gym, work up a sweat. That does the trick. You should try it."

Celine shook her head modestly. "I get all the exercise I need running up and down the stairs all day, and I usually walk to work."

"Well, whatever you're doing, it must be working. You always look bright eyed. The picture of health."

"Oh, thank you."

"I mean it. I suppose it helps to have a partner in healthcare. Patrick's a physiotherapist, isn't he?"

"Yes, but he's still training. He's in his final year."

"That's right. I remember now. Well, good for him. I couldn't do that kind of work, not at any price." Seb smiled at her. "Will Patrick be coming to the get-together on Friday?"

"No," Celine said. "I wasn't invited."

"What? That's no good. Our top IT person, left out?"

The blood rushed to Celine's cheeks, and she looked down in an effort to hide it. He'd mock her now, flaunting his status. But Seb didn't say anything, and when she looked up, he was watching her with real concern in his eyes.

"Is everything all right, Celine?"

"Yes. Fine."

"You're getting on with Tom?"

Celine nodded firmly.

"He can be a bit standoffish," Seb went on, "but I hope he treats you with the respect you deserve."

"Everything's fine. We've been busy, what with the expansion plans and everything, but it's all good."

Seb looked her in the eye. "Celine, I meant what I said

about respect. You're a hard worker, and we all know this place wouldn't function with you."

Celine started to protest, but Seb didn't give her a chance. "I know what you're up against, Celine. This office wasn't built for the twenty-first century. For years, we've been adding to the network until nobody knows where the cables run anymore, and as for that so-called server room, it's far too small for our needs."

"It is getting a bit cramped in there," Celine admitted.

"You can say that again. I'll see what I can do."

"Really? That would be great, but Tom always says there's no money in the budget."

"Where there's a will, there's a way. The problem with Tom is he's a stick-in-the-mud. Sometimes, I wonder if we ought to have somebody new as our IT manager. Somebody young and full of ideas. Somebody like you. Would you be interested in an opportunity like that?"

Celine laid her hand on her chest. "Well, I... I hadn't thought about it."

"You should."

The lift juddered to a halt, its door sliding slowly sideways.

"I really don't have the experience to run the department," Celine said. "Tom has been doing his job for years and years."

"But he wants everything to stay the way it was, and that's just not good enough. This company is moving on. There'll be new opportunities, a new building, and new ways of doing things. We'll need a whole new network, and you could be there to build it. Think about it, Celine. When the opportunity comes, be ready to grab it with both hands."

"Right. I'll give it some thought."

"Good." Seb gestured to the doorway. "After you."

Celine stepped out into the corridor and Seb followed. "I'm glad I bumped into you," Seb went on. "Listen, you really ought to come to Batworthy Castle on Friday. Knock off early for a change."

"Oh, I don't—"

"Don't worry about Tom," Seb interrupted. "I'll square it with him. You *must* come. It'll give you a chance to impress Doug and the others. Remember what I said about grabbing an opportunity."

Celine nodded.

"That's settled then," Seb said. "I'll look forward to it. Bring Patrick."

"Okay."

Seb sent her a last smile and then marched away, a swagger in his step.

What just happened? Celine asked herself. *Did he mean all that or was he just flirting with me?* She couldn't decide, but as she made her way toward Dan's office, she wasn't sure whether she minded a little banter, so long as it meant Seb was on her side. There was no harm in it, and besides, it felt good to be the centre of someone's attention. Patrick was so wrapped up his work, he didn't make much of an effort to be charming anymore, but Seb had made time for her, and there was nothing wrong with that. As a matter of fact, it was really rather nice.

CHAPTER 8

Dan stepped out of the staff toilets and looked up and down the corridor. He'd changed into his running gear, and he couldn't help feeling self-conscious, even though there was no one around. He'd been in two minds about whether to go for a run, but after a full day spent hunched over his laptop, he needed to stretch his limbs, needed to send the blood pumping around his body.

He strode back to his office, intending to collect his laptop, but while he'd been changing, someone had been in and attached a pair of bright-pink sticky notes to the laptop's lid. Written in neat capital letters with a black felt-tip marker, the first note read: *Dan, this laptop mustn't leave the building.* The second note said: *Lock it in your desk. I'll encrypt it tomorrow.* The second note was signed with a capital C and a smiley face.

Celine, Dan thought. *Why didn't she tell me earlier?* Celine had appeared to be extremely efficient, so to leave out such an important detail seemed out of character. But their interaction had been rushed, and Celine had explained that she'd been busy. When people had too much on their plates, they made mistakes, it was as simple as that.

Dan tapped the lid of his laptop thoughtfully. He'd wanted to take it home so he could do some work in preparation for tomorrow, but he was tired and the rest would do him good, give him time to think. He slid open the top drawer of the cabinet beneath his desk and slipped the laptop inside. The drawer had been empty so there was plenty of room, and when he'd closed it, he turned the key and tested the lock. It was secure enough, and Dan stored the key safely in the front pocket of his backpack before hefting the backpack onto his shoulders. It was heavier than he'd have liked, and on such a warm day it wouldn't be much fun to run with it on his back, but he'd be fine.

Dan had mapped out a route that would take him down to the River Exe. From there he'd join the paved walkway that ran along the riverbank. He'd run along the river, using his Garmin smartwatch to keep track of his progress, and when he'd covered a decent distance, he'd head to the car park and drive home. The path along the river was flat, it was smooth, and at this time of day it wouldn't be too busy. While he ran, the rush hour traffic would subside, leaving him with a clear drive back to Embervale. Perfect.

He took a quick look around the office then headed out. He didn't particularly want to trot down the main stairs in his running gear, so he turned right from his office door, quickly finding the entrance to the stairwell Celine had told him about. Beyond the fire door, the stairwell was distinctly unwelcoming. It was lit only by a few small windows set high on the wall, but a row of wall lights flickered into life as Dan made his way downstairs. When he reached the lowest level, he pushed open another fire door and found himself in a short corridor. The ceiling lights were out of action, but there was a wooden door at the end of the corridor and its narrow window of reinforced safety glass allowed a faint glow to permeate the gloom.

Dan hurried along the cramped corridor, his running

shoes squeaking on the tiled floor, the sound setting his nerves on edge. *I'm not sure I should even be in here*, he thought. The place smelt of damp and neglect, the walls pressing in on him. He passed a door on his left and idly wondered where it led, but he was not about to linger long enough to find out.

Reaching the outer door, Dan hesitated before turning the handle. What if opening the door triggered an alarm? It wasn't long past four o'clock, so any burglar alarms wouldn't be switched on yet, but what about fire alarms? Celine had told him he could use the stairwell in the event of a fire; she hadn't said anything about opening the door under other circumstances. Still, Dan could see no warning signs beside the door, so he took a breath and pushed the handle.

The door wasn't locked, but it was reluctant to budge, as though disuse had allowed it to become fixed in its frame. Dan needed to give it a determined shove before it would open.

He stepped out into the alley he'd seen from his office window. Facing him, the stone wall that ran along the alley was taller than he'd thought and it cast a long shadow. To his right the alley was blocked by a steel-barred security gate, beyond which stood a row of wheelie bins. On his left the alley led along the side of the building and offered a narrow view of the street beyond. Good.

Dan pushed the door closed, noting the combination lock mounted above the handle. Maybe he could ask about the code when he had the chance; it would come in useful if he ever wanted to pop back inside without going through the main entrance.

He broke into a jog, starting slow and giving his muscles time to warm up. When he met the road, he turned right, but the pavement ahead was blocked by a gaggle of dawdling teenagers, so he decided to cross over to the opposite pavement. Here, Southernhay West widened as it met its counterpart, Southernhay East, and Dan checked for oncoming cars before jogging into the road, making for the other side. His way was clear and his muscles were ready for a workout, so he lengthened his stride, his backpack bouncing on his back. He pulled the straps a little tighter, fastening the strap across his chest to keep the bag in place. But as he glanced down to adjust the strap, his world was suddenly filled with the roar of an engine, the sound bouncing from the buildings, battering his ears.

Startled, Dan half turned, stumbling over the kerb, the engine's growl growing louder every moment. A sleek black saloon barrelled toward him, its engine screaming, its dark mass filling Dan's field of vision. The car raced closer, its wheels squealing, sliding over the tarmac, its body shimmying as if the driver was fighting for control. With a juddering jolt, the car mounted the pavement, and still it accelerated toward Dan.

Dan threw himself back, losing his footing, staggering as he fought to stay upright. He was going to fall, sprawling on the ground, helpless. But his back met a solid wall, and he pressed himself against it. There was nowhere else for him to go. In a split second, he'd be crushed against the wall. There was no time to get away.

But he was going to try.

Tearing his gaze from the oncoming car, Dan turned and ran, pouring every ounce of energy into a headlong dash. He couldn't outrun the car, but he refused to stand still and be mown down like a stupefied rabbit.

Arms pumping, legs powering him forward, he ran like he'd never run before. But there was an obstacle in his way.

The building beside him was old and had stone steps leading to the front door, and on either side of the steps, sturdy wrought iron handrails extended onto the pavement. To skirt around the rails would take Dan closer to the road and make him an easier target. But he knew what to do.

Launching himself at the handrail, Dan grabbed the metal

bar tight, swinging himself up and vaulting over. He landed on his feet on the stone steps, but his momentum carried him forward and he overbalanced, tumbling against the door. Before Dan could right himself, the car's wing collided with the handrail, the gloss-black saloon's body buckling, metal screeching against metal. Dan shielded his head with his arms. The car was so close he felt its slipstream wash across his face. If it stopped now, Dan had to be ready to face the driver, had to be ready to defend himself.

But perhaps the driver panicked, because the car swerved back toward the road, bumping down from the pavement and slewing across the street. Then it was racing away, speeding down the road, the whine of its engine fading rapidly.

Dan gasped for air, the acrid stench of scorched rubber and exhaust fumes burning his throat. He staggered down the steps, his legs unsteady, and stood on the pavement, peering down the road. But the car was gone. It had vanished into the ever-changing stream of city traffic.

"Are you all right?"

Dan looked back to see the company's receptionist, Samantha, standing nearby, her eyes wide in alarm.

Dan nodded, walking slowly toward her. "Did you see that? Did you see what happened?"

"Not really. I heard a noise and looked around, and I saw that car hit the railings then drive away, but I didn't see what caused it. The driver must've been drunk or something. When I saw you come out from there, I could hardly believe it. You came outside at the wrong moment, didn't you? That railing saved your life." She nodded toward the building behind him. "What were you doing in there? Were you at the gym?"

"What?"

"You've just come out of Amberley Court, haven't you?"

"No. I wasn't inside."

"Oh, I see. Sorry." Samantha made a face as if embarrassed

at her mistake. "I shouldn't have assumed. I know it's very exclusive in there. The gym is only for the people in the flats above, but when I saw your sports kit…"

Dan glanced down at his running clothes. "I certainly wasn't in any kind of gym. I was going for a run, and I had to jump over the rail because some lunatic tried to run me over. He tried to bloody well kill me."

There was a pause before Samantha replied. "You've just had a lucky escape from what could've been an awful accident. It must've been a terrible shock. Do you want me to get you a glass of water?"

"No, thank you. I'll be okay." Dan took a steadying breath. "You didn't get a good look at the driver did you?"

Samantha shook her head.

"What about the car? Did you recognise it? Or maybe you saw what kind it was?"

"No, sorry. It was a black car, maybe a BMW or something like that, but I think it had tinted windows. I couldn't see inside."

"Dammit!" Dan muttered. "Damn, damn, damn."

Samantha stepped closer and placed her hand on his arm. "Mr Corrigan, I really think you should go back to the office and sit down. You're white as a sheet. Listen, there's a water cooler in reception. I'll come with you. A cold drink will make you feel better."

Samantha spoke to him as if trying to pacify a bad-tempered toddler, and Dan wanted to argue with her, to tell her that it wasn't shock that had made him angry; it was sheer, bloody-minded rage at the fact that someone had just tried to kill him. But she was being kind, and after what had just happened, the simple offer of a cup of cool water suddenly seemed very generous.

"Thank you," Dan said. "That's probably a good idea." Dan followed Samantha back into the building, and she made him sit down in the waiting area while she fetched him a drink.

Samantha was right. The first sip of ice-cold water made Dan feel a lot better.

"I know that car was going far too fast," Samantha said, "but if you want to run in the city centre, you really must be careful. The roads get quite busy, and they're too narrow. People are always having accidents."

Dan took another slurp of water. "I was being careful. I'm always careful. I used to run in London all the time. I'm used to traffic, and I'm used to running by the road, but that car wasn't there when I crossed the road. It came out of nowhere."

Samantha stared at him. "You don't really think someone went after you on purpose, do you?"

"I do. Why else would they drive on the pavement like that?"

"Maybe the brakes failed, or it could've been joyriders. They stole that posh car, and when they tried to get away, they lost control."

"I just happened to be in the way?" Dan said. "No, I don't buy that. As I said, I'd just checked the road and it was clear. That car must've been parked, and when they saw me run across the road, they took their chance."

"I'm sorry, Mr Corrigan, but that sounds a bit far fetched."

"Does it? Then how would you explain it?"

"It was a coincidence. They came tearing along, going too fast for whatever reason, and you didn't notice. Maybe something distracted you. All it takes is a second."

Dan thought of his rucksack, and the way he'd been adjusting the strap as he'd crossed the street. He'd had a busy day, he'd felt mentally exhausted, and it had been the first time he'd run on that particular road. It *was* possible that he'd had a momentary lapse of concentration, wasn't it?

"No," Dan muttered. "I didn't make a mistake. That car was driven at me deliberately."

"Surely not. That doesn't make sense."

"No, it doesn't," Dan said. "Not yet. But it will by the time I've finished."

"What do you mean?"

"Someone just tried to run me down, Samantha. I'm going to find out who, and then I'm going to make them wish they'd never tried."

CHAPTER 9

Years earlier, when Dan had first driven into Embervale, he'd grumbled at the lack of lay-bys on the narrow lane that connected the village to the main road. He'd since learned that there were several places where the lane widened enough to let two cars pass, so long as one driver was prepared to pull over as far as possible and wait until the way was clear.

Driving home from Exeter after his disastrous attempt to go for an invigorating run, Dan was forced to stop in the lane on three separate occasions, each time reversing his RAV4 into a passing place, pulling in so close to the hedge that branches poked in through his open car window. But he did all this without so much as a muttered complaint, driving on autopilot while his mind replayed a disturbing montage of scenes from his brush with death, the black car swerving toward him again and again in his mind.

Several times, Dan convinced himself that Samantha was right; the whole thing had been an unfortunate accident, a joyrider losing control of the car. Now that he'd had time to think about it, he recalled Alan mentioning something about car thefts recently. Apparently, there'd been something in the local news, though Dan had listened to Alan's anecdote with half an ear, and he couldn't remember the details.

Later, he'd call the police to report his near miss, and he'd ask if any cars matching his description had recently been stolen. Of course, the police might not be forthcoming, and they'd be less than impressed when he couldn't tell them the make and model of the car. He'd tried to concentrate, to bring the image of the speeding vehicle to mind, but in Dan's memory, the black saloon was a blur: a muddled amalgam of sleek lines and reflected sunlight. Only the sounds remained vivid in his mind: the engine's growl rising to a crescendo, the tyres screeching over the tarmac.

Dan gripped his steering wheel tight and stared at the lane ahead, forcing down a rising sense of frustration. He was good at recognising cars, especially the more expensive models, but for some reason he was drawing a blank. Samantha had suggested the speeding car was a BMW, but he would've recognised the distinctive grille. He used to drive a BMW for goodness' sake, so Samantha must've been mistaken. What alternatives did that leave him with? If the car had been an Audi or a Lexus, he would've spotted the logo on the front, and the same went for a Mercedes.

However hard he tried, he couldn't recall any aspect of the car that distinguished it from the common herd. *Something will come to me*, Dan thought as he pulled into his parking space in front of The Old Shop. *I just need to be patient.*

But by the time he'd dropped his bag on a chair in the kitchen, the last vestiges of Dan's patience had dissolved. He couldn't sit and wait for his memories to resolve into a coherent picture. He had to do something. A car driving so erratically through the city centre must've attracted attention. There was a chance it had been reported to the police already, and Dan knew exactly who to contact.

His call was answered quickly: "Mr Corrigan. It's been a

while since your name appeared on my phone. To what do I owe the pleasure?"

"Detective Sergeant Spiller. I'd like to report a crime."

"That's very public spirited, but it's Detective *Inspector*, if you don't mind, Mr Corrigan."

"You've been promoted?"

"Try not to sound too surprised."

"Sorry, I didn't mean..." Dan paused. Why did every conversation with Spiller have to descend into antagonism? They were supposed to be on the same side, weren't they?

"No offence taken, Mr Corrigan. Now, I'm very busy, so if you'd like to report a crime, you can dial 101 if it's non-urgent, and they'll direct you to the appropriate—"

"I'd rather talk to you," Dan blurted. "It's important."

Spiller sighed. "Go on then. But I want to make one thing perfectly clear. As an inspector, I have a lot of additional responsibilities, so I can't drop everything and get involved in one of your... what shall we call them? Shenanigans?"

"I beg your pardon?"

"All right, your personal projects. Whatever you want to call them, if you need help, you'll have to go through the proper channels like everyone else."

"But I thought..."

"What? That you'd given me a couple of tips in the past, so you could pick up the phone and I'd come running?"

"Not exactly, but I thought you might return a favour."

"The police force doesn't operate in that way, Mr Corrigan. There's no *quid pro quo*. That would be a fast track to corruption, wouldn't it? But let's get down to brass tacks. What kind of crime are we talking about?"

"Someone tried to kill me today."

"Oh dear, oh dear," Spiller drawled, a hint of smug satisfaction in his tone.

"I need you to take me seriously," Dan said. "There was an attempt on my life."

"But you're all right? You weren't injured?"

"I'm fine. A few bruises, that's all."

"That's something," Spiller said. "Go on then. Let's have the details."

"It happened in Exeter, not long after four o'clock. I was coming out of work when someone tried to run me over. They went straight for me. The car mounted the pavement. If I hadn't jumped out of the way, I'd have been killed."

"Someone tried to run you over? It wasn't in a Volvo S90, was it?"

Dan stared at the wall. "That's it! It was a Volvo. That's why I didn't recognise it. I would've spotted a high-end car straight away, but a Volvo, that's a different matter."

"I've always sworn by them."

"Sure, they're fine, but you know what I mean. They're fairly anonymous, aren't they?"

"In my line of work, that's one of the best things about them," Spiller said. "Where did this incident take place?"

"Southernhay. But how did you know it was a Volvo? CCTV?"

"You know I can't discuss an ongoing investigation, Mr Corrigan, but I'll send someone to see you. One of my subordinates. An old friend of yours, as it happens."

"DC Collins? I'd hardly describe him as a—"

"I think you'll be pleasantly surprised," Spiller interrupted. "Mind how you go, Mr Corrigan. Look both ways before you cross the road, eh?"

Spiller ended the call, and Dan replaced the handset in its cradle. *An old friend?* DI Spiller was poking fun at him in some way, but for the life of him, Dan couldn't see the joke.

He'd find out soon enough. It was only a matter of time.

CHAPTER 10

Sitting at the kitchen table, Dan picked at the remains of his chickpea curry. It was one of his favourite recipes, but today he hadn't got it right. The spices had taken on a harsh taste that caught at the back of his throat. He obviously hadn't been paying attention, throwing in the ingredients one after the other without giving any time for the flavours to develop.

There was a knock at the front door, and Dan pushed his plate away and jumped to his feet. This might be the police officer Spiller had promised, and he was eager to tell his story. Marching to the front door, Dan readied his opening remarks. But when he saw the smartly attired woman standing by the doorstep, his mind briefly went blank. "Detective Constable Kulkarni. I wasn't expecting you."

Kulkarni smiled. "DI Spiller said you'd be surprised. Nice to see you again, Mr Corrigan, but for the record, I've been a detective sergeant since I transferred to Exeter."

"Congratulations. Please, come in."

"Thanks."

Dan stood back and Kulkarni strolled inside, casting her gaze around the hallway.

"Come through to the front room." Dan led the way and Kulkarni followed. Apart from Alan, Dan didn't have many visitors, and a twinge of embarrassment nagged at the back of his mind. The front room was comfortable enough, but his modern sofa and chairs still looked out of place in the old cottage, and the overall effect was slightly chaotic, as if the furniture had been thrown in at random. Seeing the room through Kulkarni's eyes, Dan realised it was very much a bachelor pad: functional but not appealing. If he was going to invite Sam around, he'd have to spruce the place up a bit, buy a couple of pictures for the wall.

But DS Kulkarni scarcely glanced around the room before gesturing to the sofa, saying, "Mind if I sit down? I've been on my feet all day, apart from the drive over, that is."

"Please, go ahead. Can I get you a cup of tea or anything?"

"No thanks. I'm fine." Kulkarni sat down, crossing her legs. She wore a simple pair of black trousers that emphasised the length of her legs, and Dan vaguely wondered if she was a runner.

Dan shifted a chair so that he'd be facing her, then he sat down, forcing himself not to perch on the edge of his seat. "I appreciate you coming to see me," he began. "I'm sure you must be busy."

Producing a black notebook, Kulkarni nodded. "There's always plenty to keep us occupied. Never a dull moment."

"When did you transfer from Newquay?"

"It's been a few months, but let's get back to the reason I'm here. If you could tell me exactly what happened, it will help us in an ongoing investigation."

"An investigation into what?"

Kulkarni regarded him for a second. "We'll come to that later, sir. I understand that you were almost hit by a speeding car, and when DI Spiller suggested the make and model of the vehicle involved, you agreed. Is that correct?"

"He happened to mention it, and that's when it clicked. I realised he was right about it being a Volvo."

"Hm." Kulkarni made a note in her book. She did not look pleased.

"I suppose some might say that DI Spiller asked me a leading question," Dan said. "But it wasn't like that. I knew straight away that he was right, but he didn't change my mind in any way."

"Even so, it's best if we discuss the case after you've given me the facts as you see them. I'll jot down the sequence of events and we'll take it from there. Okay?"

"Yes, that makes perfect sense," Dan said. "Memories are much more fluid than most people realise. Give people a narrative, and their memories shift to fit the story."

"I couldn't have put it better myself."

"Well, I've worked with a lot of marketing firms. They know more about manipulating people's perceptions than anyone."

Kulkarni laughed at that, and Dan relaxed. She was easy to talk to, and as he told her what had happened as he left work, Kulkarni listened and made notes, occasionally looking up to ask clarifying questions. She wanted to know who else was on the street at the time, and she asked about Samantha.

"I'm afraid I don't know her full name," Dan admitted. "It's my first day in a new job."

"Quite a day. Do you have any reason to suspect that someone in your new workplace might want to do you harm?"

"No. I'm a freelance consultant, and not everyone appreciates me being there, but no one has been aggressive toward me. Not really."

"*Not really?* Does that suggest a degree of ill will?"

"I wouldn't put it that strongly," Dan said. "There's a certain amount of antagonism, maybe, but that's business. It's not a popularity contest."

"I see. Is there anything else you'd like to tell me?"

"Not that I can think of. It all happened so fast."

"Okay." Kulkarni closed her notebook. "Thanks for your co-operation, Mr Corrigan. It might put your mind at rest to know that you almost certainly weren't the target of an attempted hit and run."

"Oh? Can you be sure of that?"

"Within reason. You see, a vehicle matching the description you gave was stolen shortly after three o'clock this afternoon from a location near the city centre. Unfortunately, the car was taken directly from the owner, and there was some violence involved."

"It was a carjacking?"

"It looks that way. The owner was seriously injured."

"Oh no. What happened?"

"I can't go into it with you, but we're following every lead."

"The owner, are they all right?" Dan asked.

"He's stable, but we haven't been able to speak to him yet. He needs time to recover."

"That puts my near miss into perspective," Dan said. "The poor guy."

"I'd say you had a lucky escape, Mr Corrigan. We're dealing with some dangerous people here, and this isn't an isolated incident. We're looking at a string of similar car thefts across Devon, and all of them involved injury to the owners. However, we're pursuing several avenues of enquiry, and we're working hard to identify the culprits."

"I'm sure you are, but did you find the car? It was badly damaged, so that would make it difficult to sell, wouldn't it?"

"We're unlikely to find it. It looks as though the thieves are organised. By the time they've finished with that car, it'll be virtually untraceable, but we'll keep looking."

Kulkarni stood, producing a business card and offering it

to Dan. "Thanks for your help, and if you think of anything…"

"I'll call you right away." Dan took the card, noting that DS Kulkarni's first name was Anisha. He ought to have remembered that, but it had been some time since they'd met in Newquay, and so much had happened since then, it seemed a lifetime ago.

Dan saw Kulkarni out, and then he was left alone with his thoughts. Which perhaps was just as well. There was a lot to think about.

CHAPTER 11

I *ought to have gone home by now*, DI Spiller decided. It was late, and he'd had a full day of meetings, one much like another, but he was behind on his admin and that wouldn't do. If he started the week with a backlog, he'd never catch up, so he sat alone in his office, staring morosely at his computer's screen, his eyes skimming over the densely packed lines of text: *Regional reported crime statistics... month-on-month increase... upward trend... antisocial behaviour... acquisitive crime... violence.*

It all came down to one thing: the world was going to hell in a handcart. "I could've told them that," Spiller muttered. "And it wouldn't have taken me twenty-eight pages to do it."

He sat back in his seat, interlacing his fingers in his lap, his thumbs fidgeting. *Look at me*, he thought. *I'm literally twiddling my thumbs.* He almost laughed out loud, but what would be the point? There was no one in the office to share the joke, no one to chuckle and take the mickey, knowing that it would be their turn to be the brunt of some barbed remark sooner or later.

In any nick in the land, the banter wasn't always kind, and it could be downright cruel, but whenever he was stuck behind his desk on his own, he missed it all the same. Clicking his mouse to close the document, Spiller rose slowly and made his way into the main office, his hands thrust deep in his pockets. The place was almost empty, but one officer sat at his desk, his brow furrowed as he leafed through a stack of papers.

As if sensing Spiller's presence, DC Collins glanced up from his work. There was a fraction of a second before Collins lifted his chin in acknowledgement, but the accompanying smile was warm enough. *Good lad*, Spiller thought. *He's got over it.*

Spiller sauntered over to Collins and leaned against the edge of the desk. "How's it going?"

"All right, sir. Busy. As per usual."

"Good lad. Erm…"

"Yes, sir?"

"You can drop the *sir*, Collins."

"Okay. To be honest, I have to keep reminding myself not to call you Sarge or Skipper. It had better be guv'nor from now on."

"Every time someone says guv'nor, I look over my shoulder, expecting to see a DI behind me. It takes some getting used to."

"There's been a lot of changes," Collins said, his voice growing heavy. "For some more than others."

"Yes. As it happens, I've been meaning to talk to you about that. You know, the sergeants' exam is tough. It's meant to be that way. Plenty of people don't pass it the first time."

Collins smiled bravely. "Yeah, so people keep telling me. But I know where I went wrong. I'll have another crack at it, and I'll get there next time."

"That's the spirit. Learn from it, that's the main thing. I sometimes think this job is one long learning experience, and the people who take some knocks along the way, well, I reckon it makes them better coppers in the end."

Collins looked unconvinced, so Spiller added, "Think about it. Most of the people we deal with have made mistakes in their lives, one way or another. It's good for us to know what that feels like."

"I get what you mean. See the other side."

"That's right, lad." Spiller smiled. "So, what are you up to at the moment? Getting any closer to our friendly, neighbourhood carjackers?"

"There's not much to report. The victims haven't given us much to go on. They're getting out of their cars, or just about to get in, and they get hit from behind, we think with a steel baton. We're still ploughing through the CCTV. Plenty of sightings of the cars they take, but nothing on the individuals. They're smart. They pick places where there are no cameras, or else there's always something blocking the view."

"Like what?"

"A tree or a van. Something like that."

"What kind of van?"

"A big transit van usually," Collins said. "It could be the same one, but we haven't been able to see the number plates."

"This van, was it already there, or did it pull up just before the theft?"

"Already there. In each case, the van was parked. We figured it's someone making a delivery."

"Any markings on the vans? DPD, UPS?"

"Not as far as we can see, but like I said, the CCTV footage isn't much help. There are so many white vans on the road, and we've got no way of narrowing it down. It seems like a dead end."

Spiller nodded thoughtfully. "It could be, but if a van being present is a common factor, I wouldn't be too eager to dismiss it."

"I'll take another look at it," Collins said. "If I visit each scene and ask around, I should be able to find out whether anyone had a delivery at around the right time."

"Also, check if a courier called to collect something," Spiller suggested. "With a bit of luck, you'll find someone who recorded the exact time they took a delivery or handed a parcel over. Receptionists sometimes keep a log. That'll give you the name of the courier company, and then it'll be a short step to the driver."

"Yeah, and even if they weren't involved, they might've seen something."

"Now you're thinking. Good work. Make sure you tell DS Kulkarni what you've come up with. No need to mention my name."

Collins beamed. "Cheers, guv'nor."

"Think nothing of it, lad." Spiller pushed himself off from the desk. "Now, I'd better get back to my paperwork. Regional crime statistics make riveting reading, I can tell you. Almost as good as a Jeffrey Archer."

"Who?"

"Never mind, lad. Before your time." Spiller chuckled and Collins joined in.

"Talking about ancient history," Collins began, "have you heard what the army boys unearthed?"

"No. What's that?"

"You know that unexploded bomb on Belmont Road," Collins said. "When they blew it up, it left a bloody great crater, and guess what was in the bottom of it. A bunch of bones. Human, they reckon. Must've been there for decades. Since the war, probably."

"Has anyone been to take a look?"

"There's a crime scene team over there, bagging everything up and taking it back to the lab. I'm surprised you haven't heard about it."

"Contrary to popular opinion, you don't get given an all-seeing eye when they make you a DI. You'd be surprised how much stuff never makes it to my desk. Besides, I don't expect a few bones will amount to much. It's probably some poor sod who was killed in an air raid. There must've been plenty of bodies that were never recovered."

"Yeah, I reckon you're right. They won't bother us with it." Collins returned his attention to the sheaf of papers on his desk.

"Pity really," Spiller said. "A body that's lain undiscovered for all these years. Intriguing. You never know what other evidence might turn up. If it turns out to be a case of foul play, well, that's the kind of case that might attract attention. Could be good for somebody's career. Still, I'd better get back to my office." Spiller rocked back and forth on his heels, but he made no move to leave. "I certainly can't go poking my nose in to what is almost certainly a stone-cold case, just because it's cropped up on my ground. Not when I've got all those reports to read and time ticking away."

Collins looked up at him. "Unless…"

"Unless what?"

"I was thinking, it's late and the crime scene crew are probably finished for the day. If we were to swing by and have a peek, it wouldn't do any harm."

"That's an intriguing idea, Collins. I'd be happy to come with you. Not that you need my help, but it can be useful to have an inspector in tow."

Collins stood, grabbing his jacket from the back of his chair. "I'll drive if you like."

"Right. I'll get my things," Spiller said, and as he headed back to his office, there was a spring in his step.

THE SMALL CAR park on Belmont Road was almost empty, and DC Collins drove into a space, the tyres of his Vauxhall Insignia crunching over the gravel and debris littering the surface.

"Cheers," Spiller said, climbing from the passenger seat.

When he stepped back from the car, the soles of his shoes grated on the tarmac and he glanced down, scraping his foot through the grit. "Sand."

"Yeah," Collins said. "They covered the bomb with four hundred tonnes of the stuff, to absorb the blast."

Spiller scanned his surroundings. Set back from the road, the row of terraced houses seemed to be undamaged, but a modern block of flats hadn't fared so well. Despite being protected by scaffolding and some kind of mesh, there were broken windows and chunks missing from the walls.

"I suppose it worked after a fashion," Spiller said. "I don't know how much damage a thousand kilos of high explosive would've done if it hadn't been controlled, but I'm guessing it would've been a hell of a lot worse."

"You can say that again, guv'nor." Collins indicated a stretch of bare ground on the other side of the road. "The bomb was over there."

In the distance, Spiller could make out a line of blue-and-white police tape fluttering in the breeze. "Lead the way, Collins."

They strode over the uneven ground, Collins setting a brisk pace. "See that dip in the ground?" he asked Spiller. "That's where they dug a trench around the site to reduce the ground shock."

"You seem very clued up. Have you been following the news?"

"Sure. Got to keep up to date with what's going on."

"Absolutely." Spiller studied his colleague from the corner of his eye. Generally, Collins showed little interest in anything other than the football scores. What had got into the lad? First, he'd put himself forward for the sergeants' exam, and now he was keeping up with current affairs. He seemed brighter too, more alert. *Maybe he's finding his feet at last,* Spiller thought. *Good for him.*

Arriving at the cordoned-off area, Spiller presented his ID

to the uniformed officer who'd stepped forward to meet them. It was a godforsaken spot to be stuck on duty, and the young officer looked relieved to have something to do, smiling as he made a note on his clipboard. The routine was repeated for DC Collins, then the officer lifted the blue-and-white tape and ushered them through, saying, "The CSM says you don't need overshoes or anything up here, but you'll need to suit up if you want to go down into the crater."

"Thanks. Who's running the show?" Spiller asked.

"Ms Haig, sir."

Spiller shared a look with Collins, both men raising their eyebrows. Nicola Haig was the senior crime scene manager at Exeter. Her presence was not insignificant, and both men had a sudden glint in their eyes.

"Reckon they must've found something juicy," Collins said.

"Count on it."

Spiller led the way toward the crater, slowing as he reached its edge. The rectangular crater was the size and depth of a swimming pool. A white forensics tent had been erected at one end of the crater, and as they watched, the tent's flap was pushed open from within. A petite figure emerged, clad in a hooded white forensic suit, complete with face mask. The figure stopped short on seeing Spiller and Collins, blinking up at them, and despite the sexless outfit, there was no mistaking the piercing, pale blue eyes of the CSM, Nicola Haig.

"Nicola," Spiller said. "How are you getting on?"

Nicola removed her face mask. "Tim, I wasn't expecting anyone from CID. I told Chief Superintendent Bradbury that he'd get my preliminary report tomorrow."

"Don't worry, we're not here to put the pressure on," Spiller said. "We came along to indulge our professional curiosity, that's all."

"I see." Nicola hesitated. "You're not expecting to go inside the tent, are you? Only—"

"No, no," Spiller interrupted. "We wouldn't dream of trampling all over your crime scene."

"But you'd like to know what we've found, even though we haven't begun to analyse it yet. Does that cover it?"

"You've got me bang to rights," Spiller said with a smile. "I'll tell you what, it's been a long day and you look like you could use a drink. How about we reconvene in the nearest pub?"

"I don't know," Nicola replied. "I haven't quite finished yet. I only popped out for a breather."

"When you're ready. We can wait, can't we, Collins?"

Collins nodded. "Definitely. There's the Star Inn five minutes down the road. They ought to be open by now."

"How do you know that?" Spiller asked. "It's hardly your local."

"They've got a big screen. I sometimes come down to watch the football."

"Ah. Well, so long as they can rustle up a cold lager, that'll do for me. What do you say, Nicola? Must be hot, wearing that suit. Thirsty work."

"All right," Nicola said. "I give in. I'll see you there in fifteen minutes or so. Unless something crops up."

"It's on Sidwell Street," Collins chipped in. "You can't miss it."

Nicola raised her hand in a weary wave, then she replaced her mask and trudged back into the tent.

There was nothing to be gained from hanging around, so Spiller and Collins headed back toward the street, nodding to the uniformed officer as they passed.

"That went well," Spiller said. "What do you think?"

"I don't know. She seemed pretty cagey. She might not tell us much."

"Yes, but why is she keeping her cards so close to her

chest? And why is she reporting directly to the chief superintendent?"

Realisation dawned on Collins' expression. "Could be something big."

"It could indeed," Spiller said. "So, let's go and find a quiet table at the Star. I don't know what Nicola's discovered, but whatever it is, it's going to be a hell of a lot more interesting than the regional crime figures."

CHAPTER 12

Dan hadn't been sure about going to the pub, but Alan had talked him into coming along. Now, sitting at a corner table in the Wild Boar, waiting for Alan to bring their drinks over, Dan felt himself beginning to unwind. He'd had a lousy day, but everything in the pub was exactly as it should be, from the gentle murmur of background conversation to the scent of brewed hops hanging in the warm air. Sam was busy behind the bar, and when Dan had walked in, she'd favoured him with a warm smile. That alone had made the trip worthwhile. He'd have a chat with her later, but first he wanted a pint and a few minutes to decompress.

As if on cue, Alan arrived with a couple of pint glasses, sliding one across the table to Dan as he sat down. "Get that down you. Three Hares. It's the guest ale."

"Thanks." Dan took a mouthful of beer. And another. Then he let out a sigh.

"It's not bad, is it?" Alan said. "Fruity with a hint of honey, according to Sam. It's put some colour back into your cheeks. You look better already."

"I needed that."

"No wonder. You were telling me about your phone call with DS Spiller."

"They've made him an inspector."

"Oh. Good for him. What did he have to say?"

"Not much," Dan said. "But he did promise to send someone to see me."

"I suppose Embervale's too small-time for him now. Did anyone turn up?"

Dan took another sip of beer. "Remember when we stayed in Newquay? There was a detective constable. DC Kulkarni."

"I remember her well. She was very attractive, in a sporty sort of way."

"Detective Sergeant Kulkarni now. She's been promoted and I'm not surprised. She has a sharp mind."

"Coming from you, that's high praise," Alan said. "I suppose, with Spiller moving up to inspector, there was a vacancy for a sergeant. Is that how it works, do you think?"

"I've no idea. At any rate, she was convinced that I was in the wrong place at the wrong time. The car thieves were making a getaway, and they lost control."

"Joyriders?"

"No. It was a carjacking. The driver was seriously injured. It sounds as if they left the poor man for dead."

Alan shook his head in dismay. "Terrible. I never thought I'd hear of such a thing around here."

"Criminals have no respect for postcodes, Alan. You ought to know that by now."

"Yes, but Exeter is hardly a hotbed of crime, and for all we know, the thieves came from elsewhere."

"Unlikely. DS Kulkarni said there's been a spate of similar thefts across the county. That points to a local gang."

"Ah well, at least your old Toyota will be safe. I can't see anyone pinching that in a hurry."

"True, and your Golf isn't what you'd call a performance car."

Alan pulled a face as if affronted. "That car is a classic, and unlike your bucket of bolts, my VW is solid as a rock."

"There's nothing wrong with my car."

"Apart from the hideous screech coming from the fan belt and the way the suspension creaks every time you turn a corner."

"Does it still do that? I must've got used to it." Dan smiled. "It's about time I traded it in, and once this job has paid out, I'll be able to afford something better."

"I'll drink to that." Alan took a draught of his beer.

Dan followed suit, but he sipped his pint distractedly, lost in thought until he realised that Alan was watching him intently. Returning Alan's unwavering gaze, he said, "What?"

"You tell me. Something's on your mind."

Dan hesitated, but there was no point trying to fool his friend; they knew each other too well. "All right. Despite what I've just said, I'm not totally convinced that my near miss was an accident. It just doesn't feel right. There was no reason for that car to mount the pavement. The road ahead was clear."

"These things happen. People make mistakes, especially in the heat of the moment."

"But according to DS Kulkarni, the thieves aren't just a bunch of amateurs. They know what they're doing, so why would they drive so erratically? They weren't being chased, so they could've blended in with the traffic and gone on their way."

"Maybe something spooked them, made them panic."

"That's one possibility," Dan said. "But you should've seen it, Alan. I can't help thinking they went straight for me. It felt deliberate."

"Okay, let's say you're right. Why would anyone target you?"

"I don't know, but it could be connected to CEG. There's something going on there, something not quite right."

Alan sat up a little straighter. "Something worth investigating?"

"It could be. There's an odd atmosphere, and it makes me wonder what's at the root of it. I get the idea there's been some kind of problem and it's been swept under the carpet."

"What kind of problem?"

"I can't pin it down. No one has done or said anything particularly strange, but I keep feeling as if there's something going unsaid."

"Your instincts are often right," Alan said. "On the other hand, it can take a while to settle into a new job, get to know your workmates."

"That's what I thought at first. I assumed people were taking their time, sizing me up, but it's more than that. There's a sense of secrecy, as if too many people are holding something back. For instance, the man who hired me was called Neil, and it turns out that he's left the company. They say he took early retirement, but it seems very sudden, and everyone else is reluctant to talk about it."

"Do you think he left under a cloud?"

"That would be my guess, and there's something else. I was told not to ask too many questions about the past."

"A red rag to a bull."

Dan laughed. "I've been told not to poke my nose in, and it's piqued my curiosity? Is that it?"

"It has been known, although no one has ever succeeded in getting you to stop asking questions, so will this time be any different?"

"It might be. I've got more to lose. They can terminate my contract at a moment's notice."

"But you're going to do it anyway," Alan stated. "You're going to do some digging."

"I'm tempted."

"I say go for it. You know you want to, so you may as well get stuck in and to hell with the consequences."

Dan studied Alan for a moment. "You're in a very cheery mood."

"I've had a good day. I'm sorry about what happened to you, but it won't help anyone if I'm down in the dumps as well."

"You're right. It's been an odd day, but I've lived to tell the tale and I'm in the pub with a mate, so enough of me banging on. What've you been up to this afternoon?"

"After I left you, I did a bit more shopping in Exeter, then I came home and got down to work. I rattled off three thousand words, just like that." Alan clicked his fingers. "I tell you, when the writing goes well, there's nothing quite like it. This book has been like pulling teeth, but now it's got a whole new lease of life."

"Good. Maybe the pep talk with your agent gave you the boost you needed, and do I detect the signs of some subtle pampering? If I'm not mistaken, you've had a haircut. A good one too."

Alan ran his hand over the back of his head. "Yes, but I'm not sure about it. It's a bit trendy for me. People might think I'm trying to look younger."

"Trust me, it's a damned sight better than your usual short-back-and-sides at that barber in Newton Abbot."

"Do you think?"

Dan nodded firmly. "Definitely."

"I'll take your word for it. I hope you're right. I've got a photoshoot tomorrow. My author photo isn't up to scratch, apparently."

"Where? Exeter?"

"No. She's coming here. To the house. To beard me in my den."

"That sounds fun. It's a shame I'll miss it, but it's back to work for me tomorrow."

"The first day of a new case, perhaps?"

"Possibly," Dan said. "I suppose you're keen for me to

start digging because it plays into your new image as the amateur detective."

"That's not true at all. I'm encouraging you because I know what you're like. You've sniffed out a problem, and it will eat away at you until you do something about it. You won't rest until you get to the bottom of it."

Dan held up his hands. "Sorry. I shouldn't have said that. I'll tell you what, I'll get the drinks in. Same again?"

Alan regarded his glass which was still three-quarters full. "There's no rush, and there's no need to apologise. You've had a rotten time of it. Almost being run over is enough to make anyone a bit tetchy."

"Even so, I'll get the drinks in." Dan stood. "Besides, I want to have a word with Sam."

"In that case, I'll have the same again. By the time you've finished chatting with Sam, I'll have dispensed with this one."

"Fine."

Dan headed to the bar and was immediately under Sam's watchful gaze. He offered a warm smile, but she merely raised an eyebrow and said, "What can I get you?"

"Hello to you, too," Dan said cheerfully, trying to lighten the mood. "Had a good day?"

"Not bad, but I've got to go down to the cellar and fetch up some lagers in a minute, so…"

"I could give you a hand if you like."

"You? Seriously?"

"Of course. Why not?"

"Because it's a bit grim down there, and you're all dressed up in your smart shirt."

"That's okay. It's not new or anything."

Sam folded her arms. "So, if it was new, I'd be on my own, is that right?"

"No, I would've offered to help no matter what I was wearing." Dan maintained his smile, fighting off the sinking feeling that settled in his stomach whenever he did battle with Sam. "I'd like to help. Really."

"I can manage a couple of crates, you know. This place is better than any gym. I'm up and down the stairs all day."

"I'm sure you can manage, but my offer stands."

Sam didn't reply for a full second, then she tilted her head to one side. "Go on then. Come through. But don't blame me if you get mucky."

Dan marched to the end of the bar and lifted the hinged section so he could cross the threshold. He'd never been behind the bar before, but he didn't have time to look around; Sam was already heading through the archway that led to the kitchen. He caught up with Sam in the short corridor where she was unlocking a plain wooden door. Pulling it open, she said, "Mind your step as you go down."

She disappeared inside and Dan followed, his eyes adjusting to the gloom. The stone steps were steep and uneven, the treads too shallow for his feet, but Sam wasted no time in reaching the bottom and she waited for him, her hands on her hips. "I'll bet you've never been in a pub cellar before."

Joining her, Dan said, "No. Never. It's not what I expected."

"It's an old pub. What did you think it would be like? All shiny and new?"

"It's not that. It's... a bit more rustic than I'd imagined." Dan kept his tone light, but in truth, the cellar was almost enough to put him off beer for a while. Lit by a single bare bulb hanging from the ceiling, the place looked as if it had been neglected for years. The flagstones were cracked and chipped, and it had been far too long since they'd seen a broom. At one time, the walls had been painted white, but the paint was flaking, clusters of white crystals showing where the damp had penetrated the stone walls. Aluminium barrels stood in a haphazard arrangement around the room, shoulder to shoulder with steel canisters of CO_2. Stacks of plastic crates, all full of glass bottles, seemed in danger of toppling over at any moment, and a jumble of broken chairs were piled against the far wall. The corners of the room were lost in shadow, and if rats lurked there, Dan wouldn't have been surprised. The musty smell of damp and decay filled Dan's nostrils, and the dank air raised goose pimples on the back of his neck.

"Rustic?" Sam cast her disparaging gaze around the room. "It's a dump, that's what it is. I've been on at Craig for ages to sort it out, but he doesn't get it."

Dan pictured Craig Ellington, the pub's owner, shambling down the steps in his olive-green corduroys and waxed cotton jacket. "He probably thinks this is exactly what a pub cellar should be like. Authentic — that's what he'd call it."

"You know what? That's exactly what he said. Authentic. And something about olde worlde. He said we ought to bring the punters down here, give them a taste of the past or some such rubbish. I told him he could forget about that. I said, 'What about insurance? What would happen if some daft bugger slipped on the stairs?' That shut him up."

"Good for you. But is he going to get the place cleaned up?"

"Is he hell," Sam said. "It'll be up to me, like everything else around here."

"You could use some help. You work hard, but it's too much for one person."

Sam's expression softened, and despite the harsh overhead light, when she looked up at him, her pupils were wide. "I knew you had something on your mind. Why else would you come down here?" She took a step closer to him. "This is your way of applying for the job, is it?"

"Oh. Not exactly. I mean, I would be happy to help out occasionally, if you really want me to, but I've just started a new job, and I'm going to be pushed for time, so—"

"I should've known," Sam interrupted. "Of course, you wouldn't get your hands dirty, would you? You wouldn't dream of it. You must want something else. You want a favour, don't you? You want me to do something for you." She let out an exasperated sigh. "Come on then, out with it. What do you want?"

"I…" Dan swallowed. "Actually, I was going to ask you out."

Sam's face froze in an expression of horrified disbelief.

"But obviously I've misjudged the situation," Dan went on. "I'm sorry." He summoned a rueful smile. "It seems to be my night for apologising. Of course, I'll happily carry something upstairs for you. I promised to help, so—"

"Never mind all that," Sam blurted. "You were going to ask me out? Like, on a date?"

Dan nodded.

"Where? Where were you going to take me?"

"Batworthy Castle. For afternoon tea. I've heard it's nice there, and I thought you'd enjoy it."

"I went in the bar once, ages ago, but I've never…" Sam looked down at her hands, her left hand clasping the fingers of her right. "I've wanted to go there for years, but no one's ever…" She looked up sharply. "Are you making fun of me?"

"Not at all. The company I work for are hosting a get-together on Friday, afternoon tea at Batworthy, and partners are invited. I thought that you and I might go together."

"Partners?"

"I know that might sound like I'm jumping the gun, but as soon as I was invited, I thought of you. I wanted you to come with me."

"You wouldn't want me hanging around, not with all your new business friends."

"But that's it, Sam. I do want you to come, as my date. As for the others, I don't give a damn what they think."

"You say that now, but when I don't know what knife and fork to use, it'll be a different matter."

"It's just afternoon tea. Sandwiches and scones. You won't need—" Dan cut himself short and took a breath, and when he went on, he made his tone as gentle as he could. "Sam, none of that stuff matters. As far as I'm concerned, you'd be the most important person in the room."

Sam studied him. "Really?"

"Really."

"I don't know. It sounds a bit..." Sam bit on her lower lip. "It was nice of you to ask. Don't think I don't appreciate it, but it wouldn't work out. I might scrub up all right, but as soon as I opened my mouth, they'd be looking down their noses at me. You'd be embarrassed."

"No, I would not," Dan stated. "I'd be proud to have you beside me."

A silence crept through the chill air and planted itself firmly between them until Dan plucked up the courage to break it. "That's a *no* then, is it?"

Sam nodded. "Sorry."

"Right. Well, the tea party isn't until Friday, so if you change your mind..."

"I don't think so. Anyway, I've been away from the bar too long. I just need to grab the lagers." She selected a plastic crate of bottles, lifting it easily.

"Let me." Dan held out his hands, but Sam made no response. "Come on, Sam," Dan said. "Let me do this, at least."

"All right." She passed the crate to him, then hefted another. "If you could leave it by the chiller, that'd be great."

They climbed the stairs in silence, Dan leading the way. He placed the crate carefully behind the bar.

"Thanks," Sam said. "I'll get you a pint if you like. On the house."

Dan saw that his half-empty glass still sat on the bar. He

didn't really want it, but he picked it up anyway. "Thanks, but I still have this."

"Don't be like that."

"I'm fine, but I don't need another drink yet. I'd better go and see how Alan's doing. He'll be wondering what's happened to me."

"Okay. I'll see you later. If you still want that drink…"

"Maybe. But I might have an early night. It's been a busy day." Dan managed a brief smile, then he walked away quickly. *I made a total mess of that*, he thought. *Where did I go wrong?*

He ran back though his exchange with Sam, but try as he might, he couldn't figure out what he should've said. Joining Alan, Dan sat down heavily with a sigh.

"You changed your mind?" Alan asked.

"About what?"

"Er, you went to get another round in." He picked up his own glass, swilling the remnants of his drink meaningfully.

"Oh, sorry. I was helping Sam carry up some bottles, and it slipped my mind. Do you still want another? I was thinking of going home."

Alan looked from Dan to the bar and back again. "What happened? What did you say to Sam?"

"Nothing much."

"I'm not buying that. She looks upset. Have you two been arguing again?"

"No."

"Well, something's upset her. She's looking anywhere but at you."

Dan sighed. "All right. I asked her out. I offered to take her to the tea party at Batworthy, and she said no. Okay?"

"I see." Alan finished his drink. "And are you going to accept that?"

"I don't have much choice."

"Faint heart never won fair lady."

"But no means no," Dan said. "I should've guessed she wouldn't be interested. She doesn't think of me in that way."

"I don't know what to say to that. But you'd better think of something, Dan. She's coming over."

"What?" Dan turned to see Sam advancing toward him, a pint glass in each hand.

With a guarded smile, Sam slid the drinks onto the table. "There you go. Two pints of Three Hares. On the house."

"Thanks," Alan said. "Er, I was just going to the loo." He stood, walking away at a brisk pace.

Dan nodded to the brimming glasses. "You didn't have to do that, but thanks all the same."

"That's all right," Sam said. "And about that other thing... I've been thinking."

"Oh?"

"Yeah. If I did go with you to Batworthy, you wouldn't go off and leave me on my own with a load of strangers, would you?"

"No. Of course not. I'd be with you all the time."

"So, when you said I'd be the most important person in the room, you really meant that?"

"Yes." Dan steeled himself. There were times when you had to lay your cards on the table, and this was one of them. "Sam, it'll be true on Friday and it's true right now. You're the most important person in any room. To me, anyway. That's not some stupid line. It's how I feel. I've felt that way for a while."

"Why didn't you say something?"

"I wanted to, but..." Dan looked into Sam's eyes. "I could make excuses, but to tell you the truth, I don't know why I've never told you how I felt. I'm an idiot. I shouldn't have waited so long, but I like you, Sam, and I'd really like you to come out with me. If you do, I'll make sure I look after you. If you aren't enjoying it, for whatever reason, I'll take you home. I promise."

Sam took a slow breath. "You're a pain in the arse, Daniel Corrigan."

"But—"

Sam silenced him with her raised hand. "Let me finish. You're a pain in the arse, but you've never lied to me. Not once. I reckon that's worth something, so..."

"So, you'll come out with me? On Friday?"

"Yeah. Providing I can get someone to cover the bar, and if I can get my hair done in time."

"You don't need to do anything special. You look wonderful as you are. You always do."

"Rubbish," Sam said. But her lips curled in a modest smile. "I'll see you on Friday. Text me the time, and I'll be ready."

"Great. That's just... great."

"All right. I'd better get back to work." Sam grabbed Alan's empty glass, then she headed back for the bar.

Dan watched her go. Was there a lightness in her step, or was that his imagination?

"What are you grinning about?" Alan sat down, pulling his fresh drink toward him.

"Nothing much."

"Pull the other one. You're in a world of your own. I just walked right up to the table, and you didn't even see me. I could've pinched your wallet and you wouldn't have noticed."

"Yeah. Right."

"Did you just hear what I said?"

Dan pried his eyes away from Sam for long enough to smile at Alan. "Not really. Was it important?"

"No, but would I be right in guessing that Sam has agreed to go out with you after all?"

"You would."

"Finally. I'm really pleased for you." Alan lifted his glass then added, "And the cherry on the top is Jay Markham now owes me a tenner."

"You had a bet on whether I'd ask Sam out or not?"

"It was only a bit of fun. It was Jay's idea, and in my defence, I was backing you all the way. Jay thought you'd never get around to it, but I knew."

"I don't know why I'm surprised," Dan said. "Everyone thinks they ought to know everyone else's business in this village."

"There'll be talk, but who cares? You're the one Sam said yes to, and she's great, she really is. She'll be good for you."

"I'm not counting my chickens," Dan said. "We haven't even been on our first date yet, and that's days away. In the meantime, anything could happen."

CHAPTER 13

The Star Inn boasted two large-screen TVs, both playing different sports at full volume, but Spiller and Collins found a table in the outdoor seating area at the back of the building. The sign by the pub's front door had promised a beer garden, but that was stretching the definition a bit thin in Spiller's opinion. The paved yard offered a few tubs of flowers and a climbing plant that had crept along the high wall, but most of the space was taken up by wooden tables with bench seats.

Still, it made a convenient place to sit while they waited. Collins and Spiller were the only two customers who'd ventured outdoors, so they could chat without fear of being overheard.

"So," Collins began, "how's life as a DI?"

Spiller chewed his words before he replied. "You know, I didn't really have any illusions. I knew it was going to be hard work, but…"

"Go on."

"It's not what I'm used to, that's all. Old habits die hard."

Collins nodded, then he sipped gingerly at his half pint of lager as if anxious to eke it out.

"How are you getting on with Anisha?" Spiller asked. "No hard feelings?"

"No, it's all fine. She made it to DS and I didn't. I don't hold it against her. She's easy to work with."

"That's good to hear. Teamwork, that's the most important thing."

"She's a lot better than my last DS, that's for sure. A right grumpy old sod he was."

"Very funny," Spiller drawled, but he found himself chuckling. This was more like it. "You'd do well to learn from the likes of Anisha," he went on. "The future belongs to bright young things like you and her. Old-fashioned coppers like me are a dying breed."

"I wouldn't say that. You taught me a lot, and I reckon there's life in the old dog yet."

Spiller tried to pull a face, but it somehow turned into a smile. "We'll see."

"Can I ask you something?" Collins said. "What made you want to come down and look at that bomb site?"

"I could say it was my unerring instinct, but in all honesty, I fancied a taste of some real police work, and I didn't think anybody else would be interested enough to chase it up. Everyone else is busy, and this was low-hanging fruit. There's a lesson for you. Don't worry about chasing after high-profile cases. Sometimes it's the littlest things that end up being the most interesting, while the big cases fall flat. You can think you're on to a murder, then it turns out the victim had too much to drink and fell down the stairs. Another time, you might be chasing up a burglary and find a meth lab in someone's cellar. It's not how a case starts that matters, it's—"

"How it ends," Collins interrupted. "Yeah, you might've mentioned that before." Collins leaned across the table, lowering his voice. "But let's talk about this bomb. How come the bones have survived? Why weren't they blown to bits when the bomb went off?"

"That's one thing we can ask Nicola." Spiller peered over Collins shoulder to focus on the pub's window. "In fact, that looks like her. Pop inside and check. If you're quick, you can intercept her at the bar and buy her a drink."

"I thought you were getting the drinks in."

"I'll owe you one," Spiller said. "Now, get in there before it's too late. Get her anything she wants."

"Fine." Collins stood and made for the pub door.

"Oh, and get me a packet of crisps while you're there," Spiller called after him. "Salt and vinegar."

Without looking back, Collins raised a hand as he marched inside. Spiller smiled to himself and savoured his pint of lager, content.

He didn't have to wait long before Nicola appeared, glass in hand, with Collins following sulkily behind. He looked distinctly put out, but at least he was clutching a couple of packets of crisps, and as he neared the table, he tossed a packet to Spiller's waiting hands.

"Ta," Spiller said, then he turned his smile on Nicola. "That looks posh. What are you having?"

"A G and T." Nicola sat down facing Spiller then took a sip of her drink, ice cubes tinkling in her glass. "Salcombe Gin with Luscombe tonic. Delicious."

"At that price, it ought to be," Collins grumbled as he retook his seat and opened a packet of crisps.

"Now, now," Spiller said. "Don't begrudge Nicola a decent drink. We invited her, remember. Our treat."

"Thanks." Nicola took another sip of her drink then set her glass down with an appreciative sigh. "This is all very nice, but there's not much I can tell you. Not yet. Besides, this isn't even your case, is it?"

"Let us worry about that," Spiller replied. "We're not about to go treading on anyone's toes. At this stage, we're taking an interest, that's all."

Nicola gave him an appraising look. "I see. Then you'll

understand if I don't go into details. I don't want to say anything that might jeopardise an investigation."

"So, there will be an investigation?" Spiller asked.

"Oh yes. There's no doubt about that."

"What are we looking at?"

There was a pause before Nicola replied. "An unexplained death."

Spiller searched her expression and said, "There's something else, isn't there?"

Nicola glanced back toward the pub as if to check that no one was listening, then she nodded. "There are signs of police involvement. We found a pair of handcuffs."

"Police issue?" Spiller asked.

"It looks that way. They were stamped or engraved. We haven't had time to study it properly, but we can make out that it says Exeter City Police."

Collins puffed out his cheeks. "Sounds a bit off. In the old days, we were the Devon and Exeter Constabulary, weren't we?"

"That only existed for about a year, and that was in the late sixties," Spiller said. "We've had a few different names over the years, but if you go back to when that bomb would've been dropped, we were officially Exeter City Police."

Nicola's eyes lit up. "I didn't know that. I was going to look it up later, but you've saved me a job." She hesitated. "There was a two-digit number as well. Seventy-three. Could it identify a particular officer?"

"I doubt it," Spiller replied. "Not with only two digits. But I'll put some thought into it. Maybe you could see your way clear to sending me a photo?"

"That should be okay," Nicola said slowly. "But you know what I'm going to say, Tim. Everything should be done through the proper channels. If you're on the case, that's one thing, but if you're not, I've probably said too much already."

"I understand." Spiller offered a reassuring smile. "I'll square it with the chief superintendent. In the meantime, perhaps you can help settle an argument."

Nicola regarded him levelly. "Go on."

"Well, young Collins here thinks we might be wasting our time looking into this case. He reckons there won't be much to go on, because the explosion would've blown the bones to bits. But bones can be preserved quite well when they're away from the air, can't they? I think they might've survived more or less intact, so long as they weren't right next to the bomb."

"You're fishing," Nicola said.

"Who, me?" Spiller asked. "No, we're just having a chat. You know what coppers are like when it comes to talking shop."

"Indeed. But all I'm hearing is a lot of idle speculation, and in my line of work, that's something we steer clear of."

"On the other hand," Spiller said, "I couldn't help noticing that your tent is right at the edge of the crater, which lends a bit of weight to my side of the argument."

"How so?"

Spiller held out his hands. "It suggests that the bones weren't directly hit by the blast, but when the dust settled, they were exposed. Not totally, perhaps. Just enough for some sharp-eyed soul to spot them."

Nicola mimed applause. "Well done, Inspector. You've got me bang to rights."

"So, the bones are in decent shape?" Collins asked.

"They're not bad," Nicola admitted. "But it's early days. You know how long these things take."

"There's no rush," Spiller said. "The poor sod has been down there for a while. Assuming that the remains are from the war, that is." He turned a questioning gaze on Nicola.

"Assume nothing," she said. "But the bones were beneath the block of flats they demolished a couple of weeks ago, and the building was put up in 1950, so the victim was almost certainly interred before then."

"Interred. Interesting choice of word," Spiller said. "Does that mean he wasn't killed in an air raid, buried under the rubble?"

"I didn't say the victim was a man."

"Most victims of murder are," Spiller replied smoothly.

Nicola let out an exasperated sigh. "There you go again. Who said anything about murder?"

"No one," Spiller said. "But I figure there are only a couple of ways the victim could've been buried with a pair of handcuffs. Either he was a copper and he had the cuffs with him, or he was wearing them when he met his untimely end."

Nicola drew her lips tight.

"Bloody hell," Spiller breathed. "That's it, isn't it? The victim was handcuffed. He was killed while he was in custody."

"You're jumping to conclusions," Nicola said. "There could be any number of explanations."

"Someone could've got hold of a pair of handcuffs," Collins suggested. "Stuff goes missing all the time."

"That's not likely," Spiller said. "Old cuffs didn't snap shut. You needed a key to lock them. Is that right, Nicola?"

Nicola nodded. "Perhaps now you can see why the chief superintendent wants this dealt with carefully."

"Who better to handle it than an experienced detective like myself?" Spiller said. "I'll have a word with the guv'nor in the morning." He smiled at Collins. "Do you fancy a crack at this? If I asked for you, I reckon the guv'nor would agree."

Collins looked down for a moment.

"I know what you're thinking," Spiller went on. "This case could go either way. If it all ties up nicely, you'll get noticed. But if it turns out that something dodgy was covered up a long time ago, no one will thank you for dragging it back into the light."

"You could put it like that," Collins said. "And I've got a lot on my plate. There's the carjacking for a start, and there are a couple of things coming to trial."

"You can handle it, and it's not like there'll be a lot of witnesses to chase up. Most of them will have passed away by now. This will be more of a research job. Old-fashioned police work, ploughing through the files. If we can find any files."

"Doesn't sound too bad," Collins said. "All right, guv'nor. I'm in."

Spiller patted him on the arm. "Good lad. We'll make a DS out of you yet."

Nicola had been following their exchange as if mildly amused, but now she leaned toward Spiller. "When you retire, you could have an excellent future in sales."

"That's one good reason to stay on the job," Spiller replied. "And since we're probably going to be working together, can I get you another drink?"

"Not tonight. I'm driving." Nicola drained her drink and set her empty glass on the table. "But next time, it'll be your round, Tim, and I'll be having a large one. I have a feeling I'm going to need it."

TUESDAY

CHAPTER 14

I t was mid-morning, and the IT office was usually filled with the clicking of mechanical keyboards and the background buzz of conversation, but Celine had the place to herself. Sitting at her workstation, she plucked the sticky note from her central monitor, frowning as she deciphered the clumsy scrawl of black ink: *Post room laser busted - J+R.*

"Great," Celine muttered. The main laser printer in the post room was notorious for failing at critical moments, so Justin and Rob had obviously rushed off to coax it back into life. *I keep telling Tom to replace the damned thing,* Celine thought. *But he won't listen to me.*

Celine dropped the note in her waste bin. She needed to have a word with Justin and Rob about effective communication. They had software to keep track of technical support requests. Each task was allocated a ticket number and assigned to a technician, but her colleagues tended not to use the system, making it hard to know who'd done what. Small wonder then that Tom would never admit they were understaffed; every time she raised the issue, he showed her the lack of open tickets and claimed they were managing just fine. Then he'd give her a patronising look, as if she were being hysterical. Meanwhile, Justin and Rob got to be the golden boys. Sure, they never had a bunch of unresolved tickets to deal with, because they never opened the damned tickets in the first place. It was all fly-by-the-seat-of-your-pants with them.

Celine realised she'd picked up a pen and was clutching it tight in her fist. She felt the pen's plastic body flexing beneath her fingers. If she squeezed any harder, it would snap, shattering into jagged pieces.

She closed her eyes, breathing deeply, in through her nose and out through her mouth, extending each exhalation as long as she could. She let go of the pen, bringing her hands together in her lap, letting one hand rest gently on the other, just as the meditation app had suggested. *That's better*, she told herself. *Let it go.*

And she heard a voice.

Celine's eyes snapped open. She tilted her head, listening. It was Tom talking to someone in his office. He had his door closed, but he'd raised his voice. Celine couldn't quite make out what he was saying, but if she moved a little nearer to his door...

I shouldn't, Celine decided. But she gripped the edge of her desk and pushed her chair backward, its castors rolling almost silently over the thin carpet.

"It's no bloody good," Tom was saying, his voice cracking as if it cost him some effort to keep it under control. "I'm sorry but I cannot do it. I just can't."

A quieter voice replied. A woman. Her tone was gentle, and Celine couldn't pick out a single word.

"No!" Tom snapped. "I won't listen. It's wrong. Can't you see that? What you want me to do... it's wrong. I've already done too much."

A chill crept along Celine's spine. What the hell had Tom got himself into? And who was he talking to?

The handle on Tom's door was wrenched down from within, the click of the catch as sharp as a gunshot.

Bloody hell! Celine pushed her feet against the floor and sent her chair gliding back toward her workstation. Still sitting, she whirled around, grabbing the edge of her desk and pulling herself closer.

She sat up straight, staring at her monitors and reaching for her mouse, clicking on Microsoft Outlook just to put something on the screen. She heard Tom's door opening, someone marching across the room. Celine looked up, trying desperately to appear unruffled, but she quailed inwardly at the sight of Melanie Steele storming toward her.

Forcing a smile, Celine said, "Morning. Everything okay?"

Melanie stopped a few paces away from Celine's desk, pulling herself up to her full height and lifting her chin as though preparing to make a regal proclamation. "How long have you been sitting there?"

"I..." Celine took a moment to regain control of her breath. "Only a minute. I've just come in. I've been upstairs, encrypting a laptop for Dan Corrigan."

Melanie's nostrils flared. "Oh, *him*."

Unsure how to respond, Celine simply nodded.

"Just now," Melanie went on, "you may have heard my... exchange with Tom."

"No, not really. I mean, I heard voices. I knew someone was in the office, but as I said, I've only just come in."

"You didn't hear what Tom said?"

"No." Celine hesitated. "Is he okay?"

"Of course he is. Why wouldn't he be?"

"I don't know. But I don't normally hear him at all. Usually, you'd never know he was there, so when I heard his voice, I wondered if he was all right."

Melanie seemed to consider this while her gaze swept rapidly around the room. Finally, she said, "Tom takes his work very seriously. This place, this office, it's his world, do you understand?"

"Yes," Celine said. "He's been here a long time." Sensing an opportunity to show a little solidarity, she added, "Men. They like to have their own territories, don't they? They're like little boys."

"I wouldn't know," Melanie shot back, but she studied Celine as though seeing her anew, and her expression softened. "They don't have our emotional resilience, that's for sure. I came down here to tell Tom about the IT budget for the next quarter, and he didn't much like it."

"Ah, that's a button we don't like to press."

"I can see why." A smile lit Melanie's eyes, and in a conspiratorial tone she added, "He'll get over it. He always does."

Returning Melanie's smile, Celine relaxed. *She's not as cold as people make out,* she decided. *You just have to get to know her, that's all.* But her thoughts were derailed by Melanie's next words:

"Tell me about Daniel Corrigan."

"Er, how do you mean?"

Melanie took a step closer. "You've just been up to his office. What are your impressions?"

"He…" Celine broke eye contact. She needed to choose her words carefully, and it was impossible while Melanie was staring at her like that.

"Go on," Melanie said. "I'm not asking you to betray a confidence. Remember, he's only here temporarily. He's not on the staff like you and me."

"Well, if you'd asked me yesterday, I'd have said he was fine. He came across as very professional, like he was on the ball. But today, he seemed different."

"In what way?"

"I don't know really. He had a lot of questions."

"What kind of questions?"

"Well, he wanted to know about Neil, about why he left the company. I asked him why he wanted to know, and he said he was just curious because he's in Neil's old office."

"Was that all there was to it? Or did he have some kind of agenda?"

"I'm not sure, but I thought he might've been feeling a bit insecure. He kept going on about Neil getting the sack, as if he was worried that he might be next."

"Neil wasn't sacked," Melanie said. "He left voluntarily, as you well know."

Celine blushed beneath the force of Melanie's glare. "Yes. Sorry. I didn't mean…"

"Never mind. You might be right about Dan feeling insecure. He's got a lot to prove, and if he doesn't get results, we'll have to let him go."

"Maybe that was it. There was definitely something on his mind. He seemed very distracted."

Melanie nodded. "You know that Dan was almost run over last night. Right outside."

Celine's face fell. "What?"

"Hadn't you heard? Samantha has been broadcasting it far and wide."

"That's awful."

"I know. I've told her not to spend her time gossiping. It does no one any good."

"No, I meant it was an awful thing to happen to Dan."

"Well, that too," Melanie said. "It goes without saying."

"What happened?"

"Apparently, he got in the way of somebody driving a stolen car. It's unbelievable, isn't it? There's been a spate of car thefts around here. I thought twice before driving to work today, but where I live, I really don't have much choice." She gazed at Celine with concern. "Do you drive?"

"No. I don't have a car at the moment. I walk, but if it's really awful weather I take the bus."

"Very wise. Good for the environment too." Melanie brightened. "I went electric as soon as I got the chance. Tesla. It's a dream to drive, and so quiet."

"Nice." Sensing a chance to steer the conversation in a different direction, Celine screwed up her courage and went for it. "I can't afford to run a car at the moment, but I'm looking for the opportunity to progress, you know, to develop my career."

"Are you thinking of leaving us?"

Celine's heart sank. Melanie might've offered some encouragement, but she appeared utterly disinterested, and already she was taking out her phone and checking the screen.

"It's not that I'm keen to leave," Celine said. "I thought that, after the expansion, there might be possibilities within the company. I'd like to take on more responsibility. I think I'm ready."

"I see," Melanie said distractedly. "I suppose something might come up, but I wouldn't want to raise your hopes. Things are going to be tight in this department."

"Oh, it's just that Seb said—"

"Seb?" Melanie interrupted. "What's he been saying?" Melanie raised an eyebrow and offered a sardonic smile. "Has he been promising you the moon?"

"Not exactly, but he mentioned that we could be moving to new premises, and that we might need a whole new network."

There was a pause before Melanie replied. "Seb has big plans, but he doesn't hold the purse strings in this company. That's my job. As long as I'm in charge of the finances around here, we won't be splashing out on unnecessary infrastructure. There'll be no new money for IT, not in the short term. That's what was making Tom so irate. One of the things, anyway." She lowered her voice. "A word to the wise, Celine. I asked about Dan Corrigan because he's become a touchy subject as far as Tom's concerned. If I were you, I wouldn't mention the man's name while Tom's around."

"Why?"

"Unfortunately, Tom has somehow found out the size of Dan's fee and he's spitting blood about it. He thinks we're throwing away good money, when we should be investing in new hardware. What was it he kept asking for? A backup system, that was it."

"Actually..." Celine began, but Melanie went on as if Celine hadn't spoken.

"Tom just doesn't get it," Melanie said. "He doesn't see the bigger picture. As far as he's concerned, the company starts and ends in this dingy little place." She cast a disparaging glance at the cluttered workstations. "God knows what he thinks we do on the fifth floor. He talks as if we sit on our hands while everyone else runs around doing the real work. He has no idea." She shook her head as if dismissing a thought. "Right, I have a meeting in five minutes. Must dash. Good to catch up with you, Celine. Good luck with your job hunting."

"Thanks," Celine murmured, but Melanie was already marching from the room, leaving Celine on her own.

Thanks for nothing, Celine thought bitterly. For a second, she'd thought Melanie might've been an ally, but she should've known better. Tom always said that the management didn't appreciate the importance of IT, and it looked like he had a point. Celine felt a pang of sympathy for the man. Tom was a company man to his core. When they told him what to do, he buckled down and got on with it. He might grumble and whine, but he got the job done. He wouldn't have raised his voice to Melanie unless something had seriously upset him, made him see red.

Celine shivered. The air con must be playing up again, because the temperature in the room had suddenly dropped. She brought her mind back to her work, trying to concentrate as she read through her emails, but an insistent thought kept pushing itself to the front of her mind. There was something wrong at CEG, seriously wrong, and Melanie's parting words took on a new significance: *Good luck with your job hunting.*

It might be wise to make a serious search for a job at another company. If there was going to be trouble at CEG, she didn't want to get caught in the fallout. She ought to say goodbye to the company. Before it was too late.

CHAPTER 15

S tanding in the sunshine in his back garden, Alan pulled in his stomach and squared his shoulders, beaming at the camera. But Suzie Henshaw did not press the shutter. Instead, she lowered her camera and frowned. Dressed in black, and with white-blonde hair and a pale complexion, Suzie had the appearance of a monochrome photo come to life. Her dark eyes completed the picture, and right now they were focused on Alan so intently that he shifted his weight from one foot to the other and asked, "No good?"

Suzie shook her head. "Please don't smile unless I ask you to. Okay?"

"All right, but I would hate to come across as looking unfriendly. I write children's books. I don't want my readers to think I'm grumpy."

"I know that, Alan, but these aren't family snapshots. You want to look your best, and I can do that for you. So please, relax and enjoy the experience. Put yourself in my hands."

"Okay. I'll try." Alan tugged at the collar of his leather jacket. "Actually, I'm a bit warm in this. Maybe we should try something else. I've got a linen jacket inside."

"Stay as you are for now, Alan. Let me get some shots and

then you can take a break." Suzie raised her camera and said, "Okay, turn to your right a little. Good. Nose to the left. Now, lift your chin and set your jaw, like you're determined. That's it."

Alan could make out the click of Suzie's camera, and he wondered why a digital camera should make a sound at all. Perhaps he'd ask her later. For the moment, he'd better follow her instructions as best as he could.

"That's great!" Suzie called out, her voice startlingly loud. "Fantastic!"

I hope the neighbours aren't listening, Alan thought. At least, with Dan out at work, there was no danger of him peering over the garden fence. "How about this?" he said, folding his arms and turning toward the camera.

"Yes. Try out a few different poses. The more the merrier."

"I'll give it a go." Feeling slightly foolish and hoping he didn't look too much like a model from a menswear catalogue, Alan tried as many combinations of facial expressions and gestures as he could muster.

Finally, Suzie seemed content. She put her camera down and swigged some water from a brightly coloured insulated bottle.

"Can I get you anything?" Alan asked. "A cold drink or a cup of tea?"

"I'm good thanks, but you can grab something if you like. Take five while I go through what we've got so far."

So far? Alan thought. *How many more photos could she possibly want?* But he smiled and stepped into the cool of his kitchen, glad to take a break. He shrugged out of his leather jacket and hung it on the back of a chair, then he took a deep breath. That was better. Now for some tea.

As he put the kettle on, it occurred to him that he must've seen thousands of portrait photos of famous people, but he'd never really thought about the time and effort that went into making each one. It was a backstage business, carried on out of sight of the public eye, and each image was a construct: a lie of a kind. Mind you, the same could be said of his own work. It was a mixture of make-believe and artifice. Fiction: the word said it all.

The kettle boiled and Alan made to grab a teabag from the jar on the counter, but he changed his mind. There was a packet of lapsang souchong in the cupboard, and it was the only thing for a hot day.

Alan brewed his mug of tea, but he'd only taken a sip when Suzie joined him in the kitchen.

"Don't worry," she said before Alan could speak. "Take a couple of minutes and finish your tea. Then I'd like to take a few shots indoors if that's okay."

"That's fine. I think the place is reasonably tidy."

Suzie smiled as she looked around the room. "Perfect. The light in here is great. Bright but not too harsh."

"Yes, I like it in here," Alan said. "I often bring my laptop in here and work at the kitchen table."

"Even better. I'd like some shots of you at the table, tapping away at the keys." She grinned. "You haven't by any chance got a vintage typewriter lying around the place, have you?"

"I've got an Olivetti portable, but it's stored in a box somewhere, and it'll need a good clean. I've been meaning to restore it for years, but I keep forgetting about it."

"It's a pity, but I don't think we've got time to go hunting for it. Let's stick with the laptop for now. Could you get it, and I'll get set up while you finish your tea."

"No problem." Alan set his tea aside and went to retrieve his laptop. He was only out the room a few minutes, but when he came back in, Suzie had brought her bag inside and she'd already erected a small tripod on the table, complete with some kind of light. "My portable studio," she explained while she unfolded a circular panel of white cloth that sprang into shape. "This is a reflector. It'll help me to control the light and get rid of any shadows that we don't want."

"Fascinating." Alan seized the chance to gulp down some tea, then he set up his laptop in its customary place.

"That's perfect, but before we get started, do you have the hat? I was told we needed some shots of you with a hat."

"Ah. I'm really not sure about that."

"It was in the brief," Suzie said. "Leather jacket. Fedora. The client was very specific."

"Am I not the client?"

"Nope. You're not picking up the bill, Alan. You're the model. This is your chance to shine, and it's my job to make you look good. I've done this hundreds of times, so just go with it, okay? Trust me."

"I do. But if I feel uncomfortable, I'll end up looking silly."

Suzie's smile seemed to say that she was used to dealing with models and their jitters. "Okay. Let's just chat for a second. You write detective stories for kids, right?"

"Not exactly. They're adventure stories."

"Oh. I thought that was the point of the hat: to look like one of your characters."

It was Alan's turn to smile. "The hat is part of my new look. It's my agent's idea. You see, in real life, I've been involved in a handful of investigations, some of them very serious."

"So, you're a private investigator on the side?"

"Not officially. More of an amateur." Alan explained his history of tackling cases with Dan, keeping the tale as brief as he could, and Suzie hung on his every word.

"Now I get it," she said. "I wish I'd been briefed on this from the outset. It makes all the difference."

"Does it?"

Suzie nodded firmly. "Context is everything." Suzie scooped up her camera and snapped back into picture-taking mode. "Now, pop your jacket back on, Alan, and get that

hat." Alan was about to protest, but Suzie added, "If the hat doesn't work out, that's fine, but we ought to give it a whirl."

"Okay." Taking a long breath, Alan trudged into the hall and retrieved the brand-new grey fedora from a coat hook. Pausing in front of the mirror on the wall, he plonked the hat onto his head and adjusted the brim. *Ridiculous*, he decided. But Suzie had been insistent, and there was little point in arguing with her. She clearly took her work very seriously.

He smiled as he returned to the kitchen, determined to make the best of an awkward situation. After all, Suzie was a guest in his home. "How's that?" he said.

"Not bad, Alan. I'll have to work with the shadows, but I think we're on to something. You look good."

"Flatterer. But seriously, I'm sorry if I was being difficult."

"No worries. Compared to most models, you're a treat, believe me." Suzie switched on the tripod-mounted light and adjusted it carefully, then she fixed Alan with a purposeful look. "Okay, let's get you comfortable at the table, and we'll see what happens."

For the next few minutes, Alan did as he was told, pretending to type at the keyboard or gazing thoughtfully toward the window. Meanwhile Suzie flitted around him, moving the light or the reflector, and keeping up a stream of encouraging comments as she clicked away with her camera. Caught up in Suzie's enthusiasm, he began to enjoy himself. He even forgot he was wearing the hat. And then suddenly Suzie was switching off the light and packing up her gear.

"All done?" Alan asked.

"Yeah. We've got plenty to work with."

"Do I get to take quick peek?"

Suzie wrinkled her nose. "Sorry, but there are too many to go through them now. It would take too long, and anyway, they're not edited yet. I need to look at them properly, but you won't have to wait long. I'll pick out a fairly broad selection for editing, then I'll send them through to your agent in the next couple of days. I got some good shots, so I'm sure everyone will be happy."

Alan tried to hide his disappointment. "Well, that's something to look forward to. Will I get to choose which ones we use?"

"That's between you and your agent," Suzie said. "If I were you, I'd let a professional choose. You need someone with a good eye, someone who knows the market you're aiming at." Suzie stowed the last piece of equipment and hoisted her bag onto her shoulder. "Right, that's me done. Thanks very much, Alan. It's been a pleasure working with you."

"Thank you. It's been fun." Alan shook hands with Suzie. "Do you need anything before you go, or are you dashing off?"

"I'm fine, thanks. I've got to go." Suzie plucked a business card from a side pocket on her bag and offered it to Alan. "If you need to get in touch, my details are all there."

Alan took the card. "Thanks. I'll see you out."

At the front door, Suzie took her leave quickly, and the house suddenly seemed very quiet. Alan padded back toward the kitchen, but he stopped when he caught sight of himself in the hall mirror. He was still wearing the fedora, but this time it didn't strike him as so odd. "It's not that bad," he muttered, then he took off the hat and the jacket, returning both to their hooks.

From outside, he heard a car engine start. Suzie had used Dan's parking space, and Alan had told her that was fine. She'd be long gone before Dan returned from Exeter. But it sounded as though Suzie was in no hurry to leave after all. He could hear her car ticking over.

Alan wandered into the front room and peered out of the window. Suzie's car was still there, and she was in the driving seat, looking down at something in her lap. Alan wondered if she was having trouble finding directions for her journey home, but then Suzie looked up, lifting her phone to her ear. She began talking, her lips moving rapidly and her eyes on the house. She didn't seem to notice Alan, so he raised his hand and gave her a friendly wave. Her eyes snapped to his, and she gave a start.

Alan smiled and Suzie recovered her composure, returning his wave. She put her phone down, then she put her car into gear and reversed out of the parking space. She turned the car around, then she drove away. She didn't look back.

Alan stood at the window for a moment, distinctly unsettled. In his mind, he replayed Suzie's reaction when she'd seen him standing at the window. Had there been a flash of guilt in her eyes? It was hard to be sure, but Alan had been a teacher for long enough to know a mischievous expression when he saw it. Suzie had been up to something. He'd put money on it.

WEDNESDAY

CHAPTER 16

At lunchtime, Dan strode through the streets of Exeter. He marched past the cathedral, taking little notice of the young people picnicking on the well-kept grass of Cathedral Green, and he ignored the cafes crammed with tourists. He had a destination in mind. Some time ago, Alan had shown him Rougemont Gardens: a pretty piece of parkland hidden away behind the Royal Albert Memorial Museum. The gardens had been built on a site that had once been part of the defences of Exeter Castle. If you knew where to look, you could still see sections of the ancient city wall built by the Romans, and there were traces of the defensive ditches dug at the time of William the Conqueror. But for Dan, the value of the park lay in the fact that it was generally quiet. He could stroll along the leafy paths until he found a peaceful place to eat his lunch.

It didn't hurt that on an earlier jaunt to Exeter he'd discovered an excellent coffee shop nearby. The Burnt Bun Bakery was pretty much perfect, and they did a brisk trade in take-out lunches. He could get a decent cup of coffee and a vegan sandwich, sometimes made with deliciously fresh sourdough, on any working day.

The quickest route to the cafe took him through a narrow passageway that led from Cathedral Green to the bustling high street. The alley ran between two buildings and was just about wide enough for two people to walk side by side, but Dan halted at the alley's mouth. A group of tourists, led by one of the city's official, red-jacketed tour guides, was coming toward him. Dan stood back, and while he waited, he cast a look back toward the cathedral, admiring the play of the soft summer sunlight on the mellow stonework. The building almost glowed.

But something snagged Dan's gaze.

A tall man perched on the low wall that surrounded the green. He was alone and he had his back to Dan, but even so, there was something vaguely familiar about him. The man was facing the cathedral, but he wasn't looking up at it. His head was down, as though he was staring at the ground, and his shoulders were hunched. A footsore tourist, perhaps. But if the man was flagging, it was probably his own fault. *Who wears a raincoat on a day like this?* Dan thought. *Some people have no idea.*

"Thank you kindly, sir."

Dan turned to see the tour guide smiling at him.

"No worries," Dan said. He cast his eye over the party of tourists as they filed past. Most of them looked hot and tired too, but their expressions changed when they saw the cathedral, and cameras and phones were raised in readiness.

The guide gathered his charges, and smiling to himself, Dan resumed his quest for lunch.

A short while later, reusable cup and cardboard carton in hand, Dan made his way into Rougemont Gardens and let the scent of sun-warmed greenery wash over him. Today's vegan special was a wrap filled with roasted vegetables and seasoned with harissa. Dan could hardly wait to get started, but with his hands full, he'd find it easier, and enjoy his lunch more, if he could find somewhere to sit in the shade.

He stopped to look around. The gardens were almost deserted. A pair of young women pushed their strollers along a path, chatting as they went along, their young charges fast asleep. Further along the path, a man hurried to the nearest bench and sat down, turning his face away.

Dan stared. The man was tall and he was wearing a long raincoat. This was the man he'd spotted near the cathedral. And he'd seen him somewhere else too.

Yes. On Dan's first day in the office, he'd looked outside when he'd heard the explosion, and in the alley outside, he'd seen someone who looked remarkably similar to the man sitting on the bench.

He wasn't just similar, Dan decided. *It was the same man.* Of course, that's why the raincoated figure had seemed familiar when he'd spotted him by the cathedral.

A coincidence, Dan told himself. *Why would anyone follow me?* He could think of no reason, but then, he had no idea why anyone would try to run him down in the street, and that had happened just a couple of days ago.

He should march up to the man and demand to know what the hell was going on. But there was still a chance that Dan was mistaken, and the man didn't seem to present a threat. He had the slightly stooped posture of someone who took little exercise, and Dan guessed he might be middle aged. The man was above average height, but apart from that, he looked ordinary in every way. Besides, if the man was up to no good, he'd only deny it. A direct challenge would achieve nothing.

But there was another way.

Dan turned around and strolled away, looking around as if he didn't have a care in the world. He'd come to know the routes around the park quite well; ahead, the path forked. Dan took the smaller path on the right, smooth tarmac giving way to rough gravel. His footsteps were loud on the gravel, but that was good, it was what he wanted.

The path took him into a shady part of the park where mature trees would provide plenty of cover. In seconds, the leafy canopy closed overhead, and Dan picked up the pace, almost jogging as he sought out a place to lie in wait. There. A huge chestnut tree had a trunk wide enough to conceal him, and Dan cut across the grass toward it. He glanced back to make sure he was unobserved, then he darted behind the tree and he waited.

A breeze riffled though the leaves above. Birds sang. But otherwise there was silence. No one was following him. He'd made a mistake.

Dan exhaled, almost laughing at himself. He leaned back against the tree and took a sip of his coffee. It was good and still hot. He drank some more, savouring the taste.

And then he froze.

Footsteps crunched on the gravel. Hesitant, nervous footsteps. Slowly, Dan placed his cup and the carton containing his lunch on the ground. He pressed himself back against the tree trunk and, staying low, he crept forward.

The tall man shuffled along the path, looking around him as though frightened, his gaze flitting from one shadow to the next.

Dan waited while the man drew closer. Closer still. Something told Dan he ought to recognise this odd figure, but the man moved in a strange, stiff manner, his chin down as though he hardly dared to look up at the world, and Dan couldn't get a good view of his face.

But the man was hunting for something, that was plain, and for some reason, he'd chosen Dan as his quarry.

The man was almost level with Dan now, and Dan was ready.

Pulling himself up to his full height, Dan strode out from behind the tree, marching toward his pursuer. "Can I help you with something?" he demanded. But when the man stared straight at him, Dan halted in his tracks. "Neil? Is that you?"

But Dan already knew the answer. He'd never met Neil Hawthorne in person, but he'd seen photos. The straggly grey beard was new, and the unkempt hair tumbling over the deeply furrowed brow was enough to alter the man's appearance, but Dan was in no doubt. This was the former head of online operations at CEG, a man Dan had spoken to on the phone several times before starting his new job.

Neil's fingers went to his lips and he plucked at his beard nervously, then he nodded. "Dan. It is Dan, isn't it?"

"Yes." Dan stepped closer to Neil, moving slowly. "What are you doing here? And why are you following me?"

"I wanted to talk."

"There are simpler ways, Neil. You have my phone number."

"I couldn't risk it. It had to be offline, and I needed to get you away from the office. I had to talk to you alone."

A sense of foreboding stirred in Dan's stomach. He knew how it felt to cling to the corporate ladder, knowing you'd climbed too far, even as the treacherous treads slipped from beneath your feet. Neil had that look about him. Failure. It was in the stoop of his shoulders and the shabbiness of his shoes; it was in the limp folds of his stained raincoat and the slackness of his jaw. Neil was a broken man.

As if to confirm Dan's fears, Neil sidled closer to him, bowing his head and looking up at him in an oddly lopsided way, his bloodshot eyes burning with a fierce need. When Neil spoke, his voice was hoarse with repressed emotion. "You know the old saying, follow the money?"

"I've heard it in films and on TV. But—"

"Forget the fairy stories," Neil blurted. "This is real life, not some ridiculous soap opera. In real life, there are consequences. People get hurt. Do you understand?"

"Not really. I can see you're worried, Neil, but I have no

idea what you're talking about. When people say follow the money, they're usually talking about trying to uncover a crime. Is that what you mean? A crime has been committed?"

"You're getting there. But think plural. Crimes. Going back years, decades."

"Okay, and who is responsible for these crimes?"

Neil shook his head. "Oh no. You don't get me that easily. I'm admitting nothing, and it'd be better for you if you never found out."

"You're not making sense. Listen, you're obviously upset. Why don't we find somewhere for you to sit down?"

"I'm fine right here. There's no one to overhear."

Time to change the subject, Dan thought, and making his tone gentle he said, "You look as though you could do with a rest. Why don't you get away from it all for a while? I was told you had a boat – that sounds like a great way to relax."

"Ha! I did have a boat. I had to sell it, and quickly too. I couldn't hang around trying to get a good price. I had to let it go."

"Why's that?"

"I needed the money. I had to have something to live on."

"Really? Didn't they give you a good retirement package?"

"Don't make me laugh," Neil sneered. "I didn't retire. I was kicked out. Thrown under a bus."

"I'm sorry to hear that. I know what that feels like."

"Do you?" Neil studied him for a moment. "Yes, I believe you do. I can see it in your eyes." A hesitant smile twitched at the corners of Neil's lips. "Maybe this'll be okay. Maybe you're not one of them."

"And by *them*, you mean the management at CEG?"

"Yes." Neil raised his hands as though he'd have liked to grab Dan's arms in a brotherly embrace. "You see? I was right, you *do* understand."

Dan kept his expression neutral. There had to be some

way to let Neil down gently, to calm his anxiety and persuade him to go home. But before Dan could come up with anything, Neil said, "I need your help, Dan. I've got something to ask you. A favour."

"Okay. Go ahead."

Neil ran his hands over his hair as if preparing himself. "Okay. Listen. What if there is no money, Dan? Nothing to follow. No way to prove a damned thing."

"I don't know what you mean, Neil. What are you trying to say?"

"Think about it. No money. What else is there?"

"Stocks? Gold? Diamonds?"

A cackle of dry laughter burst from Neil's lips. "I thought you were smarter than this, Dan, but you're not getting it." Neil glanced over his shoulder and cocked his ear as though listening to a sound only he could hear. "Just the wind," he muttered. "Nobody there. Nobody."

Poor guy, Dan thought, and he held out his hands, his fingers spread wide. "There's only you and me, Neil. So, why don't you tell me what all this is about?"

"I can't. I can't do that. It's too dangerous. But listen, you can still help. You need to find my old office. It's at the end of the corridor."

"I know. They've put me in there. I've been using your old office since Monday."

"Bloody hell. They put you in that hole. You must've rubbed someone up the wrong way. Who did you upset? Was it Seb? You need to watch out for him. There are a lot of skeletons in his cupboard. A lot of demons."

"Okay, that's enough," Dan said. "Neil, you're overwrought. Go home. Get some rest. But then you need to see someone, someone who can help: a therapist or a counsellor. Maybe I could find someone for you."

"There's only one person who can help me, and he's standing right in front of me. Are you in or out?"

"Neil—"

"Simple question. In or out?"

Dan drew a breath. "I'll try and help if I can, but I'm not going to make any promises."

"All right. It's very simple. I left something behind in my office, and I need you to let me in so I can find it."

"I can't do that, Neil."

"Yes, you can. We can use the back stairs. Nobody will see us. I tried to let myself in, but they changed the code."

"Was this on Monday?"

"Might've been."

"I saw you outside the office on Monday," Dan said. "You were walking away when that bomb went off."

"Maybe I was, maybe I wasn't. But if you won't let me in, you'll have to find it for me, bring it out."

"Find what? The office was empty apart from the furniture."

"It's just a photo, a picture of my wife, Felicity."

"I didn't know you were married."

Neil's face fell as though something inside him had crumpled. "I used to be. Felicity died, six years ago. So that picture... it's got sentimental value. I've got to have it."

"Yes, of course. I'm sorry for your loss, but I didn't see any photos. Do you have another copy? Or perhaps you can get another one printed."

"No. It has to be that one. There's a note on it, okay? On the back. It's personal, and I need to have it. It's one of the few things I have to remind me of her. Do you understand?"

"Yes. I'll try and find it. Really, I will. I'll have a good look around."

"It's in the desk, under the drawers."

"I suppose it could be," Dan said. "You think it might've slipped down the back?"

"It didn't get down there by accident. I hid it."

"Why? And if you knew it was there, why didn't you take it with you when you left?"

"Because I didn't have time, you bloody fool. They marched me out of the building. I barely had time to get my coat. Joseph bloody Clayton came in with some big bloke from the post room, and they escorted me off the premises. I didn't even get to say goodbye to anyone."

"That's awful."

"You don't have to tell me. Oh, they were very polite about it. Can't have anyone making a fuss, can we? But at the end of it, I was on the street, and that was that. Goodbye, Neil. Bugger off and don't come back."

Fighting back his own memories, Dan said, "I'll find your photo, Neil. Today. How can I get it to you?"

"I'll find you. I'll wait outside. What time do you finish work?"

"Around four, depending on how it's going, but I don't think you should be hanging around the office. I park near the quay. Why don't you wait down there?"

"Okay. There's a bar. The Quayside Inn. I'll get a drink, sit outside."

"I'll find you."

"Great." Neil exhaled, closing his eyes for a moment, then he fixed Dan with a look. "Don't let me down, Dan."

"Don't worry," Dan said. "Go and sit down, get something to eat. I'll see you later."

Neil nodded, then he turned and walked away, his shoulders slumped.

Dan watched him leave. *That's a lot of anxiety over a photograph,* he thought. But Neil probably felt as though he'd lost everything, and Dan could sympathise with that. The photo had become a symbol in the man's mind: a token that stood for the life he'd once had. If restoring the photo to its rightful owner could bring the poor man some peace, it was the least he could do.

Dan went to retrieve his lunch. He'd have to eat the wrap while he walked back to the office, but perhaps he had time to drink his coffee. He lifted the lid and took a sip. It was just about warm enough, and he drank it quickly, then he headed back, hardly noticing his surroundings as he trudged through the park.

CHAPTER 17

Someone was knocking on his office door, but DI Spiller kept his attention fixed firmly on his computer. "Hang on," he called out. "With you in a minute."

He typed out the last sentence and read it through, checking it carefully. *Nailed it*, he told himself. *It's in the bag.*

He heard the door open and a woman's voice said, "You're looking very animated."

Spiller looked up to see Nicola standing in the doorway, a tablet computer in her hand. She was watching him with undisguised amusement. "Which is it?" she asked. "Candy Crush or today's Wordle?"

"Hilarious." Spiller saved his file and closed it, making sure it was in the right folder, then he met Nicola's gaze. "I'm more of a solitaire man myself, but as you well know, such things are frowned upon during working hours, so if I look pleased with myself, it's because I've just put the finishing touches to the budget for the Belmont Road case."

"That's why I'm here. The chief superintendent called me up himself. I've been instructed to give you every assistance."

There was an icy edge in Nicola's tone, and Spiller sent her a questioning look. "Something wrong?"

"No, it's just the usual, run-of-the-mill bullshit. I shouldn't let it get to me."

"Let me guess. You tried telling the guv'nor you were up to your eyeballs in work, and that this isn't really in your job description, but he told you to drop everything and do it anyway."

"Something like that. He doesn't mince words, does he?"

"He's a Scot," Spiller said. "He prides himself on plain speaking, but he can come across as a bit heavy handed. Why don't you take a seat? Tell me all about it."

"I didn't come looking for tea and sympathy. I'm just venting. Forget I said anything." Nicola sat down on a chair facing Spiller, lifting her tablet and tapping on the screen. "I'm here, I've got my preliminary report, so let's get started."

"Sure. But you could have emailed it to me, saved yourself a trip."

"Oh no, that wasn't good enough for the chief superintendent. I had to come in person."

"Something's lit a fire under him," Spiller said. "When I asked to take this case, I expected to have a fight on my hands, but he was all ears, eager to help."

"That's all very well, but I don't see the rush. You attended the post-mortem examination, and you know what we're dealing with."

"Yes. Dr Bunting was very thorough, as always, but she was somewhat cagey about the cause of death. I'm hoping you can work your magic and give me something to work with. After all, a crime has been committed, and it looks like there's been some kind of police involvement. What should we do? Ignore it?"

"No, of course not, but we should be focusing our resources on the here and now, on cases where we can actually make a difference. Lab tests take time and they cost money. You know that as well as I do."

"Let me worry about the pounds and pence," Spiller said.

"If we need to outsource some work or call in specialists, I can get that taken care of."

"Seriously?"

"Oh yes. The guv'nor wants this case cleared up." Spiller offered a patient smile. "Think about it. Sooner or later, the facts about this body are going to come out. We can keep a lid on it for a while, but eventually some plucky journalist will hear about those handcuffs, and that will be that. It's a nice juicy story, and there'll be no stopping it. The only safe approach is to get ahead of it, clear it up fast."

"It's a PR issue, is that it?"

Spiller's smile vanished. "Come on, Nicola, you know better than that. It's a public trust issue. We can't do our jobs without it."

"All right." Nicola held up her hands. "Let's start again."

"Fine. Let's run through your report, shall we?"

"Certainly." Nicola looked down at her tablet. "I'm sending you a copy now, and you can read all the details later, but I'll go through the main points with you while I'm here. Okay?"

"Perfect." Spiller glanced at his screen. The email arrived, and he opened the attachment, but he focused on Nicola. He wanted to watch her as she delivered her report, gauging her level of confidence in each point.

"To begin with, I want to make clear that these are initial findings," Nicola said. "They're subject to change in the light of future results."

"Understood. Let's begin at the beginning. From the post-mortem examination, we know that the victim was an adult male, and he would've been approximately 185 cm tall. That's about six foot one in old money. He was middle aged, and there was enough hair to tell us that he had straight, dark hair." Spiller paused. "Any chance of getting some DNA?"

"There's always a chance, but who would we be matching

it against? When this man was killed, DNA wasn't well understood and DNA profiling hadn't even been invented."

"We might find a family member of the deceased."

Nicola looked doubtful. "If we do manage to retrieve some DNA, and if you can find a relative, we could try that approach. A familial match won't conclusively prove the dead man's identity, but it can tell us whether someone might be related to the victim."

"Might be?"

"Yes. We can give you a measure of probability, nothing more."

"Fair enough. Let's run through the pathologist's report together. I'd like to get your perspective, Nicola."

"All right. The victim suffered a range of injuries sometime shortly before his death. The pathologist found multiple fractures that hadn't had time to heal. The most likely candidate as a cause of death was probably blunt force trauma to the skull, but as I'm sure you appreciate, at this stage we can't categorically say that the injury actually caused his death."

"Tell me more about the broken bones. Take me through them."

"Starting with the smaller injuries, the pathologist found three cracked ribs, but they're non-specific traumas, meaning that they could've resulted from a fall, or a kick, or something else entirely. Moving on, there was significant blunt force trauma to the metacarpals of the victim's right hand. The metacarpals are the bones that run from the wrist to the base of the fingers, and it would appear that four of them were fractured at around the same point along their length, suggesting an impact with something long and thin, such as a narrow-edged implement. It certainly wasn't a crushing injury. In fact, the pathologist found no evidence of crushing injuries." Nicola sent Spiller a meaningful look.

"So, we can rule out the idea that our victim might have been buried by falling rubble during an air raid?"

Nicola nodded. "The victim was lying on his front, but his body lay in a straight line, his arms behind his back. He was surrounded by soft earth rather than masonry or timbers. It would appear that he was buried quite carefully."

"Can we say he was dead at the time?"

"Almost certainly, but we'll come to that." Nicola swiped the screen of her tablet, scrolling through the pages. "Next we come to the patellae. There was blunt force trauma to both kneecaps, and again, the fractures were clean, suggesting an impact with a narrow implement. There were also fractures on the tibia of the right leg."

"The same kind of breaks?"

"Not exactly, but then the shin bone is very different to the metacarpals or the patellae. It's a thick bone and strong."

"Could the same implement have been used?"

"We can't rule that out. But now we come to the skull. There was non-specific blunt force trauma to the malar bone, and that would indicate a blow to the cheek, but much more significantly, the victim's frontal bone had been fractured. Again, the trauma was linear. According to Dr Bunting, this would've been a serious injury, with significant bruising, bleeding and swelling in the brain. This injury *could* have caused the victim's death." Nicola paused for a breath. "Now, because the fracture was on the frontal bone, and the victim was lying face down when we found him, it's highly likely that the injury occurred before he was placed in the ground."

"What about the handcuffs?"

"He was wearing them when he was buried, and this might interest you," Nicola said. "We found the key. It was right next to him."

Spiller raised his eyebrows. "As if someone threw the key into the man's grave?"

"Exactly so."

"Any sign of clothes? A uniform, perhaps?"

"Not yet. We're testing the soil, looking for fibres, but I'm not expecting to find much. There was hardly anything except bones and some hair. At this stage, we don't know if his clothes have decomposed or if they'd been removed."

"So, we're looking at someone who was beaten up, possibly stripped, handcuffed, tortured and then murdered."

"Thankfully, it's not my job to put those kinds of scenarios together. I'll leave that to you. But as a working hypothesis, I'd say that your version of events is consistent with the evidence we've found so far."

"It's beginning to look like a gangland interrogation. First, he's taken. They punch him in the face, but they hit his cheek rather than the mouth because they want him to be able to talk. But he doesn't give in, so they knock him down and give him a kick in the ribs. Maybe he's dragged off somewhere. They'd need somewhere quiet where nobody would hear what was going on."

"You're straying beyond the evidence."

Spiller waved her objection aside. "Think about it. It's very methodical. They hit his hand with a crowbar or a piece of lead pipe. It must've been excruciating, but he still won't talk, so they cuff him and go to work on his legs, breaking his shin and both kneecaps. Maybe he gives them what they want, maybe he doesn't, but either way, he knows too much. They have to kill him, so they finish him off with a blow to the head."

"All right," Nicola said. "But if this was the work of a criminal gang, then how do the handcuffs fit in? Surely, they'd have been much more likely to tie their victim up with a piece of rope or a length of cable."

"True, but I can think of one explanation. They wanted to make a point."

"To whom?"

"To the rest of the gang," Spiller said. "If they'd found a

rat, they might well have made an example out of him. The police informant, or an undercover officer, was cuffed and then murdered."

"You're ignoring a simpler, more obvious explanation. The crime was committed by a rogue police officer: someone who wanted information from the victim and was prepared to stop at nothing in order to get it."

Spiller shook his head. "A police officer wouldn't have been so stupid as to leave his handcuffs at the scene. No, this was ruthless and vicious. It has all the hallmarks of organised crime."

"I'll take your word for it, but listen, I have to head back to my office. I can tell you which tests I've ordered if you like, but to be honest, they're all listed in the report and there's not much more to say. We're still waiting for the results."

"Don't worry about it," Spiller said. "If you could let me know as soon as any results come in, that would be great."

"No problem. Was there anything you wanted to know before I shoot off?"

"Nope. I'll let you go. I know how busy you are."

"Believe me, you don't know the half of it." Nicola stood. "So, who have you got working with you on this one?"

"Just DC Collins and me at the moment."

"Really? I thought the chief superintendent was going to pull out all the stops."

"We felt it was best to keep the team small," Spiller said. "For the moment, anyway."

"Right. I suppose he's trying to keep the case under wraps for as long as he can."

Spiller summoned an inscrutable smile. "I can neither confirm nor deny that statement, but Collins and me make a good team. The lad might be a bit wet behind the ears, but he's got potential. We'll get a result."

"Let's hope so. Where is he, anyway? I didn't see him on the way in."

"Collins is delving deep into the archives, searching through the old records, seeing what he can unearth."

"Rather him than me." Nicola headed for the door. "We'll talk soon," she called over her shoulder, and then she was gone.

I wouldn't be too sure about that, Spiller thought. He had a feeling that this case wasn't going to hinge on the forensics. Nicola's team had probably found everything of significance already. No, this was going to be old-school police work, and that suited Spiller down to the ground.

CHAPTER 18

DS Kulkarni made her way to the reception desk in the offices of CEG and presented her warrant card to the blonde woman behind the counter.

"I'm Detective Sergeant Kulkarni, Devon and Cornwall Police. I'm here to see Daniel Corrigan."

Without batting an eyelid or so much as glancing at the proffered card, the receptionist said, "Do you have an appointment?"

"No. I don't need one. I'm here on police business, so I'd appreciate it if you could tell Mr Corrigan I'm here, unless he isn't in the office, in which case, I need to know where he is."

The receptionist tapped at her keyboard and without looking up from her screen said, "Please take a seat. I'll let Mr Corrigan know you're here, and I'm sure he'll come down as soon as he can."

"I can go up to his office. Just tell me where it is. I'll be able to find it."

The receptionist turned her cool gaze on Kulkarni, but there was a flash of alarm in her blue eyes. "I'm afraid I'm not allowed to do that, not when I'm on my own. If there was someone available to take you up—"

"Never mind," Kulkarni said. "I'll wait." She paced across the lobby, her hands clasped in front of her. She did not sit down. Instead, she stood beside the main doors, keeping her gaze fixed on the receptionist. Was the young woman a little flustered? She was avoiding eye contact, looking anywhere but at Kulkarni. At first sight she'd appeared poised and unflappable, but all that had changed when she'd discovered Kulkarni's reason for being there, and now the receptionist's posture seemed stiff and awkward.

It's not uncommon, Kulkarni decided. The announcement of her rank tended to inspire a certain amount of guilty panic in law-abiding folk. She ought to be used to it by now. There were only two kinds of people who didn't worry when a detective arrived: the truly innocent, and those who were so corrupted by criminality that they'd gone past caring. The difficulty came in deciding which people fell into each camp.

She checked the time on her watch. It was almost four o'clock, and she still had a mountain of work waiting for her back at the nick. But thankfully, it wasn't long before the lift doors opened and Dan Corrigan appeared, hurrying to meet her, an uncertain smile on his lips.

"DS Kulkarni," he said, a hint of nervousness in his voice. "What can I do for you? Is everything all right?"

"Nothing to worry about," Kulkarni replied. "But there's something we need to discuss. Is there somewhere quiet we can talk?"

"Er, actually, I was just about to head out. We can go outside if you like."

Kulkarni examined Dan for a second, noting the messenger bag hanging from his shoulder. Yes, he had his jacket on and he looked like a man who was ready to head home. "Okay," she said. "If you don't mind walking and talking, that's fine with me."

"Great." Dan gave the receptionist a friendly wave and said goodbye, then he patted his jacket pockets as though checking he'd got everything. He gestured to the door. "Shall we get going?"

"Sure." Kulkarni led the way outside, then she halted, facing Dan. "Where are you parked?"

Dan hesitated. "By the quay. In the car park."

"Do you use that one every day?"

"Yes. Why do you ask?"

"No reason. I was just thinking that it must work out expensive. The park and ride is cheaper."

"Thanks. I'll look into that. I'm still finding my way around the city."

"Me too. Shall we head for the quay then?"

Again, Dan seemed hesitant, his gaze flitting up and down the street. But before Kulkarni could press him to make a decision, a smartly dressed, silver-haired man appeared from the building and strolled over to join them.

"Hello, Dan," he said. "Off home?" Without waiting for an answer, he turned his attention to Kulkarni as if expecting to be introduced.

Dan obliged. "Doug, this is DS Kulkarni. She just dropped in to see me."

The man did not look best pleased, but he extended his hand for a shake. As Kulkarni took it, he said, "I'm Doug Petheridge, the CEO. Is this a private matter, or is there something I can help with?"

"I'm following up the incident that occurred here on Monday."

Doug lowered his eyebrows. "Here? At my company?"

"No, sir," Kulkarni said. "Literally here, on this road. Mr Corrigan was almost hit by a speeding car."

"Yes, of course." Doug's expression lightened, and he sent Dan a sympathetic smile. "I was so sorry to hear about that, Dan. Dreadful thing to happen. I've been meaning to pop in and see how you're doing, but I was assured you weren't hurt, and you know how it is. I've been tied up in back-to-back meetings."

"Too busy to check on an employee who was almost killed?" Kulkarni asked.

Doug's smile tightened but did not slip. "As I said, I knew that Dan was all right after the accident, and he's a big boy. I'm sure he can look after himself. Isn't that right, Dan?"

"Yes, I'm fine," Dan said. "It's in the past. There's no point dwelling on it."

"That's the spirit." Doug patted Dan on the arm. "Good man. I'll leave you to your chat with the detective sergeant. But since it's nothing to do with CEG, I'd prefer it if you'd move somewhere more discreet."

"Why's that?" Kulkarni asked.

"I'd have thought it was obvious," Doug replied. "A police officer on the doorstep gives a certain impression. I don't want the other employees to be worried unnecessarily."

"I'm in plain clothes, sir," Kulkarni said with a smile. "You didn't know I was a police officer when you first saw me."

Doug's posture stiffened. "Even so, I'd ask that you conduct your business elsewhere. I don't want to be the man who says he knows the police commissioner, but as it happens, I play golf with Stephen from time to time, and I'd hate to bother him with a complaint. He has enough on his plate already."

"It's all right," Dan chipped in. "We were just about to leave. We're heading into town."

"That's right," Kulkarni said, pushing aside a flush of irritation at Dan Corrigan's intervention. *Typical man*, she thought. *Stepping in to save the lady.* She needed no protection, especially when it came to dealing with a stuffed shirt like Doug Petheridge; the man was all bluster and hot air. She should ignore Petheridge's thinly veiled threat, but she couldn't help looking the man in the eye and adding, "I'd be happy to send you a copy of our complaints policy, sir. Would you like me to do that?"

Doug's only reply was a superior smirk. He nodded to Dan then he turned on his heel and walked away. Kulkarni watched him as he stopped beside a car parked at a meter. A muted beep announced that the car had been unlocked, and Doug climbed in. A moment later he drove past, looking straight ahead. Kulkarni took a good look at the car. It was a Jaguar XF, sleek, black and very powerful, its engine barely making a sound as the car accelerated away.

She thought of the recent car thefts, imagining how easily it could be done. People felt safe as they got into their cars, their minds on other things. Someone only had to approach them at the right moment, ready to strike.

Interrupting her thoughts, Dan said, "Shall we go?"

"Yes," Kulkarni said. "But what was all that about heading into town? You said you were parked by the quay."

"I forgot earlier, but I have to pick something up in town, so if you don't mind, we could talk on the way."

"No problem," Kulkarni replied, but as they began walking along Southernhay West, a suspicion stirred into life. Daniel Corrigan didn't seem like the kind of man to forget when he had an errand to run, and it was telling that he hadn't specified exactly what he was supposed to be picking up. If she pressed him on the subject, would he be able to come up with a credible story? *I won't ask him yet*, she decided. *I don't want him to feel threatened.*

They turned a corner into Cathedral Close, heading toward the cathedral itself, and as they entered the quiet street, Dan appeared to relax. Smiling, he said, "So, what can I help you with?"

"We think we've found the car that almost ran into you. Unfortunately, it's been burnt out, but I'd like you to look at some photos and see if you recognise it."

"I'll try. The car clipped a metal railing, and it left a deep dent all along the wing. That ought to be obvious."

"Exactly, and the car we found has damage that ties in with your account." Kulkarni took out her mobile phone and located the photos, then she held her phone out to Dan. They stopped walking while she scrolled through the images one by one with her thumb.

Dan studied the photos intently, then he met her gaze. "That looks like the same car, but it's hard to be sure. It's in a hell of a state."

"Yes. It could be that the damage made the car hard to shift, so the thieves decided to cut their losses and tried to destroy any evidence that might be inside."

"But you're not convinced of that, are you?"

Kulkarni shook her head slowly. What had given her away? Had Dan picked up the doubt in her voice, or had there been something in her body language? Either way, she'd have to be more careful. *I'm supposed to be questioning him*, she thought. *Not the other way around.*

Kulkarni started walking once more, and as Dan matched her pace, she said, "Assuming it's the same gang, this is the first car we've recovered. There's been no sign of the other cars at all. Not a trace."

"If they've established a pattern, why would they change it?"

"There could be a number of reasons, but I've learned to avoid too much speculation. It gets you nowhere."

"I disagree," Dan said. "Sometimes, when you haven't got much else to go on, it's good to indulge in a bit of speculation. It frees the mind, leaves the way open for creative thinking."

"That's what you did back in Newquay, was it?"

Dan shrugged. "It worked, didn't it?"

"After a fashion, but you managed to get yourself into hot water. It's a good job we were there to help, and we got there by solid police work: reviewing the evidence, interviewing witnesses, following procedure."

"I'm grateful for everything you did, but I have successfully solved a number of cases, so you must admit, there's room for different ways of working."

Kulkarni raised an eyebrow. "I've been hearing about some of your so-called cases. When you interfere in a police investigation, you consider that to be *work*, do you?"

"Ouch. Okay, so I'm an amateur, but it's not as if I treat these things as a hobby. It's much more important than that, and it hasn't been all fun and games."

"So why do it? Why get involved?"

"I keep asking myself the same question. All I know is that when a problem presents itself, I try to solve it. If people are dishonest, if they try to hide what they've done, then I look into it. Is that so different from your line of work?"

"If only my life were that simple." They'd reached Cathedral Green and Kulkarni gazed across the grass to the stained glass and carved stone of the venerable building beyond. "If you want to go looking for a solid line between right and wrong, you should go inside and talk to a priest. You won't find that kind of cast-iron certainty out here."

"I'm not religious, and I know real life can be messy, but that doesn't mean we can't try and untangle truth from lies."

"With guesswork? Intuition?"

"If it helps, why not? For instance, a while ago you said, 'Assuming it's the same gang.' That means you're starting to doubt whether that car was stolen by the same thieves. What led you to that conclusion? Intuition?"

Kulkarni had to look away from Dan, hiding her smile, but the man didn't miss much and he said, "Ah, I'm right, aren't I? You think someone else took that car."

"It's a possibility we're considering. The other thefts have been reported in the media, so it might've given someone the idea."

"A copycat crime. Interesting. That would explain why the car was burnt out."

"It might," Kulkarni said. "But there's another possibility that we have to consider."

Dan looked thoughtful for a moment, his good humour slowly vanishing. "You think this might not have been about stealing a car. You're beginning to wonder if I was right when I said the car was driven at me deliberately."

Reluctantly, Kulkarni nodded. "It's a possibility that I can't rule out, so I have to ask you a few questions. For instance, do you know of anyone who might wish to do you harm?"

"No. No one."

"What about someone who's affairs you've looked into? Could someone be bearing a grudge?"

"Not as far as I know."

"Put some thought into it," Kulkarni said. "There are people who've been sent to prison because of the things you've done. Try to remember if anyone has ever made any threats against you."

"I can't recall any, and I don't think I'd forget something like that."

"You live in a small village, a close-knit community. If you go around getting people arrested, it's going to be noticed. People have family and friends nearby, and some of them might want to pay you back for what you've done."

"You sound as though you have someone in mind."

"Not exactly, but I want to run a name past you. Kevin Pearson. He used to be the landlord at the village pub."

"I remember who Kevin is, but we're not likely to see him around for a while yet, are we?"

"No, but I had a quick look at his file, and he has a brother. Keith."

Dan seemed to weigh this up. "I think I might've seen him at the trial, but I've never actually met him."

"We have. I can't go into the details, but Keith's been in trouble in the past."

"What kind of trouble?"

Kulkarni thought about the criminal career of Keith Pearson: the string of convictions leading from teenage petty theft to the gang-related violence of his adult life. It was a sad catalogue of misery dealt out to others, culminating in a spell in prison for possession of a firearm, but she couldn't divulge confidential information to a member of the public. Instead, she made her tone grave and said, "Serious trouble. The kind you want to avoid if you possibly can."

"Do you think he might be coming after me?"

Again, Kulkarni weighed her words before replying. "There's no evidence to suggest that. As far as we know, Keith is living in Plymouth and keeping his nose clean. I only mentioned his name because, if you come across him, you should steer well clear. Do not confront him. Make sure you're safe then call us."

"I'll do that," Dan said. "Thanks for the warning."

"That's all this is: an informal word of warning. I still think it's unlikely that you were targeted. There are other, more plausible explanations for what happened. There's every chance that you were unlucky, but as a precaution, I suggest that you think about what I've said, and if you have any concerns, call us."

"I will."

"Good." They'd reached the edge of Cathedral Green, and Kulkarni stopped, smiling at Dan to let him know their chat was over. "Which way are you headed?"

Dan looked around. "Oh, I've got several things to pick up. I'll probably have to pop into a few different shops."

"Okay, I'll let you get on. Thanks for taking the time, Mr Corrigan. Remember, there's probably nothing to worry about, but if you need to call, you have my number."

"It's stored on my phone," Dan said. "Thanks again. Bye."

Dan walked away, striding purposefully toward an alley that would take him to High Street. She watched him until he was out of sight. He didn't hesitate, didn't look back. There was nothing shifty in the way he moved. But something was wrong. Dan's story about running errands had been just that: a fiction. What had been his intention? Had he wanted to lead her away from his true destination? *I could follow him*, she thought, but she had no legitimate reason to suspect Dan was breaking the law, and she simply didn't have time to go traipsing around Exeter on a whim. There was work enough waiting on her desk.

Kulkarni headed back toward Southernhay, barely registering the cathedral as she passed by. Daniel Corrigan was hiding something, but for the life of her, she couldn't guess what that might be.

CHAPTER 19

Dan glanced back over his shoulder as he neared the quayside, but there was no sign of DS Kulkarni. The memory of their conversation made him cringe. He'd never been much of a liar, and DS Kulkarni had a disarmingly frank gaze. He was sure that she'd seen right through his pathetic subterfuge. For a moment, he'd thought she might follow him, forcing him to go through the charade of tramping around the shops, but thankfully she'd left him alone. Once he'd left DS Kulkarni behind, he'd made for the quay, taking a circuitous route through a series of meandering side streets to make sure he didn't bump into her again.

Earlier, he'd done as Neil asked, and he'd found the photo easily enough. It had been hidden beneath the desk drawers, just as Neil had said it would be, and Dan was prepared to accept that the woman smiling in the photo was Neil's wife. She'd looked happy and relaxed, sitting at a table outside a restaurant or bar, a glass of red wine on the table in front of her. But when Dan had turned the photo over, he'd found something written on the back: a couple of dates and a quote from Shakespeare, all written in a firm hand with a black ballpoint pen. Something about the note triggered a twinge of anxiety in Dan's stomach. Did it contain a code or some hidden meaning?

As Dan had studied the note, he'd been struck by a vision of Neil adding the photo to a pinboard littered with newspaper clippings and scribbled notes, strands of string stretched from one to another, forming a complex web of imagined connections.

Dan had seriously considered walking along the corridor and showing the photo to Seb Cooper. Seb had worked with Neil, and he might've been able to help, but Seb didn't seem like the sympathetic type. He probably would've poured scorn on Dan's efforts to help, seeing any kind of altruism as a form of weakness.

Dan had held on to the photo until the end of the day, and it was in his pocket as he passed the Old Custom House and spotted the Quayside Inn.

As arranged, Neil was sitting alone at a table outside the pub, his elbows on the table, his head resting on his hands as he stared out over the slowly moving water.

"Hi," Dan said as he approached, and Neil looked up with a start, his gaze sliding past Dan as if to search for someone else.

Dan sat down facing Neil, and he tried not to count the empty pint glasses clustered in the centre of the table.

"What took you so long?" Neil asked, his words slightly slurred. "Did something happen? Did you get it?"

"I got it. Don't worry. I've got it here."

Neil held out his hand. "Come on, then. Give it to me."

"I will. But first, tell me what all this is about, Neil."

"Nothing to tell. I want that photo. It's mine."

"Okay, but why did you hide it?"

Neil's bloodshot eyes flashed with alarm. "That's my business. Give it to me."

Dan sat back. "Neil, have you spent the entire afternoon drinking?"

"What's it to you? Besides, what else was I going to do? Now, hand over that photograph."

"In a second. Why don't we order a couple of strong, black coffees? We could grab some food too. Have you eaten?"

"Save it," Neil snapped. "I don't want your bloody sympathy, and I don't need your charity."

Neil's voice had grown louder as he'd spoken, and Dan spotted several of the other customers looking over; some concerned and some amused at seeing a man who'd clearly had one drink too many.

"Fine," Dan said. "I was trying to help, but here's your photo." He pulled the photo from his inside pocket and offered it to Neil, who snatched it from his hand.

Neil gazed at the image intently before turning it over to glance at the back. "Thanks," he muttered, then he stuffed the photo into his coat pocket. He nodded to Dan, then he stood and walked away, shambling over the cobbles unsteadily but without looking back.

Dan watched him for a second, but there was nothing he could do. He'd tried to help Neil, but he barely knew the man, and Neil had made it clear that he wanted to be left alone.

Having no reason to stay, Dan had made his way back to the car park and drove home. On the journey, he paid little attention to the news on the radio. He couldn't help thinking of his encounter with Neil. A profound feeling of disquiet had taken root in his mind. *It's over and done with*, Dan told himself. *It's best forgotten*. But though he tried to push the whole business from his mind, he couldn't shake the image of Neil shuffling away, his shoulders slouched like a man whose spirit had been thoroughly broken. *There but for the grace of God*, Dan thought, and he reminded himself that he had some worries of his own. DS Kulkarni's words of warning were decidedly disturbing. Could it be true that someone wished him harm?

"I'll soon find out," Dan muttered to himself. If someone really had tried to run him down, they'd already crossed a line, and before too long, they'd try again.

THURSDAY

CHAPTER 20

When Spiller arrived at work, he found Collins already beavering away. Collins' desk was cluttered with papers and cardboard folders, and his neck was craned forward as he peered at his computer's screen.

"Good morning," Spiller called out. "You're bright and early. You have been home, haven't you, Collins?"

"Morning. Don't worry, I haven't been here all night." Collins sat back and rubbed his eyes with his fingertips. "Feels like it though."

"You need a mug of coffee."

"Yeah. Good idea." Collins made to stand but Spiller gestured for him to stay put.

"I'll get them."

Collins raised his eyebrows. "Thanks."

Spiller made them a mug of coffee each, then he carried the drinks carefully to Collins' desk. A little encouragement went a long way, and the lad looked like he'd been working hard. He deserved a pat on the back. "There you go," he said, placing a mug in front of Collins. "Get that down you, and then you can tell me how you're getting on."

"Cheers." Collins took a slurp of coffee, then he set his

mug down and rubbed his hands together. "Right, guv. I've got lots to tell you."

"Glad to hear it." Spiller made a show of studying the jacket that hung on the back of Collins' chair. "Judging by the dust on your sleeve, you got stuck in at the records department yesterday. I take it that you had a good day."

Collins half turned to frown at his jacket, but he wasn't about to be derailed. "Yeah. It was hard work, and at first I thought I wasn't going to have any luck. I went through a ton of unsolved cases, but nothing seemed to fit."

"You ought to have asked old Geoff Higgins for help. He's still in charge down there, isn't he?"

"Haven't you heard? Higgins is no more, guv."

"Really? I didn't know that. Poor old Geoff."

"Yeah. He disappeared a few years back, but they finally found him, filed under Missing Persons."

"Ha ha," Spiller intoned. "I walked into that one. I presume Geoff is still with us."

"Oh yes, and as it happens, he did help me out. When I told him about the bomb and the air raids and the possible police connection, he said I ought to check the records for officers who were killed while on duty."

"Good idea. I suppose there must've been quite a few. They would've put themselves in harm's way, trying to keep people safe, and they would've helped in the rescue effort after a raid. That must have had its own dangers."

"It made me think, I can tell you," Collins said. "I'll never complain about working a late shift again. It's nothing to what those blokes went through. It must've been hellish."

"Without doubt, but what did you come up with? Any promising leads?"

"Only one. This guy." Collins clicked his mouse, opening a grainy image of a scanned black-and-white photograph.

Spiller leaned forward to study the photo and the caption beneath. "DS Anthony Barnett," he read. The man had probably been in his forties when the photograph was taken. His round face had a careworn look, the forehead furrowed by deep wrinkles, and he had the jowls of the man who liked to overindulge. It was a typical mugshot, the expression giving nothing away, and the man's eyes looked cold as stone beneath his thick dark eyebrows. "He looks like a nasty piece of work," Spiller concluded. "But what makes you think he might have been our victim? Or did you have him pegged as the perpetrator?"

"Victim." Collins pulled up a document and began reading from it. "DS Anthony Barnett was declared missing, presumed killed while on active duty, on the 13th of May, 1942." He looked up at Spiller. "Barnett would've been forty-five at the time. That fits with what they said at the post-mortem examination, and he was the right height too. Six foot one."

"Let's have another look at that picture."

Collins obliged, enlarging the photo so that it filled the screen, and Spiller gazed at it, seeing it anew. Was this the man who'd ended his days in such a brutal way? A serving police officer, tortured and killed. The thought sent a chill racing down Spiller's spine. "Follow this up," Spiller said. "Look for dental records or anything else that might identify him. I'll get on to Nicola and see if she's been able to get a sample of DNA. I want you to look for any surviving family members, and we'll get samples to see if we can find a match." He patted Collins on the shoulder. "Good work, lad. You've got us off to a flying start."

"Cheers, guv. I'll get on it."

Spiller took a mouthful of coffee, the lukewarm, bitter liquid making him wince. "Blimey, this stuff doesn't get any better," he muttered, then he headed for his office, his head held high. The news might be grim, but at last he was getting stuck into some real police work, and nothing, not even the coffee, could dent his determination to see this case through.

CHAPTER 21

Dan drove into Embervale, tired and hungry. He'd put in a solid day's work, pounding the keyboard with scarcely a break. Between sessions of data wrangling, he'd tried to keep on top of his inbox, but since he'd been issued with an official CEG email address, the flow of corporate communications hadn't stopped. He ought to have a word with someone about that. They clearly had no idea how much time they were wasting.

As he parked outside The Old Shop and turned off the ignition, he longed for a hot meal and a cold beer. But for some reason, he stayed sitting in his car, staring into space while the RAV4's radiator beat out an irregular rhythm of clicks and ticking noises, like a clockwork mechanism winding down.

Why didn't he want to go inside? It was as if he didn't have the energy to move on, to leave the day's labours behind him, and it wasn't just the endless emails that had stretched his patience thin. *I'm scarcely making headway with this project,* he admitted to himself. *It's bigger than I expected. Much bigger.*

Had he taken on a task he couldn't handle? It was one hell of a lot of work for one person to tackle, that was certain.

Really, the company ought to have brought in a specialist agency, and from the figures he'd seen, they could easily afford it.

It's no use being defeatist, Dan thought. *I took the job, so I'll just have to push on through, tough it out.* He'd get there in the end, but first he'd need to clear his mind, focus his energy. Ever since his conversation with DS Kulkarni, Dan had been on edge.

Driving to and from work, he'd kept an eye on his rear-view mirror, and all day long he'd been hypervigilant, keeping track of the comings and goings beyond the glass door of his office. But nothing out of the ordinary had happened at work, and his commute had been entirely without incident.

I'm home now, Dan told himself. *Nothing is going to happen. Let it go.*

Dan climbed from his car, but he didn't head to his own front door. Instead, he crossed the path that separated his house from Alan's and let himself into his friend's back garden. He knocked on the back door, and a minute later Alan appeared, smiling.

"The hunter returns," Alan said, but his expression quickly turned to one of concern. "Is everything all right? You look done in."

"I'm fine. It's been a long day, that's all." Dan hesitated. "Have you got a minute?"

"Of course." Alan stepped back, beckoning him inside. "Tea?"

"Thanks. That would be great." Dan sat heavily at the kitchen table, making himself at home and shrugging out of his jacket while Alan busied himself with the kettle and clinked mugs onto the counter.

I'm not sure why I'm here, Dan thought. But as soon as Alan handed out the drinks and joined him at the table, Dan found himself relating the full story of his meetings with Neil.

Alan listened carefully, sipping his tea, and when Dan had finished he said, "This sounds intriguing, especially the dates on the back of the photograph. Did you take a copy of them?"

Dan nodded, reaching for his phone. "I made a note of the dates and the quote, and I took a picture of the photo. I'm not sure why."

"Because the whole thing is a puzzle, that's why. You couldn't resist it."

"Maybe. I'll send them to you." Dan found the note and the photo, and shared them with Alan, who took out his own phone and studied the screen carefully.

"The dates don't mean anything to me," Alan said. "Have you looked them up?"

"I haven't had time."

"Let me get something to write on." Alan fetched a pad and pen from a drawer in the kitchen and sat back down, lining up the pad carefully in front of him. "That's better. We'll start as we mean to go on."

"You're going to help me figure it out?"

Alan grinned. "Try and stop me."

"I wouldn't dream of it." Dan returned Alan's smile, suddenly feeling absurdly grateful. He'd never found it easy to ask for help, but with Alan it wasn't necessary to even try. A true friend, Alan saw what was needed and stepped up to the mark.

"It'll be just like old times," Alan said. "But I don't think we're looking at a cipher." He copied down the information from the photograph, laying it out across the page in a neat hand. "The quote is from *Henry V*, obviously, but I'm not sure what to make of it. There's something about it. It doesn't look quite right."

Taking his phone back, Dan ran his eyes over the words: *Once more unto the breach dear friends once more!* "I know what you mean," he said. "It's a strange thing to have on the back of a photo of your wife."

"Perhaps it was a private joke, something they said to each other before tackling an unpleasant job. But that wasn't what I was getting at. For one thing, the punctuation isn't right. There ought to be commas on either side of *dear friends*."

"Trust you to notice that," Dan said. "But people don't always punctuate scribbled notes, and he probably didn't expect anyone else to see this one."

"That shouldn't matter. Punctuation is important. But let's go on to the dates. One of them could be the date the photo was taken, but it's a shame we've only got two digits for the year. We don't know for certain which century we're dealing with."

"I assume we're looking at this century, so the first one, 19/2/16, refers to the 19th of February, 2016, and the second date, 8/1/12, refers to the 8th of January, 2012."

"Assuming that the lady in the photograph is Neil's wife, you said that she died some time ago," Alan said. "Could one of the dates be the day she died?"

"I already thought of that. Neil said that his wife died six years ago, so that would have been in 2015 if he was being precise, but on the other hand, he may have been rounding the years up, so it's possible that she died in February 2016."

"I'll check. What did you say her name was again?

"Felicity."

Alan made a note. "The other date could be an anniversary or a birthday. Did Neil have children?"

"I'm not sure, but I could find out if I drop it into the conversation at work."

"Good. Now, what about this number that sits on its own? Five. What could be the significance of it?"

"The quote came from *Henry V*, so it could be a reference to that."

Alan looked thoughtful for a moment, then he set down

his pen. "It's not much to go on, is it? Perhaps you're reading too much into it."

"It's possible, but you didn't see the way Neil acted. He was deeply worried about something, and he said that crimes had been committed. Something financial by the sounds of it, but he was talking in riddles. I couldn't make much sense of it."

Alan pursed his lips.

"You think I'm being overly suspicious," Dan suggested. "And you think Neil was being neurotic and he drew me into his delusions."

"I think that Neil has lost a great deal. A handful of years ago he lost his wife, and now he's lost his job. Either one of those things could've knocked him off balance, but taken together, who knows what effect they may have had? The poor man must be reeling."

Dan considered this for a second, then he said, "There's more to it than that. Neil was convinced that something shady has been going on at CEG, and I'm inclined to believe him. I know I've only been there a few days, but there's something about the place. It just doesn't feel right."

"You mentioned that the other day, when we were in the pub."

"The feeling hasn't gone away, and I haven't told you what DS Kulkarni said. She came to see me yesterday, and she suggested that someone might have a grudge against me. She mentioned our past cases, especially that business with Kevin. He has a brother, apparently, and he's an ex-con."

"She thinks that Kevin's brother tried to take revenge by running you down?"

"Yes. But I think there could be another explanation."

"Such as?" Alan asked.

"I'm not sure, but someone tried to put me out of the picture, and then a couple of days later, Neil appeared and started talking about crimes at the company where I've just started working. I can't help feeling the two events are connected."

"Okay."

"Okay? What do you mean?"

"I mean, that's good enough for me," Alan said. "Your intuition isn't always right, but I've learnt to trust it. Leave the dates to me. I'll do some research and see what I can come up with. I could try to do a little background research into the company, but you're better placed to sniff out anything suspicious."

"I'll see what I can find out," Dan said. "I don't really get an opportunity to ask questions when I'm in the office. I'm mostly in a room on my own with my head down, but tomorrow I'm going to the afternoon tea at Batworthy Castle. That should give me a chance to ask around."

"So long as you don't neglect your other duties."

"I'm just a guest. I don't have any other duties."

Alan let out an exasperated sigh. "I'm talking about Sam. You need to look after her, make sure she has a good time."

"Yes, I'm aware of that, Alan."

"I hope so, because if you muck her about, she won't take it lightly."

"I know that, but what's she going to do, crack me over the head with a bone china teapot?"

"Quite possibly," Alan replied. "But only if you're lucky. If there's anything heavier to hand, I don't fancy your chances."

CHAPTER 22

D S Kulkarni thought she knew Plymouth reasonably well, but the back roads at the city's edge were a new experience. Away from the wide streets and bustling thoroughfares of its centre, the city showed a different face: a drab hinterland of neglected terraced houses interspersed with clusters of tired little shops that were somehow hanging on. You could get a takeaway out here and booze from a 24-hour off-licence, but that was about all.

Kulkarni drove on, checking her satnav, and she was finally rewarded when a metal sign beside the road announced that she'd found the Plym View Trading Estate. She steered her Honda Accord through the open gateway and across an expanse of cracked tarmac, then she found a parking area and pulled in, making a mental note of her arrival time. She'd arrived much later than she'd hoped, but there were still a good number of cars in evidence, so with a bit of luck the man she wanted to see would still be here.

Climbing from her car, she paused to take a look around. The trading estate was home to a score of businesses, all housed in grimly functional buildings made from concrete and sheet metal. A shade of dull green was the predominant colour of choice, and apart from small signs here and there, the buildings were almost identical and stolidly anonymous.

The estate was surrounded by a tall chain-link fence topped with razor wire. Kulkarni spotted a few floodlights dotted around the compound, all mounted on tall metal posts, but if there were CCTV cameras, she couldn't see them. *That's a shame*, she thought, but she'd make enquiries about cameras anyway. You never knew who might've decided to set up their own CCTV system.

The company Kulkarni was looking for, a printing firm going by the name XpressPrint, was based in Unit 14, and it didn't take her long to find it. As she approached, a tall, well-built man eyed her warily from his position beside a wide-open loading bay. The man puffed at a cigarette then snatched it from his mouth and ground it underfoot, scowling as though irritated that his break had been interrupted. He bent to retrieve his cigarette stub and threw it in a nearby waste bin. Once that had been dealt with, his demeanour altered, and he turned to Kulkarni with a pleasant enough expression. "Can I help you? You look lost."

Kulkarni smiled. "It's not true what they say then."

"Sorry?"

"A lot of ex-cons reckon they can always spot a copper."

"I wouldn't know."

"Is that so? It is Keith, isn't it? Keith Pearson?"

"Yeah, I'm Keith, but before I say another word, I'd like to see some ID."

"Sure." Kulkarni showed him her warrant card. "I wondered if we could have a little chat, Keith. Shouldn't take more than ten minutes."

"Maybe, but I'll have to check with the boss. We've got a lot on today."

"Business is good?"

Keith nodded.

"You've got time to slip out for a fag break though?"

"Just about. If you really want to know, I'm waiting for the machine to finish its run. Nothing much I can do once it's started, so I came out for a breather, all right?"

"What are you printing?"

"Catalogues for the lifeboat people. You know, the RNLI. They sell merchandise to raise cash. We do a lot of work for charities."

"Sounds very worthwhile."

"We do a good job. Always on time. People like that, so they come back for more." Keith glanced at his watch. "I've only got a couple of minutes. What do you want to know?"

"I thought we had to check with your boss?"

Keith shrugged. "Make it quick and I won't need to bother him."

"Meaning, you'd rather keep quiet about your criminal record?"

"No, he knew about it when he took me on, but all that mess was a long time ago. I don't think about those days anymore, and I haven't kept in touch with anyone from back then, so if that's what you're after, you're wasting your time."

"Actually, it was your brother I wanted to talk about. Kevin."

The change in Keith was immediate. He looked crestfallen, his eyes dim with worry. "Is he all right? Why didn't you say something straight away?"

"It's okay. As far as I know, Kevin is fine. I haven't come to bring you bad news."

"Thank God for that." Keith drew a deep breath. "Why'd you mention him then?"

"His name came up in a routine inquiry. You know how it goes, Keith. Probably nothing in it, but we have to follow these things up."

"What kind of inquiry? He's inside. What's he supposed to have done, dug a tunnel?"

Kulkarni humoured him with a smile. "Have you been to see him recently?"

"A few weeks back. He was doing all right, keeping his head down."

"What did you talk about?"

"Anger management, mainly. He's doing a course. Seemed to be getting a lot out of it. I was chuffed for him."

Kulkarni raised her eyebrows, and Keith added, "No need to look like that. My brother isn't as daft as he looks, but he's easily led, and that woman strung him along. She played him, and he fell for it. He was always a mug for a pretty face. Even when he was a kid, there were girls who'd take advantage, get him to do stuff. I used to tell him not to be so bloody soft, but he didn't listen to me. If he'd taken a bit of notice, he wouldn't be in this bloody mess."

"You sound a little angry yourself, Keith."

"No, life's too short. It vexes me, that's all. I ought to have looked out for him."

"Is that what you're doing now, taking care of things on his behalf?"

Keith stared at Kulkarni from beneath lowered eyebrows. "What are you talking about?"

"I'm talking about the possibility that you and Kevin might harbour a grudge against the man who put him inside."

"DS Spiller? No. I saw him at Kev's trial, and he remembered me. He nicked me when I was a lad. I'd been in a fight, but I didn't get charged. Spiller had a word with my dad, and they both gave me a talking to. Can't say it did much good, but at least he tried. I suppose he's all right — for a copper."

"I'll be sure to pass on your regards. It's *DI* Spiller now, but I wasn't referring to him. I was talking about the member of the public who got involved."

Keith grunted under his breath. "You mean that bloke

who stuck his oar in. Dave something or other, wasn't it? Irish sounding surname. I saw him at the trial. Why would I bother with him? The bloke's a bit of a nutter, isn't he? Not quite right."

"In what way?"

"I dunno. He looked a bit crafty to me. Sly. He was always watching, and not just the judge and the briefs; he was checking out everyone in the room. He clocked me, and I reckon he figured out I was Kev's brother. I gave him a look, you know, to make him mind his own business, but he took no notice. He just kept staring, like he was weighing me up."

"Sounds like he made an impression on you. Are you sure you don't remember his name?"

"Positive. It was a while ago, and it's all done and dusted. Why?"

"His name came up in a recent investigation, and we're chasing up the loose ends."

"Oh, I get it. Something's happened to this bloke, and you think I tried to get back at him because he got Kev banged up." Keith's expression soured. "You took one look at my record, and you made your mind up. Bloody typical."

Before Kulkarni could reply, a side door opened, and a man appeared, his gaze going from Kulkarni to Keith. "What's up? Problem?"

"No, boss." Keith gestured to Kulkarni. "This lady was asking about my brother and me, that's all."

The man's eyes narrowed as he studied Kulkarni. "You're with the police?"

"Yes, sir." Kulkarni showed her ID. "And you are?"

"John Sykes. I'm the manager, so if you have any business on this site, you ought to have come through reception and signed in. We can't have people wandering about the place. Health and safety."

"Understood. I would've come in through the main door,

but I bumped into Keith outside, and we've been having an informal chat."

"Are you going to be much longer?" John asked, then to Keith he added, "Your print run has finished. We need to get it packaged before the mail man gets here."

"Right." Keith looked to Kulkarni. "Are we done?"

"Almost. There are just a couple of things I need to know. When were you last in Exeter, Keith?"

Keith's expression became blank. "I don't go that way much. The last time was probably for Kev's trial. Yeah. That would've been it."

"Did you go by car?"

"Yes. So what?"

"Was it your own car, Keith?"

"Obviously. I've got a Vauxhall Astra. Silver. But I thought you had all that stuff on computer."

"We do. Do you have access to any other vehicles?"

"No. It's bad enough running one car. What would I want with another?"

John cleared his throat. "Listen, Miss…"

"Kulkarni, and it's DS or Detective Sergeant."

"Right. I'm sorry, Detective Sergeant, but Keith has work to do, and he needs to see to it now. If you want to ask him anything else, I suggest you make an appointment."

"We're done for now," Kulkarni said. "Thanks, Keith. You've been very helpful. If there's anything else, we'll be in touch."

John hooked his thumb back toward the building. "Right, Keith, you'd better get inside and make a start. I'll come and give you a hand in a minute."

"Cheers, boss." Keith made his way inside without so much as glancing at Kulkarni.

Once Keith was out of sight, John said, "What's all this about?"

"It's just a routine inquiry. Keith's name came up, and I wanted to talk to him in person."

"Well all I can say is, Keith's a good worker. I know he's been in trouble in the past, but if you ask me, he's put all that behind him."

"That's good to hear."

"But what was all that about his car? What's that got to do with anything? He hasn't been speeding, has he? Keith's always struck me as a careful driver."

"We're looking into an incident in Exeter, and it involves a stolen car. There was a possible connection with Keith's brother, Kevin."

"Keith told me about his brother," John said. "He was cut up about it. Keith might look like a thug, but he's all right, and I can tell you for sure, he'd never steal a car. Not him."

John's gaze flicked sideways. Kulkarni turned to see where he was looking but saw only the row of ugly industrial buildings. "Mr Sykes, is there something you'd like to tell me?"

"I'm not sure. It's probably nothing."

"Even so, why don't you tell me about it? You obviously have your suspicions about someone or something, and in my experience, people are pretty good at judging when something isn't quite right."

"I don't want to stir up trouble. Forget about it."

"The people we're looking for haven't just stolen a few cars. They take high-end cars, probably stealing to order. They're carjackers, and they don't care who they hurt. They need putting away." She cast her eye over the car park and spotted one expensive car among the herd of grimy hatchbacks and tired saloons. "Is that your Audi by any chance?"

"Yeah. It's a company car. The only perk I get."

"It's nice, but it makes you a target as far as these crooks are concerned. For a car like that, they'd hit you on the head and leave you in the gutter. They've done it before and they'll do it again, unless we stop them."

John looked down. Kulkarni knew the signs, and he was about to walk away, but even as she began to protest, John inclined his head toward the side door and said, "You'd better come inside."

"Fine."

John held the door open. "It's noisy, and we've got fork-lift trucks operating, so stick close to me."

"Got it." Kulkarni followed him inside, looking around as John took her through a small office and into the print works itself. There were very few people in evidence, so she presumed that the collection of futuristic machines scattered throughout the cavernous space were automated. Conveyor belts whirred, motors hummed and the repetitive thuds of mysterious contraptions reverberated in a relentless rhythm.

John led Kulkarni to where Keith was working hard, stacking neat piles of glossy catalogues into a large cardboard carton. Keith glanced at them as they approached, but he didn't stop working.

"Leave that for a second, Keith," John said over the noise of the machinery.

Keith picked up another pile of catalogues and placed them in the box. "I can't. The mail man will be here any minute. He won't wait."

"It'll be all right," John said. "I'll help you catch up in a minute, so you can stop what you're doing and talk to the detective. It's important."

"Yeah? So's this." Keith cast a worried glance at the catalogues that remained unpacked, then he let out an exasperated sigh. "Go on then. What do you want?"

"She wants to talk about some stolen cars," John said. "High-end cars."

"Why didn't you say so?" Keith demanded. "What was all that about my brother?"

"I was following up a possible connection between two cases, but let's put that to one side. The car thieves are top of my list. They're a nasty bunch. We need to get people like that off our streets."

Keith looked at John as though seeking approval.

"Go on," John said. "Tell her what you told me."

"All right." Keith moved closer to Kulkarni, and lowering his voice as much as he could in the noisy room, he said, "There's a bloke who has one of the units along the way, and I saw him talking to someone I recognised. Someone from back in the day."

"What's this man's name, and who was he talking to?"

"I don't know the bloke's name, but the guy I recognised goes by Jez."

"Surname?"

Keith shrugged.

"Seriously? You can't remember your friend's full name?"

"Jez was never a mate of mine. I knew him by sight, that's all. He's a nasty little sod, and he's been up to no good."

"What makes you say that?"

"Well, he was always a loser. A snot-nosed kid with a bad attitude. But when I saw him the other day, he looked very sharp. Suit and tie, smart shirt, shiny shoes."

"So, he's come up in the world. Maybe he's got a decent job, turned himself around."

"Not likely. Jez hasn't got two brain cells to rub together, but he's done all right for himself somehow. I saw him drive away, and he was in a Lexus. Brand new. Very fancy. Kind of silvery grey."

Kulkarni's expression froze. A Lexus had been taken in Exeter on the 7th of May, the driver attacked and badly injured. "When was this, Keith?"

"It was when we were doing that big order for the university. I worked late for three nights in a row, and that was when I saw Jez."

"Five weeks ago," John put in. "We started just after the May bank holiday, and we were flat out all week. We finished on the 7th. Right on time."

Kulkarni allowed herself a satisfied smile. It wasn't often you caught a break like this, and you had to appreciate it when one came around. "Tell me more," she said. "What happened between Jez and this other man. Did you see anything change hands?"

"No. They were talking, then Jez drove away. I don't think he saw me."

"Okay, so what do you know about this other man? The one who has the unit?"

"Not much," Keith said. "I've seen him around now and then, but not very often. I only see him when I've been working late. I'll be heading home, and I'll see him turn up. He drives down to his unit, parks outside."

"He goes into Unit 18," John said. "It's usually shut up during the day, nothing going on. Like Keith says, the bloke usually arrives after most people have gone home. What he does in there at night is anybody's guess."

Kulkarni made a note. "You say he rents the unit. How do you know he doesn't own it?"

"They're all rented," John said. "They're owned by Plym View Management. Their office is in Plymouth. I can give you their phone number if you like."

"That would be very helpful, thank you." Kulkarni pocketed her notebook. "Does this place have CCTV?"

"Yes, but it only covers our premises. You can get to Unit 18 without going past us."

"Even so, I'd like to take a look at the recordings."

"All right," John said. "But first, I need to help Keith pack this lot. He's right about that mail man. The bugger won't wait."

"Royal Mail?"

"Yeah. He'll be marching through that door any second."

"You two finish up here, and I'll head him off. He won't argue with me." Kulkarni made for the door, and behind her, she heard Keith saying, "You heard the detective, Boss. Let's get going."

Kulkarni smiled to herself. She almost hadn't made the trip over to Plymouth, but now it looked like it could pay off, although not in the way she'd predicted. Was that a happy chance, or had some intuition led her here? *Maybe Dan Corrigan knows what he's talking about*, she thought. Unlikely as it seemed, there just might be some method in his madness after all.

CHAPTER 23

B loody hell! How could I have been so stupid?
It should've been simple, but still, it all went to hell.
It couldn't have gone more disastrously wrong.

I could scream, yell, beat my fists against a brick wall.

But I don't have that luxury. I have to keep it together, lock my anger in a trunk and bury it in the earth.

This course of action has set me on a path, and there's no going back.

Because, despite the fact that I failed, the attempt set my senses alight in a way I've never before experienced. For a moment, I held the power of life and death in my hands, cradled it in my palms.

I was filled with the thrill of it.

It changed me.

So, I move on, hoping I've done enough to cover my tracks, and I regroup.

Time is precious, but my life and liberty are even more valuable. They are priceless.

I must watch and wait, think and plan.

Because next time, I cannot fail.

Next time, there can be no mistakes.
Only certain death.

FRIDAY

CHAPTER 24

S piller and Collins climbed from Spiller's car, pausing on the broad gravel driveway to inspect the Derryvale Care Home. Both men tilted back their heads to admire the building's large sash windows and its spotless cream-coloured walls. *It must've been a grand house at one time*, Spiller thought. *It's in a good spot too.* It had only taken them fifteen minutes to drive to the care home, but the leafy neighbourhood sat high on a hill and felt worlds away from the city centre. The garden was enclosed by high hedges, but Spiller guessed the house would offer fine views from the upstairs windows.

"Nice place," Collins said. "I wouldn't mind ending up somewhere like this."

"On a police pension?" Spiller scoffed. "You'll be lucky. It must cost an arm and a leg to live here. Look at the size of that garden. You could play bowls on that lawn."

Collins cast a brief glance at the pristine expanse of grass and the artfully laid out flower beds. "Maybe they do. It's an old man's game, isn't it?"

"It's a sport appreciated by many senior citizens, certainly, men and women alike. But I wasn't speaking literally, Collins. For a start, you need a little ditch around a bowling green."

"I'll take your word for it, guv."

Spiller sent his subordinate an austere look. It was good that the lad was feeling more confident, but there was banter, and there was cheek, and that line was not to be crossed. "Let's not waste time, Collins," he said. "Ring the bell and we'll crack on with the job."

"Sure." Collins sprang up the stone steps that led to the imposing front door, and Spiller trudged along behind him. As he joined his colleague, the door was opened by a smartly dressed woman in her fifties. Slim and silver haired, she had the upright bearing of someone for whom brisk efficiency was a way of life and she looked down at them with a clinical gaze, as if measuring up their potential as future residents.

Spiller had his warrant card ready, and he took care of the introductions, adopting a business-like smile to show Collins how it was done.

The woman nodded in acknowledgement. "I'm Elizabeth Jones. We spoke on the phone."

"Pleased to meet you, Mrs Jones. Thank you for making the time to help. We appreciate it."

"It's no problem. Come in, and please, call me Liz. Everyone does." As she ushered them inside, she smiled, a gentle warmth in her brown eyes, and Spiller found himself standing a little straighter, pulling in his stomach.

Gazing appreciatively around the spacious hallway, Spiller was struck by the sense of opulence. Yes, the place had been modified for its present use, so the carpet was hard wearing rather than luxurious and the staircase had been fitted with a stair lift, but even so, the building had retained something of its past glories. The tall sash windows let in the light, and the doorways leading from the hall were on a grand scale: wide and with polished brass knobs.

Watching his reaction, Liz said, "Not what you were expecting?"

"Not by a long way," Spiller admitted. "I'm impressed."

"Good. We want Derryvale to be a home in the truest sense of the word. It's all about attention to detail." Liz chuckled softly. "Forgive me. You're not here to join the waiting list. You have a job to do, so I'll take you through to meet Mr Davies. He's in the conservatory, but before we go through, I do ask that you keep it brief, and please be gentle with him. He puts on a good front, but he's an elderly man, and we don't want him distressed."

Spiller held up his hands. "Don't worry, Liz. We'll be on our best behaviour. It's just a few questions, that's all."

"All right. Well, you'd better come through. It's this way." She set off along the hallway, and Collins and Spiller followed her into a conservatory that spanned the back of the house. The room was simply furnished with sturdy rattan tables and chairs, and a few elderly gentlemen and ladies were sitting quietly or taking a nap.

Collins wrinkled his nose, but Spiller sent him a withering glance, and that was enough to keep the younger man quiet.

Liz stopped beside a gentleman who was sitting near the centre of the room, where he had an uninterrupted view of the garden; despite the warmth he was swaddled in a woolly cardigan. "This is Mr Davies," she said to Spiller. To the man, she said, "Hello, Rodney. I've brought some gentlemen to see you. I expect you remember me telling you about it this morning. They're from the police."

The man looked around, appraising Spiller and Collins with a swift glance. "I remember."

"Hello, Mr Davies," Spiller said. "I'm Detective Inspector Spiller, and this is my colleague, Detective Constable Collins."

"Detectives, eh? Must be important." Rodney nodded toward an empty sofa at his side. "Well, sit down then. Let's find out what this is all about."

"Thank you, sir." Spiller and Collins sat down, and Collins produced his pocket notebook and pen, ready to start. But Spiller waited, taking a moment to make eye contact with Rodney. *Spry*, Spiller thought. *He looks better than I will at eighty.*

"Can I get anyone a cup of tea or coffee?" Liz asked.

Rodney shook his head, smiling. "Not for me. I'm sloshing with the stuff."

"And we're fine, thank you," Spiller said. "We won't be stopping long."

"Right." Liz clasped her hands. "Okay then, I'll leave you to it. I'll be back in ten minutes. If there's anything you need, Rodney, you know what to do."

"Yes, yes," Rodney replied, but he never took his gaze from Spiller. "So, are you going to tell me what's so important or do I have to guess?"

"All in good time, sir. It's nothing to worry about." Spiller nodded to Liz, letting her know he'd take it from there, and she took the opportunity to make her exit, hurrying away as if she had a hundred things to do.

"Well?" Rodney prompted. "Are we going to get down to brass tacks or what?"

Stifling a grin, Spiller adopted his friendliest tone and began. "Mr Davies, your grandfather was a policeman, wasn't he? Anthony Barnett."

Rodney blinked as if taken aback. "Yes, but if that's what you've come to talk to me about, you're wasting your time. He died when I was a baby. Killed in an air raid. I can't remember when exactly."

"1942," Collins put in. "He was posted as missing in May of that year."

"Sounds about right." Rodney rubbed his chin. "Tony, that's what he was always known as, but I can't tell you much more than that. Why are you asking after all these years?"

"Your grandfather was presumed to be dead in 1942," Spiller said, "but his body wasn't recovered."

"That's right. My mum told me all about it. She always felt bad about not being able to bury him, but she said it was the same for a lot of folk in the war. It was the way things were."

"So I understand. But there's been a development and new evidence has come to light." Spiller paused, giving Rodney time to digest this information. "You may have heard about the unexploded bomb that was found in Exeter recently. Well, when it was detonated, it uncovered some human remains that had been buried for many years."

Rodney shifted in his seat. "I see, and you think it might be him."

"That's right," Spiller said. "And naturally, as his closest surviving relative, we wanted to let you know."

"Right." Rodney sighed, and he seemed to shrink in his chair, suddenly looking frail. Spiller recalled the warning Liz had given him. Rodney had, indeed, been putting up a front. His feistiness only went so far, and there was no need to risk distressing him with talk of handcuffs and broken bones.

"Well, I appreciate you coming out to tell me in person," Rodney went on. "If you have found my grandad, we'll be able to lay him to rest properly. Mum would've liked that. It's a shame it never happened in her lifetime, but she died years ago."

Spiller nodded sympathetically. "I understand. But before we can release the remains, we have to be absolutely sure of the victim's identity."

"Victim?" Rodney's eyes widened. "What do you mean by that?"

"Just a turn of phrase," Spiller said. "I should've said, *the deceased*. But whoever he is, he didn't die of natural causes, so we have to look into the case."

"Oh, that makes sense, I suppose." Rodney thought for a second, then added, "You'll be wanting to check my DNA."

Spiller wasn't quite able to hide his surprise. "Yes, that would be most helpful."

"I thought as much. I watch *Silent Witness*. I like that Emilia Fox."

Rodney chuckled and Spiller joined in. Tipping Rodney a wink, he said, "She's great, isn't she?" He tried to share the moment with Collins but received a blank look in return.

"I don't know who that is," Collins admitted. "I don't really like crime shows. They always get the details wrong."

"Never mind," Spiller said. "But I'm afraid, Mr Davies, that we're not quite as clever as our TV counterparts. It'll take us a little while to get results. We'll get there in the end, and you can help. All we need from you is a quick swab from the inside of your cheek. It only takes a second, and it's completely painless."

"Now?" Rodney asked.

"No, we'll send someone around to see you, make sure it's done properly."

"A CSI," Rodney said. "That makes sense. So, is that it? Have you got what you came for?"

"We're almost done," Spiller replied. "But if it's okay with you, I do have a few more questions. We'd like to know a little more about Tony and your family. It'll help us in our enquiries, and the sooner we can tie the whole thing up, the sooner we can release his remains."

"Like I said, I don't really know much about my grandad, but go on, ask your questions."

"Thank you." Spiller made a show of looking around the conservatory. "Nice place, this."

Rodney nodded. "It's all right. I can't complain."

"More than all right," Spiller said with a smile. "You've done well for yourself, Rodney. If you don't mind me asking, what did you do before you retired?"

"I was an accountant. I worked for the county council."

"Paid well, did it?"

"Not bad." Rodney straightened his cardigan, fidgeting with the buttons. "I worked there a long time, and I built up a good pension pot. I watched the pennies and I saved what I could. It wasn't always easy, but it worked out for the best."

"Good for you. You've always lived in Exeter, have you?"

"Oh yes. Married a local girl. Valerie. She passed away five years ago, but we had a lot of happy years together. We married young, settled down. It was what we did back then."

"Before that, did you live at home with your parents?" Spiller asked.

"That's right. Mum was called Beverley. Beverley Barnett until she married my dad."

"What did they do, your parents?"

"Dad worked in a bakery. His full name was Frederick, but no one ever called him that. It was always Fred. Mum was a housewife. Before she had me, she worked in a shop. A greengrocer's I think." Rodney raised his hand to his temple. "I've just had a thought. The tapes. Why didn't I think of that before?"

Spiller smiled indulgently, waiting, but Collins wasn't so patient. "Tapes?" he asked. "What tapes would those be, Mr Davies?"

"Cassettes, really. I recorded my mum. I was forty-something, and I'd just got a new stereo. Beautiful it was. Pioneer. I was a bit of a hi-fi nut in those days, and I got a bee in my bonnet about recording everything. I had shelves full of cassettes, all labelled and organised properly. Anyway, I recorded my mum, talking about the old days, and I'm sure she said something about her dad. I'd put money on it."

Spiller leaned forward. "Do you still have those tapes?"

"I don't have them here. They were in a big box, and I haven't the room. But my son, Nathan, should have them. He took a lot of my old stuff and stored it for me."

"Is Nathan local?"

"No," Rodney said. "That's the trouble with boys; they move away. I have two boys, and they both live miles away. Nathan is up in Hull, so he doesn't visit much, but we talk on this thing." Rodney delved into his cardigan pocket and retrieved a smartphone. "We use Skype."

"Excellent. If we can take Nathan's contact details, we'll see what we can arrange." Spiller turned to Collins. "Have a word with Mr Davies' son, and then get onto the local police in Hull. Have someone drop in on Nathan and collect the tapes and get them down to us pronto."

"I expect they can digitise them," Collins said. "That'll be much quicker."

"The wonders of technology, eh?"

"Hang on a minute," Rodney said. "I don't know what you're getting all excited about. I'd have thought the DNA would be enough to tell you whether you've found my grandad or not. Why do you want to know all this other stuff?"

Spiller took a moment to frame his reply. "Remember that the remains we found might not be anything to do with your grandfather. It could be someone else entirely. But for reasons that I can't go into, we're treating the man's death as suspicious."

Rodney paled. "He was murdered? Is that what you're saying?" He flicked his hands at Spiller as if shooing him away. "My grandad was killed in an air raid."

"That's a possibility," Spiller said. "But we have to consider every eventuality, and each bit of information helps us to put together a picture. I'm sure you understand."

"It might mean that we can rule your grandad out," Collins put in. "If we can eliminate him from our inquiry, then we can move on, and you can forget about the whole thing. But it's best to get these things over with, get them done and dusted."

Rodney lowered his eyebrows and looked ready to argue, but he said, "All right. If it helps, I'll tell Nathan to look for the tapes and hand them over. That's the best I can do."

Collins took a note of Nathan's contact details, and then Spiller said, "Thank you very much, Mr Davies. We're grateful for your assistance. I think we've taken up enough of your time, so we'll be on our way." He glanced at Collins, and both men stood. "We'll be in touch," Spiller went on. "We'll let you know what we find out. Look after yourself, Mr Davies."

"Goodbye," Rodney said, his voice faint, and he looked away, his eyes losing focus.

Spiller inclined his head toward the door, and they made a swift exit, pausing only to thank Liz Jones on their way out.

Outside, Spiller said, "You didn't say much in there, Collins. If you want to make sergeant, you need to think about speaking up a bit more, make your presence felt."

"Right. Okay, guv." Collins looked crestfallen.

"On the other hand, what you *did* say…" Spiller paused as if considering the matter carefully. "Well, it was excellent."

"Really?"

Spiller nodded. "You saw the old boy was getting wound up, and you reassured him. When you said that bit about ruling his grandad out, it gave Mr Davies something to cling on to. You've got to throw people a lifeline now and then. It helps them to feel like there's a bit of give and take. Do you see what I mean?"

"Yes, guv."

"Good lad. Now, we'd better get back to the nick. I'll send someone out to sample Rodney's DNA and get it matched against those bones."

"I'll liaise with the police in Hull," Collins said. "Shouldn't be too hard to get those tapes digitised and the files sent down."

"It might be better if I call our brethren in the grim North.

If the request comes from a DI, they might pull their fingers out. Plus, I want you to get cracking on the computer. Use the names Rodney gave us and see what you can find out about Tony Barnett's family."

"Okay, but what if the DNA match comes up negative? There's no point looking into Barnett's background if they're not his bones."

"It's him," Spiller stated. "I'd bet on it."

"What makes you so sure?"

Spiller turned to look back at the building. "Look at this place. Does it seem like the kind of retirement home an employee of the county council could afford? I don't care how much he scrimped and saved, Rodney Davies doesn't belong here."

"He was an accountant, guv. They get a decent wage."

"Even so, he had commitments. A wife and two kids. That wouldn't have left him with much to squirrel away, and a county council pension wouldn't cover the fees in a place like this."

"He seemed anxious when you asked him about that," Collins said. "Do you reckon he was hiding something?"

"Bingo." Spiller smiled and gestured toward his car. "Let's go."

They set off across the driveway, the gravel crunching underfoot. "Mr Davies married young and had kids," Spiller went on. "In those days, that would've put the kibosh on his wife's chances of a decent career, and I don't think it's likely that he married into money. He doesn't come from the right stock. His mum was a housewife and his dad was a baker, but somehow he seems to have struck it rich."

"I expect he had to sell his house before he came here. That could've given him a decent lump sum."

"Then why didn't he mention it?"

"Maybe he didn't think of it," Collins said. "He's an old man."

"He's as sharp as you or me, and as you pointed out, he was an accountant. I'll bet he knows where every penny came from, but he wanted to keep it under his hat."

Collins nodded thoughtfully. "We could look at his financial records, but that could take ages unless we bring someone else in to help."

"I'll see what I can do, because I'm sure it'll be worth it. My gut tells me Rodney is sitting on a nice little nest egg, and I want to know two things." He gazed at Collins expectantly.

"Where did he get the cash?" Collins offered. "And how does it connect to Tony Barnett?"

"Spot on," Spiller said. "I didn't buy Rodney's story about his pension, and people don't need to lie about honest money. If we can prove a link between Rodney's assets and Tony Barnett, we could be on to a winner. If Tony had money, our two questions become one: was it enough to get him killed?"

CHAPTER 25

"We're here," Dan said unnecessarily as he drove between the stone-pillared gates of Batworthy Castle.

"Finally," Sam replied. "We're late."

Dan sighed quietly. So far, their date wasn't going as he'd hoped. Sam had been tense from the moment he'd picked her up. He'd told her she looked good, and he'd meant it. Sam wore a long, sleeveless dress in a pale-green paisley print, and it accentuated her curves and showed off her tanned shoulders. But Sam had brushed off his compliments, and when he'd opened the car door for her to climb in, she hadn't been impressed. "I'm not helpless," she'd said, and after that the atmosphere in the car had been strained.

It hadn't helped that the journey took longer than Dan had expected, the winding lanes defeating his sense of direction and confounding his phone's satnav. Sam had set him right, but it irked him that he'd been forced to rely on her.

As he parked his car between a Range Rover and a BMW, he knew he had to do something to save their first date from being their last, but what could he say without coming across as patronising? Because he didn't want that; not with Sam.

But before he could utter a word, Sam said, "Come on then." And she let herself out of the car.

Inside the hotel, they were greeted by the young man on the reception desk, who informed them that afternoon tea was to be served in one of the lounges. He pointed the way and offered to take them through.

"Thanks, but I'm sure we can find it," Dan replied. "I'll follow the scent of freshly baked scones."

The young man looked a little taken aback, as if he was unused to the guests making light-hearted remarks, but he recovered quickly and said, "The scones are very good. I hope you enjoy them."

"We will," Sam said, but she seemed reluctant to set off in search of the lounge.

"Are you okay?" Dan asked.

"Yes," Sam replied. "But do I look all right?"

Dan made a show of checking Sam's outfit. "Perfect."

"I don't know about that," Sam said, but there was the hint of a smile on her lips, and she looked at Dan expectantly.

Dan hazarded a guess and offered his arm, and for the first time that day, he'd apparently done something right.

Sam took his arm, and they set off together.

The lounge was easy to find, and when Dan and Sam walked in through the door the room was already quite full. Some lounged on leather sofas while others stood in small groups, huddled together, champagne flutes in hand. In the centre of the room, Joe Clayton was in conversation with Doug, their heads close together, but they both looked over at Dan and smiled, Joe lifting his hand in a wave. Dan returned the gesture, but Doug and Joe had already gone back to their conversation.

"Who are those two?" Sam asked.

"The distinguished looking one is Doug – he's the CEO – and the man who waved is Joe. He's in charge of online operations."

"They ignored me. Looked right through me."

"I'm sure they didn't mean anything by it." Dan offered a reassuring smile. "Don't worry. They don't bite. I'll introduce you to a few people and you'll be fine."

Sam gave no sign of having heard him. She was scanning the crowd nervously as if expecting to be thrown out at any moment. "I knew this dress was no good," she muttered. "It might be okay for the village fair, but here..." She cast a disconsolate gaze around the room, and Dan had to admit that the place exuded an aura of timeless wealth. The walls were panelled with polished oak, the leather sofas gleamed with the patina of age, and even the coffee tables looked like cherished antiques.

"I know what you mean," Dan said. "I felt a bit self-conscious when I parked my old Toyota amongst all those posh cars."

"That's different. You might have a clapped-out car, but you fit in here, and I don't."

Unsure what to say, Dan searched for inspiration and spied a young man weaving through the crowd with a tray of champagne flutes. He'd expected tea, but he should've known that no corporate shindig would be complete without a glass of fizz.

"Can I get you a drink?" he asked Sam, and when she hesitated, he added, "It's all paid for, so you may as well enjoy it."

"All right, then."

With a practised wave, Dan attracted the young man, who bustled over and offered them a choice of champagne or orange juice. Sam opted for champagne, and after a moment's indecision, Dan did the same. *One drink*, Dan told himself. *Just one*. The first sip of cold champagne hit the spot, and he took another mouthful, savouring the sensation of bubbles popping on his tongue.

Sam followed suit, her eyes widening. "Ooh, that's nice."

"Good. I'm glad you like it. I'm sorry we got off to a bad start, but I'll make it up to you. I want you to have a good time."

"I will. But you don't have to apologise. It takes two, and I reckon we're both a bit on edge."

They shared a smile, and Dan's spirits rose. It was going to be fine. Things were bound to be awkward between them at first; their relationship was changing and this was just the start. But they'd got over the first hurdle, and now they could move on, relaxing into their new roles.

"If you're ready, we could go and say hello to a few people," Dan said. He spotted Celine standing at one side of the room, a dark-haired man at her side. "That's Celine. She works in IT."

"She's very young," Sam said. "And very pretty."

"I suppose so. She's just a colleague. The man with her must be her partner. I've never met him."

"So, how do you know they're together?"

"It's the way they're standing so close, and I can tell he's not from the office. He looks uncomfortable in that suit, and he could do with a shave."

"He's the strong and silent type," Sam said. "He's got that smouldering look, like that bloke who does *Poldark*." She sipped her champagne, then said, "What do people see when they look at us, do you think?"

"They probably don't notice me at all," Dan replied. "They see you, and if they happen to glance in my direction, they wonder how I could be so lucky."

Sam nudged him with her elbow. "Don't waste your smooth talk on me, Dan Corrigan. Save it for flirting with the office girls, like *Celine*."

"I don't..." Dan started to protest, but Sam's wicked grin stopped him from completing his sentence. Somehow, he'd thought Sam might stop teasing him when they started going out together, but that had been optimistic.

"You're way too easy to wind up," she said. "I know you're not a lech. Unlike that bloke over there. He's been giving me the glad eye since I walked in."

"What? Who?" Dan looked round sharply, only to find Seb Cooper leering at him. Seb lifted his glass of orange juice in acknowledgement, a glint in his eye as though he and Dan were complicit in some way.

Dan nodded in return, his expression grim, and Seb seemed to find his response amusing. Seb said something to the statuesque woman beside him, but she appeared disinterested, barely sparing a glance at Dan and Sam.

"That's Seb," Dan explained to Sam. "He's a bit..."

"A bit of a creep," Sam said. "I bet he thinks he's God's gift."

"I don't really know him that well, but you're probably right."

"Oh, I'm right. He's a nasty piece of work. Is that his wife with him?"

"I presume she's his partner, but I don't know if they're married." Dan noted that the slim woman beside Seb was slightly taller than her companion, due in part to her glittering high-heeled shoes, the straps criss-crossed around her ankles. As long legged as a model, the woman made her simple blouse and skirt look like something from a Milan catwalk. *Not just taller than him*, Dan thought. *Younger too.* By all appearances, she was finding the occasion dull, her vacant stare skimming over the assembled company as though she wondered how she'd come to be here. But then something caught her eye and her pale lips curled in a hungry smile.

Following her gaze, Dan saw that the woman's attention had been caught by Celine's partner, and the young man didn't mind one bit. Returning her smile, he raised his hand to smooth his eyebrow, effectively shielding his face as his gaze lingered on Seb's companion.

Dan wasn't the only one to notice. "I know that look,"

Sam said. "There'll be trouble there. Blimey, Dan, what kind of a tea party have you brought me to?"

"They're not all like that. Let me introduce you to Joe. He's a nice guy. You'll like him."

"Okay."

Dan and Sam made their way over to where Joe stood with Doug, and Dan made the necessary introductions. Doug seemed relieved to break off his discussion, and he was all charm, greeting Sam like a favourite niece.

"How good of you to come," he said. "We're a stuffy old bunch, so it's particularly good to see a fresh face. It's a shame my wife isn't here to meet you, but she doesn't come to our office parties anymore. She'd have loved to have a chat with you. You look a picture, you really do. That dress is delightful, isn't it, Joe?"

Joe nodded. "Sure. It's very pretty."

"Oh, I just got it at New Look." Sam brushed the fabric with her fingertips. "It was on the sale rail. Forty quid."

Joe had been about to sip his drink, but he froze with the glass halfway to his lips. "How much?"

"Forty quid. I didn't think that was too bad, but it was all I could find. I didn't have much time."

"It was a bargain," Joe said. "I must introduce you to my fiancée, Teri. She came home with an armful of outfits, and don't get me wrong, she looks great, but I think my credit card almost melted."

"Now, now," Doug gently reprimanded him. "My daughter has always had exquisite taste. She gets that from her mother, bless her."

Joe's cheeks coloured. "I didn't mean anything, Doug. You know I'd never begrudge Teri a single thing."

"Quite." Doug patted Joe on the shoulder. "You're a good sort, Joe, but when are you two going to name the day? I'm looking forward to dusting off my morning suit and writing my speech."

"We'll let you know. Teri's been talking about venu
months, but you know how it is. She wants everything t
perfect."

Joe looked around their little clique as if seeking
affirmation. Doug provided an indulgent chuckle, and Sam
said, "Good for her." But Dan smiled and said nothing. He
was thinking of a remark Celine had made when they'd been
talking about the rapid progress of Joe's career. 'There's a
whole different way to tell that story,' she'd said, and now
Dan understood. Joe was marrying the boss's daughter. It was
the oldest trick in the book, and a drop of disillusionment
tainted Dan's image of the man.

"I'm afraid I must ask you to excuse me for a moment,"
Doug said. "I have some people I absolutely must see. Good
to see you, Dan. Sam, it was lovely to meet you. I do hope
we'll have the chance for a proper chat later. But now I must
go and schmooze. Time to stiffen the sinews, summon up the
blood and do battle. Wish me luck." And with a smile, Doug
made his exit.

Joe appeared wistful as he watched Doug leave.

"Unfinished business?" Dan asked.

"Am I that transparent?" Joe asked. "Teri always says I'm
an open book. Maybe that's how she manages to wrap me
around her little finger."

"Where is your fiancée?" Sam asked. "She *is* here, isn't
she?"

"Oh sure." Joe turned around. "There she is, talking to
Tom Hastings, having a heated debate about some book or
other, I shouldn't wonder. They're both big readers."

Dan looked across to the woman who was engaged in a
lively discussion with Tom. From Joe's description, Dan had
half-expected Teri to be a princess-like character, dressed up
to the nines, but Teri wore a pair of lilac linen dungarees and
a plain white T-shirt, and her floral-patterned boots looked
like Dr Martens. She gesticulated energetically as she spoke,

and when Tom said something, she shook her head, her chestnut, bobbed hair flying from side to side.

Perhaps registering Dan's surprise, Joe said, "My fiancée is what you might call a free spirit. She's an academic. Literature. If she asks you about George Eliot, you'd better be careful what you say."

"I've never read any Eliot," Dan admitted.

"We did a bit of *Mill on the Floss* at school," Sam said. "I didn't like it."

Joe ran a hand down his face. "Don't say that to Teri, I beg of you. Pretend you haven't read it. It's safer."

"Noted," Dan said. "I didn't know you were engaged to Doug's daughter."

"It's no secret, but I don't make a song and dance about it. I'd hate for people to think I'd taken advantage of Teri. I got where I am through hard work. It took a lot of long days, missed weekends and not enough sleep."

"I know what that's like," Dan said.

Joe regarded him for a moment. "I'll bet you do. But it's important to take time out, so forget about work for a while. Enjoy this fantastic place. Have fun."

"We will," Dan replied. "But there was one thing I wanted to ask you."

"Oh?"

"Does the date, the 19th of February 2016 mean anything to you?"

Joe looked nonplussed. "Not at all. Why?"

"It's just a reference I found. How about the 8th of January 2012?"

"No. What's this in connection with, Dan?"

"The dates were on a note I found in my office. I thought they might be important."

"Was there anything else on the note?"

"Just the number five and a line from a Shakespeare play."

"That's odd, but without something to give it a context, I can't help you. Where was this note?"

"I found it in the desk. I thought it may have belonged to Neil."

Joe lowered his eyebrows. "That's unlikely. Your office was professionally cleaned before you started. Maybe someone dropped a scrap of paper by accident. I wouldn't worry about it. I'm always scribbling notes to myself, and half the time I can't remember what they mean. Really I should keep my notes on my phone like everyone else, but it's an old habit and hard to break."

"I always think there's something satisfying about putting pen to paper," Dan said. "I wonder if Neil felt the same. He struck me as an old-school kind of guy when I spoke to him the other day."

"You talked to Neil? I thought he was on his boat."

"No. I saw him in Exeter. Actually, he was in a bit of a state. He seemed to feel aggrieved at the way he'd left the company."

"Ah, I'm sorry to hear that. I liked Neil. I guess it can be difficult when you have to move on. Maybe he's finding it hard to adjust."

"Yes. I've been there myself."

"I didn't know that," Joe said. "But then, I'm not in charge of hiring and firing. Not at the management level anyway. That kind of thing is above my pay grade, thankfully."

"Who would've handled Neil's redundancy? Doug?"

"Seb Cooper. But listen, Dan, this sounds like something we should be discussing in the office. It can wait until Monday, can't it?"

"Yes," Dan said. "I thought someone at the company should know about Neil, that's all. He was in a bad way."

"As I said, I'm sorry to hear that. I'll be sure to pass it along at the appropriate time."

Joe's tone had grown stern, and an uncomfortable silence sprang up between them.

"Why don't you tell us about your fiancée?" Sam said brightly. "Where does she work? Exeter University?"

"Yes. She's with the English Department. It's all very highbrow."

"Is that where you met?" Dan asked. "Did you go to the uni as well?"

"No, I studied at Reading."

"Me too," Dan said. "When were you there?"

"Oh, it feels like a lifetime ago, but I'm sure Sam doesn't want to listen to us going on about our student days." Turning to Sam, Joe said, "You'll like this story, Sam. Teri and I met in Seattle. She was over there for a conference, and we met in a bar. I'd gone to see some guys playing jazz, and she'd been dragged into the place by her friends. Teri hates jazz, so she wanted to get out of there. Fortunately, she heard my accent and thought a fellow Brit might bail her out."

"And did you?" Dan asked.

"Of course. Some people are worth missing a band for, and I knew right away she was special. I took her to a great little Italian place I'd found. We talked for hours, and that was that."

"Aw, that's so sweet," Sam said. "You see, that's much more interesting than spreadsheets and profits."

Joe arched his eyebrows as though hearing heresy, then he laughed. "You're absolutely right, Sam, and that's my cue to leave you two alone so you can relax and enjoy some quality time. Meanwhile, I'll go and separate Teri and Tom before they come to blows over the three-act structure or something." Joe bowed his head to Sam and shook hands with Dan, laying his free hand on Dan's arm and adding, "Glad you took my advice, Dan. She's a keeper." To both of them, he said, "Have fun." Then he strode across to join Teri and Tom.

"What did he mean by that?" Sam asked. "What advice did he give you?"

"Nothing really."

"Tell me. It was something about me, wasn't it?"

Dan chose his words carefully. "I wasn't sure what this get-together would be like. Some of these corporate events are all about networking, and I didn't think you'd enjoy that. But Joe told me it would be a social occasion and said that partners were welcome."

"So, you weren't talking about me?"

"I told him there was someone I'd been wanting to ask out, someone special, and he encouraged me. Then I asked Alan about this place, and he said it was great."

"I see. Before you asked me on a date, you ran it past two other people, and then you finally got around to talking to me."

"I wanted to be sure. I didn't want to blow it."

Sam regarded him for a moment. "You're a strange one, Dan Corrigan. Half the time you jump in with both feet, but with me..." She broke off, shaking her head. "I don't know. You tiptoe around me like I'm made of glass, but I'm not. I might not be as clever as you, but I'm not stupid. If you ever have something to say to me, just come out and say it, because I like to know where I stand. If this is going to work, we've got to be straight with each other. Okay?"

"Okay." Dan gazed into Sam's eyes, the sights and sounds of the room fading away, and he found himself saying, "Since we're laying our cards on the table, I'd like to kiss you, if that's all right."

"Go on then."

"Right." Dan moved closer, and Sam tilted her face toward him, but in that moment, a woman's voice rang out, her cut-glass tones demanding attention: "There's a surprise! Dan Corrigan, what on earth are you doing here?"

Dan froze, unable to turn around.

Sam stared over his shoulder, her eyebrows tented. "Bloody hell," she murmured. "Who's she?"

"No one." Dan kept his attention on Sam. "We were about to kiss."

But Sam was still staring past him, and he knew exactly who she was looking at. Behind him was a woman who he'd never expected to see again; a woman he'd tried very hard to forget. He opened his mouth to explain, but the right words eluded him.

"She's never been a no one," Sam said. "She looks like Keira Knightley and she knows you. She's coming over."

With a supreme effort of will, Dan plastered a bland smile onto his features and turned to meet the new arrival.

Frankie Herringway, sheathed in a black dress that was tight enough to show her hip bones, homed in on him, stalking across the room, her leopard-like gaze unwavering. Each step she took was an elaborate choreography of high heels and swishing fabric, her long dress subtly slashed to the knee, offering glimpses of firmly toned calves. She smiled, and Dan found himself holding his breath. It was as if he was waiting for his heart to skip a beat. In the past, she'd always had that effect on him, reducing him to a shy, stumbling schoolboy. But not now.

He looked at Sam. She was nervous, her earlier confidence gone. She'd been afraid that she wouldn't measure up, and now her worst fears were coming to life before her eyes. Carefully, Dan reached out and held Sam's hand, squeezing it tight. Leaning toward her, he whispered, "I'm here with you. To me, that means everything."

Sam looked up at him, her eyes moist, and for a split second he thought he might be able to claim a kiss after all. But then Frankie joined them, confronting them, hands on hips as she cast her eye over them, amused. "Well, look at you two lovebirds. Don't you look absolutely gorgeous?" She focused on Dan. "Well, Dan, aren't you going to introduce us?"

"Of course. Frankie, this is... I mean, Sam, this Frankie Herringway. An old friend."

"Less of the old." Frankie thrust her hand at Sam for a shake, and as their hands touched, she pulled Sam closer, kissing the air on each side of Sam's startled face. "Aren't you divine?"

Pulling back, Frankie sighed in delight. "You really are too cute. Both of you." Studying Dan's clothes, she added, "You still have your Armani. It always looked good on you. Everyone's going in for something a bit different this year, but the classics never go out of style, do they?"

"It's just a jacket," Dan said. "I don't really think much about these things anymore."

Frankie's lips formed an O. "Goodness, you have changed. Someone told me you'd swapped London for the quiet life, but I never believed it. I just couldn't see you roughing it in the sticks, but here you are, and I must say you look well on it. It must be all that fresh air. You look simply marvellous. What's your secret?"

"I'm enjoying life," Dan replied. "I'd recommend it to you, but I'd say you're doing very well as you are. You look five years younger than when I last saw you."

"Only five?" Frankie pouted. "I shall have to ask for my money back."

"I'm sure that can be arranged," someone said, and Dan realised that Frankie hadn't arrived alone. A middle-aged man was loitering at arm's length from Frankie, his hands behind his back and his expression serious.

"Ah, this is Walter, everybody," Frankie said. "Walter Drake."

They exchanged handshakes and greetings, Walter beaming all the while.

"Frankie told me all about you," Walter said to Dan. "You're into high-tech start-ups, am I right?"

"Not so much these days. I moved away from London and I have other interests now."

"Me too," Walter said. "Not that I'm leaving London any time soon, but I've moved away from the high-tech arena. It was fun for a while, but it moves so fast, and the competition is brutal, isn't it?"

Dan nodded. "It tends to be that way. Who did you work for?"

"Walter was at Microsoft," Frankie said. "He was based in Seattle for years, weren't you, Walter?"

"Yes, it was great experience, but I'm glad to be back home."

"You might know Joe," Dan said. "He was at Microsoft too."

"Joe...?"

"Joe Clayton." Dan pointed Joe out. "The smart young man talking to Doug Petheridge."

Walter peered across the room. "No, I've never seen him before in my life. It's a big company, but even so, his name doesn't ring any bells, and I *never* forget a name."

"Walter's like a human computer," Frankie said. "That's why he's so good at what he does."

"Which is...?" Dan asked.

Walter smiled. "Financial analysis."

"Walter can do things with a spreadsheet that you wouldn't believe." Frankie bestowed a proprietorial smile on Walter, adding, "That's why he's my wingman on this operation."

Dan tried not to show his surprise. "You're here on business?"

"Didn't you know?" Frankie glanced at Walter then lowered her voice. "I'm sorry, Dan, but I have to check. Are you with CEG?"

"Yes, I'm working with them as a freelance consultant. I'm a business intelligence analyst."

"Didn't they tell you what's going on?"

"I know they have big plans, but I'm not on the inside track. What's happening?"

"Oh look," Sam said. "They're putting the food out. Shall we go and sit down?"

"In a sec." Dan focused on Frankie, a question on the tip of his tongue, but before he could say a word, Sam hooked her arm through his, and in a firm tone said, "No, let's go and sit down now. You've had enough shop talk for one day. We're meant to be enjoying ourselves."

One look told Dan that Sam was not to be contradicted, and anyway, he'd made her a promise. "Sure. Where would you like to sit?"

"Over by the window." Sam gestured to a small table flanked by two chairs, where a waiter was arranging plates around a multi-tiered cake stand filled with sandwiches and tempting treats.

"That looks great." Dan nodded to Frankie and Walter. "We're off to get some tea. Good to see you again, Frankie. Nice to meet you, Walter. I hope you have a nice time."

"We could grab a couple of chairs and sit with you," Frankie said, but Walter held up his hand.

"No, let them have a little space, Frankie. Besides, we said we'd have tea with Doug."

"Ah yes. See you later, you two. Have fun." Frankie blew them kisses, then she turned on her heel and strode away with Walter following in her wake.

Sam let out a small sigh of relief. "I thought she'd never go. It's a good thing Walter got the message. I was about ready to stick one on that woman, and he knew it."

"Really?"

"Yeah. He saw the look on my face when she wanted to sit with us. That's why he took her away."

"She's gone now, so let's forget about her."

Dan made to move away, but Sam held her ground, her arm interlocked with his. "An old flame, is she?"

"Yes," Dan admitted. "We went out together for a while, but that was a long time ago."

"Did she dump you or the other way around?"

"She finished it, not that it makes any difference. It's in the past, and I didn't know she was going to be here. It came as a complete surprise, and not a pleasant one."

"That's all right then, but let's steer clear of her, okay?"

"Fine by me. But hang on a minute – were you jealous, Sam?"

"Don't flatter yourself. It was the way she talked down to me that got my back up."

"She talks like that to everybody. She didn't mean any harm."

Sam raised an eyebrow. "If you think that, Dan, you have no idea about women; no idea at all."

"Maybe, but I only need to know about one of them. For a start, I'd better find out what you like to eat. Let's go and sample all those little sandwiches and cakes, and you can tell me which ones you like best."

"It won't be vegan. I like cream and butter and all kinds of cheese."

"That's fine. I won't make a fuss. I'm sure they'll be able to find me something I can eat, so don't worry about it. Enjoy."

"I will."

Sam drained her champagne, then they made their way over to the table and claimed their space. Everyone else flocked to the other tables, leaving them in peace, and while Sam poured them both a cup of tea, Dan tried to relax.

Even so, he couldn't help thinking about his encounter with Frankie. The last time he'd seen her, she'd been working for Stein Waterhouse, a major financial institution known primarily for buying up businesses and shutting them down, stripping their assets and making a fast buck. Frankie had been in charge of acquisitions. If she was in Devon to snap up CEG, Dan had better make sure he submitted his invoice before the hammer fell; otherwise, he could be left out in the cold.

"Look at these cute little sandwiches," Sam said. "They're so tiny." She turned the cake stand around, inspecting its contents carefully, smiling like a kid in a sweet shop. "When I make a sandwich, you need two hands to pick it up. These things are barely a mouthful."

"Try one."

"All right." Sam plucked a sandwich from the stand and nibbled at it. "Mm. Have one of these, Dan. I think they're cucumber, so you should be all right."

"In a minute. I just want to drink my tea, clear my head after the champagne."

Dan sipped his tea, watching Sam as she finished one sandwich and selected another. She deserved his full attention, but he couldn't help worrying about work.

What about my reputation? he thought. *How will it look if the company gets liquidated so soon after bringing me in?* No one would ever hire him again.

Right from the beginning of his time at CEG, it had struck him as odd that they'd hired a lone freelancer when they could easily have bought in a whole team of experts. Now he was beginning to see why. He was a pawn in a much larger game. Whether he was to be a fall guy, set up to fail, or a distraction, put in place to cover up the board's plans, he couldn't say. But something was wrong at CEG. Neil had known it, and he'd been kicked out and left a broken man.

They won't get rid of me so easily, Dan told himself. *I won't let them make a fool out of me*. But it was easy to feel strong when he was sitting in an oak-panelled dining room with Sam. On Monday, in his bleak little office, it would be harder to know what to do.

Still, that gave him the weekend to come up with a plan of action, and it had better be a good one. He'd worked damned hard to build up his new career, and he wouldn't stand by and see it destroyed. He'd do anything to protect it. He'd learned a few things in his time in the City, and if the management at CEG thought they could mess him about, he'd soon show them what he was made of.

Whatever happened, he would not go down without a fight.

CHAPTER 26

As best as she could in the confines of the driving seat, DS Kulkarni arched her back and stretched her legs. She'd been parked in the Plym View trading estate for over an hour, and the wait was starting to place a strain on both her nerves and her body alike. Staring out through the windscreen, she decided that the place had been bleak in the full light of day, and the encroaching darkness had done nothing to improve the view.

It's a shame about the CCTV, she thought. As John Sykes had said, the cameras on his building were set up to focus on his small patch of the trading estate and they hadn't captured any passing cars, luxury or otherwise. She'd ploughed through enough of the footage to guess that it was unlikely to yield anything significant, and she hadn't been able to get hold of the mysterious tenant of Unit 18, so here she was, waiting for him to arrive.

The floodlights around the compound's edge weren't switched on, and the lights from the main road were doing little to penetrate the shadows between the darkened industrial buildings. Still, at least there wasn't much chance of her car being spotted. She'd parked in a neglected corner of the compound, positioning her car carefully so that it was partially obscured by the rusting hulk of an abandoned transit van, while allowing her clear lines of sight towards the site's entrance, the car park and, most importantly, the squat building labelled Unit 18.

As she watched, a figure emerged from behind a stack of junk by the fence and jogged towards her car. *About time*, she thought. *Come on, Collins.* There was no way she would've come on this job alone, and DC Collins had been the obvious choice. He was young and ambitious, and he seemed reasonably capable, but in his company the time had passed slowly. Despite the fact that they'd been working together for a few weeks, she'd found no common ground, and she couldn't help thinking he resented her being promoted over him. *That's his problem*, she told herself. *He'll have to get over it.*

DC Collins climbed into the car without a word and settled himself in the passenger seat.

"Better?" Kulkarni asked.

"Yeah. Sorry to leave you on your own. Call of nature. I shouldn't have had that last cup of coffee."

"You're lucky. Harder for me to nip out for a pee."

Collins looked uncomfortable. "I suppose so. Still, we shouldn't be much longer, eh?"

"Hopefully not. He should be here any minute." Kulkarni glanced at Collins. "I hear DI Spiller has been keeping you busy. How's it going?"

"It's slow. A lot of dead ends. But it's a cold case, so I'm not expecting much excitement."

"You never know. Spiller seems keen to get a result. He's got that look in his eye, like someone's holding his feet to the flames, and that can make all the difference."

"We'll see how it goes," Collins said, and there was something in his tone that made Kulkarni pause for thought. Collins was trying to sound casual, but he was holding something back: some nugget of information that he wanted to keep for himself. She could probably get the truth out of him, but it would have to wait. The beams of a car's headlights were sweeping across the car park.

"That's him," Collins said. "Red Renault Espace." He reached for the door handle. "Ready?"

"Give him a minute. Let him get out of his car."

Kulkarni waited, watching while the red car halted outside Unit 18, parking close to the building. The engine and headlights died, the sudden darkness forcing her to narrow her eyes. The Renault's interior light flared, and she heard its door open. A man emerged, slamming his car door and locking it before heading for Unit 18.

"Hang on," Kulkarni said. Starting her car, she flicked on the headlights and put her foot down, gravel grating beneath the wheels as her Honda accelerated across the compound.

She saw the man turn and stare, blinking in the glare of her headlights, and then she swung her car into position behind his, blocking it in.

Collins was already climbing from the car, and Kulkarni followed suit. Warrant card at the ready, she marched toward the man who still stood, frozen to the spot.

"Mr Williams?" she said. "Darrell Williams?"

The man held out his hands as if to ward off impending doom. "Listen, I'll pay the rent. I will. I just need a couple of days, that's all."

"Sir, we're police officers," Kulkarni said. "I'm DS Kulkarni and this is DC Collins. Are you Darrell Williams?"

"Police? Why? What's going on?"

Collins stepped forward. "Sir, we need you to confirm your name."

"Okay, I'm Darrell Williams, but what's this about?"

"We need to talk to you," Kulkarni said. "Inside would be best."

"All right, all right. Let me catch my breath." Darrell

exhaled loudly. "You put the fear of God into me. Hang on while I open up."

Darrell had been in the process of letting himself into the building, and his keys still hung from the door. Turning his back on them, he unlocked the door, and Kulkarni made sure she was standing close behind him as he turned the handle. As soon as he pulled the door open, Kulkarni grabbed it, making sure he wouldn't try to duck inside and shut them out.

Darrell sent her a guilty glance, as though the thought of escape had been very much on his mind, but he entered the building and stood back meekly to allow Kulkarni and Collins to follow, then he switched on the lights and closed the door. Facing the police officers, his shoulders back as though braced against bad news, Darrell composed himself, then said, "So, what's the problem? Has someone made a complaint?"

Kulkarni met his gaze. "Is there any reason why someone might do that?"

"Not really, but I work late, sometimes very late, and I thought someone might've been annoyed by the van coming and going. We try and keep the noise down, but there's only so much you can do."

"I see," Kulkarni said. "But is it vans that come and go in the night, or is it cars?"

"I sometimes use my Renault, but it isn't big enough, so I have a mate with a van, and he helps me out."

"Right." Kulkarni looked around, taking her time. The building's interior comprised a single space, much of it taken up with ranks of metal shelving. Plastic crates were stacked on every shelf, each one placed neatly and labelled. There was only one work surface: a simple workbench that ran the length of one wall. The bench was empty apart from a single desktop computer, its monitor, keyboard and mouse arranged tidily beside it. In front of the bench, an office chair looked slightly forlorn, its upholstery repaired with strips of carefully applied gaffer tape.

Kulkarni wasn't sure what to make of it. Given the building's tatty exterior, the place was suspiciously clean. The floor looked as though it had been swept, and there was not so much as a scrap of paper in sight. She exchanged a look with Collins. If this place had anything to do with processing stolen vehicles, it was clear that they'd both be very surprised.

"Mr Williams," she began, "what's the nature of your business?"

"Erm, I sell crafting supplies. It's all online. People order on the website, and I package it up and send it out. Usually, I take the parcels myself in the car, but when it gets busy, like at Christmas, my mate helps me out with his van."

"Crafting supplies?" Collins asked. "What's that when it's at home?"

"You know, card and paper, beads and boxes, paints and inks and all that kind of thing."

Collins looked perplexed. "So, stationery, then?"

"No, it's more than that. There's all the tools and equipment for a start, and I sell sheets of foam, wooden boxes, even feathers."

A sinking sensation descended on Kulkarni. Looking again at the plastic crates crammed on the shelves, she could see that Darrell was telling the truth. Some of the crates had translucent sides, and she could see the bright colours of their contents.

Turning back to Darrell, she said, "Why do you work at night?"

"No choice." Darrell regarded his kingdom sorrowfully. "I aim to run the business full time one day, but it doesn't pay the bills. Not yet. Until it does, I've got to have a day job. I stack shelves at Tesco. Fruit and veg."

Collins muttered something under his breath, but

Kulkarni ignored him. "Okay, let's move on to your association with a man called Jez. How do you know him?"

"Jez? He's the guy who helps me out with his van. We go to the same pub. That's how I know him."

"What's his full name?" Collins asked, taking out his notebook.

"Jeremy Parker, but everyone calls him Jez."

Collins made a note, and Kulkarni said, "Is Jeremy an employee?"

"Not really. It's casual. When I get a lot of orders, I give him a few quid and he loads up at night and takes the parcels to the depot in the morning." Darrell hesitated, uncertainty in his eyes. "I don't know if he declares the money. Me, I pay my taxes. I do my books every week. I was going to do them tonight, as it happens. It's all on the computer."

"We're not tax inspectors," Collins said. "But we need to know more about Jez. Tell us about the car he was driving a few weeks ago."

"I don't know what you mean. I've never seen his car."

"Really?" Kulkarni asked. "According to our information, he turned up here in a Lexus, about five weeks ago."

"Oh, that wasn't his. He was just delivering it to someone. That's what he does. He's a driver, or so he says."

"You don't sound too sure," Collins said. "Who does he work for?"

"To be honest, I can't say exactly what he does. I think he's self-employed, but I don't really know what he gets up to when he's not working for me. I've heard him talk about delivering cars, but he's never brought any of them here, except for that one time. When he turned up in that Lexus, he said he'd come to ask if I needed him, but I reckon he was just showing off. He was all dressed up and everything." Darrell smiled wistfully. "I suppose when you get a car like that delivered you don't want it turning up with some scruffy sod behind the wheel."

Kulkarni studied Darrell for a moment. She'd met plenty of crooks who could smile and plead ignorance, and she wasn't easily taken in, but this man was almost certainly telling the truth. He knew nothing about the stolen cars, but he had given them a lead. "Do you have an address for Jeremy Parker?"

"No. I've got a mobile number, but he keeps changing it, so it might not be right."

"If he changes his number, how do you get in touch with him?" Collins asked.

"I see him in the pub. The White Swan on Alexandra Road. If I finish work in time, I call in for a swift half on the way home. Jez is there most nights."

Kulkarni looked to Collins. "The White Swan. Do you know it?"

"No, but we can find it easily enough."

"I'm sure we could." Kulkarni nodded to Darrell. "Thank you for your help, sir. It's been useful. We'll leave you to get on with your work."

"No problem." Darrell tried to smile but his expression faltered. "I hope I didn't... I mean, I wouldn't want to get Jez into trouble or anything. He's a decent enough lad. Not the sharpest tool in the box, but he's all right. I don't think he'd do anything wrong. He's just a driver."

"Then he has no need to worry," Kulkarni said smoothly. "All the same, we'll have a chat with him. It's best to straighten things out in person, isn't it?"

"Yeah. If I see him, should I tell him you're looking for him?"

"It's probably best if you don't. He might take it the wrong way, and I'd hate for him to be angry with you."

Darrell looked thoughtful. "He does have a bit of temper. I'll keep schtum."

"Good idea. Goodnight, Mr Williams." Kulkarni took a last look around the place then nodded to Collins. "Let's go."

"Fine," Collins said, though he kept his gaze on Darrell as though handing out an unspoken warning.

Practising his police officer's stare, Kulkarni thought. *Fair enough.* She headed for the door and heard Collins fall into step behind her.

Outside, Collins said, "Do you want to try the pub now?"

"No. Sorry to disappoint you, but the last thing we want is to go trawling through the pubs of Plymouth, waving our warrant cards. We don't want Jez to disappear into the woodwork. We'll run a background check on Jeremy Parker, but it can wait. We can go home. Thanks for tonight. You did a good job."

"Cheers." They walked back to the car in silence and climbed inside. As they set off, Collins said, "I don't know about you, but I'm starving. Fancy stopping off somewhere for something to eat?"

"Er, maybe, but I'm not sure if it's a good idea."

"Oh, I didn't mean... I wasn't trying to ask you out or anything."

It was hard to tell in the car's dark interior, but Kulkarni had the distinct impression that Collins was blushing. He'd protested a little too strongly, and she knew his game. She'd noticed him checking her out a couple of times, and it hadn't bothered her. He'd never said or done anything to cross the line, and that was actually quite refreshing. Plus, he wasn't bad looking, but he was younger than her, and she was his superior officer. It wasn't going to work. *Poor lad*, she thought. *Let him down gently.* She cleared her throat and said, "It's a nice idea, but I've got some work I want to catch up on. Another time perhaps."

"Okay. No worries."

"I'll tell you what, why don't you come with me when I follow up with Jeremy Parker?"

"At the weekend?"

"No, I think it can wait until Monday."

"In that case, I'd be happy to tag along, so long as the guv can spare me. I'd like to see the case through."

"I'll square it with him and I'll put in a good word, tell him how helpful you've been."

"You don't have to do that. I didn't do much."

"Don't do yourself down. This thing tonight, it could've gone either way, but the guy decided to cooperate. Having you there was a big help."

"Thanks."

They didn't talk much for the rest of the journey back to Exeter. Collins seemed satisfied to tap on his phone, and that was fine with Kulkarni. She needed the time to think.

SATURDAY

CHAPTER 27

F resh from his morning run, Dan was standing in his kitchen with a welcome glass of cold water when his phone rang. Grabbing his phone as he swallowed a mouthful of water, he checked the caller's name and he almost choked.

Spluttering, Dan wiped his mouth and composed himself. Only then did he answer the call. "Frankie. This is a surprise. How are you?"

"I'm good," Frankie said. "But have I called at a bad time? You sound a little hoarse."

"No, I'm fine. I've just come back from a run, that's all."

"That's dreadfully energetic for a weekend, but then you always were a glutton for punishment." Frankie laughed gently, but then her tone changed, becoming more serious. "It's good to talk to you, Dan. I was worried you might've changed your number, and to tell you the truth, I need your help."

"Oh? What can I do for you?"

"You can let me take you out for lunch. I'm stuck in Exeter all weekend with only Walter for company, and I'm bored out of my mind."

"I see. I assumed that you'd headed back to London straight after the get-together at Batworthy Castle."

"If only. There's far too much to do. We'll be here for days."

"Do I take it that Stein Waterhouse are looking to acquire CEG?"

"Tut-tut, you naughty boy," Frankie purred. "My lips are sealed. You must promise you won't try and tempt me to spill the beans, or I shan't agree to see you."

So, there are beans to spill, Dan thought. *Or is that what she wants me to think?* He had to admire the artful way Frankie had just turned the tables on him. After their last encounter he'd had no intention of ever seeing her again, and yet now, despite himself, he had to meet up with her, had to know more.

"I don't like to make promises I might not keep," Dan said. "Where are you staying?"

"We're at the Hotel du Chambray. It's not bad, but I need to get out and about, and I don't know anyone here. It's enough to drive anyone to distraction. I simply must have some fun or I'll go mad."

"Well, I'm not sure if I can make it today. Tomorrow would be better."

"Oh dear," Frankie said, pouring a full measure of disapproval into the two small words. "What are you up to that's so important?"

I don't owe her an explanation, Dan told himself, but it would be rude not to offer some kind of excuse, so he said, "I was going to catch up with a friend."

"Do you mean Sam? She seemed nice. Bring her along. My treat."

"That's kind of you, but Sam's working today. She tends to be busy at the weekends. She runs the village pub."

In the silence that followed, Dan pictured Frankie's

delicately shaped eyebrows rising as far as her suspiciously wrinkle-free forehead would allow.

"Actually, I'd planned to go out with my neighbour," Dan went on. "We're going for a hike on Dartmoor."

"That sounds ideal. I've always wanted to see Dartmoor properly. They filmed *War Horse* up there, didn't they?"

"Yes. I'm not sure which part of Dartmoor they used, but Alan would know. He's the neighbour I mentioned."

"Ooh, is he a real, rugged countryman? I'm picturing a modern-day Heathcliff. Tell me I'm right."

Dan smiled at the thought of Alan fighting off Frankie's attentions. "I couldn't possibly comment. Alan writes children's books, but I think he's quite successful, so I guess that might make him an eligible bachelor."

"Intriguing. He wouldn't mind if I came along, would he?"

"Not at all," Dan admitted. "Alan gets on with everyone and he likes to show off his local knowledge, so I'm sure he'd love to meet you."

"There we are then. It sounds perfect. Unless you don't want me around, that is."

"I'd be happy to see you, but we're going to hike over the open moor. The views are great, but you need to be properly equipped."

"That's no problem. I can pop into town and get everything I need. I could do with a new pair of walking boots anyway."

It was Dan's turn to be surprised into silence. Frankie Herringway in walking boots? He could scarcely imagine it.

"Do say yes, Dan," she went on. "Otherwise, I'll be trapped in this hotel with absolutely nothing to do."

"Okay, if you're sure you want to come, but we aren't going out for lunch. I'll have a sandwich at home, then we'll set off around one o'clock. Could you be ready by then?"

"Easily. Where shall we meet? I've got the car, so I can come over to your place."

Dan glanced around his kitchen. It wasn't a complete mess, but it certainly looked lived in. *So what?* he thought. *I don't need to impress her.* Even so, a quick tidy up would make the house presentable, and if Frankie came to meet him, that would give him time to get ready and smarten the place up. "Okay, Frankie. I live at The Old Shop in Embervale. It's just off Fore Street, but I'll text you a map reference."

"Good idea. I'll get all the gear I need and I'll grab a bite, then I'll shoot over."

"What about Walter? Won't he mind if you run off without him?"

"Oh, he'll be all right on his own. Honestly, he's a nice man, but his idea of fun is reading the *Financial Times*, and if he gives me one more piece of advice about my pension, I'll scream."

"Fair enough," Dan said. "I'll see you here at one, and please don't be late. We need to set off in good time."

"I'll be there, Dan. I'm looking forward to it already. Bye."

Frankie ended the call, leaving Dan standing in his kitchen, lost in thought. What was he doing, allowing Frankie back into his life? She was no good for him, and anyway, he was happy with the way things were, and his relationship with Sam was just beginning.

It's just a walk on the moors, he told himself. *Nothing to worry about.* Alan would be there for moral support, and this was Dan's turf, whereas Frankie would be well and truly outside her comfort zone. And while they walked, there was a chance he'd be able to find out something about Frankie's dealings with CEG.

Stein Waterhouse wouldn't have sent her to Exeter without a solid reason. Frankie was up to something, and away from the office, she might let something slip.

~

ALAN DROVE, and naturally he offered Frankie the front seat of his VW Golf, relegating Dan to the back. Alan had changed their plans when he'd heard they were bringing a visitor along, so instead of tackling a stretch of open moor, he took them to Hound Tor, a spot that was popular with families and tourists.

Dan had gone along with the idea, but as the car headed up the hill from Bovey Tracey, he gazed out at the now familiar scenery without much interest. *We should've stuck to our plan*, he thought, *shown Frankie the real Dartmoor.*

Still, Frankie appeared to be having a fine time. She'd scarcely stopped talking during the entire journey, asking Alan one question after another, and Alan clearly hadn't minded the attention; he hadn't minded one little bit.

The car park in sight, Alan said, "I could show you Jay's Grave later."

"Ooh, that sounds a bit spooky," Frankie said.

"Not at all. It's just by the road. According to legend, Kitty Jay was a young housemaid who was betrayed by her lover. She hanged herself, and that meant she couldn't be buried in consecrated ground. In those days, I'm afraid there were a lot of silly superstitions about people who'd killed themselves. They thought that the spirits of the dead lingered and caused mischief, so they'd take the bodies right to the edge of the parish and bury them there, often by a crossroads. The theory was that the crossroads would confuse the spirits, so they wouldn't be able to find their way back to the place they'd died. Poor Kitty was buried without ceremony, but a local farmer dug up her body and reinterred her properly, setting some stones to mark her grave. To this day, there are always fresh flowers on the grave, though no one ever sees who puts them there."

Frankie sighed theatrically. "What a dramatic story. I'll bet you know lots of local folklore, Alan. You've obviously found your spiritual home in Dartmoor, and I can see why you love it."

"It has a certain rugged charm," Alan replied. "It gets under your skin."

"I can imagine. It's the sense of space that appeals to me. Looking out over the moors, it all seems so peaceful. You can't imagine anything stressful happening out here."

"It has its moments," Dan chipped in. "It's not all cream teas and strawberry jam."

In the brief silence that followed, Dan knew he'd sounded like a petulant child moaning from the back seat, but seriously, what did Frankie think she was playing at, fawning all over Alan?

Let it go, Dan told himself. *It's nothing to do with me.*

"Well, here we are," Alan said, pulling the car into a space. "Time to wrap up. I need to put my boots on, but it won't take me a minute. They're in the boot." Alan climbed out the car, and Frankie began fussing over her coat.

"Where do we pay for the parking?" Frankie asked. "I can take care of it."

"You don't need to pay for this one," Dan replied. "It's free."

Frankie turned in her seat to stare at him. "Really?"

"Yes. It stops people parking all over the place. Are you ready?"

"Yes, I think so."

They joined Alan at the back of the car where he was tying his bootlaces. Glancing up at them, he said, "I thought we'd head up to the top and take it from there. If you fancy a longer walk, we can stroll down to the ruins of the medieval village. That's always interesting."

"That all sounds lovely," Frankie said brightly. "I'm raring to go."

"Good." Alan slung a backpack over his shoulders, then he slammed the boot shut and locked the car. "Let's go."

The path up to the tor was an easy one, but they took it slowly, Frankie keeping up a stream of questions and Alan seemingly content to chat.

"Let's pick up the pace a bit, shall we?" Dan asked. "When we get up to the tor, we could stop for a break. There's a great view."

"Challenge accepted," Frankie said.

"That's what I like to hear." Alan tightened the straps of his backpack as if he meant business and he strode forward. Setting out to match his pace, Frankie appeared to stumble, and though she didn't fall, she let out a hiss of frustration.

Alan and Dan rushed to her side at the same moment, then eyed each other uncertainly, an unspoken challenge hanging in the air between them, neither willing to give way.

Sending Dan a frown, Alan turned his attention to Frankie. "Are you all right?"

"Yes, I'm fine. It's just these new boots. I'm not quite used to them yet, and I slipped."

"I'm sorry," Alan said. "I shouldn't have set off so quickly."

"That's all right, Alan. It wasn't your fault."

"Maybe so, but I knew you'd bought those boots only this morning, and I should've advised you to wear them in for a bit. New boots are always stiff to begin with."

"I know," Frankie said. "I'm quite a keen walker."

"Are you?" Dan asked. "That's new."

Frankie regarded him levelly. "Yes. A friend introduced me to the South Downs, so I head out there whenever I can find the time. It's wonderful up there. It's different to Dartmoor, but I get fresh air and exercise, and I use the time to think and unwind."

"Same here," Alan said. "There's nothing like a good walk. But how's your ankle? Shall we head back to the car?"

Frankie made a show of studying Alan as though seeing him for the first time. "You are one of nature's gentlemen, Alan. A rare find."

Alan made a valiant attempt to shrug off Frankie's compliments, but Dan could see that he was inordinately pleased.

"I don't know about that," Alan said. "I'm supposed to be showing you around, and I'd hate for you to be hurt on my watch, so to speak."

"Well, you needn't worry, I'm tougher than I look. Why don't you two go on while I sort my boots out?"

Alan started to protest, but Frankie raised her finger to silence him. "Go on," she said. "I can look after myself, and I don't want you fussing over me."

Dan nudged Alan's arm. "Come on, we'd better do what we're told."

"There's a phrase I never thought to hear from you," Alan replied. "I suppose there's a first time for everything." Alan looked ahead then pointed to a crooked hawthorn tree some distance up the slope. To Frankie, he said, "We'll head for that tree, but we won't go too fast, and you'll be able to keep us in sight. Is that okay?"

"Of course, but don't slow down on my account. I won't be long."

"Right." Alan seemed somewhat reluctant to move away, so Dan headed off, setting the pace.

Alan quickly caught up with him. "Will Frankie be okay?" Alan asked. "I don't like leaving her behind like that."

"Don't worry. She's probably fitter than either one of us, and she's very independent."

"So I gathered."

They walked in silence for a few steps, then Alan said, "Tell me if it's none of my business, but I was wondering…"

"About what?"

"I was wondering how you feel about Frankie being around."

"I'm fine with it. It doesn't bother me in the least."

"That's good, because when I first met you, you were pretty broken up about her."

"That's all in the past. I've moved on, and you can bet she has."

Alan glanced briefly over his shoulder as if to check Frankie was out of earshot, then he said, "She's very glamorous, isn't she? Like a film star or something."

Dan didn't reply. He'd heard the hushed awe in Alan's tone, and he wasn't sure how he ought to respond. Alan was a grown man, and if he'd taken a shine to Frankie, that was up to him. Even so, Alan wasn't used to people like Frankie. She worked hard and played hard, and as Dan had found out to his cost, there wasn't much room in her life for emotional attachments. *I made a fool of myself over her*, Dan thought, *and I'm not sure if she even noticed.* Still, he was different now, and it seemed that Frankie had changed too. At any rate, he shouldn't harbour a grudge; that would be childish.

Dan looked back, expecting to see Frankie following. She was exactly where they'd left her, but she wasn't adjusting her boots. Frankie was standing with her back to them, a phone pressed against her ear. With her other hand, she was gesticulating, thrusting her fingers in the air as though jabbing at an opponent.

Dan stopped, Alan halting beside him.

"What's up?" Alan asked. "Is she all right, do you think?"

"Wait and see."

As they watched, Frankie turned and gave them a reassuring wave. A moment later, she pocketed her phone and set off toward them.

"Everything okay?" Alan called out to her.

"Yes. I had a notification of a missed call, and I tried to call back, but it didn't work. No signal."

"There aren't many phone masts on Dartmoor," Alan said. "It can make life difficult, but on the other hand, it's nice to escape from mobile phones once in a while."

"Very true," Frankie replied. "Shall we get going then? Come on, I'll race you to the top."

She strode away, and Alan followed hard on her heels, Dan tagging along behind.

What is she up to? Dan asked himself. *And why did she lie about her phone call?* She'd definitely been having a conversation with someone, and her body language said that it had been a heated exchange, so why the pretence?

It wasn't that Frankie was obligated to explain herself; she could've simply said that the call had been personal, and they wouldn't have thought anything of it. But covering it up had piqued Dan's curiosity. And what about the sudden trouble with Frankie's boots? Had that been a pretext for hanging back while she made a call?

Her stumble had seemed genuine, but it wasn't like Frankie to make a misstep. She was the epitome of poise and posture, and to all outward appearances she was as fit as ever. Even now, she was marching up the hill alongside Alan, walking perfectly well. They were chatting away, enjoying each other's company. But what was this? Alan offered his hand to guide Frankie over a rocky section of the path, and she took it, accepting his help, linking her arm through his as they walked on.

A pang of dark jealousy stirred in Dan's heart, and he dropped his gaze to the uneven ground as he trudged uphill. He was being ridiculous, that was for sure. He had no part in Frankie's life anymore, and she had no part in his. As for Alan, he could look after himself. If they enjoyed each other's company, that was fine. *Good luck to them*, Dan thought. *It's no business of mine.*

He caught up with Alan and Frankie at the top of the hill,

where they were standing side by side, admiring the view over the rolling expanse of Dartmoor in silence.

Swathes of coarse grass were softened by the flattering sunlight, stands of verdant bracken rippled in the breeze and the dark smudges of prickly gorse bushes were embellished with highlights of bright yellow blossom. In the distance, a small herd of ponies wandered over the moor, their coats a mixture of colours. Occasionally, a few of the ponies lowered their heads to graze, and there were a couple of foals among their number, trotting gamely on spindly legs, determined not to be left behind.

For a minute or two, no one spoke, then Frankie drew a deep breath and said, "Glorious, isn't it?"

"Without a doubt," Alan replied. "You won't find a better view anywhere."

Dan's foul mood dissipated as he watched the fleeting shadows of clouds chase across the sunlit landscape. "On a day like this, Dartmoor is pretty spectacular," he said. "There's no denying it."

"Well, well." Frankie sent him a knowing look. "You love it, don't you? I can tell."

"I wouldn't go that far," Dan replied. "Over time, I've learned to appreciate it."

"He doesn't like to admit it," Alan put in. "But Dartmoor has a way of working its magic on people."

"So I see." Frankie turned her attention back to the view. "Now that I've seen it for myself, I must visit more often. What do you say, Alan? If I were to pop back, how would you feel about taking a city girl on a tour, showing me all the delights of Dartmoor?"

"I'd consider it a privilege. Any time you like. Just give me a call."

"Perfect. I'll check my calendar, then I'll be in touch." Taking out her phone, she added, "There's no time like the present. Let's see if we can't work something out. We must swap numbers."

As Frankie and Alan went into a huddle over their phones, Dan said, "I thought you had no signal."

"It's fine up here," Frankie replied without looking up. "High ground is usually best."

"That's true," Dan said. "But are you really planning on coming back soon, Frankie? I seem to recall that your diary is usually full."

Frankie glanced at him. "That was then, this is now. I make sure to leave myself some free time. It was my coach's idea. He's very good. He works with a lot of execs in the City, helping them to perform at their best, and he says that it's important to refill the well now and then, or you end up…" Frankie bit back her words, her lips stretched tight over her teeth. "Never mind."

"Why, what were you going to say?" Dan asked.

"Nothing. Forget it."

"Oh, I see," Dan said. "You were you going to say something about getting burned out. Or maybe you were going to go for 'having a breakdown' or plain old 'cracking up'. God, wouldn't that be awful, ending up like that poor sod Dan Corrigan?"

Dan hadn't intended to launch into a rant, but he'd done it just the same, and Frankie paled, shaking her head as though lost for words.

"That's enough of that," Alan said firmly. "Frankie didn't mean to cause any offence, Dan, as you well know. You've no right to talk to her like that. She's our guest and you owe her an apology."

Frankie lifted her hands. "It's all right, Alan. I was insensitive. I should've thought before I opened my mouth. I'm sorry."

In the silence that followed, Dan cursed himself silently. This wasn't the first time he'd behaved like an idiot around Frankie. It wasn't her fault, but whenever she was around, he felt unbalanced, his emotions out of kilter. He'd thought his feelings for her had faded, but it hadn't taken long for them to re-emerge, just as powerful and just as dangerous. That couldn't continue.

Dan let out a long, steadying breath. "It's not your fault, Frankie. I should be the one apologising. Alan is right, and I'm sorry. I overreacted, and that wasn't okay."

"Don't worry about it," Frankie said. "Let's forget it ever happened." She looked up at Dan, her eyes filled with compassion. "You've been through a lot, Dan. I can see that. But you seem happier now than you ever were before, and that's wonderful, it really is. You've built a life here, and I don't want to intrude on that, but I hope we can be friends."

Dan nodded. "Of course."

"Good, because, as a friend, there's something I want to say to you. I might be speaking out of turn, but I want you to be careful at CEG."

"In what way?"

"I think you need to watch your back. I don't know the full story, but Walter said something the other day, and it's been bothering me ever since."

"What did he say?"

"He wasn't specific, and he wouldn't be drawn on the details, but he said that there's something not right at CEG, and I take that as gospel. Walter doesn't deal in anything other than cold, hard facts."

"You've had some misgivings yourself, haven't you, Dan?" Alan said.

"Nothing definitive," Dan replied. "There's certainly a strange atmosphere of secrecy. Having hired me as a consultant, they seem determined to keep me in the dark. The board members keep saying that the company is about to expand, but if they're in talks with Stein Waterhouse, that sounds as if they're planning to sell up. Is that right? Are they going to sell the business?"

Frankie's expression tightened. "You know I can't talk about that, Dan."

"Then what *are* you warning me about?"

Frankie stayed silent for a moment as if weighing her words, then she said, "What do you think of Seb Cooper?"

"I don't know if he's good at his job, but on a personal level, he comes across as a bit brash."

"He's a player, that's for sure," Frankie stated. "Be careful around him. That's all I can say."

"You can't leave it at that," Dan said. "What's he been doing?"

"That's confidential, but I'll tell you this. We had one of our security people look into Seb's past, and they didn't like what they saw. They flagged him as high risk."

Dan thought for a moment. "From what I know of Seb, he only looks after number one. I'm guessing he's tried to cut a deal with Stein Waterhouse, going behind the backs of everyone at CEG in an effort to save his own skin."

Frankie didn't react.

"Am I right?" Dan asked.

"I couldn't possibly comment." Frankie looked away, staring into the distance as though the conversation was at an end. But then she added, "Being out here, it gives you a sense of perspective, doesn't it?"

"It helps," Alan said. "But before we change the subject, there's something I want to ask you, Frankie."

Frankie regarded him with open curiosity. "Go ahead."

"A couple of times, you've warned Dan to be careful. Are you implying that he might be in danger? Real danger, I mean."

"I don't know if I'd go that far," Frankie said. "I was thinking more about Dan's livelihood and his reputation. I'm worried that he could get caught up in a situation that's

233

beyond his control. Why do you ask?" She looked at Dan. "Has something happened?"

"It's nothing," Dan replied. "Nothing for you to worry about."

"Dan was almost run over," Alan stated. "He could've been killed."

"Let's not exaggerate," Dan said. "It was an accident."

"That's not what you said the other day," Alan replied.

"When did this happen?" Frankie asked. "Since you've been at CEG?"

"It was on my first day, and it happened right outside the office," Dan said. "Talk about a bad omen."

Frankie looked Dan in the eye. "If I were you, I'd be taking this a lot more seriously. Whatever happens at CEG over the next few weeks, there'll be a lot of money at stake. Millions. People have been hurt for less."

"I appreciate your concern, but I'll be all right. This is Exeter, we're talking about. It's quiet."

"Dan, you're not thinking straight," Frankie said. "It doesn't matter where you are; money can always be moved. CEG owns businesses all over the world, and money flows from company to company. Walter's been going through CEG's finances – at least, he's been looking at all the figures he can lay his hands on – and he doesn't like what he sees. Walter might not seem like the most dynamic man around, but I've learned to trust his advice. If he says there's something wrong, I believe him, and if I were you, I'd sit up and take notice."

"What are you saying? Are they dodging their taxes? Falsifying their profits? Insider trading?"

Frankie pursed her lips.

"Come on," Dan insisted. "You must have some idea."

"No," Frankie said. "Beyond what I've already told you, I don't know a thing, not yet, anyway. When Walter digs deeper, he might change his tune and give the company a clean bill of health, but my instincts say otherwise, so I'm giving you a heads-up. Until we know more, you should use the time to prepare, make some plans. Do you see what I'm saying?"

Chastened, Dan bowed his head. "Yes, I understand, and I appreciate the warning. Thanks."

"You're welcome." Frankie exhaled, puffing out her cheeks. "Now, all this talking has left me with a dry throat. Where's the nearest pub?"

"You want to go to a pub?" Dan asked. "Already?"

"Why not?"

Dan and Alan exchanged a look. "I dare say I could think of somewhere," Alan said. "We'll have to go back to the car, but it's a short drive to Warren House Inn, or there's The Old Inn at Widecombe, or if you prefer, there's a restaurant in the hotel at Two Bridges."

"I think you'd better choose," Frankie said. "I fancy trying a local ale, and unless I'm mistaken, you're the right man to ask, Alan. I trust your judgement implicitly."

Alan looked thoughtful for a second as though considering a weighty matter, then he nodded wisely. "The Rugglestone Inn near Widecombe. It's a bit of a drive, but I think you'll find it's worth it."

"I second that," Dan said. "The Rugglestone will be perfect."

"That's settled then." Frankie set off down the hill, then she called over her shoulder. "Come on, you two. What are you waiting for?"

Lowering his voice, Alan said, "You know, I reckon Frankie might be even more impatient than you, and that takes some doing. As a matter of fact, she reminds me of you, in a funny sort of way."

"What on earth are you talking about?"

"Never mind. Let's catch up. I'm quite looking forward to a beer. I'll have to make do with a half, I suppose, but since I'm doing the driving, I reckon the first round is on you."

Without waiting for a reply, Alan marched away in dogged pursuit of Frankie, leaving Dan alone. Dan took a last fleeting glance at the view, then he set off to join Alan and Frankie. He wasn't sure what to make of Frankie's warning, but Alan had been hasty when he'd added the incident with the stolen car into the mix.

Dan needed some time to think, and a moment's peace in a country pub with a pint of good ale suddenly sounded like an excellent idea.

SUNDAY

CHAPTER 28

In his front room, Alan set his half-finished mug of coffee on the table and perched on the edge of his armchair, letting his gaze wander. Sunday mornings were for reading the paper with a hot drink and an endless supply of toast, but for some reason, he couldn't settle into his usual habit.

What was niggling him?

He thought back to the day before and the time he'd spent in the pub with Frankie and Dan. They'd had a good time. Dan had been a bit on edge at first, but a pint of ale had mellowed his mood, and he'd relaxed, regaling Frankie with tales of their investigations. Alan had joined in, and Frankie had lapped it up.

In hindsight, he wondered at the way Frankie had been so keen to talk about their past cases. Had she been steering the conversation away from Dan's job and the company he worked for? If so, she'd achieved her objective artfully, and with a certain degree of flattery. When she'd heaped praise on the pair of them equally, using words like 'brave' and 'daring', Alan's chest had swelled, and he'd noticed Dan sitting up a little straighter.

Alan had even wondered, once or twice, if there was

anything more to the admiring way that Frankie had looked at him. Was she attracted to him? *Probably not*, he told himself. *What would she see in a man like me?* Alan waited in case a likely answer might present itself, but none came.

Frankie was charming, intelligent and wonderful company, but she was out of his league. Alan sighed. No, it wasn't Frankie who was occupying his thoughts. It was something else.

It's this trouble with Dan, he decided. Since he'd started at CEG, Dan had lost his usual drive and lust for life. He smiled less and was easily irritated. The way he'd snapped at Frankie on the hill was a case in point. Dan could be stubborn and confrontational, but it wasn't like him to be so bitter.

Perhaps seeing Frankie had brought back unpleasant memories, reminding him of the life he'd once had. But surely, Dan ought to have moved on. He had a new life now and a budding relationship with Sam. Dan ought to be contented; he was anything but.

He's lost, Alan decided. *Like he was when he first came here.* It was as if going back into the corporate world had robbed Dan of something. He seemed adrift in the events of his own life, buffeted by the tides of change.

Why couldn't Dan see that he was in danger? Someone had tried to run him down, and he'd narrowly escaped with his life. If that weren't bad enough, he'd been warned by Frankie that he needed to watch his back at work. But Dan still planned to turn up at the office on Monday, carrying on as if nothing had happened. He was in denial, turning a deaf ear to common sense in the hope of clinging on to his job.

But what can I do? Alan asked himself. There was one thing, of course.

Jumping to his feet, Alan hurried through to the kitchen and stationed himself at the table, pulling his laptop toward him. He'd upgraded recently, and the new Dell booted in seconds. Retrieving his phone, he found the note with the mysterious dates and the Shakespeare quote that Dan had sent him, plus an image showing the front of the photograph. Dan had probably taken a picture of the photo using the camera on his phone, and the image quality wasn't great. It looked as though Dan had been indoors when he'd taken the shot; some parts of the original photo were obscured by reflections from overhead lights, and the image was slightly blurred as if Dan hadn't held his phone steady enough. But it would have to do, and fortunately Dan had taken the time to type out the text he'd found on the back.

Alan began by searching for the name of the man who'd owned the photograph: Neil Hawthorne. Surprisingly, he found very little about the man online. There were a handful of references to Neil on local news sites. CEG had supported several local charities, and Neil had been the man they'd wheeled out to present the cheques. Also, there were mentions of Neil in connection with a couple of sailing events, but otherwise he seemed to have lived an unremarkable life.

That's a damned shame, Alan thought. *It doesn't give me much to work with.* Returning to his phone and scrolling to the copy of the mysterious photo, Alan studied the woman pictured. Dan had told him that this was Neil's wife, Felicity, adding that she'd passed away. In the photo she'd been captured in a happy moment, without a care in the world, and the scene struck Alan as incredibly sad.

Reluctantly, he searched for her name online, but he could find nothing, and he was quietly relieved; he had no real wish to rummage through the online vestiges of the poor woman's life, and he would've hated to intrude on the personal grief of Felicity's family and friends.

His optimism fading, Alan turned to the dates from the back of the photograph. The dates were almost certainly personal to whoever wrote them. They'd probably refer to birthdays, anniversaries or significant milestones, but with nothing else to go on, he had to hope that the dates might be important in their own right.

He began with 19/2/16. The first two digits proved that the date was written in the British system, so he was looking for the 19th of February, but whether it was 2016 or 1916, he couldn't say. "Try both," he muttered to himself. An online search took him to a website that listed historical events on a given date, and he began with February 2016 as the twenty-first century was the most likely candidate. After all, the dates had been written on the back of a photo, not an old document.

He soon learned that Harper Lee had died on that day, so too had Umberto Eco. Though interesting, these facts didn't suggest a line of enquiry. Trying the same date in 1916, he found that an American jockey named Eddie Arcaro had died on that day.

Alan frowned. This wasn't a promising start. Even so, he repeated his searches for the second date: 8/1/12. The results for the 8th of January 2012 and 1912 were even less helpful. A Bulgarian pianist died on that date in 2012, and the Denver Broncos defeated the Pittsburgh Steelers. Meanwhile in 1912, members of the African National Congress in South Africa declared their aim of bringing all Africans together as one people.

Again, he'd struck out. There'd also been the number five written on the photo, but what that signified was anybody's guess. *They might not be dates at all,* Alan thought. *What if it's a code?*

If each number represented a letter of the alphabet, that could give him a starting point. He looked online and found a handy table listing the alphabet with numbers alongside. 19, 2, 16 spelled out S, B, P, and 8, 1, 12 added H, A, L. He thought briefly of the computer in *2001: A Space Odyssey,* and the snippet of trivia that claimed the name HAL was chosen because the three letters were each one place removed from I

B M. Could that be a clue? If he shifted S, B, P one place along, he got T, C, O. That wasn't much help, so he checked the number five and saw that it might represent E or possibly F.

"This is no good," Alan grumbled. He might have more luck with the Shakespeare quote. "Once more unto the breach dear friends once more!" he read aloud. He knew it was from *Henry V*, and he thought it was from act three. A search confirmed it. Act three, scene one, but what was its significance?

He watched Olivier's performance of the speech online and it brought a smile to his face. But when he found himself clicking from one video to the next, he knew he was procrastinating. "I need a break," he said, and putting his laptop aside, he went to put the kettle on.

While he waited for it to boil, he checked his phone. He'd put it on silent for the morning, and much to his surprise, he found he'd missed several calls, and a handful of text messages were awaiting his attention, all from his agent, Katy Emsworth.

Tackling the texts first, he read: *We need to talk, Alan. Please call me as soon as you get this.* The second one was shorter and had the tone of a command: *Call me.* Katy had obviously been in no mood to bandy words, but by the time she'd sent her third message, she appeared to have calmed down. It simply said, *Crisis averted. All will be OK. I've handled it.*

Katy had left several voicemails, but they followed a similar pattern to the texts, and none really explained why she'd been so anxious to get in touch. Alan checked the time. He didn't like to call Katy on a Sunday, but it wasn't too early in the day, and she had been remarkably eager to talk to him.

Katy answered his call on the second ring: "Alan, at last. How are you? Okay?"

"Fine. Sorry I didn't see your messages earlier. The phone signal around here can be a bit sketchy."

"That's okay, Alan. I hope I didn't worry you, but we had a situation, and I wanted your take on it before I acted."

"Oh? What's the problem?"

Katy sighed. "It's that photographer, Suzie Henshaw. She's been misbehaving, causing me all kinds of grief."

"What's she done? She seemed nice when she was here. Were the photos no good?"

"The photos were fine. Very good, actually. She caught your rugged side, just like we wanted, and if she'd stuck to doing her job, everything would've been wonderful."

Alan remembered watching Suzie leave, recalling the look on her face as she'd made a phone call. He'd sensed that she'd been up to something, and it sounded as though he was about to find out what.

"Apparently she fancies herself as something of a scribbler," Katy went on. "Meeting you was enough to make her swing into action."

"You mean she's writing a novel? How is that a problem?"

"If only it were that simple. No, young Suzie has set her sights on breaking into journalism, and she thought you might be her meal ticket. She's written up a feature-length piece all about you and your investigations, and she's been hawking it to every newspaper in town."

"She didn't breathe a word about this," Alan said. "What a cheek."

"Quite. Unfortunately, she's nothing if not persistent. I don't know how many media outlets she approached, but I've been fielding calls left and right, mainly from interested parties who wanted to verify the facts before they paid Suzie for the story."

"But nobody's called me. Apart from you, that is."

"That's exactly as it should be," Katy stated. "Google your name, and you'll find only one set of contact details: mine. I represent you, Alan. It's what you pay me for."

"A fact for which I'm profoundly grateful. Here you are, working hard on my behalf, and on a Sunday."

Sounding somewhat mollified, Katy said, "Yes, well, I must confess that of all my clients, you've given me the least trouble over the years. If they were all like you, Alan, I wouldn't have to spend so much time having my grey hairs tinted."

"Oh, you're too young for that, surely."

"Very smooth, Alan, but let's get back to the point. Suzie could've damaged your reputation. She's clearly done her research, and she's turned your life into a true crime piece. It's very dark, and not at all what we want for a children's author."

"That's awful. But you said 'could've'. Does that mean you were able to keep a lid on it?"

"Thankfully, yes. I've built up a good number of contacts in the media, and more than one editor owes me a favour. I let them know the situation, and they saw the sense in keeping me sweet."

"That won't be enough, will it? If it gets posted on the internet…"

"Don't worry about that. I've talked to Suzie myself. She has aspirations of making it as a serious journalist, and nothing less will do, so I gave her a lesson in ethics that she won't forget in a hurry. I told her that if she wants to make a name for herself, she's going about the wrong way. I dropped a few names, and she decided to shut up and listen, which makes a refreshing change."

"You marked her card," Alan said. "I almost feel sorry for her."

"Don't waste your sympathies. She got off lightly, and anyway, if she's going to survive as a reporter, she'll need the skin of a rhino."

Alan chuckled. "I expect you're right. Thank you for handling this, Katy. I appreciate it."

"Think nothing of it. But, Alan, she'll probably get her story out somewhere, so this changes the timetable for your relaunch. We need to get ahead of this now."

"Relaunch? I thought it was more of a rebranding exercise."

"It's both, because it's also become a damage-limitation exercise. It's about protecting your reputation, and to do that, we'll need to wipe Suzie's story off the face of the earth."

"That sounds a bit drastic."

"The situation has changed, and we need to respond. We want to be sure there's only one story anyone is talking about, and it has to be our version. Yes, it's a bolder strategy than we originally discussed, but it's necessary, and I think it will work out for the best."

"I'm not sure about this," Alan said. "Can't we discuss it before you—"

"It's too late for that," Katy interrupted. "It's time to take some decisive action. But don't fret. I've been in talks with your publisher, and they're on board. They'd like to crack the American market just as much as we would. It's all systems go, so I've told Clive to move things up a gear. He'd already done the groundwork, and he's putting the finishing touches on the media kits as we speak."

"You have the poor chap working at the weekend?"

"He's young and he's a pro. He's doing a first-rate job, and he assures me that everything will be ready this afternoon. As soon as he's done his bit, I'll be starting in earnest, hitting the phone and firing off emails to all and sundry. Be prepared to make a splash in the papers and online. Are you across all your social media accounts? Are they all up to date?"

"Yes, I, er, that is, I think they're all fine."

There was a brief silence before Katy replied. "Alan, we've discussed this. It's important to keep your image consistent. I'll have Clive send you some materials: graphics and so on.

Can you deal with them, or do I need to arrange for that to be taken care of?"

"I'll handle it. Sorry, Katy, I meant to get everything shipshape online, but with one thing and another…"

"Never mind. So long as you're getting on top of it, that's fine. I'll leave it with you for now, but I'll ask Clive to check in with you later today, and we'll take it from there. Okay?"

"Yes, that would be good. Thanks, Katy. Again."

"No problem. We'll talk soon. Bye."

Katy hung up, and Alan placed his phone on the counter. He'd forgotten about the kettle, and it had long since boiled and switched itself off. Flicking the switch to boil the water once more, he grabbed his teapot and spooned loose-leaf English breakfast tea into the integral strainer. It seemed that he had a bit of work to do on his online presence, and one mug of tea simply wouldn't be enough.

I was supposed to be helping Dan to decipher that cryptic note, he thought. But it wasn't as if he'd been getting anywhere with it. It felt as though there was some important part of the puzzle that he didn't have, and without it he didn't stand a chance. Anyway, with Katy standing by to breathe fire in his direction if he didn't get his act together, he didn't have much choice. Dan's project would have to wait.

CHAPTER 29

I'm almost ready.

An operation this subtle takes time. You have to do it properly or not at all, and in this case, inaction is not an option. All must be done correctly.

Ultimately, it comes down to a question of logistics.

First you plan, then you source your materials, making sure you have everything you need, and then you apply a little finesse. You can't rush into these things.

I've had to do a lot of research, but I'm a fast learner, or a quick study as our transatlantic cousins would say. I've had the weekend to work through the details, put the pieces together.

This time, I won't be rushed. My earlier attempt was a disaster from start to finish. For a while, I was angry, furious with myself, but I've set those useless emotions aside.

My haste was my undoing, I see that now. I should've known better, but I was hot headed, impulsive. That can't happen again.

We must master our circumstances or be mastered by them. Who said that? Whoever it was, they would've made an excellent criminal.

I am not a passenger on this journey, I am the driving force, the architect, the visionary, and I *will* master my circumstances.

Soon, my design will be complete. All it needs is a few finishing touches.

Which, when you think about it, is really rather an appropriate term.

MONDAY

CHAPTER 30

On the fifth floor of Corinthian House, Celine stood by the lift and stared at the illuminated row of numbers. She'd pressed the button to call the lift several times, but there was no sound of movement and the lift remained stubbornly on the ground floor.

She could use the main stairs instead, but that would deliver her, flushed and out of breath, to the lobby and Samantha's watchful gaze. *Sod it*, Celine thought, and headed for the little-used stairs at the far end of the building. But when she pulled the door open, she hesitated on the threshold. Someone was in the stairwell. It sounded like two people, a man and a woman, their voices echoing from the bare walls. They were some way below her, but one thing was for sure: they were engaged in a heated argument.

I should make a noise, Celine told herself. *Let them know I'm up here.* She certainly shouldn't stand there and eavesdrop. But she couldn't help it. She'd recognised the hoity-toity accent of that snooty Herringway woman, and by the sounds of it, Ms Herringway was in the grip of a blind fury, letting fly with the full armoury of her upper-class vocabulary.

Celine listened for a few seconds, her eyes widening, then

she backed into the corridor, closing the door as quietly as she could. There was no sense in interrupting Frankie Herringway; she was clearly in no mood to tolerate any kind of interference.

Good for her, Celine thought as she walked away. *Show them who's boss.* Celine allowed herself to daydream about picking a few battles of her own. She'd like to lay into some of her male colleagues, teach them the error of their ways. It was about time she stood up for herself, and not just at work but at home too. The memory of her latest quarrel with Patrick crept into her mind.

He'd been acting strangely toward her for a while, and they'd been bickering over stupid little things like whose turn it was to fold the laundry or empty the dishwasher. The arguments were nothing new, but lately their petty squabbles had grown bitter, their words more barbed.

Mulling it over while she traipsed along the quiet corridor, she decided that Patrick had been acting coolly toward her ever since that awful tea party at Batworthy Castle. To her colleagues, she'd introduced Patrick as her partner, and he'd corrected her in front of everybody, referring to himself as her boyfriend. *Boyfriend!* They'd been living together for three years, and for most of that time she'd supported him while he trained as a physiotherapist. She deserved some level of commitment in return, didn't she?

Celine passed the lift, but it was still on a lower floor, so she headed for the main stairs, her mood darkening. *Men are like children*, she thought bitterly. *Overgrown schoolboys.* One day soon, she'd fight back, starting with the other techs, Justin and Rob, and working her way up to the smugly superior Seb Cooper. *Smarmy Seb*, she thought. He'd led her on, and she'd allowed herself to be taken in by his charms. But not anymore. She'd seen him for who he was. She'd witnessed the way he'd fawned over Frankie Herringway at Batworthy Castle, and it had sickened her.

He'd flirted with Frankie despite the fact that his wife had been at his side.

Not that his chat-up lines did him any good, Celine recalled. *Frankie looked down her nose at him.* Indeed, she'd dismissed him with a roll of her eyes, and Seb hadn't liked that. The look on his face had been a picture, his cheeks reddening as though he'd been slapped, a fierce indignation burning in his eyes.

She wondered if Seb had been the other party in the stairwell just now. She hadn't been able to recognise the man's voice, because whoever it was, he'd hardly got a word in sideways. All she'd heard from the unknown man were low murmurs, apologetic and cringing. She'd never heard Seb speak in that way, but it could've been him. If it wasn't, then who was it?

Celine thought about going back to see for herself, but she still had work to do. She checked her phone and found that Tom had sent her an email demanding to see her immediately. No doubt he was in a flap about something, so it would be up to her to smooth his ruffled feathers. But why should she? Why should she always be the one to remain calm, the one to apologise, the one to keep her temper?

One of these days, I'm going to lose it, Celine told herself. *Then they'd better watch out. Every one of them.*

CHAPTER 31

DC Collins had a spring in his step as he marched up to Spiller's office and rapped smartly on the door with his knuckles. In his other hand he held several sheets of paper, all neatly stapled together, and he glanced down at them, smiling to himself. This was going to be good.

"Come in," Spiller called out.

Collins opened the door and stepped inside. "Got a minute, guv?"

"Always," Spiller said with a broad smile. "As a matter of fact, you're just the man I want to see. I've got news. Pull up a pew."

Collins took a seat facing Spiller, holding his papers in front of him and summoning his patience. He'd have to wait his turn, let his boss have the floor and hope it didn't take too long.

Looking pleased with himself, Spiller picked up a sheet of paper of his own and pushed it across the desk to Collins. "Unbelievably, the familial DNA matching for Rodney Davies and the body from Belmont Road has been done in record time. Nicola brought the results to me herself. It seems that the chief superintendent has been pulling strings. I've never had a result so fast."

"Blimey." Collins plucked up the sheet of paper and read it quickly. "It's a match. There's a 99.5% probability that they're related."

"Yes, and that seals the deal. Taken with the handcuffs and the dates, we can say that the bones in that crater are the remains of Tony Barnett."

"Unless the victim was a close relation of Tony's," Collins said. "We have no way of knowing for sure."

"True, but you've trawled through the archives and you've seen Tony's records. Did you find any reference to, say, a sibling?"

"No. He was an only child, but he could've had a relative we don't know about. If his father—"

"Let's not go down that rabbit hole," Spiller interrupted. "Everything points to the victim being Tony Barnett, so unless we find fresh evidence to contradict that, we'll stick with it."

Spiller gestured to the sheaf of papers that Collins still clasped in his lap. "Now, what have you got there?"

"Financials. Everything you need to know about the assets of Rodney Davies." Collins leaned forward to pass the papers to Spiller. "This is just the summarised version."

"Excellent." Spiller smiled as he picked up the papers and began leafing through them. "Clear and concise. Good work, Collins."

"Thanks. Have a look at page seven. I've highlighted the best bit."

It seemed to Collins that his boss was trying to appear unhurried as he turned the pages, but that was okay. He could wait for the penny to drop.

And there it was. Spiller furrowed his brow as he read the relevant page, and his mouth formed an O. "Well, well. That is a lot of money."

"Most of it from the sale of property," Collins said. "When

his mum died, Rodney inherited a string of terraced houses on Belmont Road."

"That *is* interesting. Do we know how Beverley Barnett came to own them?"

"I ran into problems with this. They belonged to a letting company, but the records were sketchy. It looks like the company was put in Beverley's name, but I don't know who did that or when. It *could* have been set up by her father, and maybe the paperwork went missing on purpose, but that's guesswork. I ran into a dead end but I've summarised everything I can find. If you have a look at the back page, you'll get the gist."

"Let's see." Spiller flipped to the last page and studied the detailed spreadsheet that Collins had constructed, then he looked up sharply. "You did all this?"

"Pretty much." Tempting as it was to leave it at that and make himself look good, Collins couldn't quite pull it off. "I had a bit of help putting the spreadsheet together, but I chased down all the records myself."

"You've done well. Now we know how Rodney can afford to live it up. He's quite the property tycoon."

"Well, he was," Collins said. "He rented the houses out for a while, but I guess he wanted to cash in and take it easy, and here's where Rodney was smart. He'd worked for the council in the past, so he knew the ropes, and he managed to get planning permission to tear down the houses and build a block of flats, well, luxury apartments. He sold the houses some time ago, and with the planning permission in place, they were worth a lot more than they would've been."

"By the look of his bank balance, Rodney did very nicely out of the deal."

"Too right. He's loaded. When I saw how much he's worth, I knew something was up, so I started with the present day and worked backwards."

"Well, I'll say it again, this is first-rate work, Collins. I was going to call in a few extra bodies to help you sift through his bank accounts, but you've beaten me to it. Maybe you should think about going into financial investigations."

Collins affected a modest shrug. "It wasn't that hard, guv. Rodney didn't hide anything away. He kept most of his money in the same building society he'd been using for years. He paid his taxes, and I found regular payments to a firm of accountants in town. It's all above board."

"Are we sure about that? No shell companies or accounts in offshore tax havens?"

"Not that I could find. To be honest, I can't see him going in for that kind of complicated crime. He's an old man, and he's got more than enough money to see out his days in style. Even if he lives to a ripe old age, there'll be enough cash left over to leave a fair chunk to his kids."

Spiller appeared to consider this for a moment. "I think you're probably right. If he was motivated by money alone, he wouldn't have spent his life working for the council. He could've been paid a lot more if he'd chosen to go into private enterprise, but he stayed in the public sector, and we both know what that's like when it comes to payday."

"Yeah, and he was very particular about his finances. Cautious. There were no high-risk investments. He even had a few thousand in a Post Office savings account. Who does that?"

"I do," Spiller said. "I know they don't pay much interest, but they're as safe as you can get. Government backed. I don't trust the big banks any more, not after the crash."

"That was years ago, guv. Things have moved on. I do all my banking on my phone. It's an app."

"What happens if someone nicks your phone or you get hacked?"

"I'm careful," Collins said. "You've got to move with the times, guv. It's the only way."

"I wouldn't be so sure of that. Sometimes, you need to

know about the old way of doing things, as you're about to find out."

Collins sighed, his good mood evaporating in an instant. He knew that look in Spiller's eye, and it meant trouble. He folded his arms and sat back, waiting for the other shoe to drop.

"No need to look like that, Collins. I've got a present for you." Spiller pointed to a large cardboard box in the corner, and Collins eyed it warily.

"What is it?"

"A blast from the past, that's what. Cassettes. Lots and lots of lovely cassettes."

"But I thought they were going to digitise them up in Hull?"

"I tried, I really did, but the DI I talked to wasn't budging. I guess it's true what they say about Yorkshiremen keeping a tight grasp on their pennies. He kept harping on about budgets and personnel as if I didn't know the way the world works. But at least they paid for the courier, so I managed to winkle something out of the tight sods."

"Unbelievable," Collins muttered. "I have to plough through them, do I? What a waste of time."

"Chin up. It won't be so bad. Have a look."

Reluctantly, Collins stood and crossed to the box, then he opened the flap and peered inside, staring in disbelief at the sheer number of plastic cases stacked inside. "There must be hundreds of them."

"I'm afraid so. That was the problem as far as our friends in Hull were concerned. They didn't have the time or resources to digitise them all, and they'd no way of knowing which ones we might find useful."

"They could've asked." Collins picked up a cassette case and examined the label. "I mean, look at this one. Top ten hits, October 15th, 1983. That's a fat lot of use, anyone could see that."

"Look at the bright side. At least they're all labelled."

"Great," Collins said without any trace of enthusiasm. "Oh well, he can't have recorded his mum very often. With a bit of luck, there'll only be one or two with her name on."

"That's the spirit, Collins. It shouldn't take you too long to sort the wheat from the chaff."

"The problem is, where am I going to find something to play them on?"

"There'll be a cassette player somewhere," Spiller said. "We used to have loads of them. Ask around. Someone will know where they've all been stashed away."

"Right. I'd better get started." Collins picked up the box. It wasn't heavy, but he needed both hands to keep hold of it. "Anything else before I go?"

"No, that's it for now. Good luck with the tapes and let me know if you find anything." Spiller offered an earnest smile. "I meant what I said about your work on Rodney's finances. It was meticulous, and that's what we need in this job: attention to detail."

"Cheers, guv." Collins inclined his head toward the door. "I'll go and track down a cassette recorder. I expect you're an expert on all that old-school hi-fi, aren't you, guv?"

"In my youth, I was known to dabble. I had a setup that could make the windows rattle."

Collins nodded as though impressed. "Was it electric or did you have to wind it up?"

"Very funny. The only wind-up merchant around here is you. Off you go, Collins. I'll see you later."

With a smile, Collins departed. He had a lot of work to do, but first he needed to grab a sandwich. It was lunchtime, and he was starving.

～

SITTING AT HIS DESK, Collins downed the last of his bottle of water and began sorting through the box of cassettes, checking the labels of each one. Some were plainly marked as music, and he set them aside. Collins reminded himself that Rodney had been in his forties when many of the recording were made, and it seemed that his musical tastes had been fixed firmly in the middle of the road. Amid the classic pop and easy listening albums, Elton John was one of the few artists that Collins recognised, and that was about as adventurous as it got. But then there were the personal recordings. A lot of the cassettes were labelled with the names of Rodney's children, who would've been teenagers in the eighties, so Collins doubted whether the youngsters would've set down anything worth listening to. Finally, Collins came to a cassette case labelled: *Mum - 1983*.

He opened the case carefully and was glad to see that the cassette itself had been labelled, the description matching the one on the case. *Good old Rodney*, he thought. *Very thorough*.

Collins allowed himself a small smile. The cassette collection mirrored the life of the man: well ordered, neat and built upon family ties. Rodney Davies had probably come home from work at the same time each day, sitting down for a meal with his family and spending his evenings watching TV. He was the type to wear a belt and braces. He left nothing to chance, preferring safety over risk. His mindset was nothing like that of a criminal. No impulsive decisions for him, no lust for power or overwhelming greed.

So why had he lied to them about living on his pension? He ought to have known that they'd uncover the truth sooner or later, so why try it on?

Still brooding over the contradiction, Collins slid the cassette into the player. He'd found an old set of sturdy headphones in a store cupboard, along with half a dozen cassette recorders, and he clamped the bulky cans over his ears. "Quite comfy," he murmured, surprised that he couldn't hear his own voice at all. The headphones did a better job of shutting out external sound than the expensive pair of wireless headphones he had at home.

I wonder if I could borrow these, he thought. *No one would notice.* But knowing his luck, some busybody would come along and check the cupboard's stock, and he'd get moaned at. It wasn't worth the hassle.

He pressed the play button, and with a hiss, the cassette began to play. Rodney was the first to speak, his voice sounding much younger but still recognisable. He introduced himself and then asked his mum to speak.

"I'm Beverley Barnett," she said. "Is that all right? Is it coming through?"

Rodney's reply was fainter as though he was speaking from behind the microphone, and he asked his mother to state her age.

"A gentleman doesn't ask a lady such things." She laughed. "I'm sixty-one and going strong. What else do you want to know?"

"Tell me about your life," Rodney said. "Anything you can remember. Anything at all."

"There's nothing wrong with my memory. I can tell you that for a start."

"I know. Tell me about Dad."

Beverley described how she'd met Fred Davies when he'd come into the grocer's shop where she'd been working. Fred had worked for a baker all his life, and it sounded as though he'd been content with his lot. Collins did his best to pay attention, but there was a lot of waffle and he tuned some of it out. But he pricked up his ears when Rodney finally got onto the subject of his grandfather, Beverley's father, Tony Barnett: the man who'd been murdered and buried beneath 13 Belmont Road.

This is more like it, Collins thought, and he grabbed a pen and a pad of paper as Beverley began:

"He liked the high life, my dad. Flash, that's what people said, but it was different back then. People didn't have so much. If you bought a new set of clothes, people looked twice at you, and Dad liked to dress well. He had his suits tailor made. He liked flash cars too. Oh, he was mad about cars. When we were little, we loved it when he came home in a new car. 'Come on,' he'd say, 'let's take her for a spin.' And we'd all cheer. Mum would pretend to be cross, and she'd ask him how much he'd paid for it, but he'd say. 'Don't worry about it. Jackie helped me out.'"

"Who was Jackie?" Rodney asked.

"He was one of my dad's friends, and I suppose you could say he was a friend of the family because I remember him being around the house a lot, but Jackie wasn't his real name. Now, what was it?"

There was a pause, and Collins ground his teeth together as he waited, listening to the hiss in his headphones.

"John," Beverley announced. "That was his proper name. John Blatch, but everyone called him Jackie. Goodness, he was a handsome man. Truth be told, I had a crush on him. There's no need to look so disapproving, young man. I was only seventeen, and it was all totally harmless. He never tried it on with me. He was a lot older than me, and besides, my dad would've killed him."

"Did Grandad have a temper?"

"Now and then. He was very protective of his family, and he was a policeman, so he never stood for any nonsense. He'd stand up to anybody."

"He must've been quite a character."

"Oh, he was. Mind you, he wasn't all serious. He liked to have a good time. Before the war, he was dead keen on going to the races. Exeter, Newton Abbot. Sometimes he'd go further and be away for a few days. I think that's how he met Jackie. Dad used to say that Jackie would give him tips, you know, tell him which horses to put money on. You could always tell when he'd done well, because he'd come home a bit tipsy, and he'd bring flowers for Mum. She'd nag him about the gambling, tell him not to risk his wages, but Dad would just laugh. 'It was a dead cert,' he'd say. 'It couldn't lose.' Then he'd take Mum out, treat her to a nice dinner or an evening in the pub, and she'd give in and enjoy herself."

Rodney could be heard chuckling nervously. "Gambling and boozing. It sounds a bit dodgy."

"Oh no. Dad wouldn't do anything wrong. He was very proud of being a policeman. I think Jackie knew a lot about horses, that's all. He was a clever man. He could've turned his hand to anything. It was terrible what happened to him in the war."

'What happened?" Rodney asked.

"He was killed in an air raid, just like my dad. On the same night. They never found either of them."

"Hang on," Rodney said, his voice louder now as though he'd leaned forward. "They weren't killed in the same air raid, were they?"

"Yes. It was awful. Both of them gone, just like that."

Collins stopped the tape and pulled off his headphones. He'd always thought it was bravado when old coppers like Spiller went on about their instincts and their gut feelings, but he'd just been struck by a cast iron sense of certainty.

Tony Barnett had been bent, and he hadn't been too clever at hiding it, at least, not from his own family. New cars, tailor-made suits and a taste for the high life did not fit well with the income of a decent copper, and it sounded as though his mysterious friend, Jackie Blatch, had been involved in race fixing.

As for Rodney, he probably suspected that his family's property had been bought with illicit earnings. He'd held onto the houses in Belmont Road for a while, but in his old age, he'd washed his hands of them, and he'd kept quiet about the source of his wealth.

It's all falling into place, Collins thought. *I'm getting closer to finding the truth.* So far, they'd had no real leads as to why Tony Barnett had been murdered, but that had all changed. He was on to something.

Collins made a few hasty notes in his pad, then he jumped to his feet and headed for the door.

He had research to do, and he knew exactly where to start.

WHEN COLLINS WALKED into the records archive, Geoffrey Higgins was exactly where he'd last seen him, standing at a huge scanner and stacking documents into the feed tray. Geoff looked up when he heard Collins approach the counter, and he gesticulated at the machine to indicate that he had to finish his task before he could stop to talk.

"Still hard at it?" Collins called out. "Don't they let you stop?"

"I stop, all right," Geoff replied. "I'm due a brew in a minute if you fancy a cuppa."

"Yeah, that'd be great." Collins drummed his fingers quietly on the countertop while he waited. There was so much to do, but it was no use trying to hurry Geoff; Collins had learned that on his last visit. The man was a genius when it came to retrieving information, but you had to allow him space to work his magic.

It wasn't long before the scanner ceased its whirring, and Geoff retrieved his stack of successfully scanned documents. He filed them carefully away in a box and then strolled over to meet Collins. Opening the door beside the counter, Geoff ushered Collins into his inner sanctum.

"I'll put the kettle on," Geoff said. "You're a coffee drinker, aren't you? And you take milk but no sugar, correct?"

"That's right."

"I thought so. I'll be back in a tick."

Geoff ambled over to a small side room and disappeared from view. The sound of tuneless humming drifted from the room, and it was all Collins could do to restrain himself from marching inside and wrenching the kettle from Geoff's hands. *Give him time*, he told himself. *He'll repay it in spades.*

Eventually Geoff appeared with two mugs, and he set them down on his desk before taking his seat and looking at Collins expectantly.

Collins pulled up a chair and made sure to take a sip of his drink before saying anything about his quest for information. "Nice coffee," he said. "Thanks."

"No trouble. Always happy to offer something to my regular customers." He offered Collins a conspiratorial smile. "How did you get on with those financial records?"

"Great. Thanks for helping me out with that. My DI was well impressed."

"I thought he might be. It's all about breaking down the complex and making it simple. All your average DI wants to see is a summary. Paint them a picture with the data, and you've got it made."

"I'll remember that."

Geoff nodded contentedly. "So, what brings you down here this time? More spreadsheets?"

"No, I'm looking for another person who might've been killed in the War. But not a copper. I think this guy would've been a person of interest."

"A villain, eh? Sounds interesting." Geoff grabbed a pad and pen from his desk. "Name?"

"John Blatch, alias Jackie."

Geoff stared at Collins.

"Do you want me to spell it for you?" Collins asked. "It's B, L—"

"I know who Jackie Blatch is," Geoff interrupted. "I'm just surprised you don't know about him."

"Should I?"

"There haven't been many notorious gangsters in this city, but Jackie Blatch was one of them. They say he started out as a smuggler, bringing all kinds of contraband into the country, but once the War started, he turned to the black market."

"I've found a reference to horse racing, maybe fixing the races. Could that be right?"

"If there was anything crooked going on, he'd have taken a slice of it. He might've started out as a small-time smuggler, but that wasn't enough for him. He built up a gang and from then on, he managed things, keeping his hands clean while his thugs did his dirty work."

"We'll have a file on Jackie Blatch, right?"

"Young man," Geoff said. "We have a file that'll make your head spin." Geoff took a long draught of coffee, almost draining his mug before placing it firmly on the desk. "Sup up. We've got work to do."

CHAPTER 32

After lunch, Dan was on his way back into the office when Samantha waved to him from the reception desk. "Mr Corrigan, I have a message for you."

Dan strolled over to her. "Thanks, Samantha. Everything all right? You seem a little flustered."

"Everything's fine," she replied, though the harried look in her eye belied her cool demeanour. "But Mr Petheridge wants to see you in his office. Now."

"Summoned to the headmaster's office. Am I in trouble?" Dan smiled, inviting Samantha to share the joke, but when he saw the look on her face, his smile withered. "Has something happened?"

Lowering her voice, Samantha said, "I don't know, but I'd get up there quickly if I were you. He's spitting blood."

"Right. Thanks for the heads-up." Dan made for the lift. Although he preferred the stairs, he didn't want to race up to the fifth floor and arrive looking ruffled.

A few minutes later, Dan stood outside Doug's office and tapped on the door. Doug called out, telling him to enter, and Dan heard an edge of restrained anger in the man's tone.

It's okay, Dan told himself. *I've got this.* He'd faced all manner of boardroom bullies, and Doug, even in his foulest mood, would be a pussycat in comparison. Straightening his posture, Dan pushed the door open and strode inside, his expression neutral, his eyes alert.

Facing him from behind a broad and highly polished wooden desk, Doug scowled. "About time. Shut the door."

"Certainly." Dan did as he was asked, then indicated a chair. "Do you mind if I sit?"

"Yes, I bloody well do mind. You won't be in here long enough to sit down. I didn't ask you here for a friendly chat."

Keeping his voice calm, Dan said, "So I gathered. Tell me the problem, and I'll do what I can to help."

Doug stared at Dan in complete incomprehension, as if he'd been thrown out of step by Dan's response.

"Seriously, we'll talk better if I sit down," Dan went on, and without waiting for a reply, he took a seat and made himself comfortable, prepared to wait.

"Bloody hell," Doug muttered. "You are incorrigible."

"It has been said, but I prefer to think of myself as persistent. Now, let's get down to it. What's the problem?"

"You are. On a number of fronts, you have stirred up all kinds of trouble, and now you have the gall to sit there, acting as though you have no idea what you've done."

"That's because I don't know what the problem is. I mean no disrespect, but unless you tell me what's wrong, we won't get anywhere."

Doug said nothing, but Dan saw the flare of his nostrils, the tightening of his jaw. Doug was preparing to launch into a speech he'd already prepared, and so it proved.

"Very well," Doug began. "First, I learn that you have a personal relationship with Ms Herringway, a relationship that you did not declare."

"I know Frankie, yes. She's an old friend from London, but I have a lot of contacts – I don't see that I should have to tell you about all of them."

"Really? Might I remind you that we are conducting negotiations with Stein Waterhouse, and they are at a delicate stage. Meanwhile, I discover that you, a man with access to our confidential data, have been consorting with their principal negotiator. I also learn that you have previously had an intimate relationship with said negotiator, and if that doesn't present itself as a conflict of interest, then I don't know what does."

"There's no conflict. I—"

"No conflict!" Doug spluttered. "I've never heard such nonsense. You started here at a critical point in our company's development, and a few days later, it turns out that our fate depends on decisions made by your erstwhile girlfriend. Are you honestly going to claim that it's a coincidence?"

"Yes. I had no idea that Frankie, I mean Ms Herringway, was going to be working with you. I haven't spoken to her for some time, so I had no way of knowing. Anyway, she wasn't my girlfriend as such. Not that it's any of your business, but Ms Herringway and I went out with each other a few times, and I haven't seen her since."

"You were with her at the weekend."

"How did you know that?"

"It was brought to my attention," Doug stated. "The point is, your relationship with that lady is personal and ongoing, and whatever you may claim, that is a clear conflict of interest."

Dan shook his head. "Ms Herringway and I, along with my neighbour, went for a walk on Dartmoor. We didn't talk about anything confidential. We are both professionals, and we know where to draw the line."

"I might have believed that, if it weren't for this." Doug plucked a folded newspaper from the corner of his desk and tossed it down again in disgust.

Dan glanced at it briefly, but he was sitting too far back to make out the text. "If there's a story about CEG, it didn't come from me."

"It's not about my company, it's about you. At least, you figure in it to a large extent, and I'd say that your reputation as a professional is finished."

"What?"

"Here. See for yourself." Doug pushed the newspaper across his desk as if swatting the offending item away, and Dan reached forward to take it. It was a copy of *The Telegraph*, folded open to a page near the back, and Dan scanned it rapidly, seeing nothing that might mention him. He flipped it over and there, looking out at him with a steely gaze, was a picture of Alan. Standing in an uncharacteristic pose, his hands thrust into the pockets of his leather jacket, Alan had been captured while staring into the lens, his head tilted slightly to one side as though he'd been casting a critical eye at his photographer. He looked every inch the hard-nosed private eye.

This can't be happening, Dan told himself. *Alan said he'd keep me out of this.* But when Dan's eyes raced over the feature-length article, he saw his name mentioned again and again, his identity closely associated with tales of violence and murder. Lowering the paper, he looked at Doug, and while Dan's mind raced with possible explanations, each and every one of them sounded like a lame excuse. Finally, Dan simply nodded and said, "I see."

"Is that it?" Doug demanded. "Are you not even going to offer some kind of explanation?"

"There's no sense in trying to deny it. I have been involved in a number of investigations, but they were... incidental. They have no bearing on my present role."

Doug let out a derisive snort. "What utter rubbish! You made absolutely no mention of any of this when we took you on, and that omission was clearly a deliberate act on your part. That newspaper story exposes you as a liar and a fraud."

"It does no such thing," Dan stated. "I gave you my full employment history. Anyone could see there were gaps in my CV. I didn't hide the fact, and if asked about it, I would've told the truth. The cases I helped with were..." Dan's voice faltered as an adequate explanation eluded him.

"I'm waiting," Doug said. "I'm almost looking forward to it. What are you going to tell me, that you're some kind of modern-day Poirot?"

"No, nothing like that. I happened to be in the wrong place at the wrong time."

"Interesting. I'm told that you gave pretty much the same explanation when you were almost mown down outside this very building. I dare say there's a connection."

Dan didn't reply, but he felt his resolve crumbling. He was not going to come out of this unscathed.

Doug studied him with a jaundiced eye. "You signed a contract, Mr Corrigan, and you agreed not to do anything that might bring this company into disrepute."

Dan opened his mouth to argue, but Doug didn't give him the chance.

"Further, you signed a watertight NDA, and I have to ask myself whether you've breached that agreement, especially since it seems that you are not to be trusted."

Dan stood up. "I resent that. I've worked hard for your company, and I'll remind you that a contract cuts two ways. I have rights, and since I've done nothing wrong, you can't just—"

"Can't I?" Doug snapped, jumping to his feet and pointing a finger at Dan. "This is my company, and I'll damned well do what I want. You're finished here, Corrigan. I want you out. Now."

"But that's ridiculous. It's completely unfair."

"Save your breath. You're fired."

Dan took a moment to pull his thoughts together, but he could see no scenario in which he kept his job. Doug's mind was made up, and he clearly had no semblance of trust in Dan or anything he might say. There was no way Dan could go on working at CEG. All that remained was to bow out with as much dignity as he could muster.

"Okay, if that's the way you want it, I'll leave," Dan said. "We'll consider our contract terminated by mutual agreement. Naturally, I'll have to send you an invoice for the work I've already done."

Doug's only reply was a disapproving grunt.

"For what it's worth, you're making a mistake," Dan went on. "I could've helped your company if you'd let me finish my work. It makes no sense at all to leave the job half done, but I can see there's no point arguing. I'll get my things, then I'll be on my way."

He made to leave, but Doug stepped smartly around his desk and positioned himself between Dan and the door.

"Wait," Doug said. "I'm not having you wandering about the place on your own."

Dan met Doug's stern glare with one of his own. He was tempted to push past the man, but he stayed put, waiting.

Satisfied, Doug crossed back to his desk and made a call. He only spoke a few words, his voice too quiet for Dan to make out what was said, but a moment later the door opened, and Joe hovered on the threshold.

Joe already knew, Dan decided. *It's written all over his face.*

"Dan," Joe began, then he lowered his gaze and very quietly added, "Let's get this done."

Dan wasn't sure whether Joe was addressing him or giving himself a pep talk, but he replied anyway. "Okay, but you needn't worry. I won't make a fuss."

Joe looked at him. "Thanks. This isn't easy." He stepped back, gesturing along the corridor with his arm. "After you."

"For God's sake," Doug growled. "You're firing him, not inviting him to dance. Just get on with it, Joe."

"I will, but there's no need for any unpleasantness."

Doug dismissed them both with a wave, and they took their cue to leave, Dan striding away and Joe hard on his heels.

"If it makes any difference, I told Doug he was in the wrong over this," Joe said. "It's not right, Dan."

"Tell me about it."

Dan was in no mood for conversation, but Joe was apparently unaware of the fact. "There was no talking sense to him, Dan. He just wouldn't listen. He's very touchy about anything to do with the Stein Waterhouse deal, and he hit the roof when he found out you'd been meeting Ms Herringway outside the office."

"We're old friends."

"I figured as much. I knew you used to live in London, so it wasn't hard to work out you might've known her before. I don't know, maybe I could've got through to Doug, made him see sense, but then someone showed him that piece in the paper and he went nuts."

Dan stopped walking and Joe almost collided with him. "Who showed him the newspaper, Joe?"

"Er, why? Does it make a difference? He would've seen it anyway, sooner or later."

"Not necessarily. It wasn't on the front page. It was tucked away near the back, in the arts and culture section. Does he normally read that part of the paper?"

"I don't know his reading habits, but it wasn't me who showed it to him, I'll tell you that much."

"Was it Seb?"

Joe pursed his lips. "I don't spread gossip, Dan, but if you really want to know, it was no one from the company. Nobody here wants to upset the apple cart, especially at the moment." Joe paused, and when he spoke again, his voice was leaden. "Let's get this over with."

Dan held his ground for a second, just to make a point, then he set off once more. When he reached his office, he found Celine inside, and she gave a guilty start, turning to face him. She had his company-issued laptop cradled in her arms, and she pressed it tight against her chest.

"That was quick," Dan said. "Don't forget the power supply. I left it plugged in at the wall."

Celine looked up at him, her cheeks pale. "I have to take this back, Dan. I…"

"It's all right," Dan said. "I understand. Do what you have to do."

Celine glanced at Joe, who was waiting in the doorway, his arms folded, and when she looked back at Dan, there was an odd glint in her eye. "I left your mouse on the desk, Dan. It was your own, wasn't it? You brought it in."

Dan looked at the wireless mouse on the desk. It belonged to the company, but as he opened his mouth to explain, Celine said, "Make sure you take it home. You wouldn't want to leave it here. Check the battery. I think it's gone flat."

She's telling me to pinch it, he decided. *A last act of defiance.* He gave Celine a knowing look. "Right, I'll do that. Thanks."

"Good luck, Dan. It would've been good to work together. I hope things work out for you. Bye." Celine made for the door, and after a moment's delay Joe stood back to let her leave.

Dan grabbed his messenger bag and checked through his desk drawers, taking the few items he'd brought into the office. Some pens, a pad of sticky notes and a reusable cup for getting take-out coffee. It wasn't much, but then he hadn't been there long enough to accumulate so much as a potted plant. Finally, he packed the wireless mouse and zipped his bag closed.

"That's it?" Joe asked.

Dan nodded, then he took a last look around. "This room must be cursed."

"What?"

"First Neil, and now me. If they ever give you this office, Joe, run for the hills."

Joe almost smiled. "I'll bear that in mind."

They made the journey down to the lobby together, walking quickly and taking the lift, engaging in the bare minimum of conversation.

Samantha watched them from her desk, her lips pressed together in a thin line. Dan sent her a friendly wave, and then Joe was holding the front door open for him, ushering him outside.

Dan stepped out and drew a deep breath of fresh air. Despite everything, he smiled.

"You don't care, do you?" Joe asked. "It's like water off a duck's back."

"No, it's not that. It's just..." Dan looked up at the ugly building that had been his place of work until a short time ago, then he turned to take in the bustling city street. The buildings across the road were built from faded red brick and had once been elegant townhouses. Further along the road, where the two carriageways of Southernhay East and West were separated by a grassy verge, mature horse chestnut trees spread their leafy boughs.

Dan looked back at Joe and said, "I care very deeply about my work. I'm a professional. But now that I'm out of your company, I feel free, because I don't have to put up with that sort of nonsense. I'm worth more than that. What about you, Joe? What's your life worth if you have to spend it doing exactly what you're told by your future father-in-law?"

Joe bridled. "You know what? I was just about to offer you a reference so you might stand a chance of getting another job. But after that, you can go screw yourself, Dan."

"Oh, come on, Joe. You can drop the mid-Atlantic accent. Did you ever work for Microsoft? I mentioned you to Walter Drake because he worked there, and he'd never heard of you."

Joe's only reply was a sour expression and a slow shake of the head. He turned his back on Dan and let the door swing shut.

"I thought so," Dan muttered to himself, then he hoisted his bag onto his shoulder and walked away. It was time to go home, and the drive back to Embervale would give him a much-needed chance to cool down. That was just as well, because as soon as he got home, he needed to have a word with Alan.

CHAPTER 33

H*ere he comes,* DS Kulkarni thought, watching DC
Collins making a beeline for her desk. *Let's see what
he's got.*

She pushed her chair away from her desk and turned to
face him, sitting back, her hands clasped loosely in her lap,
waiting. But if she was all patience and calm, Collins was the
exact opposite. He stopped in front of her, bouncing on the
balls of feet, his notebook clutched in his hand.

"Good news," he began. "I reckon Jez Parker must be
linked with the carjackers."

"Go on," Kulkarni said. "But take it slow, Ben. Let's not
jump the gun."

"Right. Yeah." Collins cleared his throat. "At first glance,
Jeremy Parker, also known as Jez, comes up clean. No
cautions or arrests. I couldn't find much except for an address
and a registration number for a white Ford Transit." He sent
Kulkarni an expectant look as if waiting for her response.

"Okay," she said. "My curiosity is officially piqued. Let's
get to that all-important second glance, shall we?"

"I was thinking about something you said. When you

talked to Keith Pearson, he didn't have a good word to say about Jez, did he?"

"He described him as a snot-nosed kid with a bad attitude," Kulkarni said. "Go on."

"I figured Jez might've been in trouble with us when he was a teenager."

"Just now, you said he didn't have a record. If he was arrested, even if he was under seventeen, it would've been on the system."

"Even so, I called up the Youth Offending Team in Plymouth, and they ran a check. It turns out they'd had dealings with Jez while he was still at school. They thought he'd carried out a number of thefts. There'd been a lot of gear going missing from garden sheds, and they guessed it was local kids. They talked to Jez and they were almost certain he'd been involved, but they didn't have enough to nick him, so they gave him a chance. They talked to social services and assigned him a caseworker, trying to keep him on the straight and narrow."

"That's good work, but it's nothing to get excited about, unless there's more."

"There's more. The officer I spoke to in Plymouth said it was no wonder Jez was getting into scrapes, on account of his family, then he put me in touch with DI Russell Blakey in Plymouth CID. This is where it gets interesting."

Kulkarni sat up straighter. "Go on."

"Young Jez has a couple of cousins, Aaron and Lee Parker, and they've both been through the doors of Plymouth nick on more than one occasion."

"Arrested? Charged?"

Collins consulted his notebook. "Lee has been charged with assault on three occasions, though never convicted, and get this, Aaron served time for possession of an unregistered firearm."

"They sound delightful, but I'm not hearing anything about stealing cars."

"No, but it's worth chasing up, isn't it? We've got Jez seen with the Lexus—"

"Seen with *a* Lexus," Kulkarni corrected. "We don't have the registration and there was no CCTV to back it up."

"The date fitted."

"Yes, and that's enough to take an interest in Jeremy Parker. If he's involved, he might lead us to his cousins or to someone else entirely. From what you've just told me, I'd say he's strictly a small-time crook. I'd be very surprised if he was up to handling high-end stolen cars on his own, but with his family connections, he's clearly a suspect."

Collins pocketed his notebook. "Right. Where do you want to start? I'd like to have a pop at all three of them."

"Hold your horses. Whereabouts does Jeremy live?"

"In Plymouth. An area called Stonehouse."

"Do you know it?" Kulkarni asked.

"Not really. We could swing by, take a look."

"Grab your jacket," Kulkarni said. "I'll drive and you can give me directions to Jeremy's house."

"Sure."

Collins headed back to his desk while Kulkarni logged off from her computer and tidied her desk. She was looking forward to this. It was just a routine trip, and there was a chance it would lead nowhere, but Collins was bursting with boyish enthusiasm, and his energy was infectious. He was already loitering by the door, poised and alert, like a greyhound waiting for the trap to open.

Let's see where this takes us, she thought, and donning her jacket, she went to join her eager colleague.

～

KULKARNI DROVE SLOWLY along Neswick Street in Stonehouse, scanning the cobbled-together collection of terraced houses as she passed. *Plenty of white vans*, she thought. *Luxury cars? Not so much.* Indeed, in this neighbourhood, a top of the range BMW or Mercedes would stand out like a sore thumb.

"That's where Jez lives," Collins said. "Number 17. There's his van, the one with the red DPD logos. Although it doesn't look right."

Kulkarni slowed her car to a crawl and cast her gaze over the house. It was presentable enough and better maintained than most of its neighbours, but before she could get a better look, the front door opened, a young man stepping outside.

"That's him," Collins said. "Stop the car and I'll nip out and collar him."

"No. Hang tight." Kulkarni pressed her foot on the accelerator, driving to the end of the road and making a left turn. Spotting a lay-by reserved for buses, she pulled in and turned to Collins. "Which way was his van facing?"

"This way." He grabbed the door handle. "I'll run back and stop him before—"

"No, we're going to wait and see if he takes his van, then we'll see where he goes."

Collins looked doubtful. "On our own? We don't stand much chance. Either he'll get away or he'll spot us. I could try calling Plymouth CID, but it's short notice."

"We'll manage." Kulkarni focused on her car's wing mirror.

"What if he does a U-turn, goes the other way?"

"There were too many parked cars in the road. No, if he wants to turn around he'll drive around the block." Kulkarni held her breath, silently counting off the seconds. What if Collins was right? What if Jeremy Parker had seen her driving slowly past his house? If she'd spooked him, he might go to ground, and then it might take a long while before they could find him again.

A second later, a white van pulled up at the junction behind her, a red logo and the letters DPD marked on its side.

Peering over his shoulder, Collins said, "That's him. He's hanging a right. You'll have to be quick."

"Dammit." Kulkarni executed a three-point turn, then she sped along the road, only slowing when the white van appeared ahead. There were no cars between them, so she hung back, giving him plenty of room.

At the next T junction, the white van turned left onto a main road, so Kulkarni waited until a couple of cars had passed before she pulled out rapidly, joining the flow of traffic. This was the road they'd taken on the way in to Plymouth and it was perfect: long, straight and with a speed limit of forty miles per hour. So long as Jeremy stayed on this route, she'd have no trouble keeping an eye on him.

"Where'd you reckon he's going?" Collins asked.

"Wait and see. He might be going to a supermarket for all we know."

"Or he could be making for the A38, heading to Exeter."

Kulkarni nodded. The same thought had occurred to her. She glanced at Collins. "What did you mean back there, when you said something didn't look right?"

"It's the logo on the van. I buy a lot of stuff online, so I've seen a lot of couriers, and that van doesn't look right somehow."

"Maybe they changed their logo."

"Yeah, that could be it. I'll check it out later."

The next few minutes passed swiftly, the van trundling along at an even pace, but when it reached a major roundabout, the van swerved across the road to change lanes at the last minute. It dodged in front of a slow-moving lorry, earning a honk from the truck driver's air horn, but Kulkarni reacted quickly and stayed on Parker's tail.

"Well done," Collins said. "Was he trying to shake us?"

"I don't think so. He's just a bad driver. No lane

discipline." Kulkarni kept her gaze on the road. The traffic was building up and they'd have to negotiate several sets of traffic lights before they could exit the roundabout. If just one set of lights changed at the wrong moment, they could lose the van entirely.

"Look out," Collins said. "He's moving across. I think he's going to take the next exit."

"I know." Kulkarni prepared herself, changing gear and slowing down to give herself space to manoeuvre.

"You need to speed up," Collins said. "We'll lose him."

"No we won't."

The lights changed to amber just as the van reached them. Parker could've stopped in time, but either he didn't notice the lights or didn't care. He drove on while the other traffic began slowing to a halt, but Kulkarni was ready. She put her foot to the floor and the Honda surged forward, its engine whining. Kulkarni wove her way between the other cars, but she couldn't beat the lights; they'd already changed to red. In a split second, four lanes of traffic would pour into her path, but she didn't slow down. She sailed through, making it just in time. A couple of drivers sounded their horns, but apart from a few raised heart rates, there was no harm done.

Kulkarni peered ahead and spotted the white van taking the next exit.

She followed, decreasing her speed and tucking in behind a large pickup truck. Parker might've heard the horns and looked in his mirror, but even if he'd noticed her crashing the red light, he wouldn't be able to see her now.

"Not bad," Collins said. "Not bad at all. But look, he's going for the A38, just like I said he would."

"Good guess." Kulkarni followed the white van onto the slip road, and a few seconds later they joined the A38: the dual carriageway that led to Exeter. She could hang back now and still see the van clearly. She exhaled slowly, then she realised that Collins was laughing quietly to himself.

"What are you giggling about?"

"Nothing, Sarge. It's just that, coming from Cornwall like you do, some of the blokes back in the station thought you might be a bit…"

"What? Slow off the mark?"

"Not in so many words, but you know what it's like. Someone new comes in, and people come out with all kinds of stupid stuff. It's just banter." Collins had grown more hesitant as he'd spoken, but he quickly added, "Not me though. I didn't join in. For what it's worth, I reckon you've shaken the place up a bit."

"Even though I made DS and you didn't?"

"It doesn't make any difference," Collins said. "Whatever people think, I haven't got a chip on my shoulder. I didn't pass the exam, and that's down to me. It's no use blaming anyone else."

"That's a good attitude to have." Kulkarni paused. "To tell you the truth, some of my mates in Cornwall thought I was moving to Devon for the quiet life. That's cops for you. It doesn't matter which nick you're in, they always think they've got it tougher than anywhere else. And I have to say, back in Newquay we had plenty to keep us busy. I'm not new to this, Ben."

"No, of course not. I've got nothing but respect."

"Right." Kulkarni could think of nothing more to add, so she left it that, and an uncomfortable silence crept into the car. She checked the time on the dashboard clock. Assuming that Parker drove his van all the way to Exeter, they'd be on the road for at least three-quarters of an hour. They couldn't go the whole way without talking, and Collins still looked as if he was kicking himself for his earlier indiscretion. It was up to her to say something. Without taking her eyes off the road, she said, "So, one way to make sergeant is to really push your professional development. Go on as many courses as you can."

"Yeah, I've been trying, but, you know, budget cuts."

"You can't let them fob you off with that old excuse. The squeaky wheel gets the oil."

"You obviously haven't got to know DI Spiller yet. His mind doesn't work like that. In his book, the nail that sticks out gets hammered down."

Kulkarni smiled at the mental image of Spiller gleefully flattening the spirits of any ambitious young coppers who came barking at his heels. That was no way to carry on. Spiller was a decent DI, but he needed a nudge into the twenty-first century. "Let me see what I can do," she said. "To start with, how are your advanced driving skills? When did you last go on a course?"

"It was a while ago, and I don't get the practise. I'd love to do a refresher."

"Great. Put your name down for the next course. I'll persuade DI Spiller to let you go. If he moans at me, I'll think of something to keep him quiet, okay?"

"Yeah. Cheers."

Kulkarni exchanged a look with Collins. They'd work well together, and they both knew it. She just had to make sure Collins didn't get any ideas. She was his superior, and that meant they could be friends and colleagues, nothing more. *If he asks me out again, I'll have to be firm with him*, she told herself. *I can't mess this up*. She had her heart set on progressing through the ranks, but a relationship with a junior officer would end badly and ruin everything. She knew that better than anyone.

CHAPTER 34

D I Spiller stood on the edge of the River Exe and stared down into the dark water. Languid waves lapped against the quay's stone wall, the water stained deep brown, and despite the warmth of the afternoon sun, a chill ran through him. *Hell of a place to die,* he thought. *Hell of a way to go.*

Drowning. The word stirred a vile nausea in his stomach. What would it feel like as the water closed over you, its icy fingers stroking your skin? When the liquid trickled into your nose, your mouth, robbing you of the ability to breathe, would you hold on to some faint hope of a reprieve, or would you succumb to blind panic?

Spiller repressed a shudder, steering his thoughts back to the report Collins had delivered to him that morning. Once again, the lad had done well, crafting a thoughtful summary of the information he'd uncovered. Spiller had detected the handiwork of Geoff Higgins in the neat layout of the document, but there'd been no need to let Collins know he'd been rumbled. The young man needed a chance to shine, and that was why he'd given Collins the nod when he'd mentioned the possibility of going to Plymouth with DS

Kulkarni. She had a bright future ahead of her, and yet she had a caring side. She'd take Collins under her wing, steer him in the right direction.

Meanwhile, with Collins away, Spiller had time to mull over the implications of the information Collins had unearthed.

John Blatch, alias Jackie, a villain if ever there was one, had been murdered. Drowned.

Spiller turned his back on the water, gazing instead at the shops, cafes and bars along the quayside. On a summer afternoon like this, it was hard to imagine the place as the scene of a crime. But still, on that very spot, a murder had been committed, albeit one that had occurred a long time ago.

Around DI Spiller, the quayside was moderately busy. The weather was warm, and small groups of young people, students most likely, had gathered on the benches to chat while they sipped soft drinks from bottles and cans. Mothers strolled by wheeling toddlers in fancy buggies with rugged wheels, while senior citizens strolled singly or in pairs, some holding hands.

But here, stalking through this idyllic scene was a familiar figure, someone Spiller hadn't expected to see, and he watched him for a while.

Daniel Corrigan was marching along the pavement, looking neither to his left nor his right. His shoulders were back and his expression sharp, his stony gaze presenting a challenge to the world, and no one got in Dan's way as he strode onward. *People know trouble when they see it*, Spiller thought. *And something is amiss with Mr Corrigan.*

Spiller couldn't claim that he knew the man well, but their paths had crossed often enough for him to know he was looking at a changed man. Daniel Corrigan seemed closed off somehow, as if he'd lost the inquisitive eye he habitually turned on the world.

Spiller felt a pang of pity for the man, and without

pausing for thought, he raised his hand and called out, "Mr Corrigan. Hello."

Dan stopped in his tracks, blinking at Spiller as though awakened from a deep reverie, then he nodded in acknowledgement. "DI Spiller. Hi."

Dan showed no sign of moving, so Spiller strolled over to join him. "What brings you here, Mr Corrigan?"

"I use the car park sometimes when I'm here for the day."

Spiller sucked air over his teeth. "Expensive. You'd be better off on the park and ride."

"So people keep telling me. But it's not really an issue any more. I've been working in Exeter, but that's finished now." He sent Spiller a rueful smile. "Think of all the money I'll save while I'm back in Embervale, doing absolutely nothing."

"Is something wrong, Mr Corrigan?"

"Not really. Never mind. It's nothing."

Spiller adopted his finely honed expression of disbelief, and as usual, it worked.

Dan sighed and said, "I had a job in Exeter, but it didn't work out, that's all."

"I'm sorry to hear that. Who were you working for?"

"CEG. They have an office in Southernhay."

"I know it. It's very smart, very modern. Near to Cathedral Green and handy for the city centre. I've often thought it must be a nice place to work." Spiller bit back his words. His last remark had evidently touched a nerve, and Dan looked more downcast than ever. "Listen, I was going to try that cafe over there," Spiller said. "Would you like to join me?"

Dan looked as though he was about to refuse, so Spiller added, "My treat. Go on. You can keep me company. Besides, you look like you could do with something to cheer you up a bit."

"Is it that obvious?"

"I am a detective, Mr Corrigan."

"Fair point." Dan glanced at the cafe. "They make a decent espresso. Not perfect perhaps, but good enough."

"Right. Let's grab a table."

Spiller made for the cafe, and Dan fell into step beside him. They found a table outside and Spiller perused the menu. "Tourist prices," he muttered. "Criminal."

"I can pay my way if you like," Dan said.

"No, I wouldn't hear of it."

A young man appeared to take their order, and Dan asked for an espresso, then changed his mind to a ristretto before finally settling on a macchiato made with soy milk. Spiller watched this performance with interest. Daniel Corrigan had always struck him as a man who knew his own mind, but not today. Something had knocked him off balance.

When it was Spiller's turn to order, he simply said, "Tea, please. With milk. The normal kind."

While they waited for their drinks, Spiller stayed silent, watching Dan expectantly. *What's eating him?* Spiller asked himself. *And why do I care?* After all, he'd crossed swords with Dan on a number of occasions, and they'd rarely seen eye to eye. The man was arrogant, and he stuck his oar in at every opportunity, whether his help was wanted or not. *But he isn't a bad man,* Spiller decided. *It's sad to see him brought low.*

For his part, Dan appeared content to sit quietly, his hands in his lap and his gaze on the table.

Breaking the silence, Spiller said, "This must be something of a new world record. We've been sitting here for more than two minutes, and you haven't asked me a single question."

Dan looked up at him. "Sorry, I don't mean to seem rude. I've got a few things on my mind."

"Me too. Actually, I'm here on police business. I'm working on a case, a cold case as it happens, and I came down to take a look at the scene of the crime, get a feel for the place." Spiller chuckled under his breath. "As a matter of fact, this case is right up your alley. A bit of a mystery."

Dan let out a grunt. "I don't want to know about it. The days of me getting involved in shady dealings and criminal activities are well and truly over. They've brought me nothing but trouble."

Spiller paused, taken aback, then he said, "Okay. If that's how you feel about it, I'll say no more. I just thought you might be interested, that's all."

The young man appeared with their drinks, and they accepted them gratefully. Spiller sipped his tea and tried to remain quiet, but his curiosity got the better of him. "So, what's happened to make you have this sudden change of heart?"

"I take it that you don't read *The Telegraph*."

"No. As a rule, I steer clear of the papers. I get more than my fair share of bad news at work." Spiller summoned a quizzical smile. "Don't tell me they've run a story about you."

Dan's expression remained fixed, but he nodded slowly. "They wrote about every case, in considerable detail, and it cost me my job. Well, it was one of the factors anyway. The straw that broke the camel's back."

"I see. I'm sorry to hear that, I really am."

"Thanks. But you can understand why I want nothing more to do with any kind of investigation. I'm done." He looked Spiller in the eye. "I'd have thought you'd be pleased. You've always resented me interfering. You've warned me often enough, told me to back off, and now you've got your wish."

Spiller didn't react. At one time, he'd have taken this moment to gloat, but he could take no pleasure in Dan's fall from grace. Leaning his elbows on the table, Spiller said, "Everyone at work assumes I'm about to retire. They think I wanted to make it to DI so I could bump up my pension, and now that I have, I'll be on my way."

"But you're not going to do that."

"Too right I'm not. I love the job. I want to stay in the game, and I wonder…"

"What?"

"It seems to me that you are many things, Mr Corrigan, but you're not a quitter."

"Maybe, but that hasn't always been for the best. Sometimes I think it must be nice just to, I don't know, to let things go, enjoy the quiet life. That's what most people do, isn't it?"

"Some of them, perhaps. If you don't mind me asking, are your parents still alive?"

"Yes. Why?"

"I'm curious. What do they do?"

"They're both retired, but Dad was an academic: a lecturer. Mum worked in advertising."

"Interesting. My dad had a little shop, a convenience store, and he worked every hour God sent. He wanted something different for me, something better."

"Most parents do, don't they?"

"Oh yes, but he wanted me to learn about business, go into management. Can you believe that?"

"It's a good route to a steady job."

"That's what I thought at the time, so I tried, and I started on a business studies course at college, but I didn't fit in. I changed tack and transferred to a different college, but that was no good either, so I gave it all up. After that, I had to take all kinds of jobs to earn a crust, but nothing went right until I joined the police. The rest, as they say, is history."

Dan sent him an incredulous look. "If you're suggesting I sign up for the police force, you're wasting your time."

"Oh no, you'd be a terrible copper. Despite what you see on TV, there's no room for maverick outsiders in this job. It's all about teamwork."

"Right. So why the story?"

"Isn't it obvious?"

Dan tilted his head on one side and regarded Spiller. "You think I ought to keep poking my nose in, getting involved in other people's problems. You think it's what I'm good at, what I ought to be doing. Is that right?"

"If the cap fits."

"I'm not convinced, but I know one thing. You really want to tell me about this cold case of yours, don't you?"

Spiller smiled. "It wouldn't hurt to talk it over, get a fresh perspective." He sat back. "Indulge me."

Dan hesitated, then he rolled his hand in the air, inviting Spiller to go on.

"Okay," Spiller began. "On the night of the 13th of May 1942, a notorious criminal known as Jackie Blatch left a pub in Exeter and set off for home. It was a short walk, but he never made it back to his house. There was an air raid that night, and it was presumed that Mr Blatch was killed, but his body was not recovered, not from a bomb site, at any rate."

"Where was he found?"

Dan had asked the question all too casually, making a show of being disinterested, but Spiller wasn't fooled. He pointed toward the river. "Just over there. A few days after the air raid, a teenage lad was poking about along the quay, probably on the hunt for anything of value. A nearby warehouse had suffered a direct hit, so the debris must've been scattered far and wide. Anyway, the lad spotted something in the river, a dark shape floating just under the surface. There was a rope leading down into the water and toward this odd shape, so the lad gave the rope a tug, felt it give." Spiller paused for effect, and Dan took the bait.

"Was it him? Was it Blatch's body?"

"The lad had no idea what it was. It was too heavy. He couldn't budge it." Spiller paused, making Dan wait, and why not? He had him now, hook, line and sinker.

Only when Spiller had stretched the moment to its limit, did he continue: "Fortunately, the lad was an enterprising type. He reckoned he'd found something worth having, so he rounded up his mates, and between them they fetched it out."

"Go on," Dan said.

"There, all wrapped up in canvas and weighted down, were the mortal remains of Jackie Blatch."

"Murdered, presumably."

"Oh yes. Blunt force trauma to the head. Nothing particularly unusual in that, but there's one thing that's got me thinking."

The two men exchanged a meaningful look. "You're talking about the rope," Dan said. "If the body was weighted down, why leave a rope to show where it was?"

"Exactly. The hardest part of any murder is disposing of the body, but in this case…"

"They didn't even try." Dan was smiling now. "They wanted him found, wanted to send a message to someone. A rival gang perhaps?"

"I never said anything about gangs."

"You didn't have to. This has gang conflict written all over it."

"And he's back," Spiller said. "And as always, he's jumping to conclusions based on no evidence whatsoever."

"Gangs send messages, individuals don't. A gang wants to establish dominance. They want to warn others not to mess with them."

"I've known sociopaths who wanted to make a point."

"Come on," Dan scoffed. "If there'd been a string of murders you'd have mentioned it. Besides, you'd already said that Jackie Blatch was a criminal. What was he, a mobster?"

"Something of the kind. He started out as a smuggler, and once the war started he was involved in the black market. He progressed to extortion and illegal gambling. He might even have run a brothel, though that was only rumoured at the time."

"Now who's going beyond the evidence?"

Spiller held up a hand. "Not guilty, your honour. I was referring to a reference in a police report. A complaint was made and logged, but for some reason it wasn't followed up."

"Corruption?"

Spiller frowned, the image of the bones found in Belmont Road coming to mind. Of course, he couldn't mention that to a civilian; the chief superintendent would hang him out to dry. He simply said, "Let's focus on the murder. There's something else I want to tell you."

"Go on."

"We have a recording, made in 1983, of a woman who knew the deceased. The woman died in 2010, but in the recording she stated that Jackie Blatch was killed in the air raid."

"An understandable mistake," Dan said. "There must've been a fair degree of chaos at the time."

"Granted. But this woman claimed that Jackie Blatch was a friend of the family."

"How old was she at the time of the murder?"

"Twenty," Spiller replied. "That's old enough to know what was going on, and the murder of a family friend would've made an impact."

"Yes, but she might've wanted to blot it out, wipe it from her memory and pretend it never happened. On the other hand, she might've been covering for someone."

Spiller lifted his hands then let them fall into his lap. "Sadly, there's not much chance we'll ever know her motives. If she kept a secret all the way from 1942 to 2010, she probably took it to her grave." Spiller let out a chuckle. "You've come to pretty much the same conclusions as me. I'm almost disappointed."

Dan was silent for a moment, then he drummed his fingers on the table. "You said that Blatch disappeared while walking home. Where did he live?"

"Ernsborough Court. It's near Magdalen Road, which was

where he was drinking. It should've taken him about ten minutes to walk home."

"But he ended up down here. The question is, was he brought to the quay, or did he come for reasons of his own?"

"Remember that warehouse I told you about, the one that was hit by a bomb? It belonged to Jackie Blatch, and at the time, it was assumed that he'd come down here to check his property."

"That's an odd thing to assume," Dan said. "Even before the air raid began, it would've been a risky thing to do. Most people would've wanted to stay off the streets at night, wouldn't they?"

"Leaving the way free for criminals to go about their business. I expect Jackie Blatch was used to creeping around under cover of the blackout. He probably felt safe, and who knows what he had stored down here? His warehouse could've been stuffed with valuable goods, and criminals like to keep tabs on their ill-gotten gains."

"Yes, it's what gives them their status, their power."

"No, your average criminal doesn't think that deeply about anything," Spiller stated. "They're greedy, that's all."

Dan looked a little taken aback, disappointed to have his theory shot down, but he recovered quickly, his gaze sharpening as if he'd just figured out the rules of engagement in this particular debate. "Tell me," Dan said, "what was used to weigh Jackie Blatch down?"

"Scrap metal. My guess is that they used whatever was lying around."

"More guesswork? That won't do. You need to find out the details. What kind of metal did they use? Was it all one type or a mixture? Where might it have come from?"

"Those questions may be hard to answer after all this time," Spiller said. "And I'm not sure whether they're worth pursuing."

"You could try. If we accept that the murderer wanted to

send a message, then the way the body was dealt with is part of that message, wouldn't you agree?"

"Put like that, it presents an avenue of enquiry. I'll look into it." Spiller managed a smile. "You see, this is what I was talking about. You have a knack for asking awkward questions, and you don't give in until you've got an answer. You're extremely persistent, and that can be useful. All you need to do is to harness your instincts in some way, put them to work."

"Easier said than done, but maybe you're right. I'll have plenty of time on my hands, so I'll give it some thought."

"That's the spirit." Spiller drained his mug. "I'll go and pay. Thanks for being a sounding board."

"Thank you for the coffee and, erm, everything. It was interesting to hear about your case. Good luck with it."

"I'll get there in the end, but I won't hold you up any longer."

"No worries," Dan said. "I'm not in any rush."

The two men eyed each other, and Spiller sensed an awkward parting was about to occur, so he mumbled his goodbyes and headed over to the counter to pay.

A few minutes later, as he made to leave, he realised Dan was still sitting at the table, his phone pressed to his ear. For some reason, there was a computer mouse lying upturned on the table in front of him, its battery compartment open. Beside it, there was a crumpled, bright-pink sticky note. *I don't know what he's up to,* Spiller thought. *But he already looks more like his old self.* Dan was sitting very upright, his head erect as he listened to whoever was on the other end of the phone call. He was so absorbed in his conversation that Spiller couldn't help but be curious.

On an impulse, Spiller altered his course and passed behind Dan, peeking over Dan's shoulder as he went. There was no clue as to why he'd dismantled a mouse on the table, but the sticky note revealed what looked like a phone number. Beneath the number someone had signed off with a capital letter C and a smiley face.

It didn't mean much to Spiller, but he filed the information away in case it came in handy, and he kept walking. Back on the quayside, he saw the place through fresh eyes, his gaze sweeping along the water's edge, his senses heightened.

Spiller smiled to himself. Dan had given him a few things to think about, and in return, he'd jollied his old sparring partner along a bit. It was a fair exchange.

He mentally replayed his conversation with Dan Corrigan, and he couldn't fault the man's reasoning. The murder of Jackie Blatch had been staged as a demonstration, a threat from one gang to another. It was all perfectly logical. The only strange part of their meeting was the business with the mouse and the sticky note, but there would be an explanation for that too.

The mouse was hard to fathom, but as for the note, the handwriting had looked distinctly feminine, so in all likelihood, some woman or other had given him her number. It was no wonder Dan had perked up a bit.

Cherchez la femme, Spiller thought. *Mystery solved.*

CHAPTER 35

Alan paced the length of his front room as he delivered his prepared speech.

"Dan, you have every right to be annoyed, angry even, over what happened. It must've been a terrible shock to see your name all over the newspapers, but you must believe me when I say that I had absolutely no idea they were going to do anything of the sort, and it wasn't entirely my fault. Yes, with hindsight, I can see that I should have been more careful, but..." Alan stared around the empty room, searching for a source of inspiration, but nothing came to mind. He'd have to do better than this when Dan arrived, but what could he say?

He closed his eyes and let out a slow breath. What a mess, and it *was* his fault. At least, he was responsible. Dan had specifically asked for his name to be kept out of the press, and he was not going to be happy. *I let him down,* Alan thought. *I only thought about myself, my career, my stupid public profile.*

Alan opened his eyes. It was no good raking over the ashes, and excuses would get him nowhere. There was nothing for it but to face Dan, accept all responsibility, and then trust that his friend could forgive him. Then things could go back to the way they'd been before.

Alan went over to the window and peered out toward Fore Street. It would be hours before Dan returned home. *Plenty of time to practise what I'm going to say,* Alan thought. *It's just as well.* Alan resumed his pacing, but he couldn't come up with the right words. Maybe it would help if he stepped outside and went for a walk; that was what he usually did when he was stuck for ideas.

Grabbing a jacket from the hall, Alan went through to the kitchen and donned his walking boots. As he tied the laces he glanced at the hiking stick he kept propped beside the back door. It had been a gift from Dan, and a generous one. The stick was well made and it had served him handsomely over many long walks, but he didn't need it now. He was only popping out for a quick stroll through the village, perhaps popping into the shop to get a few supplies.

He might even be able to find a little something for Dan. A thoughtful gift often helped to pour oil on troubled waters. There wouldn't be anything fancy in the village shop, but he would surely find something.

A short while later, Alan marched back toward his house, a bottle of single malt whisky in his hand, and he congratulated himself. It had been an inspired idea to pop into the pub and ask for Sam's advice. Alan was no expert on whisky – he preferred a drop of good ale – but Sam had been able to tell him the best one to buy, and he was sure Dan would appreciate it.

Alan was almost home now. He looked over at The Old Shop as he passed, and he halted. He'd caught a glimpse of movement behind one of the upstairs windows. It was odd for Dan to be home so early, but it could be a stroke of luck. He could have a word with Dan right away; face the music and get it over with. That done, he'd give Dan the whisky and hope for the best.

Alan hesitated, glancing up and down the road as though searching for some sign of trouble. He had no idea what he was expecting to see, but something wasn't quite right. The dark figure flitting past the window must surely have been Dan. The window belonged to Dan's bedroom, so it was an unlikely spot for a visitor to venture, but somehow it hadn't looked like him. Dan had a certain physical presence and he moved in a distinctive way: resolute and quick. He'd often put Alan in mind of a boxer, permanently on his toes and ready to parry a blow or launch an attack, but this figure had moved furtively, slinking out of sight as soon as Alan had looked up.

I'm being silly, Alan told himself. *Making excuses to put off the inevitable.* There was no point in delay. Dan was home, and Alan knew what he had to do. He may as well get on with it.

Striding purposefully, Alan made for the wooden gate that led to Dan's back garden. He let himself in, heading for the back door, but as he neared the house, Alan froze in his tracks.

The back door stood ajar; not wide open as if it had been left that way on purpose, but more like someone had forgotten to close it properly. *That's not like Dan*, Alan thought, and a sense of apprehension stirred in the back of his mind. Moving slowly, he went to the door and pushed it open, standing on the threshold and calling out Dan's name, repeating it and raising his voice, adding, "Anyone home?"

There was no reply, so Alan slipped in through the door, his gaze roving across the kitchen. Everything seemed just as it should, but still, he *had* seen someone at an upstairs window, and they hadn't answered his call. There could be a reasonable explanation, but his instincts said otherwise. Something was wrong.

Alan stood still, straining his ears. The house was as quiet as the grave. The door that led to the hallway was closed, and he crept toward it, keeping his footsteps as quiet as he could on the tiled floor. But as his fingers reached the doorknob, he heard a sound that made his heart beat a little faster.

The stairs in Dan's house had been sanded down and restored by Jay Markham, and he'd gone to great lengths to bring the woodwork up to scratch. Even so, there was one errant step at the foot of the stairs, and it had resisted all Jay's efforts to prevent it from creaking. Alan was used to the distinctive sound, and he heard it now. It was muted, as though someone was trying to tread lightly, but they hadn't been careful enough. In a flash, Alan realised that whoever it was, they were making for the front door.

Alan knew what he had to do, but he suddenly felt vulnerable. Why hadn't he brought his hiking stick with him? All he had was a bottle of whisky. He scanned the kitchen and spotted Dan's collection of cooking knives on the magnetic rail on the wall. But no, that could end very badly.

There was another noise from the hallway: the metallic grating of someone turning the handle of the front door. The sound came again, louder, more urgent. Dan didn't use the front door much, so he tended to keep it locked, the key in his pocket. The intruder was trapped, cornered. That might make them more desperate, but Alan couldn't stand back and wait for a second longer.

It's now or never, he told himself, and he yanked the kitchen door open and strode through.

The hallway was gloomy, lit only by the sunlight filtering through the small window above the door. From the shadows, a dark figure flew at Alan: a man, dressed in dark clothing, running straight at him, head down, face hidden by a hood.

"Stay back!" Alan yelled, but the man barrelled into him, forcing him to stagger back into the kitchen. Struggling to keep his balance, Alan dropped the bottle of whisky, heard it smash on the tiles. He grabbed at the man with both hands, but a fist slammed into his cheekbone, snapping his head back, and the world turned white.

Unseeing, Alan lashed out with his right fist and landed a

punch to what felt like the man's ribcage, but it did no good. The man spun Alan around then shoved him to the floor, following up with a kick to Alan's side.

Alan grunted in pain and planted his hands on the ground to push himself up, but another kick swept his arms from under him, and he slumped to the floor. Raising his arms to protect his head, Alan rolled onto his side, but as he struggled to stand, the man moved past him, and suddenly he was gone, the back door slamming shut in his wake.

Groaning, Alan stood and checked himself over. He was okay, but he was in no shape to give chase, and anyway, the burglar would be long gone by now. His heart heavy with defeat, Alan gazed around the room. "Hell's teeth," he muttered. "What a bloody mess."

There was broken glass and spilled whisky all over the floor, and the intruder had overturned a chair as he'd made his escape. Those things could be put right. The real problem lay in understanding what the hell had just happened. Even worse, he'd have to explain it all to Dan. Given the fiasco over the newspaper article, Alan had absolutely no idea how his friend would react to this new turn of events.

Dan's house had been broken into on the very day the newspaper story appeared. That couldn't be a coincidence. There had to be a link, and that would surely fuel the fire of Dan's anger.

He'll go ballistic, Alan decided. *He'll blame me for the whole thing.* Alan looked at the back door. He should go home and get cleaned up, then he could call in later when Dan returned home. But first, he had a couple of things to do. He took out his phone and dialled 101, the non-emergency number for the police, and while he waited for his call to be answered, a dull, throbbing ache crept from his bruised cheekbone and spread across his skull. *It's a damned shame about that whisky,* he thought. *I could use a drop of something.* But his headache and his injuries would have to wait, because a briskly efficient woman was asking him questions, and Alan wasn't sure where to begin.

CHAPTER 36

Dan's mind didn't let up as he drove home. The phone call with Celine had left him deeply unsettled. She'd sounded worried, both about Dan and about her own position in the company. She seemed to feel threatened by what she'd called 'the toxic culture' at CEG, and she'd told him about an argument she'd overheard between Frankie and someone else. Frankie could be tough, but it wasn't like her to vent her feelings at work. Perhaps he'd call Frankie later and check she was okay. In the meantime, he had problems of his own.

Jobless again, he thought, and Spiller's words came back to taunt him. What use was it to have, as the policeman had put it, a knack for asking awkward questions? It wasn't something he could put on his CV. Instead, all he had was a chequered job history that told a story all of its own. He'd been fired from his highly paid job in London, and as a freelance consultant he'd been shown the door. Those facts would be hard to explain in a job interview. *That's if I ever get that far*, Dan thought. *My applications will be thrown straight into the bin.*

Dan drove up the lane to Embervale, and as if to match his

mood, his Toyota seemed to struggle with the uphill slope, a chorus of ominous moans coming from the engine. "What now?" Dan muttered. "Bloody car."

By the time Dan reached The Old Shop, the Toyota had added a rattling rhythm section to its orchestra, and an odd smell had seeped into the car. Dan tried not to think about garage bills and the cost of replacement parts as he parked outside his house. He climbed out the car, slammed the door, and without a backward glance he headed for the garden gate.

It was only when he reached the back door and tried his key in the lock that he realised something wasn't right. The door was already unlocked, and he never left the house without locking up.

Pushing the door open, Dan strode inside, just as Alan entered the room from the hallway. The two men stopped in their tracks, staring at each other in surprise, then they both began speaking at once.

Alan raised his hands to fend off Dan's stream of questions, and when Dan paused, Alan said, "I'm afraid you've had a break-in. I did what I could, but he got away. I took the liberty of calling the police. I hope you don't mind."

Dan stepped closer to him. "*Do I mind?* Hell's teeth, Alan, never mind about me. Are you all right?"

"I'm fine. I saw someone at your window, so I came around the back and found the door open. I caught him in the act. I tried to grab him, but he was too quick for me. I expect I'll have a shiner, but I'll be all right." Alan touched his cheekbone and winced. "I'll tell you what though, I could do with good strong cup of tea." He glanced hopefully at the kettle, and Dan took the hint.

"Of course. Sit down. I'll do it."

"Thanks." Alan took a seat at the table, pulling a slip of paper from his pocket and placing it carefully in front of him.

"What's that?" Dan asked.

"The police gave me a crime number in case you need it for an insurance claim, so I made a note of it. I told them I didn't know if anything was taken. They said they'd send somebody to have a look around, but it might be a while. I had a feeling this wasn't their number one priority."

"Typical," Dan muttered. "I was talking to DI Spiller just before I headed home. I ran into him by chance, but now we need a policeman, I won't be able to find one." Dan poured boiling water over the teabag in each mug and gave the drinks a stir, then he transferred the teabags to his compost container. "Milk? And what about some sugar? It might help with the shock."

"Just the milk, please, and you needn't concern yourself. As I said, I'll be fine. Honestly."

Dan finished the drinks and brought them to the table, then he sat down opposite Alan. For the first time since he'd walked in the room, Dan noticed a pungent scent, and he sniffed the air. "Is that whisky?" Dan asked, adding quickly, "Not that I'd blame you if you'd had something to settle your nerves. After tackling a burglar on your own, you deserve a stiff drink."

Alan shook his head. "I had the bottle in my hand when the burglar ran straight into me. I dropped it, and the bottle smashed on the floor. I did my best to clear it up, but I couldn't find a mop." Alan smiled ruefully. "It's a damned shame."

"My old mop wore out, and I keep forgetting to replace it."

"No, I meant it was a shame about the whisky. It was a single malt, and it cost a pretty penny. Perhaps you'd like to put it on your insurance claim."

"Maybe, but why were you carrying a bottle of whisky? What were you going to do, brain the intruder with it? It was a poor choice of weapon."

"Actually, it was gift for you: something to try and make

up for that story in the newspaper. I presume you know about that by now?"

"Oh yes. Forget about it. So long as you're all right, that's the main thing."

Alan said nothing in reply, but there was a distinct gleam of gratitude in his eyes.

"Tell me exactly what happened," Dan went on. "Go back to the beginning. When did you notice something was wrong?"

Alan relayed the story. It didn't take long, and Dan listened intently, then he jumped to his feet as soon as Alan finished.

"Right," Dan said. "I'm going to take a look around, see if anything's missing."

"I'll come with you." Alan started to stand, but Dan gestured for him to stay put.

"Finish your tea, Alan. I can do this on my own. I know where everything is meant to be. It won't take long."

Alan acquiesced, and Dan set off, moving from room to room, searching for anything out of place. There had to be something that might hint at the intruder's intentions, but Dan found few signs of disturbance until he reached the small room he used as his study.

Dan stood in the doorway and stared sorrowfully at the scene of destruction. His desktop computer had been turned on its side, its case opened and components ripped from within. The keyboard and mouse had been tossed onto the floor, and cables littered the desk. "Bloody hell," Dan muttered. "Why?"

He moved over to the desk and looked down into the computer's carcass, and he found the answer. The internal disk drives had been removed: both the SSD drive that housed the operating system and the hard disk where he stored his documents and files.

He had a backup, of course, but the portable hard drive

was missing from its usual place beside his monitors. He crouched to peer beneath the desk, in case the hard drive had been knocked onto the floor, but his backup was gone. *No ordinary burglar*, he thought. *He knew exactly what he wanted.* Dan checked through his desk drawers, but they appeared to have been untouched. His old smartphone had been left nestling among the papers and spare cables, but perhaps the thief had thought it obsolete and not worth stealing.

A sudden thought struck him. He'd been so distracted by his ruined PC that he hadn't noticed the empty space on his desk. His laptop. He *had* left it on the desk, hadn't he? Where else could it be?

He'd used it in the kitchen recently, but when he dashed back to check, the table was clear except for the mugs of tea and the note Alan had written.

Alan looked up expectantly. "Anything missing?"

"Yes, dammit." Dan snatched up the slip of paper. "It looks like I'll be needing this. My computer's been smashed and my laptop has gone, along with a backup drive."

"That's a damned shame. I thought I might've disturbed him before he took anything. He wasn't carrying anything as far as I could see, but he had a backpack. I caught a glimpse of it as he ran away."

"That doesn't surprise me. He'll have come prepared. This was a very specific theft and carefully planned. He knew I wasn't home, and he probably saw you going out, so there was little chance of anyone spotting him."

"You think he was watching the house?" Alan asked.

"It's likely. He must've been pretty sure of himself. He had the nerve to stand in my study and take my computer apart."

"Why didn't he just take the whole unit?"

"It's a full-size tower and he'd have needed both hands to carry it. It would've slowed him down and made him conspicuous. If he'd been challenged, he would've had to ditch the whole computer, and he wouldn't have got what he came for."

"That makes sense," Alan said. "But why would someone want your hard drives? What have you got tucked away in there?"

"Nothing special. There's nothing worth stealing, but someone clearly believes otherwise. If he'd only taken the laptop, I would've assumed this was a run-of-the-mill break-in, but no ordinary burglar would've taken the hard drives; they're not worth anything to anybody."

Alan thought for a moment. "Could it be a case of identity theft? That's happened in the village before, as we both know."

"Unlikely. There was an old phone in the desk drawer, and it was untouched. Someone trying to steal my identity would've taken it for sure. I suppose you might've frightened him off before he'd found the phone, but that seems a stretch. After all, he had enough time to take my computer to pieces."

"It's a strange business, that's for sure. The police might be able to shed some light on it. By the way, they said they'll send someone to take fingerprints."

"Today?" Dan said. "Did they give a time?"

"I'm afraid not. It sounded like it might take them a while. If you call them again and let them know about your missing laptop and so on, it might get them moving a bit faster. When I spoke to them, I didn't know whether anything had been taken."

"It's worth a try. If all else fails, I can call DI Spiller. When I bumped into him by the quay, he was looking into an unsolved crime from decades ago. Hopefully, my case will be more important than that."

"There might be an alternative course of action," Alan said.

"Yes?"

"I was thinking we could try looking into this ourselves.

After all, we've dipped our toes into murkier waters than this, and when we put our heads together, we make a pretty good team."

"True, although I thought those days were behind us." Dan did his best to look serious, but he found himself smiling. "On the other hand, I'd like to find out who stole my computer and why. Whoever it is, they came into my home. They targeted me deliberately, and I need to know who I'm up against, so I can face them head on."

"That's settled then. We'll start straight away, make a plan of action."

"We could, but are you sure you want to get involved?" Dan said. "We'll be going up against a criminal who thinks nothing of breaking into someone's house. He could be dangerous."

Alan puffed out his chest. "Try stopping me. This affects me too; he made it personal when he knocked me down. Well, he might've had the jump on me today, but next time I'll be ready."

"We'll both be ready." Dan sat down and absentmindedly took a slurp from his mug of tea. His drink was lukewarm but he scarcely noticed. "There must be a connection."

"Between what and what?" Alan asked. "Come on, Dan. Don't leave me in the dark before we've even begun."

"While someone was breaking into my house, I was getting fired. I was kicked out of the building with no notice and no warning; nothing but a swift exit."

"That's terrible. Why?"

Dan hesitated, unsure where to begin. "It was a combination of things. The story in the newspaper didn't help, but—"

"Oh no!" Alan interrupted. "Dan, I'm so sorry. I had no idea. I should've been more careful. I'll never..." Alan looked down as if unable to go on.

"Don't blame yourself, Alan. It wasn't your fault. The

atmosphere in that place was strained at the best of times. It's probably just as well that things ended when they did. Too many people at CEG wanted me to fall flat on my face. I'm better off out of it."

Alan looked up. "Really? I'd have thought you'd be furious."

"No, I'm not angry. Perhaps I'm learning to roll with the punches, to take things in my stride. You've told me often enough that I'm too hot headed. It might finally be sinking in."

"That's very philosophical. Who are you, and what have you done with Dan Corrigan?"

The two men shared a smile, then Alan said, "Do you really think there's a connection between you losing your job and the break-in? Surely, no matter how badly things ended, your old employer wouldn't have broken in and stolen your computer."

"Not directly, perhaps, but they could've hired someone to do it. I wouldn't be surprised if there was something criminal going on in that company. I don't know what, exactly, but there was something simmering beneath the surface. I never figured it out. I never even came close. I was sacked before I could even begin to make sense of it."

"I wonder… could it be something to do with that car that almost ran you down? It happened right outside the building."

After a moment's pause, Dan nodded. "It's certainly beginning to look that way. First, there's the near miss, then my home is burgled. Perhaps I've stumbled on something at the company without realising its significance. Then there's the strange behaviour of Neil Hawthorne, and the cryptic message on the back of his wife's photo. There has to be a thread that ties them all together."

"I didn't get anywhere with those dates, but I'm happy to have another try."

"Good, and there's another avenue we can explore. Earlier today, I had an interesting conversation with one of my former colleagues. She's called Celine and she works in IT. Before I was thrown out, she slipped me her phone number. I called her, and like me, she senses there's something wrong at that company."

"Such as what?" Alan asked. "I hope it's something specific, because we have precious little to go on."

"There were a few things that had worried her. Interestingly, one of them involves Frankie. Celine overheard an argument between Frankie and someone else. She didn't know who the other party was, but she's certain it was a man, and according to Celine, the guy was getting a dressing down."

"That doesn't amount to much. I imagine people have arguments in offices all the time, don't they?"

"It's not unheard of, but Celine knows that as well as I do, and she was worried enough to tell me about it. This was a full-scale row, not some squabble over a parking space or the use of the company's photocopier."

Alan sat back in his chair. "Okay. The trouble started on your first day at work, so let's begin with your erstwhile employer. We need to look into CEG."

"Easier said than done. I won't be able to get past the front desk."

"Simple. Call Celine and arrange to meet her, somewhere away from the office. We can ask her a few questions and take it from there."

"It's worth a try," Dan said. "I'll arrange it, and I'll let you know the details. Would tomorrow work for you?"

"Why not?" Alan replied. "The sooner the better."

CHAPTER 37

It can't be long now, DS Kulkarni thought. *He has to move soon.* She shifted her position and peered out through the windscreen of her Honda Accord, looking past the parked cars in front of her and along Barnfield Road in Exeter. A hundred metres away, Jeremy Parker's white transit van sat in a parking space, and thanks to a slight curve in the road Kulkarni had a good view of the driver's door. Parker hadn't climbed down from the cab; he seemed content to sit idle, wisps of smoke issuing from his open window as he enjoyed the latest in a succession of cigarettes. There'd been no other sign of activity for almost half an hour, and Kulkarni's patience was wearing thin.

Sitting next to her in the passenger seat, DC Collins seemed to read her mind. "Don't worry, Sarge, he'll do something soon. Any minute now."

Kulkarni picked up the note of camaraderie in his tone and she smiled wearily. "Let's hope so. This is the third time he's parked."

"He's up to something."

"We'll see," Kulkarni said. In truth, she was beginning to wonder if Jeremy Parker had spotted them and was now leading them on a dance. At first he'd parked outside a small hotel on Blackall Road, but then he'd driven away and parked again, this time on the edge of Exeter University's sprawling campus. Finally, he'd crawled along Barnfield Road before parking on a quiet residential part of the street. Admittedly, there were quite a few expensive cars parked in the area, most of them on the gravelled driveways of large, detached houses, but this was a far cry from the busy shops and offices of the city centre.

"At least we know one thing," Kulkarni went on. "He's no courier. He's neither collected nor delivered a single parcel. Not so much as an envelope."

"That's why I didn't get anywhere when I tried to track down the van we saw on CCTV. I was looking for couriers, but he never actually makes a delivery. He's using it as a cover while he scopes for cars."

"You could be right, but it's not just the cars he's checking out." Kulkarni pointed through the windscreen, sweeping her finger from one large house to the next. "See there? And there?"

"CCTV," Collins said. "He's looking for a blind spot."

"I'd put money on it. When he parked by the university, and by the hotel, he only waited for a minute or two, then he drove away. This time he might be thinking that he's found a likely spot to take a car."

"There are plenty of posh motors around here. I tell you what, Sarge, why don't I take a stroll past him, try and see what he's up to?"

"Okay, but make sure you keep it casual. Walk past but don't look at him directly. When you've put a good distance between you and him, cross the road and come back on the other side. Make sure he doesn't spot you."

"Got it." Collins let himself out of the car and set off along the street, looking for all the world like an average passer-by, his mind on other things. Kulkarni held her breath while

Collins sauntered past the white van. If Collins showed even a hint of interest, the driver's suspicions would be aroused. Jeremy Parker was almost certainly up to no good, and he'd be on edge, looking out for any sign of trouble.

But Collins did a good job, scarcely glancing at the van as he passed. He slowed his pace a little, then he took out his phone, looking down at it as he went along: an ordinary pedestrian checking his messages.

Kulkarni lost sight of him. She kept her attention on the van but it didn't move, and a trail of smoke still drifted from its open window. It seemed that Parker was completely unaware he was under surveillance.

A few minutes later, Collins arrived back at Kulkarni's car and slid into the passenger seat, his eyes bright. "We're definitely on to something, Sarge. You see that BMW up there?"

Kulkarni followed his gesture with her gaze, but she could only see the side of a grey car and she couldn't make out the make or model. "Not really," she said. "What about it?"

"It was the only thing Jeremy Parker was looking at. He didn't even notice me going by. He was concentrating on that car, tapping something into his phone, and when I passed by on the other side of the road, he was holding his phone up, and it looked like he was taking lots of photos: the street, houses, everything. If that isn't suspicious, I don't know what is."

Kulkarni tried to hide her mounting sense of excitement. It was important to remain cool in front of Collins, but she rewarded him with a knowing smile. "It's coming together. This is how the carjackers get close to their victims. No one looks twice at a courier's van, so Parker cruises around until he finds a likely spot, checking for CCTV, and then he looks for a car to pinch. He takes a photo and sends it to an accomplice. If he gets the green light, Parker hangs around to find out what time the car's driver turns up. If he can figure out the victim's routine, he comes back another day with his mates. The carjackers won't want to risk being seen, so they'll hide in the back of the van until Parker gives them a signal, then they'll jump out, and it'll all be over in a minute."

"Yeah, and those accomplices are probably Jeremy's cousins, Aaron and Lee."

Kulkarni's confidence faltered. "We've got nothing to place them at any of the scenes. We don't even have a good reason to call them in for an interview, but we *can* follow up with young Jeremy. If we can place his van in Exeter on the right dates, we could pull him in. I'd like to get my hands on his phone. It might be a burner, but even so, digital forensics could prove very useful indeed. The more I think about it, the more I'm convinced they're stealing cars to order. That's why he took a photo of the BMW. It was good work, spotting that. Well done."

"Cheers." Collins looked quietly pleased with himself, but as he looked away from Kulkarni, his expression suddenly changed. "Look out. He's on the move."

"On it." The white van was pulling out into the road, and Kulkarni started the engine and followed suit, tucking her car into the stream of traffic and trundling along the road. The next twenty minutes passed slowly as the van picked its way through the congested streets of the city centre, but then it became clear that Jeremy Parker was heading out of town, back toward the A38.

"He's going home," Kulkarni said. "We should do the same."

"You don't want to follow him to Plymouth, see if he leads us to his cousins?"

"No. We've tailed him for quite a while, and every minute makes it more likely he'll spot us. Besides, we know his game plan. He's heading back to Plymouth because his work is done for today. He's found a mark, and if they're going to do something about it, they'll be back soon. Before that happens, we need to stop Parker in his tracks, and that means getting a search organised."

"Back to the station then?"

"Back to the station. I'll run it past the guv'nor and put the paperwork together, then we'll catch Parker at home, maybe early tomorrow morning. I assume you'd like to be kept in the mix?"

Collins nodded vigorously. "Definitely."

"Okay," Kulkarni said. "Let's go."

TUESDAY

CHAPTER 38

Alone in his Volvo saloon, DI Spiller joined the stream of early morning commuters on their way into Exeter city centre. As he approached the quay, he took the turn that led down to the car park, and as expected, a uniformed constable in a high-vis jacket stepped into the road, his hand raised and a stern expression on his face. Spiller obliged, bringing his car to a sedate halt, and the constable stalked toward him, a steely glint in his eye.

He's keen, Spiller thought. *I was probably the same at that age.* Spiller smiled to himself. Back in the day, he'd cut quite a dash in his uniform. He hadn't been weighed down with all the kit carried by the modern copper, and the clean lines of his tunic had suited him. He'd had a truncheon, of course, but he'd rarely drawn it. Most of the time, his radio, handcuffs and helmet had been all that he'd needed.

He thought briefly of the old pair of handcuffs that had drawn him into the case of DS Tony Barnett, but he dismissed that image from his mind. He was here on a different matter, and this case was anything but cold.

Spiller wound down his window and retrieved his warrant card from his jacket pocket, flashing his ID before the constable had a chance to say a word. The young officer's demeanour changed instantly. He didn't actually salute, but he looked very much as though he'd have liked to. Leaning down to address Spiller face to face, he said, "Morning, sir. They're waiting for you on level one. Keep going down until you can't go any further. You can't miss them. They're in the far corner, over by the stairwell."

"Thank you," Spiller said. "You're doing a grand job."

The constable stood back, and Spiller drove slowly through the car park, taking the downward ramps until he reached the lowest level. There were hardly any parked vehicles to be seen, and some of them probably belonged to the small knot of people who'd gathered in one corner behind a distinctive stretch of crime scene tape.

Spiller parked and climbed out of his car, then he went to the boot, where he kept several sets of disposable protective clothing. He donned the white overall and plastic overshoes, then he made his way over to the cordon, where a bleary-eyed constable recorded his details on a clipboard.

"Been a long night?" Spiller asked.

The constable summoned a grim smile. "My shift was supposed to finish hours ago, but... you know."

"Oh yes. That's the job." Spiller nodded toward the huddle of crime scene investigators beyond the cordon. They were listening to someone who was facing away from Spiller, but he couldn't tell who it was, the shapeless forensic suit rendering them anonymous. "Who's the CSM?" Spiller asked.

"Nicola Haig," the constable replied, and a grudging note of admiration crept into his tone. "She doesn't hang about, does she?"

"Not for a second." As Spiller watched, the CSI team dispersed to tackle their assigned tasks. A photographer crouched to aim his camera at a dark shape on the floor and he began firing shots, the harsh light of the flash casting the hunched shape of a lifeless body into sharp relief.

Standing back as if to keep a watchful eye on her team, Nicola turned around and glanced in Spiller's direction, acknowledging him with a nod. She strode over to join him, pulling down her face mask, then she began speaking, her voice low but her words echoing eerily in the cavernous space. "We have a male, early thirties, and we haven't seen any signs of physical injuries as yet, though that picture might change once we get started. My first impression is we're looking at a drug overdose, though whether that might've been accidental or inflicted by someone else, we can't say at this stage."

"What kind of drugs are we talking about?"

"It's too early to say, but we could be looking at opioids. There was a build-up of froth around his mouth and nose, and that's often an indication of an opioid overdose." Nicola half turned, pointing toward the huddled corpse. "When we find someone face down like this, and on their knees, it can indicate that they might've collapsed very suddenly. Their knees buckled and they fell, unable to save themselves from landing any other way."

"Any sign of needles or other paraphernalia?"

Nicola shook her head. "No needles and no obvious injection sites, but we'll be on the lookout for those later on. For the time being, we have to be very careful. There could be a needle concealed somewhere in the deceased's clothing or underneath his body, and I have to safeguard my team. We've also got to watch out for any traces of powder. If anyone were to breathe in an unknown substance, it could be fatal. For that reason, I'd like you to stay back here for the moment. There's no sense in exposing you to any unnecessary risk."

"Fair enough, but I'll need to walk through the scene properly, as soon as you're satisfied it's safe."

"Of course," Nicola said. "I'll let you know."

Looking past Nicola, Spiller watched as one of the CSI team carefully pulled something from the deceased's pocket before standing up and heading toward Nicola. "It looks like he's found something," Spiller said. "Dare I hope that it's a wallet?"

"You never know your luck." Nicola turned her attention to her colleague, and they had a hurried conversation, their heads together. The CSI was wearing a substantial face mask, safety glasses and a transparent visor, and Spiller found it hard to make out the man's words, but then he was hardly listening; he was far too occupied with the sight of the brown leather wallet in the CSI's hands. *Skip the full report*, Spiller thought. *Let's get the damned thing open.*

He didn't have to wait much longer. Nicola took the wallet, opening it carefully, while the CSI went back to his work.

"Well?" Spiller asked.

"Plenty of money," Nicola replied. "There must be at least a couple of hundred pounds in here. There's a £50 note, so I'd say that rules out robbery as a motive."

"We'll see about that in due course. What about ID?"

"We have several credit cards and a driving licence." Nicola withdrew the white plastic driving licence and held it up carefully, holding it by its edges while she peered at the photo. "Yes, this looks like him."

Spiller took out his notebook. "Name? Address?"

"Sebastian Cooper," Nicola said. "His address is 32 Florida Crescent, Exeter."

"Got it. That's a private street, just off Pennsylvania Road." Spiller finished writing and looked up. "Anything else?"

Nicola replaced the driving licence in the wallet and carefully checked through the other cards. "There's an ID card here. It could be from a place of work. It says Corinthian Enterprise Group. It looks like he was the chief technical officer." Nicola met Spiller's gaze, and she frowned. "What's wrong? Did you know him?"

"No, but I know where he works. CEG. It's an office in Southernhay, and the place came up recently, in connection with something else."

"A case you were working on?"

"Not exactly." Spiller pocketed his notebook, signalling an end to the subject, but Nicola was still watching him as if expecting more, so he added, "Have you ever come across a man by the name of Daniel Corrigan?"

"No, I don't think so."

"Oh, I expect he'll cross your path sooner or later," Spiller said. "Until then, think yourself lucky, because once he pops up, there's no getting rid of him."

CHAPTER 39

Mid-morning, and Catherine Street in Exeter was busier than Dan had expected. The narrow alley was one of several that linked the high street to the cathedral, and an eclectic mix of passers-by were making full use of it, either searching for the peace of Cathedral Green or bustling in the opposite direction to seek the buzz of the shops.

Standing beside Dan, Alan turned away from the passing crowds to admire the ruins of an ancient crumbling wall of red stone. "Saint Catherine's Almshouses," Alan said. "I wonder why your old colleague wanted to meet here. It's not one of Exeter's best-known attractions. Most people rush past without giving it a second glance."

Dan ran his eyes over the collection of broken-down stone walls that were all that remained of the almshouses. He'd never taken much notice of the ruins himself, but when he'd called Celine she'd suggested they meet here, and he'd gone along with it. It was as good a place as any.

"The glass panels represent the original doorways," Alan went on. "They're part of a modern artwork called *Marking Time*, and if you walk around the ruins, you'll see passages from the almshouse records carved into the flagstones."

"Some other time, perhaps." Dan offered a placatory smile then turned his attention back to the street, searching for Celine. He wasn't in the mood for one of Alan's lectures on local history, but his friend had the bit between his teeth.

"It really is worth having a wander around the place, you know. Look up there, you can still see the chapel bell."

Dan dutifully glanced at the top of the tallest remaining section of wall. It had obviously been a bell tower once, but now the bell looked forlorn and forgotten, forever silent. As he watched, a seagull landed atop the tower and eyed the street, searching for scraps.

"I've never noticed the bell before," Dan said. "That tower doesn't look entirely safe."

"It's been there for hundreds of years. Anyway, I'm sure the council will have made sure it's not going to topple over." Smiling hopefully, Alan added, "We can move to the safety of that cafe over the road if you like: George's Lounge. There's a free table outside, and we could have our morning coffee while we wait."

Dan studied the modern, glass-fronted cafe. He'd been there before and liked it, but they weren't in Exeter to enjoy themselves. "I'd rather stay here," he said. "I want to make sure Celine sees us, assuming we haven't missed her already."

"We were only a couple of minutes late, and we couldn't help that. We couldn't have known the quayside car park would be closed."

"True. That policeman wasn't giving anything away, was he? I wonder what's happened."

"Who knows?" Alan said. "Maybe they've finally caught the car thieves. That would be something."

"Yes. It would be nice to think they were off the streets." Dan returned to scanning the crowd. "Celine ought to be here by now. I hope she's all right."

"I expect she's tied up at work, or maybe she had to come

up with some pretext before she could slip out of the office. She couldn't very well say she was coming to meet you."

Dan nodded. Alan was right; references to his name would not be welcome at CEG. *I'll be persona non grata*, he thought. *Just like Neil Hawthorne before me.* It was strange how, only a few days ago, he'd felt sorry for Neil. He'd pitied the man, and though he'd listened to Neil's ramblings, he hadn't given them much credence. Now that he found himself in the same predicament, might it be worthwhile to reconsider Neil's story?

"What does Celine look like?" Alan asked. "You never really said."

"Yes I did. I told you she's in her late twenties and she has short brown hair. Average height. Slim."

"That's a bit vague."

"I don't know what else to say. She's very pretty if that's what you want to know."

"No, that wasn't it at all," Alan protested, but he immediately fussed over his clothes, making sure his shirt was tucked in and his collar was straight.

Dan couldn't help but smile. "You needn't worry, Alan. You're presentable. Although I still think that jacket is far too heavy for a warm day."

"Really?"

"Yes, but at least you left the fedora at home."

"Don't mention the hat," Alan said. "I've a good mind to donate the damned thing to charity. All that nonsense about my so-called image did nothing except cause a lot of trouble. I'm embarrassed to think I went along with it."

As if to prove his point, Alan shrugged out of his leather jacket and folded it carefully over his arm. "Mind you, it would be a shame to get rid of this jacket. It's beautifully made."

"You may as well get some use out of the thing. You paid enough for it." Dan lapsed into silence, eyeing Alan's jacket enviously, but not for long. Without a proper job, he'd have to be frugal. He'd need every penny to keep the lights on and food in the fridge.

Alan looked past Dan and said, "Is that her?"

Dan turned to see Celine approaching from the direction of the cathedral. "Yes. Trust you to pick a pretty girl out of a crowd. No more preening, Alan. This is a serious business, not a blind date."

"I wasn't preening," Alan grumbled. "You were the one who brought up the fact she was pretty, not me. I know exactly why we're here, thank you very much. I understand what's expected of me."

"I know. Sorry. I'm a bit on edge." Dan hesitated. "I meant to say earlier, I'm glad you came along. I appreciate it."

The two men exchanged a smile. *Just like old times*, Dan thought, then he raised a hand to attract Celine's attention. He was about to call out, but his greeting died on his lips.

Even from a distance, it was clear that all was not well with Celine. Her shoulders were hunched, one hand clutching the strap of her shoulder bag, and as she walked, she kept glancing nervously from left to right. She grew closer, and when she spotted Dan she gave a start, but she kept moving toward him, her head bowed and her gaze on the ground.

She didn't look up until she joined Dan and Alan, and her eyes were glistening, rimmed with red.

"Celine," Dan said, "are you all right?"

Celine nodded but then seemed to change her mind. "Not really. Something awful has happened. But…" Her gaze flicked toward Alan. "Is this your friend, the one you told me about on the phone?"

"Yes, this is Alan. Anything you can say to me, you can say to Alan. You can trust him. I do."

Alan looked at Dan, blinking as though taken aback at hearing his kind words, but Dan carried on regardless.

"Celine, you look as if you've had a shock. Maybe we can get you something. Would you like a cup of tea or coffee?"

"No," Celine replied. "Thanks, but I can't stay. I know I said I'd try to help you, but something's happened, and I can't…" Celine shut her eyes and sniffed as if holding back a tear, and when she opened her eyes, she looked lost, gazing around as if unsure where she was or how she'd come to be there.

"Right, that's it," Alan said firmly. "You're obviously upset, and we can't stand by and do nothing. I really think we should go through to the cathedral. There's a quiet little teashop just around the corner, and we can sit down and have a drink, even if it's just a glass of water. Would that be okay, Celine?"

Celine studied Alan for a moment, then she nodded meekly, a grateful smile on her lips. "A cup of something hot would be nice. I think my blood sugar's a bit low, but I don't feel up to talking, and I don't want to waste your time."

"You mustn't worry about us," Alan replied. "We can sit in silence if you like, but we need to make sure you're okay. Isn't that right, Dan?"

"Absolutely. It's the least we can do."

"Okay then," Celine said, and together they walked through the narrow alley to Cathedral Green. They emerged near the bow-fronted tea room that looked as if it had stood on that spot for centuries, and Alan found them a table on the pavement where they could take in the view of the cathedral.

Dan and Alan ordered black coffee, Celine opted for tea, and when Dan saw that the flapjacks were vegan, he ordered them one each. A few minutes later they were sipping their drinks, and as Celine nibbled her flapjack, the colour returned to her cheeks.

"This is very kind," Celine said. "I'm sorry to make such a fuss. I really only came to say I can't help you. Not today. But now that I'm here, I ought to tell you what's happened."

MICHAEL CAMPLING

"That's up to you," Alan replied. "If you want to talk, we're happy to listen. If there's anything we can do to help—"

"No," Celine interrupted. "You can't help. You can't do anything. It's too late." She drew a long breath as if gathering her strength. "It's Seb. Seb Cooper. He's... he's dead."

It took Dan a moment to accept what he'd just heard. "What happened? Was it an accident?"

"I don't know. We were hardly told anything. Everyone at work was very upset. Each department had a meeting at the same time, so we knew something was going to be announced, but we had no idea it was going to be so awful."

"It must've come as a terrible shock," Alan said.

"It did. They said Seb had been found dead, and it was unexpected. We were all stunned, and before it could sink in, we were told to go home. Everyone left very quickly after that. On the way out, I overheard someone talking about the quay. They thought Seb had been found there, but whether that's true or not, I don't know."

Alan sent Dan a look, and there were no prizes for guessing what he was thinking. But Dan shied away from any thoughts of Seb lying dead in a car park; it was too stark an image, too visceral, too real.

"I still can't take it in," Celine went on. "It doesn't make sense. I keep thinking he must've had a heart attack or something, but he was young and he was always so fit and healthy."

"It's a sad loss," Dan said. "I didn't know him well, but this is a terrible thing to have happened."

Alan murmured in agreement, but Dan focused his attention on Celine. The muscles around her mouth were twitching as though she had something to say but couldn't bring herself to form the words.

"Celine," Dan said, "why don't you tell us what's on your mind?"

"I've told you everything I know." Celine looked down, clasping her hands on the table.

"Everything?" Dan asked.

"Yes." Celine looked up sharply, lifting her chin in defiance, but there was a haunted look in her eyes, and now Dan was certain: she was holding something back.

Making his voice softer, Dan said, "You've told us what happened this morning, but there's something else, isn't there?"

Celine shook her head firmly, but Dan wasn't fooled. Celine was carrying a secret, the burden of it weighing heavy on her mind, but she couldn't bring herself to give it voice. Perhaps she knew something about Seb, but she didn't want to speak ill of the dead, and that was understandable.

I can't ask her about it, Dan told himself. *I have no right to intrude.* But as he thought of Seb, a memory surfaced in Dan's mind: a recollection of the strange conversation he'd had with Neil Hawthorne when they'd met in the park. Neil had hinted that there were shadows in Seb's past. There were a lot of skeletons in Seb's cupboard, Neil had said. A lot of demons.

What kind of demons? Dan wondered. *Depression? Anxiety?* If Seb had struggled with his mental health, he'd hidden it well. But Dan had known people who'd seemed bullish and hard headed right up until the moment they'd crumbled beneath the daily pressure of corporate life; he'd almost gone that way himself.

Then again, there were other kinds of demons. Leaning toward Celine, his elbows on the table, Dan lowered his voice to a murmur and said, "Celine, did Seb have a drinking problem?"

Celine sipped her tea and pulled a face. "This is going cold," she said, then she stared into space as though she'd forgotten Dan and Alan were there.

"When we were at Batworthy Castle," Dan went on,

"most people had the free champagne, but Seb chose orange juice. It seemed out of character, and I'm wondering whether Seb had a particular reason to avoid alcohol."

"Seb didn't drink," Celine said without making eye contact. "He was into health and fitness and all that kind of thing."

There's still something she's not saying, Dan decided, but he didn't pester her with more questions; he simply stayed exactly where he was, waiting.

Finally, Celine met his gaze and said, "I've heard some things about Seb. There was some talk at work, but I don't know, maybe it was all just rumours."

"What kind of rumours?" Dan asked. "And who did you hear them from?"

"It was one of the guys I work with. Justin. He got his first job at an insurance company in Bristol, and at the time Seb was head of the IT department. But Seb was fired. There was a system crash and everything went down. Justin said it was a nightmare and it cost the company a fortune to put right. Seb got the blame. They said he'd hired a dodgy contractor to upgrade the network, so they hung him out to dry."

"But there was more to it than that, wasn't there?" Dan prompted. "Please, go on."

Celine sighed. "Justin said that some of the bosses liked to party. Drink, drugs, whatever. He made it sound like something out of *The Wolf of Wall Street*. Anyway, the rumour was that Seb had screwed up because he'd been high half the time. I didn't believe it. Justin was showing off, going on about the all-nighters they'd pulled to get the system back up and running, and I thought he was exaggerating, trying to impress me. I forgot all about it, until…"

"Until you heard that Seb might've been found dead on the quayside," Dan said.

"You get some dodgy characters hanging around there at

night," Celine replied. "The bars are okay, but there are alleys I don't like to walk through on my own."

"How about the car park?" Alan asked. "Is that safe?"

Celine frowned. "Why? Is that where they found him?"

"We don't know," Dan said quickly. "The police have closed off the car park, but there could be any number of reasons for that. They might be searching for evidence, or perhaps Seb's car is there."

"No, he parked in Southernhay."

"How do you know that?" Dan asked.

"He must've told me." A silence settled over them, then Celine pushed back her chair. "I should go home."

"Will Patrick be there?" Dan said.

Celine had picked up her shoulder bag and was rummaging through it, but she stopped and looked up. "Why do you ask?"

"I thought it might be better if you weren't on your own."

"As it happens, Patrick is in college today, but I'll be fine. I don't need a man to look after me. I can fend for myself."

"Of course," Dan said, and he should've left it at that, but he was suddenly concerned about Celine. She wasn't just being defensive; she'd grown cold, a repressed anger in her eyes, as if the mention of her partner had touched a nerve. *It's none of my business*, Dan thought, but he liked Celine and he couldn't let her walk away like that. Speaking slowly, he said, "Celine, is everything okay at home?"

Celine glared at him. "I beg your pardon. What kind of question is that?"

Dan kept his expression neutral and his voice calm. "I didn't mean to offend you. I just wanted to check that you're okay. I don't know Patrick at all, but…"

"But what?"

Dan hesitated, but he couldn't tell her what he'd seen at Batworthy Castle, about the way Patrick had ogled Seb's wife. Instead, Dan said, "Nothing. I'm sorry. I spoke out of turn."

"That seems to be your default mode." Celine resumed the hunt through her bag. "I'll pay for my share."

"It's okay," Alan said. "I'll take care of it."

"Oh, but…"

"It's no problem," Alan insisted. "It'll be my good deed for the day."

Celine looked at Alan, and his smile seemed to mellow her mood. "Well, if you're sure."

"Definitely."

"Okay. Thank you, Alan."

Celine made to stand, but Dan raised a hand to catch her attention and said, "Before you go, I'd like to ask you something. It's about Seb."

Celine looked as though she might get up and walk away, but then she appeared to give in, and her shoulders slumped as she settled back into her seat. "What?"

"Have you had any more thoughts about who you might've heard arguing with Frankie?"

Celine's expression became instantly guarded. "You're on first name terms with Ms Herringway, are you?"

"We're old friends," Dan said. "We met when I worked in London."

"I see. You never mentioned that when you called me."

"There was no reason to say anything," Dan replied. "I haven't seen Frankie for quite a while, and I had no idea she was coming to Exeter."

"Small world," Celine intoned. "But if you're friends, why don't you just ask her what happened?"

"Because, to be perfectly honest, I don't know who I can trust at the moment. Something happened recently, and I don't know who's behind it."

"What happened?"

"Yesterday, somebody broke into my house and stole my laptop, and some hard drives were taken too."

"Why would anyone do that? I mean, I can see the laptop

might be worth something, but why would they take your drives?"

"I don't know," Dan admitted. "But when we spoke on the phone, you suggested that there's something not quite right at CEG."

For a moment, Celine didn't react, then slowly, she nodded.

"Let's go back to Frankie Herringway and that argument," Dan said. "Have you been able to remember any more details?"

"Not really. Whoever she was talking to, the guy barely got a word in."

"If he hardly spoke, can you be sure it was a man?" Alan put in.

"Oh, it was a man all right. He sort of bleated, like he was cringing. I almost felt sorry for him, but it sounded like he deserved it. She called him spineless and gutless. She told him he'd stepped over the line, and if he carried on like that, she'd make sure he lost his job."

"What had the man done?" Dan asked. "Did she give any hint?"

Celine lifted her shoulders in a Gallic shrug. "I really couldn't say. I couldn't make out what he said after that, but it sounded as though he was pleading with her." Celine stopped speaking, her gaze growing distant as if she were summoning a memory. "It's funny, but even though I couldn't make out what he was saying, the way he talked gave me the creeps; it stayed with me."

"Did he sound threatening?" Alan asked.

"No. It was more like he was desperate, frantic even, and kind of panicky."

"That could be significant," Alan said. "What do you think, Dan?"

"I think there's no doubt about it. Did you really not recognise his voice at all, Celine? Surely, you must know your colleagues well enough to know what they sound like."

"If I knew who it was, I'd have told you, but it could've been anyone." Celine paused, and sadness crept into her eyes. "For a second, I did wonder if it might've been Seb, but that was just me being silly."

Dan watched her carefully. "Are you sure?"

"Yes. It wasn't him. I'd have known. We talked just last week. He was..." Celine drew a breath, and when she went on, her voice faltered. "Seb could be very charming. He made me feel as though he could really see me, do you know what I mean?"

"I understand," Dan said. "Seb was quite a character, and I can't imagine him being cowed by anyone. Who else might it have been? Were there any clues in his voice? Was he young or old?"

"I don't know." Celine looked away, her gaze following the passers-by.

"There must be something," Dan insisted. "Some hint as to—"

"No," Celine interrupted. She focused on Dan, her expression sharpening. "I've told you everything I know. There's nothing else to say. I don't know what you're trying to achieve, but I don't want to get involved."

"Then why did you give me your phone number? And why did you go to such an effort to do it secretly?"

"It was a spur-of-the-moment thing, an impulse. I didn't like the way you were being treated, and I felt sorry for you."

"I don't believe that," Dan said. "You were worried, and you wanted an ally."

"No. You're mistaken, Dan. I'm upset about Seb, but I don't need you or anyone else to ride to my rescue. I'll be fine once I get home." Turning to Alan, she added, "Thank you for the tea and everything. It was nice to meet you, Alan. Goodbye."

"Please, wait a second," Dan began, but Celine was already standing up and shouldering her bag.

"Bye, Dan," she said, and then she was gone, striding away and disappearing into the throng of shoppers and tourists.

"That went well," Alan said, his voice heavy with irony. "I don't think we could've alienated her more if we'd tried."

"It was my fault. She'd just heard about Seb, and I should've been more sensitive."

"We both could've done better, but there's no point in moaning about it. What's done is done."

"Yes." Dan took a sip from his cup, but the coffee was cold and stale, the bitterness clinging to his tongue. It was undrinkable, which was a shame, because he needed something to kickstart his brain. *I wonder if Seb felt the same way*, he thought. Celine had mentioned drugs in Seb's past, and an image of the man came to Dan's mind: the broad smile that had lacked all trace of warmth, the combative tone of his voice and the glint in his eye that had looked very much like raw greed. Seb had been every inch the driven businessman, but had he relied on artificial stimulants to give him an edge? He wouldn't be the first executive who'd turned to cocaine or some other illegal drug, and all the signs had been there.

Somehow, I didn't put two and two together, Dan thought. *Why was that? Why didn't I see that Seb was a user? It was staring me in the face.*

"Are you all right?" Alan asked. "You've gone pale."

"I was thinking about Seb, wondering if things could've been different. We didn't get on, but I could've made more of an effort. If I'd taken the time to get to know him, I might've been able to help."

"Don't blame yourself, Dan. It takes time to make friends, and you weren't there for long. You didn't have a proper chance to get to know anyone. Besides, we don't really have any idea what actually happened to the poor man. We'll know more when the police make a statement. Until then, all we can do is wait."

Dan examined his friend's expression. The meeting with Celine may have gone badly, but Alan was far from daunted. If anything, he looked more fresh faced than usual: ready for any challenge. There was no need to ask whether he'd help Dan to find the truth behind Seb's death; the look in his eye was answer enough.

"We may as well wait at home," Alan went on. "I'll settle the bill." He fished in his pocket for his wallet and looked around for someone to take his money.

Dan polished off the remainder of the flapjack from his plate. Celine had barely touched her food, and the partly eaten snack sat forlornly on her plate. *Unfinished*, Dan thought. *Like every other damned thing*. Celine hadn't told him all she knew. There was more, and sooner or later, he'd need to talk to her again. Next time, he'd be better prepared.

CHAPTER 40

DC Collins shuffled his sheaf of papers and stood up from his desk with a smile. The automatic number plate recognition system had come up trumps, and he couldn't wait to show DS Kulkarni the results. He found her at her desk, hunched over a keyboard, her brow furrowed in concentration, but as he approached, she stopped typing and sat back. "DC Collins. You look pleased with yourself."

"With good reason, Sarge. ANPR can place Jez Parker's van in Exeter on the same day as every single one of the carjackings. It was also spotted several times in the days leading up to each theft."

"Not bad, but something tells me there's more."

"There is. As I thought, Jez Parker is not employed by DPD and he never has been. That's why the logo on his van doesn't look quite right; it's fake. As far as I can tell, he doesn't work for any other courier firm either." He held out his neat stack of papers to Kulkarni, adding, "It's all in here, and I've added a few notes."

"You could've emailed this to me," Kulkarni said, but she took the sheets of paper and scanned them quickly, turning the pages in silence until she reached the last one, then she looked up at Collins, her eyebrows raised. "These cousins of his, Lee and Aaron, might've been involved with stolen cars before."

"Yes, Sarge. They were never arrested, but they were questioned in connection with two counts of taking a vehicle without the owner's consent."

"Why am I only hearing this now? You said you'd checked their records."

Collins felt his cheeks colouring. "I made a mistake. There wasn't enough evidence to arrest the Parker brothers; they weren't even interviewed under caution. They were questioned at home, and the notes never made it to the national computer. The only record was at Plymouth, but when I talked to CID over there, they didn't mention anything about stolen cars, so I left it at that. I should've asked for a copy of everything they had on the pair of them."

"Yes, you should." Kulkarni turned a stern gaze on him, but she didn't hold it for long. "At least you got there in the end. I'm guessing that's a lesson learned, yes?"

"Yes, Sarge. I won't make the same mistake again."

"Good." Kulkarni returned her attention to the written report. "So, the stolen cars in question were a Subaru Impreza and an Audi Quattro. Both a bit old school and not what I'd call high-end cars. They're certainly not luxury models."

"You know cars?"

"Why wouldn't I?"

"No reason," Collins said quickly. "I was just impressed, that's all."

Kulkarni smiled. "I'll let you off the hook. It would be rude not to, especially since you've delivered the goods on the Parkers." She tucked the report under her arm and stood. "We've got work to do. Let's go and see the DI."

"Yes, Sarge," Collins said, and he couldn't keep the jubilation out of his voice.

A FEW SHORT HOURS LATER, Collins parked his car at the end of Neswick Street in Plymouth, Kulkarni in the passenger seat. To avoid being seen, they were some distance from Jeremy Parker's house, but the street was quiet, and there was a good chance they'd be able to see any comings and goings at number 17. Collins checked the time on the car's dashboard. It was almost six, and most people would be home from work, making their evening meal or settling in front of the TV while the kids did their homework or, more likely, played computer games. It was almost a shame to disturb the peace.

"Plymouth CID should be here any minute," Kulkarni said. "When I talked to DI Blakey, I got the impression he's a man who's always on time."

"I thought we'd have met him at Plymouth nick and come together."

"The DI said there wasn't time. He wants this done and dusted."

Collins hesitated. "Did he say anything about, you know, my mistake with the records?"

"It might've come up in the conversation, but he knows the score. These things happen. I wouldn't worry about it if I were you. He's pleased as punch to be having another pop at the Parker family, and you made that possible. You did all right, Ben. No need to beat yourself up about it."

"Cheers, Sarge. Appreciate it." Collins checked his car's wing mirror and spotted a black VW saloon turning into the street, closely followed by a marked patrol car. "The reinforcements have arrived."

"Good, but whatever you do, don't say that to them. This might be our case, but we're the guests here. Let the locals handle it. We're here to arrest Jeremy Parker and take him in for questioning, okay?"

Collins nodded firmly. "Understood."

"Excellent. Let's go."

Together, Collins and Kulkarni climbed from the car and donned their protective vests, then they marched along the road to join the half a dozen police officers who'd emerged from their vehicles. Four of the Plymouth police officers were in uniform, and the other two, both of them male, separated from the group and stepped forward to meet Kulkarni and Collins.

Kulkarni had her ID ready, and the formalities were run through as swiftly as possible. DI Blakey was the older of the two officers from Plymouth CID, and his colleague was introduced as DS Simon Trevor.

The detective sergeant wore a permanent grin as though faintly amused, and Collins suppressed a flash of irritation. The man was very young to have made DS; his attempt at a beard was patchy and thin, and his cheeks were pitted with the scars of acne that might've cleared up only recently. *Fast-tracked from university*, Collins decided. *Jammy sod.*

But if his sergeant had been given an easy ride, DI Blakey looked as though he'd been a full-time student at the school of hard knocks and he'd graduated with honours. From his shaven head to his scuffed shoes, he was the image of the seasoned detective. Burly and with a square jaw, Blakey cut an imposing figure, his protective vest emphasising his barrel chest, and Collins found himself standing to attention.

"Welcome to Stonehouse," Blakey said. "I hope you locked your car door."

"Yes, sir," Collins replied. "I think we got a measure of the place the other day."

Blakey lowered his eyebrows and turned a stern frown on Kulkarni. "You've been here before? You kept that quiet, Detective Sergeant. Don't tell me you've been on my patch without so much as a courtesy call."

"It wasn't intentional," Kulkarni said. "On Monday, we

followed Jeremy Parker all the way from Exeter. We didn't know where he was headed until he got here."

"Even so, a call wouldn't have gone amiss. We'll have words about this later, but this isn't the time. Let's get this done. Before we go in, is there anything else you haven't told us? Anything else we need to know?"

"No, sir," Kulkarni replied. "It should be straightforward."

Blakey directed his stare at Collins. "How about you? Anything to add?"

"No, sir, but I do have a question." Collins nodded to where the four uniformed officers were waiting. One of them was carrying a steel battering ram of the type commonly called a big red key, and two of the others wore pistols at their hips. "Why are the AFOs here?"

"It's a precautionary measure. We don't know who'll be in the building, and one of Parker's brothers has served time for a firearms offence."

"That would be Aaron," Collins said. "Possession of an unregistered firearm. Sentenced to five years. He was denied parole because he attacked another inmate, but after that he kept his nose clean. He served three years."

DI Blakey studied Collins as though measuring him up. "Good. Detail. That's what it's all about, DC Collins."

"Yes, sir."

"Right, here's how it's going to go," Blakey stated. "DS Kulkarni and DC Collins, you will stand back and keep out of the way until I say otherwise. Got it?"

"Yes, sir," Kulkarni said, and Collins echoed her words, though it pained him to do it.

Blakey nodded, apparently satisfied, then he turned to his team. "Right. You know what to do. Let's do it."

After a brief chorus of acknowledgement, three of the uniformed officers formed up behind Blakey and Trevor, while the fourth went back to the patrol car. Kulkarni and

Collins joined at the rear, and Blakey led his team at a brisk pace to Jeremy Parker's front door.

At a wave from Blakey, the team held back while he and Trevor marched up to the door and rang the bell. A few seconds later, the door opened, and Blakey stepped forward. Jeremy Parker appeared in the doorway, but before Blakey could say a word, Parker's gaze went to the uniformed officers standing by and he bolted back inside the house. He tried to slam the door behind him, but Blakey was ready, and he barged in, shouldering the door aside. Trevor and the uniformed officers streamed into the house, and at the same time, the patrol car screeched to a halt in front of the house. Collins heard a series of muffled shouts from inside, and then a yelled curse that almost certainly came from Parker.

"Sounds like they've got him," Collins said. "Do you think we'll be allowed in now?"

"Give them a second," Kulkarni replied. "I know it's frustrating, but it's DI Blakey's show, so we've got to let him run it. Think how you'd feel if the situation was the other way around."

"Fair enough." Collins glanced up and down the street, but apart from a few faces peering out from the windows across the street, there was nothing of interest. *We're wasting time standing out here*, Collins thought, but he didn't have to wait long.

A uniformed officer strolled from the house and said, "It's all clear, DS Kulkarni. The guv'nor says you can come in."

"Thanks. Come on, Ben." Kulkarni headed inside, Collins at her heels, and they found Jeremy Parker standing in the front room, his hands already cuffed. Blakey and Trevor stood facing him, while the uniformed officers seemed content to loiter in the background.

"I've already arrested him," Blakey said. "He was going to do a runner, so there was no choice."

"Thank you, sir," Kulkarni replied. "Have you checked his pockets yet? I'm keen to get hold of his phone."

DS Trevor held out his hand, a smartphone in his palm, the screen badly cracked. "He stamped on it, but I grabbed it."

"Thank you." Kulkarni produced an evidence bag from her pocket, then she took the phone and sealed it inside.

"Good luck with that," Parker jeered. "It won't work now, and anyway, I've forgotten my PIN."

"We don't need it," Kulkarni said. "We have people who can tell us every website you've ever visited, along with every text and email you've ever sent, so you might like to think about that, Jeremy. You're going to have plenty of time."

"I'm not saying anything," Parker muttered. "Not a bloody word."

"Okay, let's get him down to Plymouth nick and get him booked in," Blakey said. "He can ride in the patrol car. I'll leave a couple of PCs here to guard the house, pending a possible search. Okay, DS Kulkarni?"

Kulkarni hesitated. "Yes, sir."

Collins fidgeted and fought back a surge of frustration. They'd planned to take Parker back to Exeter, but now that he'd tried to escape and DI Blakey had arrested him, it made matters more complicated. He exchanged a look with Kulkarni, and her tight-lipped expression held a warning: don't rock the boat.

She's right, Collins told himself. *No point in arguing*. This wasn't the outcome they'd wanted, but Parker would be placed in custody, and they had his phone, so it wasn't all bad. There was no getting away from the admin and procedures that followed an arrest, so they'd just have to make the best of it.

DS Trevor led Parker from the room, the PCs following, and DI Blakey faced Kulkarni and Collins. "I suggest we carry out an initial interview at our nick," he said. "You can sit in. As soon as we've run through the paperwork, I'll let you know. The odds are we'll get nothing out of him, but you never know your luck. If we can establish grounds for a search warrant, we'll get to it right away, but he'll probably say nothing. He knows we can't hold him for long. Your best bet is to get cracking with that phone. Once we've got that in the bag, it'll give us some leverage."

"Yes, sir," Kulkarni replied. "Sounds good."

Blakey cracked a smile. "Look, I know what you're thinking, but we are where we are. So why don't you two grab a coffee and then come along to the nick in half an hour or so? That's unless you want to head back to Exeter and question him tomorrow."

"We'll stay. I'd like to talk to him as soon as we can, if that's okay."

"Fine. I'll see you there." DI Blakey made to leave, but he half turned in the doorway and said, "Get DC Collins a bite to eat. He looks like he needs it." With that, he was gone.

Kulkarni and Collins trailed after him and then made their way back to Collins' car.

"Is he right, do you think?" Collins asked. "Will we get anything out of Parker?"

"Maybe not tonight," Kulkarni said. "We'll get digital forensics started on his phone first thing in the morning, and with a bit of luck, there'll be something on there to make him squirm."

"Yeah, and hopefully there'll be enough to give us grounds for a search warrant."

"Wait and see," Kulkarni said. "Wait and see."

WEDNESDAY

CHAPTER 41

L ast night, much to my surprise, I slept deeply. There were no dreams, no night sweats, no bitter memories or dark recollections.

I slept the sleep of the innocent. How can that be?

Pouring my morning coffee, I watched my hands for any sign of a tremor, but they were steady.

I almost wish it was otherwise.

What have I become?

A life has been snuffed out, and yet I feel no remorse, no lingering sadness, no shame. I did what I had to do.

My only regret is that the job remains unfinished. There's no sense in focusing on the past. The goal is not yet within my grasp.

Soon, there'll be an end to it. Until then, I must keep on, and if needs must, then more blood will be spilled.

There are times when a small voice in my mind makes its presence known. It whispers, tells me that it might be better if someone were to stop me. Perhaps then I could rest a while.

But that isn't going to happen.

No one will be able to stop me. I'm too clever for that.

Too clever for my own good.

CHAPTER 42

S itting up in bed, his eyes still bleary from sleep, Dan stared at his phone and scrolled through the local news sites. There was no more information about Seb's untimely death, not even a new statement from the police, and Dan ran a hand down his face and slumped against the headboard.

The previous day, Dan had watched the local evening news in horror as Chief Superintendent Bradbury, an authoritative figure in his pristine uniform, had addressed a press conference at police HQ in Exeter, announcing that Seb Cooper had been found dead in the quayside car park. Without missing a beat, the chief superintendent had gone on to say that Seb's death was being treated as suspicious. An investigation was already underway.

Will they come knocking on my door? Dan wondered. His office at CEG had been close to Seb's, but there was little he could tell the police. It was damned frustrating. Dan could help to find the truth, he was certain of that, but he no longer worked at CEG and he had no authority to ask questions.

I'll think of something, Dan decided. *But not until I've had my coffee.* Dan heaved himself out of bed and trudged downstairs. In the kitchen, he put his phone on the table and set about preparing his coffee. There was enough ground coffee in the grinder's receptacle and he scooped it out carefully, the scent of Costa Rican arabica lifting his spirits. A few seconds later, everything was ready, and coffee streamed into his pre-warmed mug, the machine's spluttering hiss like music to Dan's ears.

But before Dan could lift his cup, the moment was spoiled by an insistent buzz from his phone. Snatching it up, he saw an incoming video call on WhatsApp: *Neil Hawthorne.*

Dan sat at the table, smoothing his hair with one hand, then he held his phone up in front of him and accepted the call.

Neil's face appeared on the screen, his cheeks pale and his features even more drawn than the last time Dan had seen him.

"Dan," Neil said. "Hope you don't mind me calling."

"No, not at all. Are you all right?"

"Forget the small talk. Have you heard the news? About Seb?"

"Yes. It's—"

"They killed him," Neil interrupted. "I should've seen it coming."

"What? Who killed him?"

"I don't know. At least, I don't know who actually carried it out. I don't even know who's behind it, but someone killed Seb. There's no doubt in my mind."

Dan drew a slow breath. "Neil, if you have anything to back that up, you must go to the police."

"That's just it. I've got nothing but my suspicions. I was looking for proof, but someone figured out what I was up to. That's why they threw me out." Neil moved his phone closer, so that his face filled Dan's screen. "Tell me, are you still with *them?* Are you still at CEG?"

"No, I was let go."

"On what grounds? What happened?"

"It's a long story, but there was a newspaper article about me, and they said I'd brought the company into disrepute."

"Smoke and mirrors," Neil stated. "They'll do anything to hide the truth. Anything. But this is good. You're better off out of it, Dan. Now we can talk."

"Okay, so let's talk. You say you had suspicions. Suspicions of what?"

"Someone at CEG is cooking the books. They're siphoning off money, and I'm not talking about a few thousand here and there. I'm talking about millions of pounds, and it's been going on for years."

"How is that possible?" Dan asked. "The accounts are audited. I've seen some of the reports myself."

"If I knew exactly how it was done, I wouldn't be in this mess, but you've got to believe me, Dan, the signs are there. There are all kinds of losses that occur across the group, whole shipments sometimes, and all of them are claimed against insurance. Each business in the group has its own accounting systems, and they all use different insurance companies, sometimes switching their insurers every year, so it's hard to put the picture together, but it adds up to a fortune in claims."

"These things happen."

"Every month? Every year?"

"I wouldn't know about that, but a company the size of CEG must incur a certain amount of—"

"Wake up," Neil blurted. "This is systematic fraud on a huge scale. I'm telling you, Dan, it's been done by someone who knows how to work the system. They've covered their trail very efficiently, spreading the losses as widely as they can, but when I started putting the figures together, I knew I was on to something."

"Okay, let's say you're right, Neil. You uncovered a fraud while you worked at CEG, but if that's the case, why haven't you reported it?"

"Because I can't prove it. I needed more time, but they shoved me out, left me penniless. They thought I'd give up, and I nearly did, but then you came along and I thought you might be able to help."

"Then why didn't you say something before? We talked in the park, and I asked you a direct question, but you wouldn't explain."

"You weren't ready to hear it, not then. You were still working for them, and you looked at me as if I was some kind of lunatic. I didn't know if I could trust you."

"How about now? Do you trust me, Neil? Are you ready to confide in me?"

Neil chewed on his lower lip. "I don't know. I *want* to trust you. The truth is, I wanted you brought into the company because I'd heard you had an eye for detail. I bumped into an old friend, and you'd helped him out. He said you were like a dog with a bone, and you didn't care too much about treading on other people's toes, so I persuaded the board to take you on."

"That explains why I was headhunted," Dan said. "But who gave you my name? It wasn't Craig Ellington by any chance, was it?"

"It's not important. The point is, I got them to hire you because I thought you could shine a light on what was going on. I thought you'd get me the proof I needed, but I couldn't tell you that. You might've given the game away." Neil shook his head as if dumbfounded by his own stupidity. "I thought I was being clever, keeping my cards close to my chest, and now look what's happened. Seb is dead, and maybe I'll be next."

"It won't come to that. We'll work something out." Dan paused, thinking. He needed more than Neil's wild accusations before he could go to the police, and there was only one crumb of evidence on offer. "Neil, tell me about the photograph," he said. "The message on the back; what does it mean?"

"I don't know. It was something I saw on Seb's desk one day, written down on a sheet of paper. He realised I'd seen it, and he whisked it away. He was rattled. I could see it in his eyes. I asked him if he was okay, but he lost his temper and told me to get out. He could be nasty when he wanted to be, but I'd read the whole note, and I've always had a head for figures. As soon as I got back to my office, I copied it all down."

Dan groaned inwardly. This was all he had to go on? A glimpsed note and one man's memory?

"Don't look at me like that," Neil went on. "I remembered it correctly. All of it. I'm positive."

"Okay. Assuming you got the dates right, what about the quote from Shakespeare? A friend of mine tells me that the punctuation wasn't right."

Neil's face fell. "You showed it to someone? You shouldn't have done that, Dan. You've put them in danger."

"I only showed a close friend, and I trust him completely. He won't tell anyone, and I needed his help."

"Oh hell. I don't know about this. Maybe I shouldn't have talked to you."

"Yes, you should," Dan said firmly. "Whatever's going on, I'm mixed up in it already. Someone broke into my house and took some hard drives. There has to be a connection with CEG, but I won't be intimidated, Neil. I'm not going to let them get away with that. You can trust me. I'll do my best to help."

Neil didn't respond, and for a moment Dan wondered if his screen had frozen, but then Neil sighed and said, "Okay, Dan. Talk to your friend if you have to, but please, no one else. We don't know who we're up against, but whoever it is, they have a lot to lose, and they must be getting desperate. Seb got involved and look what happened to him."

"I'll be careful. Now, tell me about the note. Did you miss out the commas or were they missing from the original?"

Neil narrowed his eyes. "There weren't any commas. If I'd seen them, I'd have remembered, but I don't see the relevance."

"We'll have to wait and see. It might be significant. I don't think Seb would've chosen that line as an inspirational quote. He never struck me as being that kind of person, and anyway, I doubt he was ever a fan of Shakespeare."

"Probably not. Seb once told me he hadn't read a novel since he left school. He was proud of it." Neil smiled sadly. "He wasn't always easy to get on with, but he could be very disarming, and you'd find yourself agreeing with everything he said. He had charisma, I suppose."

"Yes, I can imagine him being quite persuasive." Dan hesitated before going on. "It was Celine who told me what had happened to Seb. She hinted that he'd been a bit wild in the past. He drank and possibly took drugs."

"I never saw anything like that. Seb didn't even touch sugar if he could help it. He was always talking about some diet he was on. Keto, I think. I never really paid much attention. I should've made more of an effort to talk to him. I should've..." Neil's voice trailed away, and he stared out from the screen, his gaze oddly expressionless as though he'd been hollowed out.

"You look tired," Dan said. "I'd better let you go. Get some rest, Neil. The police will want to talk to you. If they ask you to go in for a formal interview, take a solicitor."

"I will. But what about you? What are you going to do?"

"I'll do some digging, see what I can find out. Sooner or later, I'll come up with something. Whatever happens, I won't give up."

"For some reason, I believe you. You know, it *was* Craig who told me about you, and he was right; you are like a dog with a bone. I just hope your persistence pays off. Good luck, Dan. Bye."

"Bye. Take care, Neil."

The call over, Dan laid down his phone and crossed the kitchen to retrieve his cup of coffee. It wouldn't be at its best, so maybe he should start again. *It's a good job I ground a fresh batch of beans,* he thought. *Something tells me it's going to be an eventful day.*

CHAPTER 43

D S Kulkarni arrived at Plymouth Police HQ and presented herself at the front desk. Hanging her lanyard around her neck and signing in, a twinge of regret sprang up in the back of her mind. Ben Collins should be with her, but DI Spiller had sent him on some errand or other. *He'll be working on that cold case,* she thought. *What's the point?* They had plenty of fresh cases to be dealing with and Ben's energies would've been better spent elsewhere.

The guv'nor must've had his reasons, but even so, she'd have liked Ben at her side. DI Blakey seemed the type to steamroller over others, and she didn't want him muscling in on her case. *This belongs to Ben and me,* she thought. *No one should be trying to take it away from us.*

Upstairs in the CID office, DI Blakey was all smiles as he greeted her. He even offered her a coffee.

"Thanks, but I'm fine," Kulkarni said. "I'd like to crack on with the interview if that's okay."

"Be my guest," Blakey replied. "We need to get something out of him today. Unless we can charge him by the close of play, we'll have to let him go, and he knows it."

Kulkarni nodded. Parker hadn't said as much, but it

seemed as though he knew the importance of the so-called custody clock. When they'd brought him in the day before, Parker had played a familiar game, insisting on a legal adviser being present and then parroting the phrase 'no comment' in reply to every question.

This morning, things would be different, and Kulkarni couldn't wait to get started.

"I've had young Parker moved to interview room three, so he's ready and waiting," Blakey went on. "By all accounts, he was a bit twitchy after a night in the cells, so with a bit of luck he might change his tune this morning."

"Here's hoping. We got a lot of good stuff from his phone, so that ought to rattle him."

Blakey rubbed his hands together. "That's what I like to hear. I'll sit in with you. If we can get him to give us something on Aaron and Lee, it'll make my day."

"You're the boss. Is his solicitor here?"

"Yes. Tim Armitage, same as last night. He doesn't say much, but he's an old hand. He won't play silly buggers." Blakey gestured to the door. "After you, Detective Sergeant. Let's see what we can do."

The interview room was windowless, and a faint smell of disinfectant hung in the air, as though the place had been swabbed down the night before. Jeremy Parker sat slouched in a chair, his solicitor beside him, and while Tim Armitage greeted Kulkarni and Blakey with a few words and a watchful smile, Parker stared into the middle distance in a display of disinterest.

Blakey indicated the seat opposite Parker and Kulkarni took it, suppressing a smile and revising her ideas about DI Blakey. She'd expected him to face Parker directly, dominating the interview from the start, but Blakey sat back, his arms folded and an expectant look on his face, like a spectator who fully expects his team to win.

Seizing the moment, Kulkarni started the recording,

placed her tablet in front of her, and ran through the formalities at speed. But before she could ask her first question, Tim Armitage cleared his throat and said, "Are you intending to charge my client today? Because if not he'll have to be released."

"That's understood," Kulkarni replied. "We'll come to the matter of charges presently. In the meantime, we have some new evidence to present to Jeremy, and we'll take it from there."

"No comment," Parker intoned.

"We'll see about that." Kulkarni tapped her tablet's screen and held it up so that Parker could see it. "I'm showing Mr Parker an image, reference zero-one-five-six, which was held on his personal phone. The image had been deleted, but we were able to recover it. The same can be said for all the images I'm going to show Mr Parker today."

Parker's eyes flitted to the screen, and though he showed no emotion, he looked away quickly. His solicitor, on the other hand, leaned forward to peer at the image.

"In this image, you can be seen clearly, Mr Parker," Kulkarni continued. "It looks like this was a selfie, is that right?"

"No comment," Parker muttered.

"Okay, well we can see from the angle of your arm that it was a selfie, and the car you're leaning against, that's a Lexus. We can tell from the distinctive angles of the radiator grille. Why did you take that photo, Jeremy?"

Parker shrugged.

"I'm going to need you to speak up for the recording," Kulkarni said. "That way, everyone can be clear on what was said. I'm sure your solicitor will agree."

"That's correct," Armitage said. "You don't have to comment, Jeremy, but if you want to respond, it's best to speak clearly. Do you understand?"

"Yeah, I'm not stupid," Parker replied. "Okay, so I saw a

nice car and I took a selfie. So what? Nothing wrong in taking a photo, is there?"

"It depends. The owner might have something to say about you leaning on his car. You might've scratched the paintwork, and that would've been a shame. Especially since it's a custom paint job."

Parker's eyebrows lowered, and he glowered at the tablet as though it had tricked him in some way.

"You see, the owner paid a packet to have this car factory resprayed in this particular shade of grey," Kulkarni said. "To me, it wasn't worth the money. It just looks dark grey, almost black, but he wanted something a little bit different. It must be nice to be able to afford these things, mustn't it?"

"This is all very interesting," Armitage said. "But my client has explained the situation. Do you have a proper question, or can we move on?"

Kulkarni smiled. "Oh, I have a question. I want to know why Jeremy took a photo of himself next to a car that had just been stolen."

Armitage opened his mouth to speak, but Kulkarni didn't give him a chance. "You see, that paint job is non-standard, so we're confident that the car in your photo is the one stolen in Exeter on the 7th of May."

"I don't know anything about that," Parker said.

"Really? Then how come that photo is timestamped on the 8th of May, the day after it was stolen?"

Armitage leaned closer to his client. "I advise you to make no comment."

"I know," Parker grumbled. "But I just saw the car in the street. I don't know anything about it being nicked."

"Fair enough," Kulkarni said, swiping the tablet's screen to bring up the next image. "Let's move on. I'm showing Mr Parker image reference zero-one-five-eight. Another selfie, this time with Mr Parker leaning on the bonnet of a BMW, Seven Series. Now, you must have an excellent camera in that phone, Jeremy, because we were able to zoom right in and look at every tiny detail." Kulkarni pulled up the next image. "We're now looking at image reference zero-one-five-nine, which is taken from the previous photo. Do you see what we're looking at, Jeremy?"

"Not really," Parker replied. "It's a bit fuzzy."

Kulkarni tutted. "Don't do yourself down, Jeremy. That was a perfectly clear photo. We're looking at a parking permit displayed on the windscreen, and I can read every word. There's even the car's registration number there, so we can be absolutely sure that this car was stolen in Exeter. Once again, this photo was shot the day after the car was taken without the owner's consent." She sat back. "Isn't that a coincidence, Jeremy?"

"Yeah," Parker replied. "Coincidence."

Kulkarni nodded as if accepting his statement. "Interesting. What are the odds, do you think? Two cars, both stolen, and you just happen to come across them the day afterwards."

"I dunno." Parker looked to his solicitor as if seeking guidance, but Armitage didn't respond; he seemed preoccupied, staring at the tablet, where Kulkarni's finger was hovering over the screen.

Meeting his gaze, Kulkarni said, "What do you think, third time lucky?" Without waiting for a reply, she swiped the screen once more. "This image, reference zero-one-six-zero, shows Mr Parker in another selfie, this time posing with a Mercedes S-Class. You really were careless this time, Jeremy, weren't you? We can see almost the whole of the registration plate, and guess what: this car was stolen the day before you took this photograph." Kulkarni paused to let this sink in, then she added, "Plus, we have data from the ANPR system that places your van in the vicinity of each of these cars on the days they were stolen, and you also took photos of the same cars a day or two beforehand. How does it work, Jeremy? It looks as though you spot the cars and take photos, then you drive someone out there to steal the cars, and you help to handle the vehicles afterwards. Is that it?"

Parker shifted in his seat. "No comment."

"You might want to advise your client to cooperate," Kulkarni said to Armitage. "We have enough to charge him with handling the stolen cars, but there's more. It's looking like he was involved in the actual thefts, and because of the degree of violence involved, that leaves him open to much more serious charges."

Armitage regarded her levelly for a moment. "I'd like some time to confer with my client."

"That's a good idea," Kulkarni said. "But before you go, Jeremy, I'd like to ask you just one question."

Parker stared at her in sullen silence.

"On your phone, we found photos of all the stolen cars, except for one. Why didn't you take a photo of the Volvo?"

Parker's features formed a mask of incomprehension.

"Come on, Jeremy, you can do better than that," Kulkarni insisted. "You know you have to respond out loud, so tell me, why didn't you take a picture of the Volvo S90? It's the only car missing from your photos, and we couldn't find any trace of it on your phone."

"I don't know what you're talking about," Parker muttered. "I've had enough of this. I want to talk to my solicitor. Now."

Kulkarni held up her hands. "Fine. That is your right." She ended the interview then she and DI Blakey left the room.

In the corridor, Blakey said, "Not bad, Detective Sergeant. He knows he's sunk, and right now his solicitor is telling him that if we get him for the thefts, he could be looking at five years inside for GBH. If he was just the driver, he'll try to wriggle out of it by giving us something, and we'll see where that leads."

"Towards his cousins, Lee and Aaron?" Kulkarni asked.

"If we're lucky." Blakey looked thoughtful for a moment. "We've got time for that coffee now. What do you say?"

"Sure."

DI Blakey led the way along the corridor, and as they walked, he said, "What was all that about the Volvo? You seemed very keen on getting an answer out of him."

"It's an odd one. There was only one theft that didn't fit the pattern: a Volvo S90. After it was taken, it was driven through the city centre at high speed, almost hitting a pedestrian, then it hit an iron railing. We found the car later, burned out. It was the only vehicle we've been able to recover."

"Makes sense to me," Blakey said. "It was damaged. They couldn't sell it on, so they torched it."

"Maybe, but did you see Parker's face when I asked him about it?"

Blakey chuckled under his breath. "Do me a favour. They learn that expression of feigned innocence at their mother's knee."

"Maybe, but I think he really didn't know what I was talking about, and if he didn't handle the Volvo, I could be looking for another carjacker."

"That's a possibility," Blakey said. "But don't go making life more complicated for yourself. Most crimes are simple, and we've got enough on our plates without looking for extra work."

"Yes, guv'nor," Kulkarni said. But the image of Jeremy Parker's bewildered expression came back to her, and she felt certain that Jeremy Parker and his partners in crime had not stolen the Volvo. That line of thought led to two simple questions: who did steal that Volvo? and was it used as a weapon in a deliberate attempt on Dan Corrigan's life?

CHAPTER 44

Collins announced his arrival in the records department with a smart rap of his knuckles on the counter, then he held on to the counter's edge, leaning forward to peer between the rows of dimly lit shelving units that dwindled into the shadows. Where had Geoff got to?

Collins considered trying the door that led into Geoff's kingdom, but it didn't do to march in uninvited. Anyway, he could make out the sound of shuffling footsteps, and a moment later, Geoff appeared, ambling toward the counter with a stack of cardboard folders tucked beneath his arm.

"That was quick," Geoff called out. "I only emailed you a few minutes ago."

"Yeah, well I want to get this job done," Collins said. "I had to follow this up right away. There must be more detail, Geoff."

Reaching the counter, Geoff set the folders down with a sigh. "It's like I said in my email. All I can tell you is that Jackie Blatch's body was weighed down with scrap metal. I'm sorry but I can't be more specific. That's all she wrote, as they say. I've been through every file I can find, and we covered most of it in our original report." He smiled. "Sorry, I mean *your* report."

Collins shook his head. "It might've had my name on it, but you did all the donkey work. Don't get me wrong, it was all good stuff, but Spiller wants more. He's got this idea that it was a gangland killing, and the weights could've been important, like a message to Blatch's gang."

"There might be something in that. Some kinds of scrap metal were sought after in the war. It's possible that Blatch had been selling metal, so a rival gang murdered him and wanted his friends to know why. But my guess is that they weighed him down with whatever came to hand. I'd have thought that his body would've been a clear enough message in itself."

"I'm with you, but that's not going to go down too well with the guv'nor. He reckons we must've missed something."

"I can't help that. We can't find what isn't there. You've seen most of the files yourself, and you know there's not much to go on. If you ask me, no one was trying too hard to find out who killed Jackie Blatch. It looks like they sat on their hands. One gangster less and good riddance." Geoff's expression was stern, but watching Collins, he seemed to relent. "What's up? Is DI Spiller mucking you around?"

"No, not exactly, but I ought to be upstairs, setting up the incident room for the Cooper case. We've got a murder inquiry on our hands, but the guv'nor keeps sending me off to run errands, looking into an old case we'll probably never solve. He's convinced that the murder of Blatch was linked to the remains we found in Belmont Road and he won't give up. I know him. If I go back empty handed, he'll send me off on another wild goose chase, and for what? We've got zero chance of success, so what's the point?"

"Maybe that's what he wants you to think about," Geoff said. "Two people were murdered, one of them a copper, and justice wasn't done. If we don't at least try to fix that, then what are we here for?"

Collins could think of no reply that wouldn't sound mean spirited, so he said nothing.

"I'll tell you what," Geoff went on. "Let me stow these files, then we'll put our heads together and see what we can come up with. Fair enough?"

"Yeah, I'd appreciate that. Thanks."

"Right. The door's unlocked," Geoff said. "Let yourself in."

∼

HALF AN HOUR LATER, sitting side by side at Geoff's desk, they stopped rifling through dusty papers and regarded each other wearily.

"We're wasting our time," Collins said. "I should go back upstairs."

Geoff heaved a sigh. "We've hit a dead end, but we're not done yet. Why don't you go and make us some coffee? I've got something I want to look up online."

Collins complied, all the while wondering how his colleagues were progressing in the incident room upstairs. They'd have allocated the tasks for the day and interviews would already be underway, the investigation gathering momentum as evidence and data was gathered and collated. Meanwhile, he was stuck in the doldrums, getting nowhere fast.

I'll stay for a quick coffee, Collins told himself. *But then I'm out of here*. That decision made, his mood lifted and he smiled as he took the drinks through to Geoff's desk.

"Here you go," he said, but Geoff didn't acknowledge him; he was concentrating on his screen. Retaking his seat, Collins leaned sideways to see what was holding Geoff's attention and he recognised a street map of Exeter with several areas marked in shades of red.

"Bomb damage reports," Geoff explained. "From the night Blatch was killed."

"Okay, but we already know his warehouse was hit. I suppose it might help us with the timing. They wouldn't dispose of a body while the air raid was going on. It would be too dangerous, wouldn't it?"

"Yes, but that's not the point. Look at the pattern." Geoff moved his fingertip across the screen from one bombed area to the next, tracing a path across the city centre. "Do you see?"

"Not really."

"Doesn't it strike you as odd that there was no bomb damage anywhere near the quay *except* for Blatch's warehouse? I don't know why it didn't jump out at us before."

"All the reports from the time say the warehouse had a direct hit," Collins said. "They wouldn't have made a mistake about that, surely."

"You think? In the chaos of an air raid, might they not have jumped to the wrong conclusion? After all, one explosion looks much like another."

"It's a stretch. We've no evidence it *wasn't* a German bomb."

"Haven't we?" Geoff asked. "The pattern tells a story. Bombers attacked in formation; they followed a plan. Looking at the damaged areas we can work out their flight path, and they were clearly targeting the city centre. Plus, we know for a fact that they wanted to hit the cathedral. The damage on the quayside just doesn't fit. It can't have come from the air raid. It's obvious."

"I get what you're saying, but anything could've happened. The pilot might've got confused and lost his way, or his plane might've been damaged and gone off course."

"That's a possibility. If he'd been hit by anti-aircraft fire, he might've dropped his payload before ditching. But think about it, Ben; does this feel right to you?"

Collins looked again at the map of Exeter, seeing it with fresh eyes. "Well, now that you mention it, the hit on the warehouse does stand out. There was no other damage in the area, so it could be suspicious, but we're not going to be able to prove it one way or the other. After all these years, there won't be any evidence."

"Never mind about evidence. What do your instincts say?"

Collins raised an eyebrow at Geoff's demanding tone, but he knew the older man was on to something. Jackie Blatch had been murdered, his body placed to make a point, and his warehouse had been blown up to make sure the message was rammed home.

"I can see what could've happened," Collins said. "Someone grabbed Jackie Blatch while he was on his way home. The sirens had sounded, so the streets would've been quiet; no one around to see them snatch him. They take him down to his warehouse, and at some point during the air raid, they kill him. As soon as they can, they dump the body and blow up the warehouse, knowing that the authorities will assume it was hit by a bomb. The only people who'll think otherwise are Blatch's gang."

Geoff nodded slowly. "Compelling, isn't it? If only we could prove it."

"We could try looking at rival gangs."

"We could have a go, but it won't be easy."

"That's not like you," Collins said. "I thought you had the history of Exeter's criminals at your fingertips."

"There are plenty of names I know, and a lot more I can find out, but that hardly scratches the surface. Crime was rife in those years. The police were short-handed because so many young coppers had gone off to fight. The authorities tried to replace them with special constables, but that wouldn't have been enough. Then there was the blackout, making it easy to get about at night unseen, and with all the shortages, a lot of people were ready to look the other way when stolen goods magically appeared on the black market. You can fill in the blanks."

"Okay, but this isn't a bit of theft we're talking about; it's two murders. I think the guv'nor is right. We're looking at an organised gang. Their names will be in here somewhere. We need some way to narrow the search."

"Such as?"

"On that old recording, there was a hint that Blatch was involved in gambling, possibly fixing horse races. Plus, there's the metal they used to weigh his body down; that could still be a clue."

Geoff looked unimpressed. "That's your idea of narrowing it down, is it? Gambling and scrap metal. I doubt whether there was a criminal alive at the time who wasn't mixed up with one or the other, if not both."

"What do we do then, wrap it up and forget the whole thing?"

Geoff's expression was an unspoken reply. They'd reached the end of the road.

Collins sat back, staring blankly at the screen.

"Don't beat yourself up," Geoff said. "That's the way it goes sometimes. No one can say we didn't try."

"True. We gave it a shot."

"We certainly did." Geoff's conciliatory smile suddenly melted away, and he gazed at Collins, unblinking, his eyebrows twitching.

"What's up?" Collins asked.

"It was what you said just now. It got me thinking. There's one thing we haven't..." Geoff stood quickly, leaving his sentence unfinished. "I'll be right back." He bustled away and returned a few minutes later, holding a stuffed cardboard folder. He placed the folder on his desk and sat down, an enigmatic smile on his face.

"Are you going to tell me what that is?" Collins asked. "Or do I have to guess?"

"This report is from Blatch's post-mortem examination." Geoff opened the folder and began leafing through it, intent on scanning the pages.

"We already know how he died," Collins said. "He was struck on the head, probably with a crowbar or something similar."

"Yes, yes, but much as I hate to admit it, your boss was right. We missed something. It was only a detail, but as we all know, that's where the devil is."

Collins tried to read the pages, but Geoff was turning them too quickly for him to make out much detail. "Are you saying he *wasn't* hit on the head, because I remember the report, and it seemed clear to me."

"So it was, but we didn't delve deeper, and that's where we made a mistake." Geoff stopped reading and pressed a page flat, running his fingers along the neatly typed text. "Here it is. When you talked about wrapping the case up, I remembered the cloth they'd used to conceal his body."

"It was canvas wasn't it? A tarpaulin."

"Yes, but look here." Geoff tapped the page and Collins moved closer.

Collins read the line aloud: "Within the canvas, the deceased was wrapped in a heavy woollen blanket, dark green and labelled as the property of the Ministry of Defence." Collins looked up. "Weird."

"Is it? Because, from where I'm sitting, it makes perfect sense. They didn't wrap him up to keep him warm and cosy. I'd say we've just found the message you were looking for."

"I don't get it," Collins admitted. "It's just a blanket."

"No. When you're cold and your kids are going to bed in their overcoats, you'd pay a lot for something to keep you and your family warm. That blanket was MoD property, probably army issue, so I'm willing to bet that Blatch had been dealing in goods that were stolen from the armed forces. It was seen as a particularly heinous crime, pilfering from our brave boys, but it happened. There were a lot of supplies being moved from place to place, and some of them found their way onto the black market. We've been wondering what Blatch had stashed in that warehouse, and now maybe we know."

"It makes sense," Collins said. "For Blatch to have been murdered, he had to have been into something bigger than a bit of small-scale theft. If he was knocking off gear from the military, he could've been shifting lorryloads of stuff, and his rivals wouldn't have liked that."

"It's a working hypothesis, at any rate, and it fits with Spiller's ideas. It could link Jackie Blatch to the body in Belmont Road. Blatch would've needed help from people on the inside. No doubt he could've paid off a few drivers and dock workers to make sure the goods went astray, but he'd need to cover his tracks, and who better to have in your pocket than a detective?"

Collins puffed out his cheeks and exhaled. "I reckon we've hit on something, but the problem is, this'll really get the guv'nor going. He won't be happy until he knows who committed the murders, even though the culprits are probably long dead. I'll be stuck on this case until I get to the bottom of it."

"I'll help if I can. It's the least I can do. I feel bad about missing that blanket."

"You were the one who picked up on it," Collins said. "You've already done a hell of a lot, but if you've got time, I'll be grateful for anything you can dig up." Collins smiled, adding, "Not literally, Geoff. I don't want you turning up at Belmont Road with a shovel."

"No, I'll stick with my files, thank you very much. If Jackie

Blatch's racket was as big as we think, his murderer will be mentioned somewhere in this very room. It's just a matter of looking in the right place."

"You're the man to find him," Collins said, standing up and stretching his spine. "I'll go and report back to the guv'nor, tell him you're on the case. With a bit of luck, he'll send me over to the incident room, give me something a bit more modern to deal with."

"Hours of staring at blurry CCTV footage, most likely," Geoff replied. "Give me a good old-fashioned paper trail any day of the week."

"Each to his own. Thanks again, Geoff. If you find anything useful..."

"You'll be the first to know." Geoff shooed Collins away. "Go on. I've got a lot of work to do."

"All right. See you later."

Collins let himself out and headed back upstairs. Geoff wasn't the only one with a lot on his plate. By now, the inquiry into Sebastian Cooper's murder would be moving up a gear, and he'd have to play catch-up. But first, he'd have to persuade Spiller to leave Blatch's case in Geoff's capable hands, and that wasn't going to be easy.

CHAPTER 45

Celine shifted her position on the sofa. How long had she been sitting there, slumped over her iPad, watching rubbish on YouTube? *Too long*, she told herself. *Far too long*. But as the video ended and the next recommended video automatically appeared, she didn't have the energy to stop it.

Nerve-jangling music emitted from the speakers, and an overenthusiastic young man began to talk about bicycle maintenance. "What the hell am I doing?" Celine muttered to the empty room. "This is ridiculous." She didn't even own a bike, for God's sake, but Patrick had obviously been using her iPad and he was mad on the damned things. He was probably out on his latest road bike now, tearing along the city streets, taking the most circuitous route possible; otherwise he'd have been home by now. His last lecture would've finished ages ago, but these days he kept coming home at odd times.

Celine rubbed her temples, pressing her fingers hard against her skin, and she closed her eyes against the glare of the iPad's screen. *Migraine*, she thought. *I ought to have known.* Over the years, she'd grown used to her condition, and she could often spot the early signs and fend off the attack before it laid her low. But not today. She hadn't been paying attention, hadn't looked after herself. She'd done little but mope around the flat feeling sorry for herself and thinking about poor Seb. Well, that would have to change. She couldn't face a migraine, not on top of everything else.

Celine needed her medication. It was strong stuff and it would halt the attack in its tracks, but she had to take it immediately or it wouldn't do the trick. Celine stopped the YouTube video and levered herself up from the sofa, tossing the iPad aside, then she padded through to the bedroom.

She opened the drawer in her bedside table, rummaging through the odd mixture of items she'd inadvertently collected: lone earrings missing their partners, an old bottle of scent and a collection of oddments from the beauty counter, most of them unwanted gifts from Patrick. But where were her pills?

Celine shut the drawer and stood still, trying to gather her thoughts. When had she last had a migraine? She'd downed a few glasses of red wine on Friday night and regretted it on Saturday, taking a pill in the late morning, but where had she left the packet? Celine drew a long breath, but the migraine was beginning in earnest, fogging her brain and scrambling her memories.

"The kitchen," she murmured and headed for the door. The kitchen was small, but they kept it tidy, and a shelf in one of the wall cabinets was reserved for their first aid supplies. There, next to the sticking plasters, was the small, white box containing her medication: rizatriptan.

Celine opened the packet hurriedly, popping a pill from its blister pack and placing it carefully on her tongue. It dissolved in seconds, and she imagined she could feel the active ingredients coursing through her bloodstream.

Celine let out a sigh of relief. She'd be okay now. She'd

need to lie down for a while, and maybe have a little nap while the pill did its work, but she'd be all right.

She put the blister pack back in its box, noting that she only had two pills left. That couldn't be right. She must've misplaced the others, but anyway, she'd need to refill her prescription soon. Celine made to close the cabinet, but something made her stop. Where was her old medication?

She moved the boxes and packets aside, but her hypodermic was definitely missing. *It was probably out of date, anyway*, she thought. *Patrick must've thrown it out*. That was the most likely explanation. He'd never approved of her taking dihydroergotamine in the first place. The hypodermic contained a large dose, and at one point she'd carried it with her at all times in case she had a severe attack. But that was before she'd met Patrick.

As soon as their relationship had become serious, he'd persuaded her to change her whole regime. As a student of physiotherapy, he'd learned a lot about pain management, including the use and misuse of medication, and he'd said that the dihydroergotamine wasn't safe for her. She'd allowed much of his technical explanation to pass her by, but for once she'd let him fuss over her, and he'd been right.

At Patrick's insistence, she'd talked to her doctor and been prescribed the rizatriptan. The doctor had told her to keep the dihydroergotamine as a standby, but she hadn't needed it. Patrick had encouraged her to go to yoga classes, and he made sure that she ate regularly and got plenty of sleep. He'd even offered to try out his newly acquired acupuncture skills on her, but she'd drawn the line at that. "When you're qualified," she'd told him firmly. Hopefully, by then his enthusiasm for alternative medicine would fade. No one was going to use her as pin cushion.

Celine thought of Patrick while she wandered back to the bedroom and lay down, the pill already making her drowsy. Patrick could be very caring. He liked to look after her, and he took care of so many little details around the place, always making sure that everything was as it should be. She'd often wondered whether he might have a touch of OCD, but that was hardly fair. Maybe she ought to be more appreciative.

Celine closed her eyes and felt the pill sapping her strength, her limbs growing heavy. If Patrick was home, he'd have brought her a glass of water, covered her with a blanket. *Why isn't he here?* she thought. *Where has he got to?*

Truth be told, she was worried about Patrick, and it wasn't just the silly arguments and the way he kept coming home late. It was as if his whole attitude toward her had shifted. He'd started treating her like a troublesome roommate: an awkward houseguest who put the cutlery in the wrong drawer and didn't know where to get a clean towel. Yes, he did lots of little things for her, but lately there'd been an undercurrent of annoyance in everything he did, as though he *had* to look after her because she was incapable of doing anything for herself. There was no warmth there. No love.

A stray thought surfaced in her muddled mind: the memory of Dan Corrigan poking his nose in, asking her if everything was okay at home. Why had he asked that? And why had he mentioned Patrick? Did Dan know something, some secret shared in a knowing smile between two men?

Perhaps Patrick was cheating on her. That would explain everything, but Celine shoved the idea aside. It was nonsense. Patrick would never do that to her. She wouldn't even have thought about the possibility if it hadn't been for Dan Corrigan and his stupid questions. But a sneaking doubt took root in her mind, and it wouldn't let her rest. *This is no damned good*, she told herself. *It's no good at all.*

Groaning, Celine opened her eyes and pushed herself up from the bed. She stomped back to the sofa and found her phone nestling among the cushions. Dan's number was stored in her contacts, and she tapped it to place a call.

Dan answered quickly, his surprise obvious in his tone: "Celine. How are you?"

"Not great," Celine replied. "Bit of a headache. But listen, I want to ask you something."

"Go ahead."

"Why did you ask me if things were okay at home?"

There was a pause before Dan said, "Are you all right? You sound a little... Celine, have you been drinking?"

"No, it's my meds. They make me tired. I get migraines, but I'll be all right in an hour or so."

"Okay. Are you on your own? Is someone there to look after you?"

"I'm fine. There's just me here, but that's not important. You haven't answered my question. Why did you ask about my personal life?"

"We should talk about this some other time," Dan said. "When you're feeling better."

"No. I want to know, right now. You started to say something about Patrick, but then you changed your mind. What was it? What were you going to say?"

"There's no need to get upset. It's probably nothing, but when I saw you with Patrick at Batworthy Castle, he... he wasn't being very attentive. I got the impression that, maybe, things between you weren't great."

"Is that so?" Celine poured as much scorn into those three words as she could, determined to bat Dan's insinuation away, but tears pricked the corners of her eyes. So that was it. Okay, Patrick looked at other women; what man didn't? She'd always known about his wandering eye, but she hadn't realised it was so obvious to everyone else. God, that was humiliating. If a relative stranger like Dan could see what Patrick was up to from across a crowded room, then everyone else must've known. Everyone must've been laughing at her behind her back.

"I'm sorry," Dan said. "I shouldn't have said anything."

"No, you shouldn't." Celine was on the point of ending the call, but something held her back. "Who was it? Who was he looking at?"

"Erm, I really don't think that will—"

"Who was it?" Celine interrupted. "Tell me, Dan. You can't drop a bombshell and leave it at that. You have to tell me."

"Okay. Remember, it was just a look, Celine, but the person he was looking at was Seb's wife."

Celine's hand went to her cheek as if she'd just been slapped. "You mean Lauren? And was she… was she looking at him?"

"Well, yes. She was."

"Oh no. That's a disaster. A bloody disaster."

"Don't read too much into it," Dan said. "They looked at each other, that's all. It probably doesn't mean anything."

"But what if it does? If something's going on between them, people might think he had something to do with what happened to Seb."

"Hold on, Celine. That's a leap."

"No, it isn't. It's a connection."

"But it might not be a meaningful one," Dan said, "I'm sure there's a much more logical explanation for Seb's death. I spoke to Neil Hawthorne, and he's sure there's been a string of financial crimes at CEG. He thinks Seb was involved."

"What are you talking about? Neil left the company. How would he know what's going on?"

"Neil says that he came across evidence of fraud and he wanted to blow the whistle. According to him that's the reason he was sacked."

Celine shook her head to clear it, but it didn't help. In her body, a battle raged between her medication and the adrenaline stirred up by Dan's wild accusations. Why did he have to make things so complicated?

"Are you still there?" Dan asked.

"Yes. But I don't know about any of this. It's too much. I need to go."

"Okay, but can I ask you one question?"

"What is it?"

"Neil saw some dates on a sheet of paper on Seb's desk. They could be important. Can I run them past you?"

"You can try."

Dan recited some dates, but Celine was feeling worse now and the numbers slipped past her, barely registering. She swallowed, and her throat felt thick, her tongue dry. "Hang on. Say those again. Let me write them down." She picked up her iPad and opened the notes app, wincing at the screen's brightness. "Go ahead."

Dan began again, and she tapped them into a note, not bothering to separate them: 192168112.

"There was also a single digit on its own," Dan said. "A five, though I've no idea what that might mean."

Celine added the five and then blinked at the screen. "They're not dates," she stated. "Any fool could see that."

It took Dan a moment to reply. "What do you mean?"

"It's an IP address. It's obvious." She spelt it out for him: "One-nine-two, one-six-eight, one, one-two-five."

"Hell's teeth," Dan breathed. "Why didn't I see that?"

"I don't know, but you're welcome. Now, I've got to go."

"Where is it?" Dan blurted. "The IP address. I mean to say, thank you for your help, but we can't leave it there. Could the IP address point to a computer at CEG? You know the network better than anybody."

"It could be at the office, but I've no idea where."

"Can we log on to the network remotely?"

"No. Anyway, whatever's at that IP address, you'll need some credentials to log in."

"Yes, but… hang on."

Celine sighed. "What is it? I don't have all day."

"There was a phrase written beneath the dates, and I think

it might represent a password. It has to be worth a try. All I need is a way to access that IP address."

"Dan, I'm not going to tell you how to do that."

"Come on, Celine. If I can't log in from here, I'll have to get into the building."

"That's ridiculous. I'm not going to let you in. You don't work there anymore."

"I know, but we could do it today. It's an ideal opportunity. There's probably nobody there."

"Goodbye, Dan," Celine said. "Whatever you're getting into, leave me out of it." She ended the call and stomped through to the bedroom, flopping down on the bed, exhausted. She still had her phone, and she was tempted to switch it off, but Patrick might call, so she left it on her bedside table, then she closed her eyes.

Bloody Dan Corrigan, she thought. *What planet is he on?* She'd called him to shed light on one problem, and he'd presented her with a whole new mountain of difficulties.

There was nothing she could do about that. Her brain was telling her to sleep, and it was time to give in. Celine drifted into unconsciousness, but that string of numbers twirled and danced through the encroaching darkness, and they wouldn't let her be.

CHAPTER 46

Dan placed a mug of hot coffee on the kitchen table in front of Alan, then he took a seat opposite, his own mug in hand, and said, "Freshly ground this morning."

"Thanks." Alan took a sip while keeping his gaze on his laptop.

"Getting anywhere?" Dan asked.

"Not really. All this stuff about IP addresses goes straight over my head." Alan looked up. "There's no chance that Celine got this wrong, is there? The numbers were written as dates, so it feels strange to dismiss that fact out of hand."

"My instincts say she's right. Someone wrote them in date format to throw other people off the scent. It's a common enough trick."

I suppose so," Alan said. "I once disguised my credit card PIN as a phone number by adding lots of digits; this could be the same sort of thing. But even assuming Celine is right, where would we find the computer that has this IP address? And what good will it do us?"

"I'm not sure yet, but we do have one more clue to work on."

Alan nodded thoughtfully. "The mysterious Shakespeare

quote. Do you really think it might be some kind of password? It's very long."

"That's because it isn't the password, it's a hint. For instance, we could take the first letter of each word and string them together."

"That would explain the lack of punctuation. Let's see what we come up with." Alan's fingers darted over the keyboard. "There. Once more unto the breach dear friends once more, becomes O, M, U, T, B, D, F, O, M. What about the exclamation mark?"

"Keep it. Adding special characters is a common way to make a password more secure, and there could be some digits. Maybe each O could be changed to a zero."

Alan renewed his efforts at the keyboard, typing quickly. "That gives us more possibilities, depending on whether one or both of the O's are changed to zeroes, but what about upper-case and lower-case letters? If we factor those in, we'll end up with a lot of possibilities. Even supposing it is a password, what will we do with it? Presumably it unlocks something in your old office building, but we can't waltz in there and try it out."

"True. Maybe we're looking at this from the wrong angle. We should focus on the human element."

"How so?"

"Celine's boss at CEG was a guy called Tom Hastings. He was the IT manager, so he'd have access to the whole network, and he's some kind of literary buff. At least, I've heard him described as a big reader, so he might well use a password inspired by Shakespeare."

Alan looked thoughtful. "It's a bit tenuous, but it's worth following up. Do you have his number?"

"I think so. Hang on." Dan dashed through to his study, and despite the mess on his ransacked desk, he found the laminated card Celine had given him when he'd started at CEG. Good. Tom's number was at the bottom of a list of IT contacts, probably positioned in the hope that he'd only be called as a last resort. Dan carried the card back to the kitchen, showing the card to Alan before placing the call.

Tom answered immediately: "Hello. Who is this?"

"Tom, it's Dan Corrigan. There's something I need to speak to you about."

"Oh? I understood that you'd been let go." A pause, and when Tom spoke again, his smirk was audible. "Or are you calling in your capacity as a private eye?"

Dan stifled the urge to argue with the man; it would do no good to rise to his taunt. "I'm calling in good faith, Tom, and it's in relation to a serious matter. I think we should meet."

"You've got a nerve, I'll give you that, but if you have something to say, say it now."

"This isn't a subject we can discuss over the phone. It would be much better if we could talk in person."

"I think not. I've given you a chance to speak and you've declined, so let's leave it at that. Goodbye, Mr Corrigan."

"It's about Seb," Dan blurted, then he waited, listening. Had Tom hung up?

No. Tom was still there, and his voice took on a sharper edge. "Choose your next words very carefully. Seb was a friend."

"I'm sorry for your loss," Dan said. "But I have reason to believe that Seb knew about a crime that had been committed at CEG. That could be the reason he was killed."

"Killed? But I thought it was…" Tom's voice faltered as if the wind had been taken from his sails.

Either he's shocked or he's a good actor, Dan thought. *Which is it?*

Before Dan could decide, Tom spoke again: "Okay. I'm probably going to regret this, but we can meet. I suggest that you come into Exeter tomorrow morning, and unless I change my mind, I'll give you five minutes."

"I'd rather meet today. This can't wait."

Tom grumbled under his breath, his words indistinct, then: "All right. Let's get this over with. I'm at Haytor. Do you know it?"

"Yes. What are you doing up there?"

"I come here a lot. It takes my mind off things, and today I needed to be here."

"I understand. I can be there within about…" Dan took the phone away from his mouth and looked to Alan, murmuring, "Haytor".

"Twenty-five minutes," Alan replied. "Call it half an hour."

Resuming his call, Dan said, "I'll be there in thirty minutes. Where shall we meet?"

"I'll be at the tor. You'll have no trouble finding me. There's hardly anyone about." Tom paused then added, "And, Dan, come alone."

"All right," Dan replied, but Tom had already ended the call.

THERE WERE two main car parks near the impressive outcrop of bare rock known as Haytor: one at the foot of the slope that led up to the tor itself, and one higher up that offered easier access for those tourists who weren't ready to plod up the hill.

Driving alone, and doing his best to ignore the racket coming from the Toyota's engine, Dan arrived at the higher car park and found it almost empty. Selecting a spot that provided a view of the tor, he steered his Toyota around the worst of the potholes and parked. When he killed the engine, its rumbling was replaced by the sound of the wind rushing over the moor, and Dan reached around and groped for the waterproof coat he kept on the back seat. Thankfully, the coat was where it ought to be, and Dan grabbed it before stepping from the car and locking up.

As he donned his coat, the wind tugged at the fabric, and Dan knew that the moor had fooled him again. Despite the blue sky, and the fact that it was supposed to be summer, the wind was fresh enough to sting his cheeks and make his eyes stream. Even so, he breathed deep, his nerves tingling, savouring the moment. *I'm finally getting somewhere*, he thought. *Tom must be involved, or he wouldn't have agreed to meet me.* But if their meeting turned into a confrontation, how would Tom react? Physically, he was no match for Dan, but then again, Seb had been young and fit, and that hadn't saved him.

Dan checked his phone, pleased to see that Alan had already sent him a text. Alan had driven to the tor separately, and he was now in the lower car park. He'd make his way up the hillside on foot, ready to step in.

Dan set off toward the tor, striding along the rough path that was part black mud and part bare rock, a grim smile on his lips. Despite the feeling of uncertainty, it was good to be outdoors and active, going up against the unforgiving landscape, and he could hardly wait to get to the top. He was finally getting somewhere, every step taking him closer to the point where he could untangle the insidious web of events that had drawn him in.

Whatever underhand game they were running at CEG, Tom was a key player, and whatever Tom threw at him, Dan would be ready.

CHAPTER 47

Crossing Southernhay East in Exeter, DS Kulkarni cast her eye over the elegant building advertising itself as Amberley Court. The tall brick building was clearly old, but it had been tastefully renovated, its double-glazed windows framed in white-painted wood rather than ugly modern PVC, and its ornate iron guttering and downpipes had been restored rather than replaced with utilitarian plastic. Kulkarni climbed the stone steps to the broad wooden door and found a brass doorbell mounted to one side. Although the building was divided into several flats, there was only one call button, so she pressed it and waited.

A second later, a woman's voice issued from somewhere above her: "Hello, madam. How may I help you?"

Kulkarni looked up. She couldn't see where the voice had come from, but she'd been addressed as madam, so there must be a concealed camera.

She produced her warrant card and held it up. "I'm Detective Sergeant Kulkarni, Devon and Cornwall Police. I have an appointment with Mr Christopher Champley."

"Thank you, Detective Sergeant. Please step inside. Mr Champley will meet you in the entrance hall."

"Thanks." Kulkarni didn't hear the door unlock, but when she pressed it, the door swung open and she stepped into a well-lit hallway: a generously proportioned space with framed watercolours on the wall and a mosaic-tiled floor that looked like an original feature.

Kulkarni tried the inner door. It was locked, but it wasn't long before the door opened and a well-groomed man appeared, his white shirt setting off his deep tan, which had no doubt been his intention. With a broad smile he advanced on Kulkarni, his arm outstretched for a shake. "Detective Sergeant, thank you for being so prompt. I do appreciate it. Busy day."

"For me too," Kulkarni replied, shaking his hand briefly. "I won't take up much of your time. Shall we go inside?"

Champley's smile became more guarded. "If you wouldn't mind, could you explain what it is that you're looking for?"

"As I said on the phone, we believe that your CCTV may have captured vital evidence that could help in an ongoing inquiry."

"Yes, but what kind of inquiry are we talking about?"

Kulkarni fixed the man with a hard stare. "Does it matter?"

"No, of course not. It's just..." Champley offered an awkward shrug, his hands making tiny circles in the air as if he'd like to help, but he couldn't possibly manage it. "You know how it is, Detective Sergeant. As the owner of the building, I have to consider the privacy of my tenants."

"That's not an issue. We're not interested in the people who live here, nor in their comings and goings. We simply want to see any CCTV that shows the street. That's a public area, so you really have no grounds to object. I'm only looking at one day: the 7th of June. You do have recordings going back that far, don't you?"

"Yes. We keep a rolling backup, but—"

"That's great," Kulkarni interrupted. "If I can take a look at that footage, there'll be no need to take up any more of your valuable time."

Champley looked distinctly uncomfortable, but he stood his ground, barring the way.

"Mr Champley, I'm investigating a serious incident that may well have been an attempted murder, and it happened right in front of your building. Now, under section nineteen of the Police and Criminal Evidence Act, I can seize the recordings, but then I'll probably have to take all the relevant hard drives for analysis, and that could take some time."

"Oh dear," Champley said. "That would be most inconvenient."

"Quite, and I'm not sure how your tenants might react when they see a bunch of uniformed officers loading your fancy computer hardware into the back of a police van."

Champley's eyes widened, and his expensive tan couldn't quite conceal the rush of blood to his cheeks.

"What do you say?" Kulkarni went on. "Might it be best if we sort this out between us, get it done?"

"Well, I suppose that might be the most suitable course of action."

"Yes. Shall we?" Kulkarni indicated the door and Champley stepped back, ushering her inside.

Beyond the inner door the hallway continued, but Kulkarni found herself walking on a luxuriously deep carpet. Ahead, a grand staircase climbed upward, but Champley opened an unmarked wooden door and led her onto a much narrower downward stairway, the treads uncarpeted but the wood sanded smooth and bleached to show the fine grain. It seemed that the style below stairs was more modern and minimalist than at street level: polished chrome, pale wood and shades of grey. *All very Ikea*, Kulkarni thought, but she kept it to herself; the remark would almost certainly render

Mr Champley speechless, and that would defeat the object of her visit.

Instead, she adopted a friendly tone and said, "You keep the security footage in the basement?"

"We call it the Garden Floor because it opens onto the walled garden at the rear of the building, but yes, the office is on this level. There's a gym and a sauna, too, but here we are." He showed Kulkarni into a small room that had all the fittings of a modern office. At the single desk, a woman looked up from her work, eyeing Kulkarni shyly from behind a pair of widescreen computer monitors.

Kulkarni presumed that this was the woman who'd spoken to her at the door, though she seemed much more timid than might've been expected. Perhaps she was more comfortable interacting over an intercom than in person.

"Shazia, this is Detective Sergeant Kulkarni," Champley said. "I'd like you to show her the CCTV from…" He looked to Kulkarni. "What date was it?"

"June 7th," Kulkarni said. "Late afternoon. Say, four o'clock onwards."

Shazia nodded nervously. "From all the cameras?"

"How many are there?" Kulkarni asked.

"Twelve," Champley replied. "It's a state-of-the-art system. Widescreen field of view, recorded in high definition with audio, plus we have night vision recordings for after dark."

Kulkarni raised an eyebrow. "That's very thorough. Any particular reason for that?"

"It's mainly for insurance purposes," Champley said. "But anything that gives my tenants peace of mind is worth it."

"I see. Now I know why you were reluctant to give me access. There can't be much that goes on without you seeing it."

"That's not the case at all," Champley blustered. "I can assure you that—"

"Never mind," Kulkarni interrupted. "All I'm interested in is the view along the street, towards the CEG office."

"That ugly heap of bricks," Champley sneered. "What've they been doing now?"

"You've had dealings with the company?" Kulkarni asked.

"No, not really, but one hears things."

"Such as?"

Champley's lips tightened as if he'd said too much, but Kulkarni wasn't going to let him off the hook. "Mr Champley, I have to tell you that I'm also looking into a suspicious death that has connections with CEG, so anything you can tell me might be helpful."

"Suspicious death? You mean someone was murdered?"

"I can't comment on that, but if you have any information regarding the company, you'd better tell me now."

Champley ran a hand over his brow. "Goodness. I'm sure I don't know anything that might help. It's just that one of my tenants is an executive there, and whenever I bump into her, she always grumbles about the place. I shouldn't have mentioned it really. I expect it's simply office politics: nothing serious, nothing to write home about."

Kulkarni produced her personal notebook and a pen. "Who are we talking about?"

Champley looked as though he might refuse to answer, but then he relented. "I suppose you'd find out easily enough. It's Ms Steele."

"Melanie Steele?"

Champley nodded, and Kulkarni flipped back through the pages of her notebook. As part of the Cooper case, she'd been assigned a number of the deceased's erstwhile colleagues to interview at home, and Melanie Steele was on the list. But according to her notes, Ms Steele lived quite a way out of town, so Kulkarni had planned to drive out later.

"That's odd," Kulkarni said. "I have a different address for Ms Steele."

"Oh, she has a cottage out in the sticks," Champley replied. "But I understand it takes her a while to drive home, and you know what the traffic can be like in rush hour, so she keeps an apartment here as a pied-à-terre."

"Very convenient." Kulkarni made a note. "Do you happen to know if Ms Steele is at home today?"

"She's not," Shazia piped up. "She told me she'd be at her cottage all day."

"That would be her cottage in the village of Church Green, is that right?"

Shazia looked to Champley for approval, and reluctantly he nodded.

"Yes," Shazia said. "Weatherdown Cottage. She showed me a photo once, on her phone. It looked lovely."

"I expect I'll have to see it for myself at some point." Kulkarni snapped her notebook shut. "In the meantime, I'd like to see that CCTV footage. 7th of June. View of the street."

"Right." Shazia chewed on her lower lip as she focused on her monitors, her right hand moving the mouse deftly, fingers clicking the buttons. A few seconds later, she looked up. "Ready?"

"Absolutely." Kulkarni moved into position next to Shazia, pleased to see a crystal-clear view of Southernhay East displayed on the monitor.

Champley made a show of clearing his throat. "I'd better see this as well, keep an eye on things."

"That's fine," Kulkarni replied, and Champley sidled up to her, screwing up his eyes as he peered at the screen.

"You can see the CEG offices just there," Shazia said. "Is that okay?"

"It's perfect, Shazia. Is this a recording?"

"No, this is live. I wanted to check I'd got the right camera."

Kulkarni rewarded her with a smile. "Well, you've nailed it. You're a star. Can we see June the 7th?"

"Sure." Shazia's second monitor showed a list of files and folders, and with a few clicks, the screen filled with a monochrome version of the same scene. "This is from just after midnight," Shazia went on. "I'll skip forward to four o'clock."

The screen altered, the image growing bright and showing a few cars gliding past.

"Can you speed up the playback?" Kulkarni asked.

"Of course we can," Champley replied. "Do you want me to take over, Shazia?"

Shazia looked like she was trying very hard not to roll her eyes. "No thanks. I know how to do it."

As the playback sped up, Kulkarni said. "You can go faster. Stop if you see anyone coming out of the CEG building."

"No problem."

On the screen, pedestrians began to race along the pavements while cars flitted past in a blur. Kulkarni had her eyes glued to the front of the CEG building, but even so, she almost missed the dark figure she was looking for. "Stop."

Shazia halted the playback, looking up at Kulkarni in confusion. "No one came out the door. I was watching very carefully."

"He didn't use the main door," Kulkarni said. "Rewind it a bit, slowly, and you'll see what I mean."

The playback reversed, and a man appeared in the mouth of an alley beside the building. It was Dan Corrigan; she'd recognise his self-confident poise anywhere. "That's the man we're looking for. Play it forward as slowly as you can."

The room was silent as the drama unfolded in slow motion on the monitor. Dan Corrigan looked around, then he broke into a slow run. Before long, he looked both ways then he set off across the road. But where was the car?

Kulkarni held her breath. She'd taken Dan at his word,

swallowed every detail of his version of events, but had he made a mistake? Or worse, had he lied to her?

But then she saw the black Volvo S90, veering out from a parking space at the limit of the camera's vision. Without pause, it lurched into the road and headed toward Dan Corrigan.

"Stop!" Kulkarni said, and the image froze, Dan turning as the car sped toward him.

"Rewind it slowly," Kulkarni went on, a deep sense of dread churning in her stomach. She'd made a mistake. Days ago, her instincts had made her wonder if Dan Corrigan had been targeted deliberately, but after her visit to the printworks in Plymouth, she'd allowed herself to be distracted by the pursuit of Jez Parker and his cousins. Here was the evidence that she'd been wrong to ignore her intuition.

As the footage ran backwards, she watched the car reverse into a parking space. It had been near the CEG building, waiting.

"Play it again, as slowly as you can," Kulkarni said.

At a snail's pace, the car pulled out and raced toward Dan. He made a spirited attempt to escape, moving toward the camera, the car swerving as it made to follow him, mounting the pavement. Dan hoisted himself over an iron railing and disappeared from the camera's field of view. The car hit the railing then veered away.

Shazia winced as she watched. "Oh no! Was he all right?"

"Yes, he was lucky," Kulkarni said, straightening her back. "You can stop the playback now. Thank you." To Champley, she added, "That's the footage I'll need."

"Yes. Naturally I'll do whatever I can to help." Champley stared at her, blinking as though befuddled. "That was horrendous. I've never seen anything like it. That car went straight for him."

"I'll make arrangements to have this footage collected," Kulkarni said. "We have a technical team who specialise in this kind of thing. You needn't worry. They're experts in what they do."

"I could put it on a memory stick for you," Shazia offered.

"Thank you, but no. This is a serious crime, and the evidence has to be handled properly. In fact, I'll have to wait here until the team arrive. I'll give them a call now. They won't be long."

"Right," Champley said. "I'll leave you to it. Unless you need me to stay, that is."

"No, that's fine. Thanks for your help, but I'll take it from here."

Seeming relieved, Champley made his exit, and Kulkarni took out her phone and called the station. When she was done, Shazia said, "I suppose you do things like this all the time."

"It's not all so dramatic, but it has its moments."

"Not like this job, then. I'm bored out of my mind half the time."

"What is it that you do, exactly?"

"Answer the door, sort the mail, keep the place tidy. I look after the gym too." Shazia shrugged. "There's not much to it."

"Would you be able to tell me on which dates Ms Steele was staying here, and when she was away?"

"Well, yeah, I could try, but I don't know what Mr Champley would say about that. I ought to—"

"I'm sure it'll be fine, Shazia. You heard what he said: anything to help."

"Yeah, he did say that, but Ms Steele hasn't got anything to do with that car trying to run that man over, has she?"

"I can't comment on that, but as I mentioned before, I'll be talking to Ms Steele in relation to another matter. It would be helpful to have an idea about her movements over the last couple of weeks. Can you do that for me?"

"I can give it a go, but it's not like people check in and out. I don't usually see the tenants unless they're complaining about something or when they use the gym." Shazia smiled. "Ms Steele uses the gym quite a lot, and she sometimes brings a man with her. He's very good looking."

Kulkarni tried not to react. She'd seen photos of Seb Cooper, professional headshots from his online profiles, and he'd certainly been photogenic. Keeping her tone neutral, she said, "You didn't happen to catch the man's name, did you? It might be important."

"I don't think so, but he was very nice. A bit of a charmer."

"Does the name Sebastian Cooper ring any bells?"

"Er, yeah, she called him something like that." Shazia frowned. "Seb, that was it."

"Okay, that's very helpful. If you could work out when Ms Steele and her male friend were here together, that would be great."

"Right. I'll try. I'll check the calendar."

While Shazia busied herself at the computer, Kulkarni watched, her mind a whirl. Melanie Steele had worked with Sebastian Cooper, so it wasn't surprising that they sometimes met after work. Kulkarni knew from the last briefing that Cooper had been a fitness buff, and Amberley Court provided a nearby gym. It might mean nothing, but she'd follow it up, just in case.

I'm going to be swamped, Kulkarni thought. *Pulled in two directions at once.* Because after the scene she'd just witnessed, she'd need to re-examine the theft of the Volvo. It was increasingly looking like a copycat crime, the car stolen not for resale, but for one explicit purpose: the attack on Dan Corrigan. Someone had tried to kill him, but who and why?

Either Mr Corrigan had an uncanny knack for landing himself in trouble, or he was somehow involved in the murder of Sebastian Cooper. She needed to speak to Dan again, because one way or another, he was in danger. Next time, he might not be so lucky.

CHAPTER 48

Have I been sent on a fool's errand? Dan asked himself as he approached Haytor, because there was no sign of Tom Hastings. Dan had passed a few groups of dog walkers on his way up the slope, all heading back toward the car park, their faces pinched and their eyes streaming. The unseasonably cold wind had grown stronger with every step of the hike up the hill, and Dan wasn't entirely surprised to find the tor itself deserted. In this weather, it wasn't a place to hang around.

But Dan was getting used to the vagaries of Dartmoor's microclimate, and he set off to walk around the tor, undaunted. He soon reached the far side of the rocky outcrop, an area out of sight of the road, and he found Tom leaning against the rock face as if sheltering from the wind.

Before Dan could call out a greeting, Tom strode forward to meet him, and Dan felt a prickling in his scalp that might've been sweat from his walk up the slope or might've been anxiety. The two men were alone, the rugged mass of the tor on one side and the bleak emptiness of the moor stretching out in every other direction. Dan looked around, hoping to find that Alan was on his way, but he couldn't see him.

Hopefully, Alan had found a way to keep out of sight as he approached. He knew the moor, and he'd be out there somewhere, marching steadfastly up the hill. *He'll be here soon,* Dan told himself. *I can depend on that.*

In the meantime, Dan focused his attention on Tom Hastings. The man was fidgety and on edge, his hands in constant motion as though he couldn't decide what to do with them. He had a glint in his eye, and an odd grin fluttered on his lips as if he'd just thought of some joke at Dan's expense.

"You found me," Tom said. "I thought you might not come. Thought you might chicken out."

"Not me." Dan made a show of looking around, unfazed. "It's an interesting place to meet."

"I like it. I like the solitude. It gives me perspective, helps me to see things clearly."

"Is that why you wanted me to come alone?"

Tom's lopsided grin was back. "No. That's because I don't trust you."

"Fair enough, and since we're putting our cards on the table, the feeling's mutual."

"I thought as much. That's why we're going to do something."

"What?"

"Follow me." Tom headed back to the tor, and Dan followed at a distance. Tom made straight for a cleft in the rock and he bent to retrieve something, dragging a heavy object into view.

Dan halted, his instincts telling him to keep back, but when Tom straightened up, he held only a large rucksack, its sides bulging.

"I won't be a jiffy," Tom said, busy with the rucksack's

fastenings, then he glanced back at Dan, adding, "No need to look so worried. It's only my gear."

"What kind of gear?"

"This kind." Tom tugged a bright orange plastic helmet from the bag, and he tossed it to Dan, who lunged forward to catch it with both hands. "Pop it on," Tom went on. "You never know when you might need it."

Dan turned the helmet in his hands, unsure how to react.

Tom heaved a theatrical sigh. "Listen, Dan, we're not going to get anywhere unless we can speak plainly, and we can't do that until we're sure of each other, so we're going to climb up the tor together. Climbing is all about trust."

"That's not—"

"I won't talk to you any other way," Tom insisted. "We'll climb up, talk at the top." He smiled. "Call it a show of faith, from both sides."

Dan ran his eyes over the near vertical face of the tor, the rugged granite worn smooth in places by the wind and rain. He'd messed about on a few climbing walls in his time, but they'd been indoors: carefully controlled environments with thick crash pads on the floor. This climb would be much more unpredictable, but even so, he could pick out plenty of cracks and grooves in the rock that would serve as handholds and footholds. He was younger than Tom and probably in much better shape. *If he can do it, so can I*, Dan thought. *It might help me to get past his defences*. Tom seemed to pride himself on being difficult, recalcitrant even, but this shared endeavour could provide a way in.

"All right," Dan said. "If that's what it takes."

"Good. Come and have a look. I'll show you the route." Tom led Dan to the foot of the tor. "The route we'll use is called Bulging Wall, and as you can see, it lives up to its name. I assume it was christened by a climber with not much imagination. Some of the other names are far more interesting." He smiled and pointed to one side. "There's a route over there called Accomplice to Murder."

Dan looked Tom in the eye. "Is there something you're trying to tell me?"

"No, I was just making conversation. I suppose the name must've been someone's idea of a joke."

"Hilarious."

"Each to his own." Tom studied the rock face, his eyes narrow. "We'll use the crack to climb up to the horizontal break, then we'll move left a bit and rest on that ledge for a second. When you've got your breath back, we'll head for the top. There are plenty of good holds. I'll go first. Follow me and you won't go far wrong. Okay?"

"Erm, shouldn't we have ropes?"

"That would take all the fun out of it," Tom said. "This is only a bit of bouldering. We're not tackling the north face of Everest."

"Still, it looks tricky. What if we slip?"

Tom screwed up his features. "You'll be all right. Admittedly, I usually have a crash pad, but I couldn't be bothered to lug it all the way up here, so my advice to you is, don't fall." Tom watched Dan as if gauging his reaction, then he added, "Ah, you're going to go for it, I can tell. Excellent. Sometimes in life, you need to take a risk. It gives you an edge, makes you push harder, makes it all worthwhile. You know perfectly well what I mean, Dan. Don't pretend you don't understand. I can see it in your eyes. You have that drive, that urge to succeed, don't you?"

"Sometimes," Dan admitted. "When it matters."

"There you go, then. If what you want to talk about is so important, you'll put your fears aside and make it to the top of this tor."

"All right. Show me the route."

"Just a sec." Tom returned to his rucksack and pulled out a

small fabric bag. Bringing it back, he offered it to Dan. "Chalk. To keep your fingers nice and dry. Help yourself."

"Thanks." Dan dipped his hand into the bag, coating his fingers in the fine powder. Tom did the same, then he hooked the bag onto his belt. It was then that Dan noticed Tom was wearing proper climbing shoes, and he glanced down at his own feet. His trainers looked clumsy in comparison, but still, they had plenty of tread on them, so they should grip the rock pretty well. He'd do his best to climb, and if it looked like he wasn't going to make it, he could always climb down. But he wouldn't back out lightly; not unless he really had to.

"Here we go," Tom said and started to climb, making short work of hoisting himself up the rock face, finding holds for his hands and feet with a practised ease.

It looks easy enough, Dan told himself. *Here goes*. Following Tom's example, he placed his foot in a small hollow and pushed himself upward, then he gripped the edge of the vertical crack in the rock and held on. The angle of his wrist felt unnatural, and he wouldn't want to hold it for long, but he could already see the holds Tom had used, and Dan kept moving, trying hard to keep pace.

Hand over hand, Dan focused on the climb, his fingers scrabbling at the unforgiving rock, his toes jammed into holes that were never quite big enough. Sweat ran across his forehead, trickling into the corners of his eyes. He'd thought himself fit, but his muscles were unused to taking his weight while stretching to their limits, and his joints complained if he stayed in one position for too long. He had to keep moving, keep reaching up.

But what was this?

Above him, Tom had stopped, his legs splayed and his feet planted firmly on either side of the vertical crack they were using to climb.

"What's up?" Dan called out. "Why have you stopped?"

"Just a second," Tom replied. "Tricky bit here. Got to pull ourselves onto the ledge. Hang on."

"Okay." Dan risked a glance down, and his head spun. Now he knew how the route got its name. Without realising it, he'd climbed onto the part of the tor's face that bulged outward, and beneath him, the rock curved inward, sweeping away beneath his feet. He tried to pick out the holds he'd used just moments ago, but the shift in perspective confused him, and suddenly the bare rock seemed brutal to the point of hostility. To make matters worse, the cold wind had grown stronger as he'd climbed, and it tugged at his coat as if determined to yank him from his tenuous perch. Despite the wind, Dan could hold on a little longer; it wasn't as if he had much choice.

"Watch what I do," Tom said, then he stretched out one leg impossibly wide, bracing his toe against a protrusion that was little more than a bump in the rock. Tom launched himself upward, both hands stretching above his head, and somehow he latched onto something Dan couldn't see. In the same motion, Tom swung his body sideways, then he vanished from view, disappearing over a horizontal lip in the rock.

Dan stared in horror, but a moment later, Tom's face appeared, looking down on him, his cheeks flushed. "This is the ledge I told you about," Tom said. "You can rest when you get here."

"I don't know," Dan replied. "I don't think I can do what you just did. I don't have the experience."

"Nonsense. It looks daunting because the face slopes outward a bit, but it really isn't all that technical. You're taller than me, so you'll do it easily."

"I'm not sure. Is there another way?"

"There is, but it's even harder. Listen to me, Dan, you can do this. There's a handhold to your right. Stretch up and get a good grip, then pull yourself up and do like I did. You want to end up with one foot on either side of the crack, okay? Can you see the handhold?"

Dan blinked the sweat from his eyes and peered upward. Yes, he could see a small hole on his right, and it might've been the one Tom had just used, but it was tiny. He could maybe get two fingers in it if he was lucky.

"Come on, Dan," Tom urged. "You'll be fine."

Dan drew a breath to clear his head. His muscles were tiring, his legs trembling, and the chalk had worn from his hands, leaving his fingers sweaty. He couldn't stay where he was, and he didn't have the energy or the skill to climb down. He needed a rest, and he could do that on the ledge. All he had to do was press on and climb a little higher. He could do that, couldn't he?

He pushed his fingers into the handhold and tested his grip. *It's okay*, he told himself. *I've got this.* Feeling a little more confident, he stretched his right leg, and his foot found a place to rest. He did the same on the left. But then came the tricky part. He'd have to brace his foot further out and shove himself up.

"You're doing well," Tom said. "Want me to talk you through the next bit?"

"Yes. Yes please."

"No problem. But first, tell me why you came here."

"You want to do this now?"

"Why not? It's as good a place as any."

"No, it isn't. You said we'd talk at the top. We had a deal."

"Change of plan. Tell me what this is about, or you're on your own."

Dan gritted his teeth. How the hell had he managed to get himself into this mess? Unfortunately, the answer was all too clear: he'd underestimated his opponent. Tom played the part of the bumbling middle-aged man, out of step and out of favour, but he'd outmanoeuvred Dan every step of the way. *I allowed myself to be taken in*, Dan thought. *But I can't let him win.*

"Help me over this next part, and then we'll talk," Dan said. "What I have to say is too complex to go into while I'm down here and you're up there."

Tom jiggled his head from side to side as if considering Dan's suggestion. "Nope. I've gone to some effort to leave you dangling, and it would be a shame for all that to go to waste. Talk, Corrigan, and don't try to bullshit me. Let's have the truth."

"Not like this. I won't play your game, Tom. I'd rather climb down, take the risk."

"I don't believe you." Tom chuckled darkly. "You know, you're too easy to read, Corrigan. It was child's play to get you to do exactly what I wanted. That's the problem with your lot; you're always so busy bleating about some perceived slight or other that you don't notice the fact that you're leaving yourself wide open."

"My lot?"

"Snowflakes. You go around, holier than thou, explaining in painstaking detail about every tiny thing that offends you, then you act surprised when someone sticks the knife in."

"Is that what happened to Seb? You stuck the knife in?"

Tom's sneer turned into a fierce glare, his eyes burning with an ice-cold fury. From between clenched teeth, he said, "Seb was my friend."

"That may be so, but he died nonetheless. I want to find out what happened to him. Are you going to help me or not?"

Tom didn't reply, and Dan knew he had to wait, allow time for his words to sink in. But how long did he have?

Dan's calf muscles were burning now, his legs trembling. He tried to take more of his weight on his arms, but one way or another, he had to move soon.

Above him, Tom muttered something under his breath. Dan couldn't make out the words, but he detected a change in

Tom's expression; he was almost ready to talk. It was a question of which would give first, Tom's defiance or Dan's grip.

Dan pressed himself against the rock, and he craned his neck to peer across the moor. Where the hell was Alan? He ought to have been in sight by now. Something must've gone wrong.

Dan looked back up, and his stomach tightened. Tom was turning, backing away from the edge as if getting ready to move on.

"Wait!" Dan called out. "You can't leave me like this."

"I can, and I will."

Tom was almost out of sight now. Dan's only chance was to make it to that ledge, with or without Tom's help.

Dan fixed his gaze on the foothold Tom had used. He should be able to reach it and then push off from there, but he'd have to commit to the move and do it in one go.

"Oh God," he muttered, then he went for it. His right foot found the place, and he transferred his weight, letting go of his handholds, his left foot dangling in mid-air. With only his right leg to rely on, he pushed himself upward as hard as he could, his arms stretched high. His fingers found the horizontal lip in the rock face, and he held on to it with all his might. Heaving himself up, he tried to swing his body up and onto the ledge. He was almost there. But he'd misjudged the distance, and he didn't have enough momentum to swing himself up. Gravity yanked his body, and he swung down, dangling from his arms, his legs flailing in empty space. Dan's hands slipped, his fingertips scrabbling for purchase, but there was nothing to sink his nails into, only bare rock.

His fingers slid closer to the edge, and he growled in frustration, focussing all his strength on the simple act of holding on. But it wasn't enough. He was going to fall, and he couldn't do anything to prevent it.

CHAPTER 49

G eoff Higgins dragged the aluminium stepladder into the narrow space between two towering shelving units. Squinting up at the labels on the cardboard archive boxes, he checked the reference number he'd written carefully on his notepad. Yes. This was the place.

It was tricky to unfold the stepladder in such a confined space, but he won in the end, and he made sure the ladder's safety latch was engaged before setting foot on the lowest tread. Geoff vaguely recalled receiving a memo about using the stepladder when he was alone in the archive. He was supposed to fill in a risk assessment form or some such nonsense, but he wasn't going to bother with that.

The stepladder creaked beneath his weight as he climbed, but it was fine. Steady as a rock.

He reached the right height, almost at the top of the stepladder, and he scanned the shelf, searching for his prize.

"Where have you got to?" he muttered. That business with the stepladder had put him off his stride, and he'd lost sight of the damned box.

Of course. He'd placed the stepladder's feet directly beneath the box, but he hadn't accounted for the angle of the stepladder's frame, so he'd ended up in the wrong place. But no matter. He spied the box, and he could still reach it. If he stood on one leg and balanced carefully while he stretched out his arm…

His fingers brushed the corner of the box, and he felt the stepladder sway, just a little.

Geoff scowled and tried again, trying to shift his weight to counterbalance his awkward position. This time, he gripped the side of the box and slid it closer. Another creak came from the stepladder's frame, and it shifted, threatening to throw him off balance.

Geoff let go of the box and righted himself, clinging to the top of the stepladder, his heart beating a tattoo against his ribs. *Idiot!*

He'd nearly gone then. How stupid would that have been?

His legs shaking, Geoff climbed down and shoved the stepladder into the right place. There. That was much better.

He climbed up with renewed confidence, and when he pulled out the right box and felt its weight, he was glad he'd been careful.

What the heck was in this box, house bricks? He had to carry it with both hands, so he couldn't grip the stepladder as he climbed down. It took all his concentration to make it down to the concrete floor without toppling, but he did it, and he beamed as he bore the box back to his desk.

Time for a mug of tea, he thought. He'd need it. Judging by the weight of the box, he was going to get through a gallon of the stuff before he was done.

He was wrong about that.

Two hours later, his half-finished mug of tea forgotten at his side, Geoff plucked a sheet of yellowing paper from a folder and read it for the second time, his spirits soaring.

"Got you," he whispered, then he pushed off with his feet, sending his swivel chair sideways along the desk. There, he laid down the new sheet of paper alongside four others, forming a neat row.

Five reports in date order, each one revealing a piece of the puzzle. He'd started in the period immediately after the murder of Jackie Blatch, then worked backwards, following a thread. Now the picture was complete.

In December of 1942, a new warehouse was being built on the land formerly owned by Blatch, but there was trouble on the site, the workers harassed, even attacked. There was speculation that the site's new owner was the real target. Strangely, the owner's name was missing from the file, but it was noted that he was an immigrant from Russia, and there was a suggestion that locals hadn't forgotten the fact that Russia had sided with Germany in the early years of the war. Nothing came of the case, and there were no arrests, so presumably the trouble had died down.

Geoff's intuition had told him to search for any hint of a Russian connection and he'd worked quickly, focusing on the war years. He'd found no record of a suspect from Russia being arrested or even interviewed, but he had found a report written in 1941 by Tony Barnett, then a detective constable. In a thinly veiled bid for promotion, Barnett cited thirteen arrests, all made with the help of a confidential informant: an informant identified only by the pseudonym Ivan.

The connection was far from solid, but it had piqued Geoff's interest. Going back further, he'd unearthed a case involving a protection racket. A handful of arrests had been made, mainly small-time thugs by the look of it, but not one of the cases ever made it to court. The prosecutions collapsed because the victims refused to give evidence, and one of them let slip that he feared retribution from someone he knew only as 'The Russian'.

In an even older case, a convicted housebreaker had tried to bargain for a lighter sentence by giving up his fence. He claimed to know the identity of a gang leader who'd come to England from Russia. The burglar's request was denied, his evidence discredited by DC Barnett. A note added to the report stated that the burglar had later been attacked by another inmate while in prison and he'd died of his injuries.

Finally, going back even further, Geoff had discovered a report from 1937 detailing a series of violent street robberies. In each case, the robber had been armed with a knife, and his victims had been lucky to survive. All the victims agreed that their assailant had spoken with a distinct foreign accent, possibly from Eastern Europe.

Geoff smiled. He shouldn't allow himself to be persuaded by so slim a chain of circumstantial evidence, but he could see a story laid out in front of him.

A Russian immigrant started his criminal career with mugging, and at this point he came to the attention of a police officer with a taste for the high life, Tony Barnett. The Russian co-opted DC Barnett and then carved out a territory for himself, handling stolen goods.

Surely, there can't have been many people from Eastern Europe in Exeter at the time, so Barnett's unimaginatively named informant, Ivan, was likely to be the mysterious Russian. The two worked together, the association benefitting both men. The Russian used Barnett to take out the competition, and in addition to any bribes, Barnett's clean-up rate earned him promotion to detective sergeant.

But DS Barnett had been friendly with another criminal, Jackie Blatch. The evidence for that connection was in the recordings Collins had found.

Perhaps Barnett had been greedy, playing both ends against the middle. As a police officer, he might've felt invulnerable, but he'd underestimated the ruthlessness of his co-conspirator. The Russian was playing for keeps, and he didn't abide by the rules.

The Russian disposed of DS Barnett, but only after

torturing him, perhaps to gain information about Blatch's routine. If that was the case, The Russian's plan worked.

Jackie Blatch disappeared on the walk home from his local pub. On such a short journey, and on his own turf, Blatch probably felt safe, but that was his undoing.

Killed and placed in the river, wrapped in a blanket he'd stolen from the Ministry of Defence, Blatch's body was left as a warning to his gang. To ram the point home, Blatch's warehouse of stolen goods was levelled.

There was a new boss in town, and The Russian celebrated his victory by buying up the land where Blatch's warehouse had stood, building one of his own. When the locals gave him a hard time, he dealt with them, and he must've found a new police officer to corrupt, because someone had kept The Russian's real name out of the records. But there would be a paper trail. Somewhere, the sale of the warehouse would've been registered, and with a nudge in the right direction, Collins would soon be able to find the identity of The Russian.

Geoff reached for his phone. He couldn't wait to tell Ben Collins the news, but maybe he should invite him over, give him the details in person. He pictured the look on the younger man's face when he saw the compelling narrative laid out before his eyes.

It would be worth the wait.

CHAPTER 50

Dan's hands slid slowly from the cold stone, one agonising millimetre at a time. But what could he do? He was spent, exhausted, panic running riot in his mind.

"Hold on!" The shout came from below, and Dan knew the voice instantly. *Alan!*

His friend was here, and Dan knew he couldn't, mustn't fall. Pouring his last reserves of energy into his fragile grip on the ledge, he held tight with his right hand, while his left groped for a more secure handhold. There was nothing, not so much as a hairline crack in the stone he could latch on to. But then his wrist was being grabbed, firm fingers wrapping around his forearm. He was being hauled upward.

"I've got you," Tom growled. "Come on."

Grunting, Dan did his best to help, and somehow his upper body crested the lip of rock. The ledge was narrower than Dan had expected, and Tom was taking up much of it, leaning back and bracing himself, the better to pull Dan upward.

With a final tug, Tom heaved Dan onto the ledge. "You're safe," Tom said. "Sit down. Rest."

Space was tight, but Dan turned around and did as he was

told, sitting on the ledge, his feet dangling over the edge. Still breathing hard, he leaned forward to peer down to the ground. Alan had reached the tor, and he was staring upward, one hand shading his eyes. Dan lifted his arm in greeting and called out, "I'm okay. I'm fine."

"Thank God for that," Alan replied. "Do you need help? Should I call someone?"

Dan glanced at Tom before replying. Tom stood at the end of the ledge, leaning his back against the rock face, and he was watching Dan as if mildly amused. If he'd intended to harm Dan, the moment had passed.

"No, it'll be all right," Dan called down to Alan. "Tom helped me out."

"I saw. Listen, I'm sorry I didn't get here sooner. I went through the quarry, and it took me longer than I thought."

"Don't worry about it, Alan. No harm done."

"Thank goodness. Are you heading to the top?"

"I don't know," Dan replied, then to Tom: "Are we?"

Tom nodded. "It's the only thing to do from here. We're almost there. Plenty of holds. It's not hard."

"That's what you said before we started," Dan said. "I almost fell. I could've broken my neck."

"That's a bit dramatic. Anyway, the next part is easier. You'll be fine."

"What about getting down again?"

"There's an easy way. I'll show you."

Dan tried to read Tom's expression, but the man gave nothing away. "All right." He waved to Alan and said, "I'll see you in a bit."

"I'll meet you at the top," Alan replied.

"There's no need. You can wait down there."

"Nonsense. I'm coming up, but I'll go around to the other side." As if to head off any argument, Alan marched off, and Dan quickly lost sight of him. *Good old Alan*, Dan thought. *I ought to have known he'd turn up in the nick of time.*

Tom sat next to Dan. "A friend of yours, I presume."

"Alan. A friend and neighbour."

"So, you didn't come on your own. You're not as daft as I thought."

"It seems we underestimated each other." Dan hesitated. "As a matter of interest, would you have helped me if Alan hadn't turned up at that moment?"

"Yes. I wanted to push your buttons, I'll admit, but I'm not a monster. You were never in any real danger."

"I'm not sure about that."

"I gave you a helmet, didn't I? Besides, I knew you'd be all right. It's amazing how we can find the strength when we really need to. When it matters, we can achieve things we never thought possible. Seb showed me that. He opened my eyes."

Dan's heart, already racing, skipped a beat. *This is it*, he thought. *This is what this whole charade was about.* Tom was the kind of man who bottled things up, but he had something he needed to say: a burden he could no longer carry alone. Tom hadn't been able to come out and say what was on his mind. He'd felt compelled to lead Dan on a dance, string him along, make him vulnerable.

Very well, if that was his game, Dan could play along. It would be worth it to get to the truth.

"Thanks for helping me up," Dan said. "I appreciate it."

"No problem. The funny thing is, seeing you dangling down there reminded me of something that happened with Seb. He introduced me to climbing, and one day he left me hanging. He wanted to teach me a lesson, and you know what? I thanked him. He was right. I needed shaking out of my comfort zone."

"Tell me about Seb," Dan said. "Was he a close friend?"

"I thought so. We climbed together whenever we could. Oh, he was so much better than me, but it didn't seem to matter, and it did me the world of good. Before I met Seb, I'd been stuck in a rut. I'd forgotten what it felt like to take risks, but risks are what makes life worth living, aren't they? It's the element of danger that lets you know you're alive." Tom smiled sadly. "That's another lesson Seb taught me. I'll always be grateful to him for that."

As if lost in a memory, Tom looked out over the landscape, his expression serene.

Speaking softly, Dan said, "What other risks did Seb encourage you to take?"

If Tom had heard Dan's question, he didn't show it.

"For instance," Dan went on, "was it his idea to involve you in the fraud at CEG?"

Tom didn't take his eyes from the rolling moorland. His only reaction was to say, "What fraud?"

"Neil Hawthorne told me all about it. Shipments go astray and are claimed against insurance."

Tom's eyebrows lowered, and he turned his cold gaze on Dan. "I have no idea what you're talking about. I don't know how Neil could've got such a wild idea into his head. Neil was head of online operations, but he didn't have anything to do with the merchandise or the logistics of moving it around. That wasn't his field."

"Nevertheless, he found the evidence and put it together. That's why he was fired."

"No, that's not right. Neil was okay, in his way, and I quite liked him, but the truth is he lost his job because he was burned out. He couldn't keep up with the pace of change, and I'm starting to understand how he felt. I've had enough of being treated like an indentured servant." The corners of Tom's lips turned down. "You know, they even asked me to spy on him. My own friend. As if I'd do that."

"Someone asked you to spy on Seb? Who?"

"It doesn't matter."

"It might," Dan said. "Why don't you tell me, let me be the judge?"

Tom studied Dan for a moment, then said, "Melanie Steele. She wanted me to ask Seb questions, find out what his game plan was and report back to her. I didn't do it, of course. Life might've been easier if I'd gone along with it, but I had to draw the line somewhere, and that was it. I defied her. My one small act of rebellion." Tom's heavy sigh ended with a rueful smile. "I expect I've shot myself in the foot. They'll never give me a decent reference now, but I'll have to manage. I won't stay at CEG, not for another day."

"Moving on before you're found out, is that it?"

"Found out? I haven't done anything wrong. Ever. That's my problem. Maybe I'd have done better if I'd broken the rules, trodden on the backs of others, been a bit more ruthless. Sadly, that's not me." Tom let out a hollow chuckle. "I'm a yes man, through and through. I might not agree with what I'm told to do, but I generally toe the line; always have done, always will."

"But you know what's been going on, don't you? You see, I've found out where the company's secrets are hidden, and I know how to work out the password. Once more unto the breach dear friends. That's the hint, isn't it?"

"Again, you've lost me, I'm afraid. I don't know what password you're referring to. I recognise the line from *Henry V*, but I've never been keen on the bard. I'm more of a Robert Louis Stevenson fan myself. *Kidnapped*, *Treasure Island*. Stirring stuff."

"He wrote *Jekyll and Hyde*, didn't he? Very appropriate."

"Is it?"

"I'm wondering if you're a man with two sides," Dan said. "After all, until today, I'd never have imagined you climbing a sheer rock face. You clearly have another side, one that, most of the time, you're careful to conceal."

"That sounds like psychobabble to me. I've never made a secret of my hobbies, one of which is reading. By the way, the title of the book is *Strange Case of Dr Jekyll and Mr Hyde*. If you're going to use my taste in literature to accuse me of something, at least get the damned thing right."

He's deflecting, Dan thought, but before he could object, Tom let out a derisive snort and said, "Anyway, we aren't defined by what we read. By that token, you'd be an avid reader of Conan Doyle. Are you?"

"No, but then I don't see myself as some kind of detective. That rumour was started by a journalist. They embroidered the truth to spice up a story, that's all."

"Pity. Here's me, thinking I'm crossing swords with an accomplished sleuth, and it turns out you're just another corporate dogsbody like me."

"Sorry to disappoint you," Dan said. "But I am persistent, and I will find out what's been going on at CEG, no matter how long it takes."

"I don't know what you're expecting to find, but there's nothing unusual at the company. Goods are made on the cheap, moved around and sold at a profit. The margins are low, so they have to shift a lot of stuff. That's all there is to it."

"On the surface, perhaps, but as I said, I know about the secrets stored on the network at CEG. I have the IP address."

"On *my* network? What a load of rubbish. There is no secret server."

"Interesting," Dan said. "I didn't mention a server."

"It was a turn of phrase. You know what I mean."

"I know that you're not much of a liar."

The two men locked eyes for a moment, then Tom pulled himself up to his feet and said, "Come on, I'll show you the way to the top."

He offered Dan some chalk for his hands, then he started climbing and Dan followed cautiously, keeping a watchful eye on every move Tom made.

The ascent was easier than Dan had feared, and Tom made a special effort to be helpful, taking his time and being careful to point out each hold.

A few minutes later, Tom sprung nimbly onto the summit and reached down a hand to help Dan up.

"It's okay," Dan said. "I can do it."

"Suit yourself."

Tom stood back, and Dan clambered up, finding himself on a rough circle of flat rock that was several metres across. He stood beside Tom, and without speaking, they admired the view.

Tom was the first to break the silence. "You think you've caught me out, but it's not like that."

"Convince me. I'll listen."

"It's simple. At the office, there's a server on the system, and I have no idea what it's for. By the look of the thing, it's been there longer than I have, and I've often wondered about it, so when you mentioned an IP address…"

"You made a connection."

"Yes, but don't read too much into it. I jumped to a conclusion, and I'm probably wrong."

"In my experience, when people have misgivings, there's often a good reason. What makes this particular server seem suspicious?"

"I didn't say it was suspicious. That's your word, not mine, but…" Tom took a breath and exhaled slowly. "The network is a mess. A lot of the servers are past their best, but this one is practically ancient. It's obsolete. It should've been thrown out years ago, but it's been stowed away in a cabinet, mixed in with a load of old gear as if someone wanted to hide it amongst the clutter. But unlike everything else in there, this server is still connected to the network, and I have no idea why, because the damned thing is never switched on."

"Never?"

"Not as far as I can make out," Tom said. "I've only seen it once, but no one ever goes near it. It's just sitting there."

"Could it be activated remotely?"

"It's a possibility, but I don't think so. It never seems to appear in the activity logs. I suppose someone could access it locally. That might not show up on the records."

"Have you tried switching it on?" Dan asked.

"No. The cabinet is always locked, and I don't have a key. That's why I've only seen it once."

"So, we're looking for someone with access to the server room."

"*I'm* not looking for anyone," Tom said. "I only told you about it because I know you can't even get into the building. So that's an end to the matter."

"We'll see about that. Who else knows about the server?"

"Hard to say. I asked if I could get rid of it, but I was told it was a legacy system for handling a redundant backup. I was instructed, in no uncertain terms, to leave it alone, and I left it at that."

"By whom?"

Tom made brief eye contact with Dan, then he said, "I'm not going to tell you that. It's none of your business, and even if you knew, it wouldn't do you any good."

"That's for me to decide. I'll find a way to access that server, with or without your help."

"And then what?" Tom demanded. "What would be the point?"

"It might take me one step nearer to the truth. If I'm lucky, I'll have some evidence that I can hand over to the police."

"They won't be interested. Believe me."

"You sound very sure of yourself," Dan said. "Do you know what's on that server?"

Tom's cheeks tightened, and Dan knew he'd touched a nerve.

"You said the server was supposedly for a redundant backup," Dan went on. "What kind of information was being backed up?"

"I don't know. Let it go, Dan. There's nothing to be gained from all this. You're barking up the wrong tree."

"I don't agree. I think Seb knew about that server, and that's why he was killed."

"I doubt that very much." Tom drew a breath, composing himself. "Listen, Dan, we're all distraught about what happened to Seb. It's a difficult time, and it's hard to process. That's why I came up here; I wanted to do something I'd shared with Seb, remember the good times. When you called and said you wanted to talk about him, it made me very angry."

"You didn't think I had something to do with Seb's death, did you?"

"No, of course not. If you must know, I'm furious with the stupid sod. I knew he'd had problems in the past, but he'd kicked all that. He didn't even drink anymore, so why did he have to go and do something so stupid? If he'd had a moment of weakness, he could've called me and I would've helped him, but he didn't give me the chance. It makes no sense. Why would he throw his life away like that?"

"You think his death was drug related. Is that a guess or have the police said something?"

"Not in so many words, but they've been asking about his habits, his lifestyle. I can join the dots. He must've been buying drugs. Why else would he wind up dead in a car park?"

"I don't know. It's very sad."

"It's tragic, that's what it is," Tom said, his voice growing harder as he went on, his cheeks reddening. "Bloody tragic. It's a waste of human life, and it makes me so... so bloody *angry!*" His last word was almost snarled, and with it, Tom's rage reached its crescendo and died away as quickly as it had risen. Tom's shoulders shook and he hung his head, wiping his eyes with the back of his hand.

Dan waited quietly, giving the man some time. He knew there was no artifice in Tom's display of emotion. This was grief; real and raw.

It took Tom only a few seconds to pull himself together. He sniffed, cleared his throat and said, "I shouldn't have left you hanging like that. I was angry and I took it out on you. That was wrong of me, and for what it's worth, I regret it."

"It's all right," Dan said. "I think I understand."

"Do you?" Tom looked at Dan as if searching for something, then he nodded. "Friends are hard to find. Yours will be here soon, so I'll make my excuses and leave." Tom offered a thin smile, though it looked like it cost him some effort. "If I were you, I'd drop all this stuff about the server. Draw a line under it. You should go home, keep yourself busy. It doesn't do to dwell on your anxieties, as I think you know."

"What do you mean by that?"

"I've heard that you had some difficulties of your own. A breakdown, wasn't it? That's why you left London."

For a moment, Dan didn't know what to say, but this was a loose thread he had to pull. "Who told you that, Tom?"

"An old friend of yours."

Dan sighed. "It was Frankie Herringway, wasn't it?"

"I don't tell tales out of school, Dan. I think you should take a long, hard look at yourself. Neil fed you some kind of conspiracy theory, and you swallowed it, hook, line and sinker. That's not rational. It's not healthy."

"This isn't about me, Tom. It's about uncovering the truth. I have an IP address and a password. When I use them, what will I find? Where will it lead me?"

Tom rubbed his brow, his fingertips leaving trails of chalk across his forehead, his expression pained. Finally, he said, "What will it take to make you drop this, Dan? What will it take to make you admit you're wrong?"

"Help me to log on to that server. Show me what's there. If I'm wrong, I'll walk away."

"Listen to yourself. You're talking nonsense, asking for the impossible."

"You won't help? That suggests you have something to hide."

"I *can't* help." Tom dipped his fingers into his bag of chalk and brushed his hands together. "I'll climb down by myself, leave you to wait for your friend. You can keep the helmet."

"No, you can have it back." Dan hurriedly unfastened the helmet and held it out, but Tom waved it away.

"You have it. It's a spare, and I don't need it. I won't be going climbing anymore."

"But—"

I shan't see you again," Tom said. "Goodbye."

Dan watched as Tom made for the edge and lowered himself back onto the rock face. He began climbing down without hesitation, and a second later, Tom moved out of sight, leaving Dan waiting alone, staring out across the moor, the wind whipping around him.

Dan silently cursed the day he'd set foot in CEG. The place was shot through with suspicion, riddled with distrust and beset by misplaced loyalties. Whenever he felt like he was making inroads, he met a veil of secrecy. His encounter with Tom had yielded a handful of clues, but new problems had sprung up to hold him back, and Dan had absolutely no idea what to do next.

THURSDAY

CHAPTER 51

In Amberley Court, DI Spiller cast his gaze over the tastefully decorated staircase as he made his way up to Melanie Steele's flat, accompanied by DS Kulkarni. "Very nice," he said. "A place like this doesn't come cheap."

"You can say that again," Kulkarni replied. "And this is her second home. I wonder what her place in the country is like."

"We may have to find out, but let's not get ahead of ourselves."

They reached the correct landing, but before they could knock on the white wooden door Melanie Steele opened it, greeting them with a few words and a firm handshake.

"Shazia called to say you were on your way up," Melanie explained. "You'd better come in."

They followed her into a large lounge, the room filled with light from the tall windows. "Have a seat." Melanie indicated a three-seater sofa in chestnut-coloured leather that bore the lustrous sheen of antiquity.

Spiller had no idea if the sofa was a modern piece dressed up as an old one or the real thing, but he sank gratefully into its embrace, and Kulkarni took her place at the sofa's opposite end.

Melanie remained standing, and despite her air of cool self-assurance, her gaze flitted from Spiller to Kulkarni as if awaiting an opening salvo.

Offering a reassuring smile, Spiller said, "We needn't take up too much of your time, Ms Steele, but this will be easier if you sit down as well, wouldn't you agree?"

"All right, so long as we're not too long." Melanie moved to the armchair that faced Spiller and Kulkarni, and she sat down carefully, smoothing her skirt. "Now, what can I help you with?"

"It's just a few questions," Spiller replied. "Nothing to worry about."

"Do I *look* worried?"

"No, not at all." Spiller turned to Kulkarni. "Go ahead, Detective Sergeant."

Kulkarni had already taken out her notebook and she referred to it briefly, although Spiller suspected that his colleague had committed her list of questions to memory.

Focusing on Melanie, Kulkarni began. "Ms Steele, when one of our officers attended your workplace after the death of Sebastian Cooper, you gave your address as Weatherdown Cottage, Church Green."

"That's my home, yes. It's where I spend most of my time."

"But on Monday night, the night when Mr Cooper died, you were here. That has been confirmed by a witness and by CCTV."

"Your point is?"

"My point, Ms Steele, is that this flat is just a stone's throw from the place where Mr Cooper's body was found," Kulkarni said. "We're wondering why you failed to mention that."

"There's nothing suspicious about it. When the officer

asked for my address, I didn't know what had happened to Seb. All we were told was that he'd been found dead, but I didn't know when or where. Anyway, I wouldn't say this building is particularly close to the quayside car park."

"It's a ten-minute walk," Kulkarni said. "But I didn't mention the car park. How did you know that was where Mr Cooper was found?"

"It was on the news. I saw it on TV, later that night."

"That would be Tuesday night?"

"Yes." Melanie turned her cold gaze on Spiller. "It's no secret that I was here on Monday, but why do you want to know?"

"We understand that you associated with Mr Cooper outside the workplace," Spiller replied. "He came here from time to time, didn't he?"

Melanie lifted her chin in a gesture of haughty defiance. "Yes. What of it?"

"It could be important," Spiller said. "Did Mr Cooper visit you on Monday?"

"No. I saw him at work but not afterwards."

"You're sure about that?"

"Yes. It's not as if he came here all the time. It was an occasional thing. When we were working together, we sometimes carried on into the evening, and it was more comfortable for us to work here."

"You were just colleagues," Kulkarni put in. "Nothing more than that?"

"We enjoyed each other's company."

"That doesn't exactly answer the question," Spiller said. "What we'd like to know is whether, at any time, you had a romantic relationship with Mr Cooper."

"Seb was married."

"Again, that's neither a yes nor a no, Ms Steele." Spiller locked eyes with Melanie, making it clear he was fully prepared to wait for a straight answer, indefinitely if need be.

Melanie looked down her nose at him while she drew a breath. "No, Seb and I did not have what you might call a *romantic* relationship. That would've been ridiculous."

"How so?" Spiller softened his tone, adding, "We're asking these questions because it's helpful if we can build up a picture of what Mr Cooper was like as a person. You see, he's not just a victim to us. He's someone who deserves justice. You can help with that by telling us everything you can about him. You'd like to help, wouldn't you, Ms Steele?"

"Of course." Melanie's imperious expression faltered, became one of dismay, and in an unguarded moment, Spiller saw the sadness she'd been trying to hide.

Composing herself, Melanie said, "Seb and I didn't see each other as potential partners. We worked well together, and we liked spending time with each other. That's all there is to it."

"You were friends," Spiller suggested.

"No, that's not it. We were too alike, too competitive. We were more like sparring partners."

Spiller nodded. "It sounds as though Mr Cooper was ambitious. Is that right?"

"Oh yes. Very ambitious. He wanted to get on, and he wasn't afraid of hard work."

"But things didn't always go smoothly for him, did they?" Kulkarni asked. "When Mr Cooper worked for Hillingdean Insurance in Bristol, he was fired."

"All the best people have gaps in their CV. When you don't accept the status quo, sometimes you win but sometimes you get elbowed out."

"I wouldn't know," Kulkarni said. "I talked to someone at Hillingdean Insurance, and they said there'd been problems with Mr Cooper's behaviour. They said they'd reached out and tried to help him, but he'd walked away, so they'd been left with no choice but to terminate his contract."

Melanie tutted dismissively. "You believe that, do you?"

"Yes," Kulkarni replied. "I spoke to the head of HR at Hillingdean, and she gave an interesting account of the circumstances surrounding Mr Cooper's departure. Very interesting indeed."

Spiller saw a flash of recognition in Melanie's eyes. She knew exactly what Kulkarni was talking about, but she wasn't going to admit it without a fight. She remained aloof as if determined to show that Kulkarni's questions couldn't touch her.

For her part, Kulkarni was beginning to look frustrated. It was time for a break.

Smiling, Spiller said, "I wonder if I might trouble you for a glass of water, Ms Steele. All this talking makes the throat dry, doesn't it?"

Melanie shook her head as if rousing herself. "I've just realised, I haven't offered you anything. I can fetch some water, but would either of you like a cup of tea or coffee?"

"Now that you mention it, a mug of tea would be much appreciated," Spiller replied. "Thank you."

"Nothing for me, thanks," Kulkarni said. "I'm fine."

"Right. I presume you take your tea white, Inspector? Sugar?"

"Just milk, please. I'm watching my waist."

Melanie gave him a judgmental look as if she thought the moment for Spiller to count the calories had long since passed, but she nodded and said, "I only have skimmed milk, so that should suit you down to the ground. I'll have a coffee. I'll go and get everything organised." Melanie stood and made for an archway that led through to a dining area, but she hesitated on the threshold and glanced back into the room. "I won't be long," she added, her gaze flitting to something behind Spiller, and then she swept from the room.

Spiller turned his head, trying to see what had caught Melanie's attention, but he saw only a tall bookcase made from pale wood, its shelves stacked neatly with books.

"What do you think, guv?" Kulkarni asked. "She's very defensive."

"That's understandable. We're intruding on her domain, and Ms Steele is used to being in control, especially in her own home." Spiller surveyed the room. "Look at this place. There's not a speck of dust, not a thing that hasn't been carefully arranged. It's like sitting in a showroom."

"She knew we were coming. She might've cleaned up before we came."

"I'm not sure I can see Ms Steele running around with a vacuum cleaner, can you?"

"Not in those heels, no, but shoes can be changed, and this place is spotless."

"We'll make a detective of you yet." Spiller stood and strolled over to the bookcase. All the books were hardback editions and they were arranged by the author's surname. Scanning the titles, he said, "Do you read much, Anisha? Fiction, I mean."

"Not really. I used to, but I don't have the time. Cramming for the sergeants' exam was the final nail in the coffin. By the time I'd ploughed through a few pages of that stuff, I could hardly keep my eyes open."

Spiller murmured in sympathy, but he kept his attention on the books, wondering if any of them had been read. They were worthy titles, classics, the kind of books that were placed for visitors to admire. Jane Austen preceded works by the Brontës; Daphne du Maurier took her place before George Eliot; Sylvia Plath rubbed shoulders with Virginia Woolf. There were other authors that Spiller didn't recognise, but he could tell that care had been given to the selection and arrangement of each book.

He was about to turn away when his eye was caught by a title that stood out. Laying a finger on top of the book's spine, he said to Kulkarni, "What do you think of this one: *On the Road* by Jack Kerouac?"

"I tried it when I was a teenager, but I didn't like it. The way he talks about women... it made me squirm."

"I can imagine. I read it a long time ago, believe it or not, and it's a bit of a surprise to find it here. As far as I can see, it's the only book by a male author."

"What are you doing?" The voice was Melanie Steele's, and Spiller turned to see her framed in the archway, a tray in her hands and her stare directed at him.

"Just browsing," Spiller replied, and he started to slide the book from its place.

"Stop that," Melanie snapped. "Leave it alone."

Spiller met her gaze and knew what he had to do. Pulling the book out, he laid it in his hand, letting it fall open, and there, in the centre of the book, a slim leather pouch had been pressed between the pages. Judging by the impression in the paper, it had been there for some time, but the most striking feature was the letter embossed in the leather: a bold *S*.

Melanie stood transfixed, visibly shaken, her tray still in her hands. "Don't touch it. It... it's not mine."

"Are you referring to the book or this little pouch?" Spiller asked.

"Both. They're not mine."

"So how did they come to be in your bookcase?"

"I can't recall."

"I see." Spiller looked to Kulkarni. "I'm willing to bet you have gloves and an evidence bag with you."

Kulkarni grabbed her handbag and stood, crossing the room to join him. She took out her phone and shot several pictures of the book, the pouch and the bookcase.

Regaining her composure, Melanie set her tray down on a table, then she stalked toward them. "You can't do that. You have no right."

"On the contrary," Spiller replied. "I have reason to suspect that this pouch belonged to Mr Cooper, so I must treat it as evidence that might relate to my inquiry."

Kulkarni had donned disposable gloves and she'd produced an evidence bag.

"Hang on a sec," Spiller said. "Before you bag it, I'd like you to open it carefully and take a peep inside. Take care not to touch any part that might hold prints."

"Yes, guv." The pouch was closed with a simple flap, and Kulkarni delicately slid her finger beneath it and flipped it upward, then she lifted the top side of the pouch with the tip of her gloved finger. Displaying a dexterity that Spiller couldn't help but admire, Kulkarni held the pouch open with one hand, while with the other she took more photos of its contents.

"There's a mirror, and I think there's a razor blade as well," Kulkarni said. "There's also a small metal spoon."

Spiller tried not to smile too broadly. "I thought as much. Bag it and label it, please. The book too."

While Kulkarni took care of the evidence, Spiller guided Melanie to an armchair and asked her to sit. Melanie complied without argument, but she maintained an upright posture, perching on the edge of her seat.

She's down but she's not out, Spiller decided. Melanie seemed determined to face them down, her armour intact.

Spiller took a seat on the sofa, waiting. If he was right about her, she'd come out swinging, and sure enough, Melanie spoke first.

"I'm sorry, Detective Inspector, but I won't say another word without my lawyer present."

"That's your prerogative," Spiller said. "We need to discuss this at the station. It'll be what we call an interview under caution. You'll be entitled to independent legal representation during the interview."

"Am I under arrest?"

"No, not at this stage, but it may become necessary. It depends on what we find. You see, we'll be looking to obtain a search warrant to have a proper look around this place."

"Why? What can you possibly hope to gain by harassing me in this way?"

Spiller knew better than to react to Melanie's strident tone. She was trying to goad him, to push him into showing his hand, but he wasn't going to let her get away with that.

"Ms Steele, you are in possession of paraphernalia related to the use of illegal drugs. Can you explain that?"

"I told you, none of it is mine. I didn't know it was there."

"Yes, you did," Spiller stated. "You cleaned up before we arrived, but you forgot about that pouch, right up until the moment when you were about to leave us alone in the room. Suddenly, you remembered it was there. I saw you looking at it. You knew exactly what was in that book. That's why you reacted so quickly when you saw me touching it."

"Nonsense. You can't just concoct a story to suit your own ends."

"No, but I'm right about this. When we search the flat, will we find traces of any controlled substances, Ms Steele?"

Melanie paled, but she shook her head firmly, her lips closed tight.

"Are you sure about that?" Spiller asked. "Our forensic teams are very thorough. You'd be amazed at what they can find. It's the nooks and crannies that give the game away: all those little spaces where the Hoover doesn't quite reach. Isn't that right, Detective Sergeant Kulkarni?"

"Oh yes." Kulkarni had been waiting to one side, but now she joined Spiller on the sofa. "I've known them to take furniture apart so they can get right down into all the crevices."

Melanie said nothing, so Spiller carried on. "Chemical analysis doesn't lie, and it's not just the flat we'll be looking at. We'll also want you to submit to a routine drugs test."

"No. I won't agree to that."

"In that case, I'll have to arrest you, then we can force you into taking the test." Spiller paused to let his words sink in, then added, "Unless you'd prefer to avoid going down that road, Ms Steele."

Uncertainty stole across Melanie's features, but Spiller waited in vain for her to speak.

"Very well." Spiller heaved a sigh. "Melanie Steele, I'm arresting you on suspicion of possessing a controlled substance. You do not have to say anything, but—"

"It's Seb's," Melanie interrupted. "It all belonged to Seb. He left it here because he didn't want his wife to know he was still using."

"Using what?"

"Coke. He left a little bag of powder here, and he told me it was cocaine, but I've thrown it away, flushed it down the toilet. I threw the bag in the dustbin outside."

"We'll have a look for that," Spiller said. "Make a note, Detective Sergeant. All the dustbins to be searched." To Melanie, he said, "A ziplock bag, was it? Transparent?"

"Yes. It was only a tiny amount. Seb didn't use it all the time. Sometimes, after a long day, he'd say he needed something to pick him up, to get his energy back. We'd come here, and he'd sort himself out, then we'd hit the gym, hit it hard, work out until we dropped."

"Work hard, play hard, is that it?" Spiller asked.

"Something like that."

"Did you partake?"

Melanie lowered her eyebrows and glared at Spiller as if he'd said something spectacularly stupid. "I've never taken drugs in my life. I tried to talk Seb out of it. Time and again, I told him he didn't need that stuff, but he swore it was under control. He could be very persuasive, and whenever I tried to argue with him, he always talked me round. Always."

Spiller registered a brief change in Melanie's expression but wasn't sure what it meant. He looked to Kulkarni, and she seemed to understand he was passing the baton to her.

Kulkarni put her notebook down and leaned slightly

forward, her hands clasped in her lap, as if she and Melanie were two women sharing a confidence. "I've seen Seb's photo, and he was very good looking, wasn't he? Then I see you, a successful woman with a certain style, and I can't help thinking you'd have made a perfect couple."

"Don't be silly," Melanie replied, but without much conviction.

"Come on," Kulkarni said softly, "there was some spark there, wasn't there, some part of you that wanted him around? You were good together, weren't you?"

"You never met him, or you wouldn't ask that. Seb could make you feel like you were the centre of his universe. But it wasn't just me. Any woman would tell you the same."

"I think I understand. When he came here to unwind, you treasured the time you had together. You looked forward to it."

"Yes. We had fun."

"But if you stopped him from using coke, he might not come around anymore. Is that what you thought?"

Melanie stared at Kulkarni, her eyes growing moist, and then slowly, hesitantly, she nodded.

"Ms Steele," Spiller began, making his voice gentle, "you told us that Mr Cooper hadn't visited you on the night he died, but that wasn't true, was it? He'd been here, hadn't he?"

"No. I told you, he didn't come here on Monday. I wouldn't lie about something like that."

"Unfortunately for you, the CCTV from the front door shows that he was here. He arrived just before half past eight, stayed for seventeen minutes, and then he left. You may want to think again."

Melanie blinked rapidly but was otherwise unruffled. "Oh. Monday. Yes. He was here for a short while, as you say. It was such a flying visit it must've slipped my mind. I'm sorry about that."

"Apology accepted, but please remember that we cross-check every detail," Spiller said. "Now, at some point on Monday, Mr Cooper ingested a small quantity of cocaine. We know that from the post-mortem examination. Did he take that cocaine here?"

"I don't know. He wasn't here long, but he used the bathroom, so he may have done."

"How was his mood?" Kulkarni asked. "Did he seem anxious or on edge?"

Melanie hesitated. "He was... excitable. In fact, we argued. That's why he wasn't here for long."

"What did you argue about?" Spiller asked.

Melanie turned her hands palm upwards. "Work. What else?"

"Things going badly at the office?"

"Not exactly, but Seb told me something that night, and it made me angry with him."

Spiller gestured for her to go on, and Melanie cleared her throat.

"We were in talks with another company. Stein Waterhouse. They're based in London. Seb sold the deal to us by saying that Stein Waterhouse wanted to invest. He said we'd use the funds to expand, but it was all just a giant smokescreen. Stein Waterhouse had no intention of investing. They wanted to stage an aggressive takeover and then strip the company's assets, selling it off piece by piece."

"Seb knew about this," Spiller suggested.

"Yes. He'd served our company up on a silver platter, and in return, Stein Waterhouse had promised him a senior management position."

Spiller and Kulkarni exchanged a look.

"Some might see that as a betrayal," Kulkarni said. "It might be enough for someone to wish Mr Cooper harm."

Melanie cocked a disdainful eyebrow. "That's nonsense. The rank and file don't care enough about their jobs to hit back. They'd have been given a decent redundancy package, and the rest of us would've been paid off handsomely. I expect Doug would've retired quite happily; his heart was never in running the company anyway. I'd have been given a golden handshake, and I'd have secured another job within days."

"You say *would've*," Spiller said. "Does that mean the deal's off?"

"Yes. It was Seb's project. Stein Waterhouse have pulled out."

"His death saved the company," Kulkarni suggested.

Melanie lifted one shoulder in a half shrug. "We'll see about that. There are hard times ahead. Hard times."

Spiller took a moment. Sometimes in an interview you had to take a break, give everyone a chance to breathe. It helped to let his thoughts percolate while he decided which threads to pursue and in what order. Kulkarni seemed to pick up on this, and she busied herself scribbling notes in her notebook.

"Are we done?" Melanie asked.

"Almost," Spiller replied with a smile. "I was just thinking, since you were going to be okay if the company was taken over, why did you argue with Mr Cooper? It sounds as though he might've done you a favour."

"We argued because, believe it or not, I do have some principles, and Seb shouldn't have behaved like that. He shouldn't have sold us all out. There's such a thing as loyalty."

"Especially between friends," Spiller said. "You thought of Mr Cooper as a friend, didn't you? A close friend. Someone who shared secrets with you."

After a brief pause, Melanie nodded.

"I see. That being the case, did Mr Cooper ever say where he obtained his cocaine?"

"No. He never told me about that sort of thing, and I didn't ask." Melanie let out a long breath. "Look, that's enough questions. I want to talk to my lawyer before I say any more."

"There are just a couple of things I'd like to check," Spiller said. "Did you ever watch Mr Cooper while he took any kind of drug?"

"No. He went into the bathroom. Why?"

"Mr Cooper was killed when he took a drug called fentanyl. In combination with the cocaine in his system, it was lethal. He probably inhaled the fentanyl from some kind of spray. Did he ever mention fentanyl to you? Or did you see him with anything that looked like a nasal spray?"

"Definitely not. The only drug I ever saw him with was that little bag of white powder. He told me it was cocaine, and I believed him. I've never heard of the other one you mentioned. What was it?"

"Fentanyl. It's an opioid. It's the same type of drug as heroin, but it's much more potent."

"That doesn't sound like Seb. He wouldn't have taken anything remotely like heroin. I never saw him with a needle or anything, and I'm sure he was never an addict."

"You'd be surprised how well some addicts can hide their problems," Spiller said. "But you're sure you never saw him with a spray? It would've been quite small."

"I'm positive." Melanie pinched the bridge of her nose as if to fight off a headache. "That's it. We're done. I'm calling my lawyer."

"Good idea, and you might want to grab your coat," Spiller said. "When you've made your call, we may as well head straight to the station."

"We'll see about that." Melanie stood stiffly and marched from the room.

Spiller nodded to Kulkarni. "Go with her. Keep an eye on her and be ready to listen. She might open up to you. You've built up a good rapport with her. Well done."

"Thanks." Kulkarni got up and made for the door, but she

paused to look back. "Do you think she's telling the truth, or does she know more than she's letting on?"

"Time will tell." Spiller stood and crossed the room to where Melanie had set down the tray, then he lifted the mug of tea. "Shame to let this go to waste." He took a swig and grimaced.

"Has it gone cold, guv?"

"I'm used to lukewarm tea, but this is Earl Grey or something. Ugh. I ought to have guessed."

Kulkarni smiled and hurried to catch up with Melanie Steele, leaving Spiller alone. He absentmindedly took another gulp of tepid tea as he looked around the room. He'd get a search warrant and have the place gone over with a fine-tooth comb, but he wasn't holding out much hope of finding anything earth shattering.

Melanie Steele wasn't a drug user. She prided herself on her self-control. She wouldn't give that up for a short-lived buzz, and she hadn't approved of Cooper's cocaine habit. Would she have tolerated his use of fentanyl? Unlikely, but by her own admission, Cooper had charmed her, talked her into providing a hideaway for him.

That begged a question. Cooper had the use of this plush apartment, so why would he choose to take his drugs in the dank and gloomy surroundings of a godforsaken car park? The two places were separated by a short walk, so why hadn't he waited until he was safely back here? The argument with Melanie wouldn't have been enough to put him off. He'd have talked her into letting him in.

He had no choice, Spiller decided. *Someone else was in control.* And there it was: the moment of clarity Spiller had been waiting for. The fentanyl hadn't been self-administered, and this wasn't just a suspicious death. Sebastian Cooper had been murdered.

CHAPTER 52

Dan and Alan strolled through the village in companionable silence, heading for home. The walk had been Alan's idea. He'd knocked on Dan's door, claiming that he needed some fresh air and exercise, and Dan had been glad of the distraction. They'd set off immediately, and it transpired that they'd each been engrossed in a project. Alan had been working on his latest book, and Dan had been mulling over the implications of his conversation with Tom Hastings.

The walk cleared Dan's mind, but he found his pace slowing as they neared The Old Shop. The case was still waiting for him, and he was no nearer to untangling it. He needed Alan's help, but should he ask? Alan had spent most of their walk saying how great it was to be getting back to his work; it seemed wrong to derail him now.

Dan kicked at a loose stone that had made its way onto the pavement, and Alan gave him a sideways look.

"Ah," Alan said. "I take it that you're stuck on the case, and you'd like me to give you a hand."

"Is it that obvious?"

"It is to me, but then I've picked up a few tricks. I've

learned from the master, and you've been very quiet for a while. It wasn't hard to guess what was on your mind."

"Well, you've hit the bullseye," Dan admitted. "Could you spare an hour or so this afternoon? I need a pair of fresh eyes."

Alan tilted his head as if giving Dan's offer serious consideration, but he couldn't maintain his po-faced expression for long and he broke into a smile. "I'll tell you what. Make me lunch, and I'll put my thinking hat on while I eat."

"Deal. If you fancy a sandwich, I've got some vegan ham you might like to try."

"Er, what's it made out of?"

"There are a lot of ingredients," Dan said. "But it tastes like ham. At least, I think it does. I haven't had ham for years."

"Is it nice?"

Dan waggled his hand in the air. "The jury's out, but if you don't like it, I'm sure I can rustle up something else."

"I'll give it a go. I'll eat anything I can keep down two times out of three, as the late Sir Terry Pratchett once said."

Dan laughed. "Is that from one of his books?"

"I'm not sure, but I heard him say it over lunch at the Cheltenham Literature Festival. I was earwigging from the next table."

"I didn't have you down as an eavesdropper. I'm not sure whether to be shocked or impressed."

"Both," Alan said. "But you shouldn't be surprised. Most writers are like magpies, always collecting, always on the lookout for snippets of real life they can pinch and save for another day."

"I'll have to bear that in mind. I don't want to end up cast as a—" Dan broke off suddenly, his attention on a sleek BMW saloon that was pulling up outside his house. "That's Frankie's car, isn't it?"

Alan squinted. "It might be. Were you expecting her?"

"No."

They carried on walking, and a moment later all doubt was removed as Frankie emerged from the passenger seat of the BMW and Walter appeared from the driver's side.

"Who's that?" Alan asked in a low voice.

"Walter Drake. One of Frankie's minions at Stein Waterhouse. He's some kind of bean counter. A glorified accountant."

"I should talk to him about my taxes."

"Please don't do that," Dan said. "We'll never get rid of him."

"He looks friendly enough." Walter had raised an arm in greeting, and Alan waved in return. To Dan, he muttered, "I hope you're not going to be…"

"What?"

"You know, irritable, your nose out of joint about Frankie."

Dan grunted dismissively, but Alan was right. The last time they'd met Frankie, he'd been peevish, playing the part of the jilted lover, and that wasn't right. It was time to let the past go, once and for all.

"Hello, you two," Frankie called out. "Out for a stroll?"

"Yes," Alan replied as he strode over to meet them, Dan trailing behind him. "We often take a walk around the village. There are some magnificent views right on our doorstep. Perhaps we could show you."

Frankie sighed. "I'd like nothing better, Alan, but we just popped in to say goodbye. We're heading back to London."

"Oh, already?" Dan asked. "I thought you were here for a few days."

"That was before things went pear-shaped," Walter said. "There's no point in staying. Not now. Not after what happened to Seb."

Dan tried to see past Walter's blank expression but

gleaned nothing. *He's like a cardboard cut-out,* Dan thought. *Dead behind the eyes.* Walter had spoken about Seb's death as if it represented nothing but a minor inconvenience. Perhaps Walter wasn't much given to showing his emotions, but then again, maybe he just didn't feel any empathy for others. Either way, Walter was an unknown quantity, and Dan had an impulse to find out what made the man tick.

"Seb's death must've come as a terrible shock," Dan ventured. "Did you know him well, Walter?"

Walter raised his eyebrows. "Me? No, not all, but Seb was the driving force in that company. He *was* the deal. Without him, the whole thing is dead in the water, so there's no point in us wasting our time."

Walter seemed unaware that the others were watching him in mute horror. "If I had my way, we'd be halfway home by now," Walter went on, "but Frankie wanted to make this little detour, so here we are."

"I think you've said more than enough, Walter," Frankie said. "We've got plenty of time." To Dan, she added in a softer tone, "I couldn't leave without saying goodbye properly. Besides, I wanted to check you were okay. I know you worked with Seb. He always spoke highly of you."

Caught off guard, Dan was mute for a moment. He ought to look sombre and say something about Seb's family and his widow, but instead, he said, "Really? I always thought he didn't like me."

"That's not the impression I got, but then you've always been competitive, and so was Seb. I expect you rubbed each other up the wrong way."

"But when we went to Hound Tor, you warned me about Seb," Dan replied. "You told me to be careful."

Frankie glanced up and down the street. "Shall we go inside? If you don't mind, that is."

"Yes, please come in," Dan said. "We were about to have lunch. You're welcome to join us."

"Thanks, but we'll grab something on the way," Walter replied. "Maybe you two could chat later on the phone. We ought to get going as soon as possible. We don't want to get caught up in traffic."

Frankie looked as though she might give in to Walter's hectoring, so Dan quickly said, "How about coming in for a coffee? It'll only take a minute, and I have some excellent Costa Rican. It's freshly ground and much better than anything you'll get at a motorway service station."

Frankie smiled. "You and your coffee. Some things never change. What do you say, Walter? I'm sure we've got time for a quick coffee."

Walter grimaced as though he'd like to disagree, but then he looked at Frankie and adopted an indulgent smile. "Ah well, Frankie's got to have her coffee. Far be it from me to stand in her way."

Dan had a sudden urge to say something, to do something that would wipe the grin from Walter's face, but he stifled it, his manners coming to the rescue. "Excellent. That's settled then. Come in, and I'll fire up the machine."

Inside, Dan showed his guests into the front room, then he hurried into the kitchen to make the drinks. Pouring fresh beans into his electric coffee grinder, he set it whirring, its growling racket filling the room. It was only when the noise died away that he sensed someone standing close behind him, and he turned around with a start.

"Frankie. I didn't hear you come in."

"Sorry. I didn't mean to make you jump. I just wanted to get you on your own for a second." Frankie smiled, taking a step closer, and despite his best intentions, Dan's heart leapt.

"About Seb," Frankie went on. "He was very ambitious, driven, and that can be good or it can be toxic. I thought he sailed too close to the wind, so I warned you about him because I didn't want you to be drawn in. You've been there, Dan, and it didn't end well."

"Those days are behind me. I can look after myself."

"I'm sure you can, but all the same, I was worried about you working with Seb. I got the impression that he lived on the edge, and that's a dangerous place to be."

"It can be. But what's all this really about, Frankie? You told me your security people flagged Seb as high risk. What had he done?"

"I probably shouldn't be telling you this, but I suppose it'll all come out sooner or later. In the past, Seb had a problem with drink and drugs. I don't know if he was still using them, but…"

"I see." Dan hesitated. "A couple of people have mentioned drugs in connection with Seb. If that's what happened, it's a terrible thing. Very sad."

Dan saw that his espresso machine was up to temperature and he measured a scoopful of coffee into the basket. Carefully compressing the grounds with his stainless steel tamper, he thought of Seb and everything Tom Hastings had said about him. Tom had been certain that, until recently, Seb had been clean. Celine had said something similar.

So how had Seb died? Had he fallen off the wagon in a moment of madness? It was possible, but it didn't add up. Seb had money and contacts. If he'd wanted to buy drugs, there'd have been no need for him to loiter in a car park. He would've had other ways to obtain his supplies, and he would've been able to afford high-quality drugs, not the cheaper stuff they sold in back alleys.

Dan placed an espresso cup under the machine's spout and held down the button to release the stream of hot water, filling the cup almost to the brim. Passing the cup to Frankie, he said, "That's how you like it, isn't it?"

"Yes. How clever of you to remember." Frankie took the cup and breathed in the steam. "That's good."

"Glad you like it. Will Walter have the same?"

"Probably."

Dan prepared to brew another cup, and while he worked he said, "Did you mean what you said earlier, about Seb speaking highly of me?"

"Yes. I know for a fact that he tried to talk Doug out of firing you over that newspaper article."

"I didn't know that."

"It's true. I stood up for you, too. I had a massive argument about it with Doug."

"I almost feel sorry for the man."

"Well, I did rather give him a tongue lashing. One of many, sad to say."

Were any of those arguments in the stairwell? Dan wondered, but before he could ask, Frankie said, "You're happy here, aren't you? The change has done you good."

"Yes, I think so."

Frankie watched Dan brew a second espresso and she seemed pensive, her perfect teeth nipping the corner of her lower lip.

"I'll take this to Walter," Dan said, but Frankie touched Dan's arm to halt him.

"Stay," she said. "I want to have you to myself for one minute more."

"What about Walter's coffee?"

"Forget him. He can do without." Frankie gently took the cup from Dan's hand and set it down along with her own, then she drew a breath. "Dan, can't you see that I'm trying to tell you something?"

"Erm..."

"I'm trying to say that I'm sorry. I'm sorry for the way things ended between us. I've been hoping to find the right moment, but there was always something in the way. I waited because I thought we'd have more time."

"It's okay," Dan said. "I'm sorry about the way things worked out too. I ought to have said something the other day when we went for a walk. I don't know why I didn't."

"It takes two, Dan. I didn't say anything either. I hate to admit it, but I was scared. I thought I was going to make a mess of it, so I kept you at arm's length and talked to Alan instead. I told myself I'd find another time, a time when we could talk, just you and me."

"Yes," Dan heard himself say. "That would've been good."

"You know, all that time ago, when I heard you'd gone away and that you'd left London for good, I missed you, and I wondered..." Frankie lowered her gaze.

"What?"

"Maybe I shouldn't say anything, but it's now or never." Frankie looked up at him. "Since you left, I've often wondered if I could've persuaded you to stay."

In Dan's mind, a voice cried, "Yes! For you, I would've stayed. For you, I would've done anything." A giddy rush of emotion surged through him. He could reach out to Frankie, take her in his arms, and everything would be all right. He could go back to London with her and pick up where he left off. It was all so clear.

But he was out of his depth, allowing himself to be swept up in the moment. The strength of his old feelings for Frankie had caught him by surprise, but what if he'd misunderstood what she wanted?

Frankie was still waiting for an answer.

"I think," Dan said slowly, "that you're talking about closure, about making amends for the way we parted."

"No, that's not it at all. I'm trying to tell you that when you left, there was a Dan-shaped hole in my life. When I saw you again, standing there in your Armani jacket, it was like coming home. I don't know how else to put it, but ever since you came back into my life, I've been thinking about you all the time."

"You didn't say anything."

"I wanted to. So many times, I thought about what to say, but I always stopped myself. After the way I let you go, I don't have the right to barge back in. I feel so awful about the way I treated you, and I didn't want to make the same mistake twice. I've been keeping my feelings to myself, but now that I have to go back to London, I knew I had to see you. I had to tell you how I felt, because I couldn't bear it if you felt the same and we didn't talk about it; if we didn't at least give ourselves a chance."

Dan looked into Frankie's eyes and saw that, this time, she was in earnest. There was a vulnerability there that he'd never seen before. She'd lowered her defences, and now it was his turn to lay his cards on the table.

Don't blow it, Dan told himself. *Get this right.* He took a moment. The next words he spoke would shape his life for years to come. One path led to Frankie, to London and all that he'd left behind; the other led to a very different future. Dan's mind raced. If he went back, he wouldn't fall prey to the pressures that had plagued him back then. He was stronger now, more rounded. He'd weathered some of life's storms and come out the other side. This time, he could jump right back into the rat race and win. So why hadn't he said yes already?

But while he tried to put his thoughts into words, he realised he'd already taken too long to answer.

Frankie closed her eyes for a moment, and when she opened them again, Dan saw only sadness.

"I understand," Frankie said. "I'm sorry, Dan. I shouldn't have sprung this on you. It's okay. You don't have to say anything."

"Yes, I do." Dan held her gaze and said, "There was a time when it might've worked out between us, a time when we could've been good for each other. But we've both moved on, and I think we want different things now. I don't know what I'm going to do here, but this is where I belong."

"I can see that, but that doesn't mean we can't figure something out. I could be happy here too."

"That's very generous of you, Frankie, but I really don't think it would work."

"Why not? You love it here, and I could learn to love it too."

"I'm sorry, but I have to do this on my own."

"You're not alone though, are you? There's Sam."

"Yes, there's Sam," Dan said. "We've only been on one date, but I like her. I like her a lot. We're very different, and I have no idea if it'll work out, but..."

"You want to try."

"Yes. Yes, I do."

Frankie smiled sadly. "Lucky girl." She stepped back, looking anywhere but at Dan. "I should go."

"You don't need to rush off. What about your coffee?"

"Thanks, but we'd better forget about it. Another time, perhaps. If you're ever in London, give me a call."

"I don't know if that would be a good idea."

"You're probably right," Frankie said. "Clean break. Unless..."

"Unless what?"

Before Frankie could reply, someone cleared their throat, and Dan turned to see Walter standing in the doorway.

"Am I interrupting something?" Walter asked.

"For God's sake, Walter," Frankie snapped. "Why don't you go and wait in the car?"

"I..." Walter's face fell, his mouth hanging open as if he'd just been slapped. "But..."

"I'll be there in a couple of minutes," Frankie insisted. "Dan and I are talking."

"I can see that, thank you. I'm not an idiot, Frankie." Walter pulled himself up to his full height, then he stalked to the back door and let himself out, slamming it behind him.

"Sorry about that, Dan," Frankie said. "I shouldn't let Walter get to me, but I've been stuck with him for days, and he's so spineless. He drives me to distraction."

Dan frowned, staring at the closed door.

"What's the matter?" Frankie asked.

"I'm not sure."

Alan strolled into the room. "Is that cup of coffee on the way?"

"He used the back door," Dan said. "Walter. He went straight for the back door as if he knew it was there."

"There's nothing remarkable about that," Frankie replied.

"There could be." Dan crossed to the place where Walter had stood when he'd entered the room. "I thought so. You can't see the back door from here. He must've known about it beforehand, and that can only mean one thing. It was Walter who broke into my house. He was the burglar."

"No, I don't think so," Alan said. "He guessed there was a door at the back of the house. You're clutching at straws."

"Am I? We thought the break-in was connected to CEG. Walter might've taken my hard drives in the hope of finding some information about the company."

Alan shook his head firmly. "I'm afraid you're wrong. The burglar ran straight into me, knocked me off my feet. He was solidly built, and Walter is much slimmer; he couldn't get the better of me if he tried."

"That's a good point," Dan admitted. "Okay, I was barking up the wrong tree, but there's something about Walter. I don't trust him." Dan hesitated, then to Frankie, he added, "You can tell me if this is none of my business, but when you were at the CEG building, did you have an argument with Walter?"

"Several. He can be very difficult."

"I'm talking about a serious confrontation. You called him spineless earlier, and I think you may have said the same thing before, when you were in the stairwell at CEG."

Frankie tented her eyebrows, but then realisation dawned. "Oh yes, I remember. We had a disagreement, but how did you know what I said to him?"

"Someone overheard you arguing. They were concerned, so they told me about it. They knew that you and I are... friends."

There was a pause before Frankie replied. "You were right, Dan, it is none of your business, but as a *friend*, I'll tell you. Walter and I have been working closely for a while, and he got the idea there might be more to it than that. He thought I was attracted to him. He was wrong, so I had to set him straight. It was unfortunate, but I didn't have much choice."

"What did he do?"

"It's not important. I can handle the likes of Walter. I'm not sure why you're bringing this up, Dan, but if you're trying to protect me, please don't. I don't need a knight to ride to my rescue."

"I know, and I didn't mean to patronise you, but he's hiding something, I'm sure of it."

"Isn't everyone?" Frankie asked. "In business, it pays to keep your motives to yourself. Walter thinks he's a player, but he can't carry it off. I know his game. He never liked the deal with CEG. He's been picking holes in it at every opportunity, and now the whole thing has fallen apart, he's rather pleased about it. It makes him look good because, right from the start, he warned everybody it wouldn't work, and it makes me look bad because I was the one who proposed it."

"You make it sound very simple," Dan said.

"It is, dear boy. It is." Frankie smiled. "Look after yourself, Dan. It really was lovely to see you again, and it was a pleasure to meet you, Alan."

"Likewise," Alan said. "Goodbye, Frankie. Safe journey."

"I'll see you out," Dan said. He escorted Frankie as far as the alley beside the house, then she turned to face him.

"This is far enough." Frankie leaned in to Dan and kissed him on the cheek. "I'll miss you, Dan. I meant what I said earlier. If you're ever in London, or if you want to talk, you know how to find me."

"Sure."

"Bye. Take care." Frankie gave him one last dazzling smile, then she walked away, leaving Dan standing alone in the alley, his soul stirred by conflicting impulses.

He heard the sound of Frankie's car starting, and watched the BMW sweep past the alley's mouth, then he headed back to the kitchen and the easy familiarity of Alan's company. They'd planned to have lunch together, and it had just occurred to Dan that the pub would be open. Sam would be there, and he could grab a sandwich and maybe half a pint of whatever guest ale was on offer.

Make that a pint, Dan decided. *Definitely a pint.*

CHAPTER 53

D C Collins turned down the offer of a cup of tea and he perched on the edge of the sofa, notebook at the ready, as Mrs Madeleine Hatfield made herself comfortable in her armchair. The lounge was bright and cheerful, the walls painted in a subtle shade of palest yellow, but it was far too warm, and Collins fiddled with his shirt collar.

Mrs Hatfield's sharp eyes missed nothing and she studied him with a smile. "I feel the cold," she said. "I'm eighty-three, you know."

"You don't look it," Collins replied, and she waved his flattery away.

"They say you're getting old when policemen start to look young, but that's all right by me. It's not every day I get visited by a tall, dark and handsome young man. Tell me, are you spoken for?"

"I'm not sure what you mean."

"You know, are you courting?"

"Er, not at the moment."

"Well, that state of affairs won't last long," Mrs Hatfield said. "Some fortunate young lady will soon snap you up. I was married at nineteen. We didn't hang around in those days."

"Actually, that was what I wanted to ask you about," Collins said. "Your husband."

"Which one?"

"Your first. Baran Petrovich."

The light in Mrs Hatfield's eyes dimmed. "Oh, yes. What do you want to know?"

"I've been looking into something that happened at a property your husband bought during the war."

"Ex-husband. We were divorced in 1973, so I can't tell you much about him, and I definitely can't tell you anything about the war. I was just a toddler. I didn't get married until much later. 1957. As I said, I was nineteen."

"Right, but you still might be able to help. Your ex-husband was from Russia, wasn't he?"

"Yes. The Kamchatka Peninsula. He came over before the war, when he was still very young."

"That fits in with what I've found so far," Collins said. "I appreciate this was all a long time ago, but when you were married, were you aware that your husband owned various properties around the city?"

"Yes. That was partly my father's doing. Father didn't approve of me stepping out with Baran, not at first, anyway. It was partly the age difference, what with me being so young, and it was partly because Baran was a foreigner, but there was more to it than that."

"How do you mean?"

"Baran wasn't out of the top drawer, as we used to say. My family were all very respectable. My father was a businessman and a magistrate, but Baran was a bit of a rough diamond. Oh, he had money, anybody could see that, but he had no idea how to behave in polite society. If things had been…"

Mrs Hatfield's voice trailed away, and her gaze lost focus.

"Are you okay?" Collins asked. "Would you like a glass of water or something?"

"I'm all right, thank you. It's just..." Mrs Hatfield tutted under her breath. "You'll think I'm a silly old fool, but things were different back then. You see, we had to get married, Baran and me. There were no two ways about it."

"You were pregnant."

"Yes. My father hit the roof, but Baran stood by me and he did the decent thing, so we made the best of it. After that, my father took Baran under his wing. He showed him how to trade property, work his way up the ladder, and it paid off."

"The property we're particularly interested in is a warehouse on the quay. Did you ever hear mention of it?"

"Not as far as I can recall. Why do you want to know about it?"

Collins hesitated. Here he was, in the front room of a genteel lady of eighty-three: a woman who'd overcome hardships and put the past firmly behind her. A word out of place could tarnish her memories, once and for all, so he'd have to tread carefully. But when all was said and done, he needed answers.

"Did you ever suspect that your ex-husband's money might've come from criminal activities?"

Mrs Hatfield's only reply was a puzzled frown.

"Do you understand the question?" Collins asked.

"Yes. I'm not slow on the uptake, young man." Mrs Hatfield shifted in her seat as though thoroughly uncomfortable. "I must say, it's very peculiar to be asking about my ex-husband after all this time. He died twenty years ago. I went to his funeral, not that I was made to feel welcome."

Collins made a note. "I'm sorry to cause you any distress, Mrs Hatfield, but we're following a routine inquiry, and your ex-husband's name came up. What we don't know is what happened to him."

"Well, I can only tell you what I know. We were doing all right until Baran let me down. He was almost fifty and he made a fool of himself, chasing after a woman thirty years younger. I wasn't going to stand for that, so I divorced him, and that was that. I met Roger and remarried, and we were very happy. We had a long marriage and never a cross word. He passed away five years ago, but I miss him every day."

"I'm sorry for your loss," Collins said. "I'd hate to upset you, but if you don't mind a few more questions, I'm hoping you can help us to work something out. You say you went to your ex-husband's funeral, and that seems strange, because Baran seems to have disappeared sometime in the fifties. It's as if he vanished from the records."

Mrs Hatfield gave him an odd look. "You are using the right name, aren't you?"

"I think so. What name should we be using?"

"Well, in 1958, not long after our son was born, Baran changed his name. Again, it was my father's idea. He told Baran to try harder to fit in, to be seen as more English, and my ex-husband went along with it. He was always Baran to me, but he started calling himself Bartholomew, and we became Mr and Mrs Petheridge."

Collins scribbled all this down as fast as he could, but the name snagged in his mind. He looked up from his notebook. "Was Mr Petheridge—"

"*Sir*, not Mr," Mrs Hatfield interrupted. "He was knighted for services to industry, but only after we were divorced, so I never got to be Lady Petheridge. No wonder they all looked down their noses at me when I went to his funeral. They're all keen to forget where he came from, but if it hadn't been for my father, he'd still have been plain old Baran Petrovich, working all hours to make a living."

Collins found himself blinking stupidly. Could a man start out in a life of crime and become a knight of the realm? Did the man known as The Russian become Sir Bartholomew Petheridge?

"Your son," Collins began, "what was his name?"

"Douglas. He doesn't come to see me very often, but he paid for this place and he makes sure I don't go without. He still works in Exeter. He took over from his father and he runs the company. You might have heard of it. Corinthian Enterprise Group."

Bloody hell, Collins thought. *CEG.* DI Spiller was going to love this. He was absolutely going to bloody well love it.

CHAPTER 54

The Wild Boar was quiet, and standing behind the bar, Sam was looking bored until she saw Dan and Alan walk in. Her smile lit the room, and Dan couldn't help but grin. Everything was going to be okay. "Hi, Sam," he said as he led the way to the bar. "It's good to see you."

"It's good to be seen," Sam replied. "I was starting to wonder if it's worth opening at lunchtimes, but now you two are here, I'm sure you'll be wanting a slap-up lunch."

"I hate to disappoint," Alan said, "but a sandwich and a swift pint are all that we're after."

"Ah, the last of the big spenders." Sam's eyes flashed with mischief. "Seeing as you're only having one, maybe I can tempt you with our range of bottled beers. They may cost a little more than a pint of draft, but they're worth it."

It was Alan's turn to smile. "Go on then. What do you recommend?"

"Well, we've got a nice range of bottled beers from Red Rock Brewery." Sam produced a bottle from under the counter. "This is a good one. Rushy Mede. It's a golden pale ale with a subtle honey sweetness and a fresh hoppy aftertaste; at least, that's what it says on the label. I tried it and it's really nice. It's local, brewed in Bishopsteignton, *and* it's suitable for vegans."

"In that case, we'll have a couple of those, please," Dan said. "It would be churlish not to."

"Right you are." Sam began preparing their drinks, pouring them expertly into branded glasses. "What can I get you to eat?"

They ordered their sandwiches, and since Sam was used to Dan's aversion to dairy products, the process was concluded with the minimum of fuss.

Grabbing his drink, Alan said he'd go and find a table, then he sauntered away.

"He doesn't want to be a gooseberry," Dan said.

"I know." Sam leaned on the bar to get closer, lowering her voice. "I haven't seen you for a few days."

"No. I'm sorry. I've had something on my mind." Dan hesitated. "I was fired, actually. On Monday."

"But you've only just started."

"Yeah. It didn't pan out. It's probably for the best."

Sam seemed to be at a loss for words.

"I'll find something else soon," Dan went on. "There has to be some way for me to make a living around here."

"You're not going to go back to London then?"

"No. Whatever gave you that idea?"

"*Ms* Herringway for one thing. Ms Snooty Britches, more like. I saw the way she looked at you. She wants to get her hooks into you, and a little bird told me you took her out to the Rugglestone at the weekend."

"We went out for a walk," Dan protested. "Alan came too, and it was all perfectly innocent. Anyway, she's gone, and that's fine by me. I'm not going anywhere."

"I'm glad to hear it."

Dan took a gulp of beer. "This is good."

"It's always good to try something new, and there's something else new around here, in case you hadn't noticed."

Dan glanced around the room and realised his mistake when he saw Sam's expression. "Oh, yes, you've got a new dress. I can't see it properly when you're standing behind the bar, but it's great. The colour suits you."

"Yeah, it does, doesn't it? After we went out the other day, I realised I could do with a few new things, so I popped into Exeter and treated myself."

"You look wonderful, as you always do."

"That's nice of you to say, but I reckon most of my old clothes are fit for the charity shop. They're definitely not what you'd call fashionable. Anyway, you'll never guess who I bumped into. Teri."

"I'm not sure I know him. Is he local?"

"No. Teri with an *i*. You know, the boss's daughter. Well, your old boss, anyway. I went into a place called Artie's for coffee. I'd never been in before, but it's nice. Teri came in and she recognised me, came over to say hello."

Dan nodded, doing his best to look interested. In other circumstances, he might've been keen to hear what Ms Petheridge had to say, but since her father had given him the sack, he couldn't care less.

"It opens as a bar in the evenings," Sam went on. "Teri says she goes there all the time. They have a jazz night on Mondays, and she goes every week. I didn't really know what she was banging on about half the time, but she's into jazz, apparently, and she said the bands are generally good. Maybe we should go. It might be fun."

"Wait. Teri Petheridge told you that she likes jazz?"

"What's wrong with that?"

"Nothing. I was just thinking about something her fiancée told me, but never mind." Dan smiled. "I know Artie's, but I've never been in the evening. It sounds good. I'd be happy to take you on Monday, if you'd like to come."

"Yeah. I reckon I could take the night off. It's always quiet in here on Mondays, so I can get someone to cover for me."

"We could grab something to eat first," Dan said. "I'll find somewhere, and I'll give you a call, okay?"

"More than okay." Sam's smile told Dan everything he needed to know, and he was still beaming when he sat down next to Alan.

"Another date?" Alan asked.

"Yes. Monday night. Jazz at Artie's in Exeter."

Alan raised his eyebrows. "Do you like jazz?"

"Not especially. But listen to this." Dan briefly related Sam's encounter with Teri Petheridge, adding that Joe Clayton had assured him that Teri hated jazz.

"This Joe character wouldn't be the first man to completely misunderstand his partner."

"Yes, but I'm beginning to wonder if he's a compulsive liar. Joe said he'd been to Reading University, but when I told him I'd been there too, he changed the subject."

"There could be a number of reasons for that."

"Also, Joe told me he'd worked for Microsoft in Seattle, but Walter worked there, and he'd never heard of him. I said as much when Joe threw me out the office, and he didn't like it one bit."

Alan looked doubtful. "At the time, were you, by any chance, being a tad confrontational?"

"Well, I wasn't at my best, but the point is, Joe didn't argue with me. He knew I'd caught him out in a lie. I could see it in his face, and like all good liars, he said nothing rather than dig himself into a hole."

"Okay, let's say your intuition is right. He's a stranger to the truth, but that doesn't mean he's done anything wrong."

"Not in itself, but it does make me wonder. Neil discovered large-scale fraud and was ousted. Who replaced him? Joe. Who's climbing up the ranks by marrying the boss's daughter? Joe. Who's well placed to defraud the company and cover his—"

"All right," Alan interrupted. "I can see that you've got a

456

bee in your bonnet about the man, but what have you done about it? Have you looked him up online?"

"Not yet. Right up until he showed me the door, I quite liked him. He's such an affable guy. I didn't have him pegged as a suspect."

"Let's get to it then." Alan produced his phone. "Is his first name Joseph? And can you spell his surname for me?"

Dan gave Alan the details, and a few seconds later, Alan held up his phone to show Dan the screen. There, standing next to a Microsoft sign alongside half a dozen similarly fresh-faced young men and women, was Joe Clayton, a shy smile on his face.

"That's him," Dan said. "Where did you find it?"

"I searched for his name plus Microsoft, and this one popped up. Joe's name is in the caption."

"Yes, but where was the picture actually posted?"

Alan tapped a couple of times on his phone's screen. "Ah, I assumed it was from Microsoft, but it was on Joe's LinkedIn profile. I'll see if I can find the official one."

"Wait," Dan said. "Look for one of the other people named in the caption, plus Microsoft. See if you can find another copy to verify it."

"Okay. Here it is. I've found the same photo, but... hang on. It isn't the same. Joe isn't in this one."

"Show me."

Alan passed his phone and Dan looked closely at the photo.

"Yes he is," Dan stated. "The name Joe Clayton is in the caption, and this photo is identical in every respect but one. Look closer." Dan pinched the screen to enlarge the photo, centring the image on an unfamiliar face. "*This* is Joe Clayton. I have no idea who I've been working with, but whoever he is, he's taken this man's name and constructed a false identity. He Photoshopped the picture, inserting himself in place of the real Joe Clayton, then he posted it on his LinkedIn profile."

"It's not hard to alter an image," Alan said. "But he'd need more than a doctored photo to get a job. Any employer would want to see some kind of proof of ID, plus a National Insurance number, and they'd have checked his references."

"I'm not saying it's easy to build a false identity, but it's certainly not impossible. I'm starting to think Joe is a serious con artist. Getting engaged to the boss's daughter is quite a commitment, even supposing he planned to break off the engagement later." Dan picked up his beer but paused, the drink forgotten in his hand. "I've just thought of something else. What if Seb Cooper discovered Joe's real identity and threatened to expose him?"

"That would be one hell of a motive," Alan said. "But how could we prove it?"

"What, precisely, are you two hoping to prove?" someone said, and Dan looked up to see DS Kulkarni walking toward them.

"Hello," Dan said. "We were just talking over that new crime drama on the TV."

Kulkarni lifted an eyebrow in disapproval. "The bane of my life, those things. A few episodes of *Line of Duty* and everyone's suddenly an expert on police procedure. But somehow I can't see you two sitting around watching TV. Which show was it?"

"It doesn't matter," Dan replied quickly. "I'm sure you have more important things to talk about. Have you come to see me?"

"Yes, I have, Mr Corrigan. I need to have a word. Perhaps we could go back to your house."

"We could, but we've just ordered lunch. You're welcome to join us."

Kulkarni's gaze swept the almost empty room then rested on Alan.

"I can take a hint," Alan said, grabbing his drink and

standing up. "I'll pop over to the bar, see if I can find out what's happened to our sandwiches."

"Thank you, Mr Hargreaves," Kulkarni said. "You're a writer, aren't you? We met in Newquay."

"Yes. That was a memorable trip. Anyway, I'll leave you two to talk."

Alan made his way over to the bar, and Kulkarni took a seat beside Dan. "Are you sure you're okay if we talk here?" Kulkarni asked.

"Here's fine. How did you know where to find me?"

"I'm a detective, Mr Corrigan. I knocked on doors, asked a few questions. It's what I do."

"You could've called. You have my number, don't you?"

"I did try to call, but it went to voicemail."

"That happens all the time. I seem to be living in a semi-permanent black spot. I have a theory that it depends on the weather, although I've no idea how that would work." Dan smiled, but Kulkarni was clearly in no mood for banter.

"Ah, like that is it?" Dan went on. "Sorry, I should've realised straight away. You obviously didn't come all this way to chat."

"No. This concerns the incident in which you were almost run down. I'm sorry to have to tell you this, Mr Corrigan, but we now have evidence that suggests you were the victim of a deliberate attempt on your life."

Dan sat back in his seat. "Oh hell. Are you sure?"

"I'm afraid so. There's CCTV footage that shows the car heading towards you as soon as you stepped onto the street."

"Right." Dan absentmindedly took a sip of beer. "Do you have any idea who was driving?"

"That's one of the reasons I'm here. We talked once before about the possibility that you might've been targeted, and I asked if you could think of anyone who might wish you harm. Now you've had time to think, does anyone come to mind?"

"No. No one." Dan looked down at the table, his mind playing catch-up as he absorbed the idea that someone wanted him dead. Why? What had he done to inspire such hatred? *I interfered*, he told himself. *As far as someone's concerned, I poked my nose in, spoiled their plans.* Dan refocused, and a thought emerged immediately. He looked up. "This must be connected to the break-in at my house. It must be the same person."

Kulkarni had her notebook out. "When was this?"

"Monday." Dan explained what had happened, and Kulkarni scribbled rapidly in her notebook.

"I'll review the case notes and follow this up," Kulkarni said. "Please tell me that someone came out to take prints."

"Yes, they turned up eventually, but they didn't really find anything. They said the person probably wore gloves."

"Of course they did. That's a shame, but I'll look back over your statement and let you know if I have any questions. Is there anything you'd like to add, anything you didn't think of at the time?"

"No. It was all over by the time I came home. Alan actually saw the intruder, so he might be able to tell you more, but he made a statement at the time, and I believe he was very thorough. He has a writer's eye for detail."

"Nevertheless, I'd like to talk to him."

"I'm sure he'll be happy to help." Dan waved at Alan and called out his name, but he got no reply. Alan was deep in conversation with Sam, their heads close together as they peered at something Dan couldn't see. *Odd*, Dan thought. *What are they up to?*

AT THE BAR, Alan thanked Sam for the two plates of sandwiches she'd provided. "I'll take them over in a minute," he added. "Dan's busy with Detective Sergeant Kulkarni."

"Oh. What's he been doing this time?"

"He's not in any trouble. At least, not as far as I know."

"I'll take your word for it."

Alan placed his phone on the bar, and while he took a bite of his sandwich, Sam glanced at the screen.

"That's Joe, isn't it?" Sam said. "I met him at Dan's office party."

"That's right. At least, we think so."

"That's Joe all right, but what are you looking at pictures of him for?"

"I've been comparing that photo to a different one. It's a long story, but we think there might be a connection between Joe and what happened to that man who was found dead in Exeter. Sebastian Cooper."

"I heard about that on the news. It's terrible, isn't it?" Sam paused. "I saw him, you know, the man who died. He was at the tea party too. But what happened to him can't have been anything to do with Joe. I've come across plenty of dodgy blokes in this job, and Joe wasn't like that. He seemed decent. He was the only one of that crowd who was nice to me. He was no friend of Seb, I'll tell you that for nothing, but he wouldn't do anything awful."

"What makes you think they weren't friends?"

"I don't like to say."

"Go on, Sam. It might be important."

"Well, I hate to speak ill of the dead, but Seb was... well, he kept giving me the eye. I told Dan about it, and I told him Seb was a nasty piece of work. That was on account of the way Seb was staring at Joe. I didn't know who Joe was at the time, so I didn't think much about it, but a lot of things have happened since then. Maybe I should've said something before."

"It's okay, you weren't to know, but are you sure about this?" Alan hurriedly ran a search for Seb Cooper's image on his phone, finding a thumbnail and showing it to Sam. "This is the man you saw staring at Joe?"

"Yes, that's him, but let's have a proper look." Sam took the phone from Alan and tapped the screen, scrolling down as she read something. "Oh, that's funny."

"What is?"

"This article. Didn't you know about it?" Sam passed the phone back to Alan.

"It's a piece from the company's website. I don't see what's important."

Sam tutted. "Men. They go around with their eyes shut. Read that bit at the bottom."

Alan did as he was told, and then he looked up, his eyes round. "I have to show this to Dan."

He hurried away from the bar. "You forgot your sandwiches," Sam called after him.

"Sorry," Alan replied, but he didn't turn back. Lunch would have to wait.

"FINALLY," Dan said as Alan marched toward him. "I've been trying to get your attention."

"I was talking to Sam," Alan replied. "I've got something to tell you."

"It can't be more important than this. DS Kulkarni needs to talk to you about the break-in. The burglar might've been the same person who tried to run me down. The police think it was deliberate."

"That's what I want to talk about too," Alan said. "On the day you were almost run over, what were you wearing?"

"My running gear. Shorts and a T-shirt. Why?"

"What kind of shirt?"

"A lightweight one."

"You can do better than that," Alan replied. "Which specific shirt were you wearing?"

"I don't know. I've got so many." Dan cast his mind back, recalling how he'd changed into his gear at work before sneaking down to the fire exit. Then it came to him. "It was a Parkrun shirt. The milestone one I claimed after my hundredth run. It's black with the number 100 on the back in large white figures. Good enough?"

Alan nodded and turned his phone around to face Dan. "Read the last paragraph."

Dan peered at the text. *Special congratulations to our Chief Technical Officer, Seb Cooper. A keen athlete, Seb has tackled many challenges, and this week he completed his hundredth Parkrun.*

"Bloody hell." Dan set the phone down on the table.

Sam chose this moment to appear with two plates of sandwiches. Placing the plates on the table, she nodded toward the phone. "You've seen it then, Dan? It caught my eye. I've heard you going on about Parkrun, and how you've done over a hundred. It's funny, isn't it, how these things happen? I know it's only a coincidence, but it's odd to think how you had something in common with that poor man."

"It's more significant than that," Dan said. "You don't automatically get the milestone shirts. You have to buy them online, so not everybody bothers. They're not common, and if Seb had one like mine, someone might've seen my shirt and assumed I was him."

"I wouldn't say you looked alike," Sam put in. "I suppose he was more or less the same height as you, and he had that look. You know, sporty."

DS Kulkarni had been listening quietly, but now she raised a hand to interrupt. "Hold on a minute. This is all very interesting, but it's circumstantial at best."

"Is it?" Dan asked. "From a distance, and in the heat of the moment, someone could easily have mistaken me for Seb. We had the same build. Someone was waiting for Seb that day and they knew he was a runner, so they saw what they expected to see. I wasn't the target of that car. Someone was trying to run Seb down, and when they failed, they found another way to get to him."

"If you're right, this changes everything," Alan said. "What do you think, Detective Sergeant?"

Kulkarni spoke slowly as though measuring her words. "This information presents an avenue for our ongoing inquiries. We'll look into it."

"You could search Seb's house," Dan said. "You need to check if he owned a milestone shirt like mine. Also, you could ask his colleagues, see if Seb ever went for a run after work."

Kulkarni's smile was tight and humourless. "Mr Corrigan, you probably know what I'm about to say, but I'll say it anyway. We are investigating a serious crime, and if you have any information that may be relevant, you should contact us, but that is the only part you play. Our investigation will be thorough and professional. We understand the law and we know what we're doing. Now, when I came in, you and Mr Hargreaves were talking about motives and proof. Maybe you were talking about a TV show and maybe you weren't, but either way, it's vital that you do nothing that might interfere with our inquiry. You must leave this to us, Mr Corrigan. I hope that's understood."

Dan held up his hands. "Naturally. We wouldn't dream of getting in the way."

"Hm." Kulkarni studied Dan for a second, then she stood. "I have to get back, but I'll consider what you've told me and I'll be in touch. In the meantime, I suggest you keep a low profile, Mr Corrigan, and if you possibly can, stay out of trouble." She nodded to Sam and to Alan, then she headed for the door.

"Blimey," Alan muttered. "She took us seriously. I think we've really hit on something. Someone must've been trying to get to Seb for a while. Sam, tell Dan what you were saying at the bar, about Joe and Seb disliking each other."

Sam explained what she'd seen at the tea party, and Dan listened without comment.

"We ought to see what we can find out about Joe

Clayton," Alan said. "Unless you can think of any other suspects we need to consider."

Too damned many, Dan thought, but he stayed quiet, staring at his half-finished beer, thinking. What if he was wrong and Seb hadn't been the intended victim of the hit and run? What if the driver had known it was Dan stepping out into the street that day? Who might want him dead, and why?

"Are you all right?" Sam asked him.

"Fine. I was just thinking about what DS Kulkarni told us."

"Good," Sam said. "She seemed all right, and I hope you take notice of what she said. You've got to keep out of this business. Both of you."

"I know," Dan replied. "But we can talk about the case, think it over. If we come up with anything, we'll pass it on to the police."

"Don't worry, Sam," Alan put in. "I'll keep Dan in line."

"Good luck with that." Sam lowered her voice, and speaking only to Dan, added, "Listen, don't go jumping in with both feet, all right? Don't do anything where you might get hurt."

"I won't. I'll let the police deal with it." Dan wore his most reassuring smile, but as he watched Sam walk away, a heaviness settled on his shoulders. His relationship with Sam was just beginning, but already he'd made a promise he couldn't keep.

He was involved in this case and he couldn't back away, especially now that he was on the right track and getting closer to the truth with every step. He'd set out on a path, and he couldn't step away from it. It wasn't clear where that path may lead, but whatever the risks, he'd have to follow it to its very end.

CHAPTER 55

Celine had woken much later than usual and found that Patrick had already left for the day. She'd felt groggy and weak, but that wasn't an unusual side effect from her migraine medication. A hot shower had revived her, and she'd followed that up with a large mug of tea and a brunch of bacon and eggs. After that, she'd run a couple of errands and tidied the flat, but boredom had caught up with her, and she'd slumped on the sofa, watching daytime TV with the sound turned low.

Lunchtime came and went, but Celine had no appetite. The minutes plodded past, each one devoid of meaning, and more than once Celine's thoughts returned to that damned phone call from the day before. Dan Corrigan. What gave him the right to pester her with his demands? Who the hell did he think he was? *One more man with an overblown ego,* she thought bitterly. *One call and I'm supposed to come running.*

But perhaps that was unfair. Whatever else you might say about Dan, he definitely wasn't like most men. He wasn't driven by narrow self-interest, but by some kind of urge that she didn't quite understand. What was it that he wanted so badly? The truth? Justice?

Whatever drove Dan, it made him the most infuriating individual she'd ever met, but he was no fool. He'd been convinced there was some kind of fraud at CEG, and he wouldn't have made such an accusation lightly. And what about the mysterious IP address he'd discovered? Celine had written it on her iPad, and she retrieved the note now, reading the digits over and over. She knew CEG's network, knew its oddities and its eccentricities, and there was something about this IP address that nagged at her. What did it lead to? She practically ran that network singlehanded, and if there was a dodgy device connected to it, she ought to know.

This was her kind of problem, and if she was going to solve it, there was only one way to begin.

CELINE GLANCED over her shoulder as she walked into the narrow alley that ran down the side of Corinthian House. As expected, the office windows were dark. An email had been sent to all employees at CEG's head office, informing them that the building would remain closed for the rest of the week and reopen the following Monday. Celine recalled the email's ersatz sincerity: *All of us in the CEG family mourn the loss of a well-liked colleague.* Was that the best they could come up with? *Well-liked?*

There'd been a phone number to call for those who felt the need for extra support 'in this difficult time', but for everyone else, the message was clear: on Monday morning, business would carry on as usual.

Celine would almost certainly be deluged with support requests when the staff returned to work and tried to pick up where they'd left off. How many of them would get in a jam when they realised their passwords had expired while they'd been away from work? And how many more would mysteriously forget how to perform routine tasks they could've done with their eyes closed a week earlier?

Celine would need to hit the ground running. *That's not why I'm here*, she reminded herself. *I've got one job to do, and then I'll get out.*

It felt wrong to sneak into the office, but she didn't have any choice. The main entrance would be locked, and she knew from experience that when the office was closed, her key card wouldn't get her in through the front door. Fortunately, the fire exit at the side of the building was another matter.

Celine made her way along the alley as casually as she could but she hesitated in front of the door, looking back the way she'd come. There was no one around, but even so, she had the uncomfortable feeling she was being watched. The alley was enclosed on one side by the office and by a high stone wall on the other. The far end of the alley was sealed with a tall metal gate, beyond which there were only wheelie bins. There was no way that anyone could see her.

Celine tapped the code into the door's lock and pulled it open, stepping inside before she had a chance to change her mind.

The short corridor was gloomy and unloved, but she wouldn't be there for long. She made for the stairs and trudged upward, her steps slow and heavy as though some part of her didn't want to reach the next level. She'd entered on the same floor as the IT department, but she couldn't access it from there. The IT office had its own fire exit, and it couldn't be opened from outside. That meant she'd have to go up to the lobby and then take the main stairs down or use the lift.

The lobby, of course, was empty, but as Celine headed for the main stairs, she heard something that made her stop in her tracks.

There was someone at main door. A man stood outside,

his head down, his key turning in the lock. As soon as he looked up, he'd spot her through the glass. There was no way for her to escape unseen. Celine had to stand still and wait. If she ran, she'd look guilty, and that was no good. The man outside must be someone official; he had a key.

A second later, the door opened and the man swept in, freezing when he saw Celine. He stared at her from beneath lowered eyebrows.

"Oh! Hello," he called out. "It's Sally, isn't it? From IT."

"Celine. Hello, Mr Petheridge."

Doug Petheridge stalked toward her, frowning. "Celine. Yes. How did you get in? The door was locked when I arrived. You don't have a key, do you?"

"No. I probably shouldn't have done it, but I came in through one of the fire exits."

"Ah. It was you who set off the alarm."

Celine felt herself shrinking beneath Doug's accusatory glare, and with good reason. Naturally, the office would have a burglar alarm; it was a no-brainer. So why hadn't she thought about that before she'd let herself in?

"It's a silent alarm," Doug went on. "A light flashes above the front door, and it notifies the security company. You ought to have known that."

"I'm sorry, I didn't think about the alarm. I've never been in the office when it was closed, so it didn't cross my mind."

"It crossed my mind when I got a phone call." Doug stopped in front of her, his expression still stern. "The security people dashed over to check the doors, but they found nothing wrong, so they turned off the alarm and called me. Fortunately, I was visiting a friend nearby, so I hotfooted it over here to check everything was all right. It was just as well. Here you are."

"I really am sorry, Mr Petheridge. I didn't mean to put you to any trouble."

Doug studied her with a professional gaze. "Why are you here, Celine?"

"Oh, you know, I'm a bit behind with work. Lots to do."

"Haven't we all? In fact, I may as well stay for a bit, now that I've gone to the effort of coming in. I can try to catch up. There's so much to take care of since... well, you know."

"Yes. Seb will be much missed."

"It's a hard time for all of us, which is why the office is closed, and I can't help thinking that you haven't really answered my question. Why are you really here?"

"Well, I need to check the backups," Celine said, thinking quickly. "They still run all the time, whether there's anyone here or not, and I think one of them might've failed. When a backup doesn't complete, I get an automated email with an error message."

"I see, but no one was here, so there can't have been much to back up. Although..." Doug's expression brightened. "There are the batch jobs, of course, processing the daily transactions. The general ledger, account reconciliations, budget allocations and a whole host of other systems that we hardly ever stop to think about. They'll have been running every night, won't they?"

"That's right. I'm impressed. I thought..." Celine stopped herself before she said something patronising to the CEO, but Doug seemed to read her mind.

"You thought that senior management had no idea about what makes this place tick." Doug adopted a self-satisfied smile. "I may look like a dinosaur, but I do know what goes on, you know."

"I'm sure you do."

"Back in the day, I was just like you. I started out in the IT department, though we called it EDP back then. Electronic data processing. I spent years loading paper into dot matrix printers and chasing cables from one room to the next."

"I didn't know that."

"It's true, believe me," Doug said. "It was my father's idea. He said it was the best way to learn the business. Information is leverage, he used to say. He told me I had to start at the bottom and work my way up."

"He must've been quite a character."

Doug's expression soured, and Celine wasn't sure how to react. She fidgeted with her hands and opened her mouth to speak, but before she could begin, a disapproving grunt burst from Doug as though he'd been holding it back until the effort became too great.

"My father was a complete bastard," Doug stated. "He had a heart of stone. He beat the hell out of me at every opportunity, and he made my mother's life a misery."

"Oh, I'm sorry to hear that."

"Yes, that's how it is these days, isn't it?" Doug's tone became edgier as he went on. "Everybody's sorry about everything all the time, so anxious to look like they're putting things right. The problem is, saying sorry never changes anything. What's done is done. The past is dead and buried, and no amount of apologising will bring it back and set it right, don't you agree?"

Celine swallowed and fought the urge to back away. She'd always thought of the CEO as a kind of bumbling uncle: a bit of a stuffed shirt, but likeable, nevertheless. Now she was seeing him in a new light. *He's just venting*, Celine told herself. *He's feeling the strain.* Aloud she said, "I'm not sure. I don't really, er…"

Doug shook his head as if trying to rid himself of an unpleasant thought. "Oh, take no notice of me. I didn't mean to start ranting and raving. I'm not myself. Losing Seb like that, it makes you think, doesn't it? We never know what life will throw at us, nor when it will all end. It's hard at the best of times, but these last few days have been awful. Just totally bloody awful."

"Yes. It's been difficult."

"Very. But things will get easier. It'll take time, but we'll muddle on through somehow. Personally, I'm keeping myself busy. Work is a great tonic. Speaking of which, I ought to leave you to check those backups. Meanwhile, I'll pop up to my office and find something to be getting on with."

"Right. I'd better get started. Lots to get through."

"Me too." Doug's gaze sharpened as he looked at Celine, tilting his head like a bird watching a worm. "Are you on your own today?"

Celine nodded.

"Is Tom not coming in? Or any of the others?"

"No, it's just me."

"I see. All by yourself, and you slipped in through the fire door. I'm not sure whether to be concerned about security or impressed by your can-do attitude. You forgot about the alarm, but still, you were keen to come to work today. Most people wouldn't show such dedication. I won't forget it."

"Thanks, and sorry about using the door. I know it's not—"

"Forget about it," Doug interrupted. "We clearly need to beef up the locks, and next time you want to come in out of hours, contact Tom Hastings. He has a key, and as the IT manager, he should be here with you."

"Yes. I'll remember."

"I'm sure you will. Right, once more unto the breach, dear friends. Cheerio." Doug nodded to her once, then he headed for the lift.

Celine let out a long, slow breath. Her excuse had convinced him, hadn't it? He'd seemed happy enough to walk away and leave her to get on, so she should be in the clear. She'd carry on as planned, but first there was something she needed to take care of. There was a drinks machine to one side of the reception desk: an upmarket model with a display case of multicoloured pods, promising a range of enticing refreshments. Celine was certain it could whip up a large Americano, and for now that was all that mattered.

~

SITTING AT HER WORKSTATION, Celine checked her coffee cup. Empty. She must've finished it without noticing while she'd concentrated on her task. She'd trawled through the branches of the company's network, one by one, looking for the IP address Dan had given her, but she hadn't been able to find it. Maybe she'd made an error when she'd tapped the numbers into her iPad. After all, she'd been labouring under an incipient migraine at the time.

Her notes synchronised across all her devices, and she opened the note on her iPhone for the umpteenth time. As she stared at the numbers, her heart sank. If the IP address belonged to a piece of hardware that wasn't switched on, and if its location hadn't been noted in the records, she'd have trouble finding it.

An undocumented device, Celine thought. *Tom will have a fit.* Celine smiled to herself, picturing Tom going off on one of his rants. But then her smile faded as a memory came into focus. There were lots of things that made Tom irate, but only once had she seen him truly angry.

Yes. She'd hit on a promising idea. Celine jumped to her feet, then she exited the IT office and hurried along the eerily empty corridor.

Celine's key card gave her access to the server room, and she slipped inside, making sure the door was properly closed behind her. This was a controlled environment, the constant whisper of the ventilation system giving her the sense of being oddly disconnected from the outside world.

As if to reinforce the idea that people didn't belong here, the wall by the door was plastered with warning notices, and beside them, a pair of respirator masks hung inside their glass-fronted cabinet.

In the event of a fire, the sealed room would flood with halon gas, forcing out the air. This would suppress the fire without the use of water, which was great for the servers but hard luck on anyone who hadn't escaped in time. Without air, anyone in the room would quickly asphyxiate; the respirators offered a chance of survival.

The ugly rubber masks always sent a chill down Celine's spine. *I'm not claustrophobic*, she told herself. *I am not claustrophobic.* But the idea of being trapped or restrained had always horrified her. Combine that with the thought of clamping a mask on her face, and it was enough to make her shudder.

The sooner she could find what she was looking for, the sooner she could get out of there. *Time to open Tom's cabinet of curiosities*, she thought. Tom Hastings had reserved an alcove at the far end of the room for his stash of obsolete hardware. The alcove was sealed off with a steel door that was always kept locked, but it had once been left open, and Celine had peeped inside.

Metal shelves had been built into the alcove, and they were crammed with an assortment of hardware, all of it old and much of it dusty. She'd shown her colleagues, Justin and Rob, and they'd been fascinated. Most of the gear was older than they were, and they'd had fun poking around and pulling out hardware that looked like badly made props from some old sci-fi movie: miniature CRT screens, clunky switches and panels with warning lights that took their colours from strips of cracked celluloid. There was even a modem with rubber cups for holding an old-fashioned telephone handset.

Their fun had been short-lived. Tom had appeared, his mood even grumpier than usual, and he'd lost his temper. Slamming the steel door shut, he'd yelled at them with a ferocity Celine had never seen before nor since, then he'd sent them packing. Afterwards, Justin and Rob had tried to make light of the whole thing, calling the alcove 'Tom's cabinet of curiosities'. But with her pride stung, Celine had told them that this was no laughing matter. She'd been the one to show them the old equipment, and she should've known better than to muck about when she ought to have been working. Annoyed with herself, she'd told the others that Tom was right: they needed to buck their ideas up and be more professional. Her relationship with Justin and Rob had never really recovered.

Since that day, Celine had only ventured into the server room when it was absolutely necessary and she'd kept strictly to her allocated tasks. She'd put the whole sorry business out of her mind and forgotten all about the alcove. Until now.

Her footsteps ringing out on the hard, vinyl-tiled floor, Celine marched up to the alcove's steel door and tried the handle. It turned, but the door wouldn't budge. She'd known it would probably be locked, but she'd had to try.

What now? Would Tom have the key with him at home, or would it be in his office? Thinking back to the day Tom had found them exploring, she realised that she hadn't seen him lock the door, he'd only shut it. Still, he would have the key somewhere. Tom had a full set of keys for the building, but if the one she wanted was in Tom's office, there was a problem. Tom always locked his office when he went out, even if he was only going to be away for a few minutes.

"Dammit," Celine muttered. She'd have to figure out a way to pick the lock. But even as she made that decision, she heard the unmistakeable sound of the server room door opening and closing.

CHAPTER 56

I n his office, DI Spiller leaned back in his chair, gazing across the desk at Collins.

"Well, well," Spiller said. "That's a turn up for the books. The late Sir Bartholomew Petheridge, a knight of the realm and the head of an organised crime group."

"It looks that way," Collins replied. "I've pulled the deed poll records, and he changed his name from Baran Petrovich in 1958. Chances are that he was the man known as The Russian. Petrovich bought the site on the quayside where Jackie Blatch was killed, and he got it dirt cheap. It had been repossessed after Blatch's death, and I doubt anyone else would've wanted to buy a bomb site at the time. Plus, I checked the connection to 13 Belmont Road, and it stands up pretty well."

"You mean you asked Geoff Higgins to search the files."

"Okay," Collins admitted. "He's better at it than me."

"You did the right thing. Delegate where it makes sense, and you'll go far. What did Geoff find?"

"I don't know how he did it, but he worked his magic and found a record from 1939. Geoff said something about a pact between Russia and Germany, but the important thing is, Petrovich was almost sent to an internment camp."

"The Russians signed a non-aggression pact with the Germans," Spiller explained. "Didn't they teach you that at school?"

"Probably, but history was never my thing. Anyway, Petrovich was interviewed, and his address was recorded. Guess where it was."

"13 Belmont Road?"

"Yes, and Petrovich wasn't the only one. Geoff found a dozen other immigrants who'd given the same address. They must've been crammed in like sardines." Collins paused as if for dramatic effect. "There's more. We finally found out who owned the house, along with four others on the same street. The letting company was in Beverley Barnett's name, but as I thought, it was set up by her father, Tony Barnett."

"Buried under his own house," Spiller said. "Well, well. Tony Barnett was a piece of work, wasn't he? Not only was he bent, but he took advantage of newly arrived immigrants, while at the same time putting his illicit earnings into property, effectively laundering the cash."

"It looks that way, and with all those people living at the same address, it muddied the waters when we were looking into the body in the basement. We've been chasing our tails, and we almost missed the Petrovich connection."

"Hindsight is a wonderful thing, but you got there in the end, that's what counts. Well done."

"Thanks, guv'nor. Geoff did most of the work. He found all the important bits."

"He's worth his weight in gold," Spiller said. "You've both done well, and it all ties in nicely. It looks as though Petrovich got rid of his rival, Jackie Blatch, but we'll never be able to prove it. I think it's safe to assume that Petrovich also killed DS Tony Barnett, or at least ordered his abduction. The link between Petrovich and the Belmont Road house can't be denied, but our prime suspect is dead, and we've gone as far as we can."

There was a brief silence, then Collins said, "Case closed?"

"To all intents and purposes, but don't be downhearted, Collins. The chances of getting a conviction in this case were almost non-existent from the start. The top brass wanted every stone turned, and we've done our best. You've learned a lot along the way, and I've been very pleased with the way you got stuck in."

Collins shrugged and tried to hide his bashful smile. "Cheers. It's a shame we can't take it a bit further. There must be a fortune in illegal earnings we could go after."

"The sins of the father are visited on the son," Spiller mused, then he shook his head. "Not after all this time. We'd have one hell of a job putting a case together. Besides, the chief superintendent wouldn't thank us for digging deeper. Tony Barnett's connection would be dragged into the limelight, and that case hasn't turned out the way our superiors would've liked. They thought we were looking for a cop killer. They wanted to be seen as seeking justice for a brave officer who was killed in the line of duty. Instead, we've given them a bent copper, and no one likes the whiff of corruption, even if it comes from all those years ago." Spiller leaned forward, his gaze locked on Collins. "As far as this case goes, our work is all but done. I'll report back to the chief superintendent and that will be end of it. We'll let him handle the press and so on. Okay?"

"You could say that this cold case has turned into a hot potato."

"Don't give up your day job," Spiller said with a smile, then he stood, grabbing his jacket from the back of his chair. "I'm going to nip out for a coffee or something. If you fancy coming along, we can talk over the Cooper case, make sure you're up to speed. We could swing by the scene, walk through it, see if anything comes to mind."

"That'd be great."

"Good. We'll go to a decent place and get one of those fancy coffees you like. My treat."

"Right. Okay."

Spiller eyed his subordinate's expression. "There's no need to look quite so surprised, Collins. I do put my hand in my pocket now and then, you know."

"Yes, guv'nor. Anything you say."

"Quite right. Come on." Spiller marched from the room, Collins hard on his heels. They were heading for the streets, where you never quite knew what was going to happen. *And not a spreadsheet in sight,* Spiller thought. *Not a single one.*

CHAPTER 57

C eline spun around.

She couldn't see the entrance to the server room; a row of tall hardware racks stood in her way. Who'd opened the door and had they come inside? If so, were they still there?

Surely, it wouldn't be the CEO. Could it be Tom? Doug might've called him to check her story about the backups, in which case she'd have some explaining to do.

Perhaps she should call out. But if someone had come in, they might not know for certain she was there. They might go away of their own accord.

Celine held her breath, listening. There were no footsteps, no voices, nothing. Maybe someone hadn't come in after all. Either that, or the person was standing stock still, just as she was.

There was nothing for it; she'd have to risk taking a peek. Placing her feet carefully, she stepped sideways until she reached the aisle that led to the entrance. There, staring back at her, an odd expression on his face, stood Doug Petheridge.

"There you are," Doug said. "I came to see how you were

getting on, and when you weren't in the IT office I wondered where you'd got to."

"I came in to check one of the servers."

"Which one?" Doug started walking toward her, his gaze never leaving her face.

Celine clasped her hands in front of her. She tried to look relaxed, in control, but her grip tightened, her fingernails pressing hard against her skin. "Oh, you know how it is. Once I started checking, I realised there were several machines I wanted to cast my eye over, make sure everything was all right."

"I see." Doug stopped, uncomfortably close, standing in silence.

"Was there something... I mean, are you having a problem with your computer, Mr Petheridge?"

"Please, call me Doug. But no, there's nothing wrong. I came down to see what you were up to. As I told you, I started in IT, and I thought I'd take a look around, for old time's sake."

"Right. There's not much to see, I'm afraid. It's all pretty much automated. There's nothing particularly interesting."

"So I see. There used to be more switches and buttons, rows of blinking lights."

"Most of the controls have been replaced with virtual dashboards. I can sit at my desk and see a full set of status reports, and I can control everything from there."

"Fascinating, but it makes me wonder. If you can run all this from your desk, why did you need to come in here in the first place?"

Celine mentally cursed her stupidity. She hadn't meant to blurt out all that stuff about dashboards, but he'd made her nervous. "Well, we can't control absolutely *everything*. There are still moving parts, like cooling fans, and they can get clogged up with dust."

"This is a controlled environment. I read the notices on the way in. There's no dust in here."

"Yes, that's true, but we do sometimes have to come in and double check, just in case." Celine smiled. "Anyway, I should be getting back to my desk."

She made to step forward, but Doug stood in the centre of the aisle, and he showed no sign of getting out of her way.

"If you don't mind," Celine said, gesturing toward the entrance. "I have to go."

"As it happens, I do mind, because you're not telling me the truth, are you, Celine?"

"I beg your pardon."

"You heard me. What are you really doing in here?" Doug advanced on her, and Celine stepped back, but he kept coming, forcing her to walk backwards.

"I don't know what you mean," Celine said, hearing the fear in her own voice.

"Yes you do. What have you been up to?"

Celine's back came up against the wall, and she stopped, a cry of surprise escaping from her lips before she could stop it. In a moment of panic, she looked to the side, trying to figure out the best way to escape, and her gaze snagged on the steel door to Tom's alcove. She looked away, but Doug hadn't missed it.

He looked from the steel door to Celine. "Have you been prying? Poking your fingers into places where they don't belong?"

"No. Definitely not."

"But you're interested in that door."

"No I'm not," Celine said. "I don't even know what's in there."

"You're lying to me. Why?"

"I'm not lying. It's a storage area, but Tom keeps it locked. I haven't seen inside for ages. It could be empty for all I know."

Doug narrowed his eyes. "What do you *think* is in there? What are you looking for?"

"I'm not—"

"Enough." Doug raised a hand to silence her. "Tell me the truth, Celine. This is my company, and I'm entitled to know what you're doing here. If you won't tell me, I'll have to call the police, and I'll have to explain that you let yourself into the building without permission. Technically, you're trespassing, and I'm starting to think you have criminal intent. I'll have no option but to contact my legal team and set them to work. I warn you, they're like a pack of hungry dogs. They won't stop until they've pinned something on you, so you'd better come clean, young lady. Now."

It was that *young lady* that did it. Something snapped inside Celine, and she was suddenly very tired of Doug's overblown, self-important bullshit. Looking him square in the eyes she said, "No. You won't do any of that."

"Yes, I bloody well will, you cheeky little—"

"Save it," Celine interrupted. "You won't go to the police, because you don't want anyone to find out the truth. I know about the hidden device, the one where someone in this company is keeping secrets. I know the IP address, and I know how to log on to it. So does Dan Corrigan. We talked about it in detail and he knows I'm here, so if anything were to happen to me, he'd know about it straight away."

It was a bluff, but Celine saw that she'd put Doug on the back foot.

Screwing up his face, Doug said, "Corrigan? Why is he involved?"

"He's the one who put all this together. He knows everything, and I've had enough of this." She took out her phone. "*I'm* calling the police."

Without warning, Doug lunged at Celine, snatching the phone from her hand. She cried out, but he pocketed her phone and grabbed her upper arm, squeezing it tight. Celine tried to free herself, but she couldn't break his grip.

"Let go!"

"Not yet. Come on." Doug pulled Celine along by her arm, moving so fast she had to take staggering steps to stay upright. She tried to hold back, but it was no use.

Doug brought her to the steel door. "If you're so sure of yourself, you'd better show me some evidence. Go on. Open it."

"It's locked."

"Obviously." Doug patted his pockets. "I have a complete set of keys at home, but I don't carry them all around with me. It's a shame. I could've satisfied your curiosity. As it is, I'll have to take an alternative course of action."

"What do you mean?"

"We'll have to see, won't we? I can't have you making wild allegations about my company, so I'll have to make you see the error of your ways."

"They're not wild allegations. Dan Corrigan—"

"Don't talk to me about that idiot. He's led you astray. He's made a fool of you. There are no secrets here, and if I could open this cupboard, I'd prove it to you."

"Tom has a key," Celine blurted

"Does he, by God." Releasing her arm, Doug fished in his trouser pocket and produced a bunch of keys, singling one out. "Stay here."

"What are you going to do?"

"Fortunately, I have my master key, so I'm going to do two things. I'm going to look in Tom's office and find the keys for this door, but before that, I'm going to lock you in here, so you don't try anything foolish."

"No," Celine protested. "Don't lock me in, please. I don't like it. It makes me anxious."

"Tough. I won't be long."

Celine held out her hands, pleading. "Seriously, I really can't stand being locked in, especially here."

"You'll be fine. I'll be five minutes, maybe ten."

"No." Celine grabbed at Doug's jacket, but he pushed her back, hard. Her body met the metal door with a hollow boom, and her shoes almost slipped on the smooth floor. Celine kept her balance, but Doug was already marching away. Celine set off after him, but he had a head start, and he was moving away with a determined stride. She caught up with him at the door, but again, he held out his arm and shoved her back. Then he was gone, the door slamming shut behind him.

"Oh my God," Celine whispered. She heard Doug walking away, and then there was only the hissing whisper of the air vents.

CHAPTER 58

Their sandwiches long since devoured and only the dregs of their drinks remaining, Dan and Alan loitered in the pub, talking over the case.

"Sometimes I envy DI Spiller," Dan said. "He could march up to Joe Clayton's house and knock on the front door, demand answers." Forming his features into a passable imitation of Spiller's hangdog expression, Dan had a stab at a Midlands accent. "Excuse me, sir, I'd like a word, if you don't mind."

"It's like he's in the room," Alan replied. "But unless you're planning on joining the force, I think we're stumped. We may as well head home."

"Yes."

"I know we've come to an impasse, but we'll work it out eventually."

"You're right. We're not out of the game yet."

"That's the spirit. We'll think of something." Alan raised his glass in a salute. "Once more unto the breach." He drained his glass then set it down firmly. "When the blast of war blows in our ears, then imitate the action of the tiger; stiffen the sinews, summon up the blood!"

Dan reached for his own glass, but something made him stop. "What did you just say?"

"It's from *Henry V*, his speech rallying the troops. I thought it might get us going. It starts with 'once more unto the breach', but then I skipped to my favourite part. It goes, 'When the blast of war blows in our ears—'"

"Not that bit," Dan interrupted. "Go from the line after the part about the tiger."

"I can't turn it on and off like a tap, you know. I'm not an actor. But let me see. The next line is, 'stiffen the sinews, summon up the blood!' Why?"

"I've heard it before."

Alan looked unimpressed. "It's a fairly common saying. You'd be amazed how many snippets of Shakespeare have made it into everyday language."

"No, I mean, I've heard someone say it recently." Dan bowed his head, searching his memory. The answer came to him, and he stared at Alan. "It was Doug Petheridge. My old boss. The CEO. He said exactly the same thing at Batworthy Castle."

"Interesting. That could be significant. On the other hand, it could just be a turn of phrase; the sort of thing people say when they want to appear educated."

"I don't think so. The words seemed to come easily to him, as though it was something he said all the time. It can't be a coincidence that part of the same speech was written on the back of that photograph. The password almost certainly belongs to Doug, and if it does, then the secret server belongs to him too."

"You think he's defrauding his own firm?"

Dan shook his head. "He's using the assets he controls to defraud his insurers. Who better to run the scam than the man who controls every facet of the company? Maybe he's working with Joe, but Doug is the ringmaster, and we can only assume that Seb got in his way."

"What are we going to do about it?"

"We have to get into CEG," Dan said. "We need to get to that server and use the password. Once we see what's there, we can figure out what to do. If we're lucky, there'll be something we can hand over to the police."

"But surely, they won't let you in."

"They won't have to. There's a fire exit on the side of Corinthian House. If I had the combination for the lock, or if I could force the door somehow—"

"Hold on. You can't do that. You'd be the one breaking the law."

"With good reason. We'd be helping to uncover a crime, and don't forget, Doug may have been responsible for Seb's death. He might not have done the deed himself, but Doug has money and influence, and that makes him potentially dangerous."

"Then we take our suspicions to the police."

"Not yet," Dan insisted. "We don't have enough."

"I'll admit that what we have is pretty thin, but I can't see any other option. We can't start breaking into buildings. If that's your only idea, I want no part of it."

Dan knew that look in his friend's eyes, and there was absolutely no point in further argument. Besides, Alan was right; breaking and entering would be a step too far. But he had to do something. "I'll call Celine, ask for her help."

"That's a much better idea."

Taking out his phone, Dan called Celine's number. She didn't pick up, and he couldn't explain properly in a voicemail, so he hung up and composed a brief text: *Please call me. I'd like to talk about that matter we discussed. Thanks.*

"Done. Now all we can do is wait, but we don't have to do that here."

"No, we can retire to my house if you like," Alan said.

"Thanks, but I'd prefer to take the bull by the horns. If Celine comes through for us, I want to be ready."

"You want to head to Exeter? What if she doesn't get back to you?"

"Then we'll think again," Dan said. "What do you reckon? Are you game?"

"Always. I'll drive."

"Okay. I'd better go and say goodbye." Dan inclined his head toward the bar.

"I'll wait outside."

Alan headed for the door, and Dan grabbed their glasses and plates and took them back to the bar. It was a small gesture, but Sam would appreciate it, and that was all to the good, because she wasn't going to approve of Dan's jaunt to Exeter. She was almost certainly going to tell him that he shouldn't interfere and warn him that he was going to wind up in trouble. All things considered, she was probably right.

CHAPTER 59

In the server room, Celine paced the length of the aisle, counting off the seconds. Every time her eye caught the respirators in their cabinet, a dizzying wave of panic rose from her stomach. She did what she could to remain calm, hugging herself to ward off the cool air from the vents and breathing deeply, in through her nose and out through her mouth.

I won't be here for long, Celine told herself. *He'll be back soon.* She pictured Doug Petheridge returning to the room. Would he turn his back on her for a moment as he shut the door? Would she be able to take him by surprise, shove him, knock him off balance? She'd only need a fraction of a second to dash out the door, and then she'd be free.

But Doug was stronger than her, deceptively so. With one hand, he'd almost sent her sprawling. She'd need something to give her an advantage. But what? She'd searched in vain for a weapon. The server room was kept tidy. There were cables she could yank out, but what use were they? She couldn't tie Doug up unless she could overpower him first.

She glanced again at the respirators, pushing away her fears and trying to assess the situation rationally. If she were to take both respirators and then set off the fire alarm, she'd have the upper hand, but it would be risky. She'd have only a brief window to escape, then the door would automatically lock, and she'd be trapped with Doug.

No. She'd have to think again.

A key sounded in the lock, and Doug stepped in smartly, facing her as he pushed the door closed behind him.

So much for that, Celine thought, but then her mind went blank, wiped clean by a flash of cold dread.

"Here we are," Doug said. "This should do the trick."

He lifted his hand, and in his fist, the object of Celine's terror gleamed dully.

The claw hammer's head was black, its shaft formed from stainless steel and its handle coated in a rugged, orange grip. To Celine it was huge, its forked claw vicious, but she couldn't tear her eyes from it.

Doug hefted the hammer, cradling its head in his other hand as he strode closer.

Celine's throat was tight. "What's that for?"

"What do you think?"

Celine's gaze flicked up to meet his and her spirit quailed. There was no anger in Doug's stare; anger would've been better. There was nothing: no emotion, no hint of empathy, no spark of humanity. He was a man without a soul.

Doug advanced on her and Celine backed away, somehow finding her voice. "What are you going to do?"

"You'll see." Doug was close to her now, and he filled her field of vision.

"Please," she started, though she couldn't find the words to finish her sentence.

Doug's mouth twisted into a mocking smile. "Don't waste your breath. It's no use looking at me all cow eyed. This is on you. I don't like this any more than you do, but you started something when you crept in here like a filthy sneak thief. You set this in motion, and you've left me no choice."

"But I didn't mean—"

"Oh, shut up!" Doug raised the hammer to shoulder height, while with the other hand he grabbed Celine's shoulder.

She tried to turn away, to wrench herself free, but her body wouldn't obey. Her legs could barely keep her upright, and a tremor shivered through her. She opened her mouth to cry out, but then Doug was pushing her away, letting her go, and she almost tumbled to the floor.

Her hand on her chest, Celine took a breath, her ribcage shaking, her throat dry. But Doug wasn't looking at her. He stood in front of the alcove's steel door, staring at it as if he'd forgotten Celine was there. A heartbeat, and then Doug brought the hammer down hard against the centre of the door, metal slamming against metal with a harsh thud that reverberated through the room.

Celine flinched, but she couldn't look away. Doug was a man possessed, a blood vessel bulging at his temple, his fierce gaze fixed on the steel door.

The metal door looked tough, but it was thin, and Doug's first blow left a long dent. Doug grunted in satisfaction, then he lashed out again and again, his teeth bared, his cheeks flushed, and the door buckled beneath the onslaught.

Celine edged away. There was no way Doug would hear her. She could make it to the door.

But Doug stopped suddenly, turning his head to fix her with a glare. "Stay there. I'm almost done. You do want to see what's in there, don't you?"

Some instinct for survival made Celine nod. *Humour him. Buy yourself some time.*

"Pathetic," Doug muttered. He flared his nostrils, straightened his back and raised the hammer high, bringing it down in a vicious swipe, aiming squarely at the door's steel handle. Something inside the lock snapped with a harsh, metallic crack, and Doug let out a bark of humourless laughter. Turning the hammer in his hands, he slid its claw between the battered door and its frame. He grunted, heaving the hammer's handle back, and with a groan of tortured metal, the door shuddered open.

For a second, Doug stared into the cabinet, then he turned to Celine and inclined his head toward the result of his handiwork. "Come on then. You'd better take a look."

Celine stayed exactly where she was. "I'm fine."

"No, really, I insist." Doug's eyes locked on hers, implacable, the hammer still in his hands, and Celine found herself complying, taking tiny, faltering steps.

"For God's sake. We'll be here all day." Doug stepped back, giving her some room. "Is that better? Happy now?"

Celine didn't reply, but she moved forward more steadily until she could see into the cabinet. "What the hell?"

"My thoughts exactly. You'd better explain."

Celine shook her head in confusion. The shelves that had been crammed with clutter were now empty, save for one item. On the middle shelf sat a broad device with a beige metal case. It bore no logo or identifying marks, and something about it, perhaps its powder-coated finish or the inelegant arrangement of its cooling vents, made it look old. This was twentieth century technology.

"Go on," Doug said. "Tell me what you think."

Celine hesitated. "I don't know for sure, but it looks like an old server."

"Spot on. We used these years ago. Workhorses. They never let you down, but sadly they're obsolete these days." Doug sent Celine a challenging look, as if defying her to extend the analogy to include him. When she didn't speak, he added, "Go ahead. Fire it up, if you can work out how."

"I... I don't know if it's connected, but I can try."

"Be my guest."

Feeling vulnerable as she leaned into the cabinet, Celine groped around the device. At the back, her fingers found a cable that was almost certainly a power lead, and there was a rocker switch beside it. Holding her breath, she pressed the switch and snatched her hand away. Inside the steel case, a cooling fan whirred into life and a light on the server's front panel glowed green.

"It's booting up," Celine said. "If it's on the network, I can find it from my dashboard, but I'll have to go back to my workstation."

"Nice try, but we have everything we need here." Standing too close to her, he reached down to the shelf below the server with both hands.

Had he put down the hammer? Celine couldn't be sure. The shelf was too low for Celine to see what Doug was grappling with. She steeled herself. Could she punch him hard enough to put him out of action? Unlikely. Close up, Doug was heavy—set, solid. It would take more strength than she could muster to have any effect on him.

And then her moment was gone. Doug was sliding something out from below the shelf: a slim device set into a metal tray that remained attached to the shelf above it. Doug lifted its lid to reveal that it was something like a crude laptop, complete with a keyboard and integral screen. Celine's heart sank. Doug had managed to keep the hammer in his hand.

"You do know what this is, don't you?" Doug asked.

"A rack-mounted console."

"Precisely. What you're going to do is this: you're going to use it to connect to this server."

"Why?"

Doug tilted his head to one side as though formulating his reply with care. "I want to see what you know."

He gestured to the console, and Celine felt impelled to lift her hands over the keyboard.

"Go on," Doug went on. "Show me."

"I've never used this model. I don't know how…"

494

"For goodness' sake. You said that you know the IP address. Boot the console up and take it from there."

Celine found the console's power button, and not knowing what else to do, she pressed it. The console responded with a muted beep and a few rows of text scrolled rapidly up the screen, disappearing at the top until only a flashing cursor remained.

"There we go," Doug said. "Now what?"

"I use the command line to access the server, then I'll navigate to the hard disk, see if I can find the file directory."

"Give it a shot."

Celine trawled her knowledge of old-school systems and tapped out the correct commands. On the console's screen, a message flashed up:

>*Password?*

"I don't know it," Celine admitted.

"Oh dear. Then perhaps you can concede that there's nothing to see. No secrets. It's just a piece of old junk, and you really have been a rather foolish young woman, haven't you?"

Celine bridled. "Dan Corrigan knows the password. He worked it out."

"Hm. In that case, there's something you're going to do for me."

"What?"

Doug took Celine's phone from his pocket. "You're going to call Mr Corrigan, and you're going to persuade him to come here, right now. We'll settle this matter once and for all."

CHAPTER 60

Dan and Alan were walking up the steps from the Magdalen Street car park in Exeter when Dan's phone rang in his pocket.

"It's Celine," Dan said, then he accepted the call. "Hi, I guess you got my message."

"Yes," Celine replied, her voice tight. "About that. Can you come into the office? It's urgent."

"Okay. But you sound upset. What's wrong?"

"Nothing. There's a bug in the system. I got an error code: three thirty-three."

"What? I don't—"

"It happened three times," Celine interrupted. "What are the odds?" She let out a shrill burst of laughter. "Anyway, you are coming to *help*, aren't you? I could really use your *help*."

"Yes, of course. I'm in Exeter, as it happens, so I can be there in a few minutes, but how will I get in?"

A pause, and then: "We'll leave the front door unlocked. Come down to the server room."

"We? Is someone there with you, Celine?"

"Dan—"

The call ended abruptly, and Dan stood still, looking at his phone.

"What's the matter?" Alan asked. "I couldn't really hear what she was saying."

"It was odd. She said something about an error code three thirty-three, but I've never heard of it. She said it happened three times as though that was significant."

"It means nothing to me. You should call her back."

"Yes." Dan tried, but his call went straight to Celine's voicemail. He left a brief message and hung up.

"I don't like this," Dan said, and he went into motion, taking the steps two at a time. "Come on. We'd better hurry."

Alan puffed as he matched Dan's pace. "What's wrong?"

"Three thirty-three multiplied by three gives us 999. Celine wants me to call the police."

"Are you sure?"

"Not entirely, but as far as I know, there's no such thing as an error code three thirty-three, and Celine sounded odd. She kept stressing the word 'help'. The one thing I'm sure of is that she's in trouble."

At a swift jog, it took Dan only a few minutes to arrive at the main entrance to Corinthian House. Alan lagged a little way behind him, his phone pressed to his ear. When he caught up, Dan said, "Well? Did you get through?"

"Yes. I talked to DS Kulkarni, and she said they're on their way. She said we should wait outside."

Dan looked up and down the street. There was no sign of a police car, no wail of sirens. He made up his mind. "I'm going in."

"Dan, I—"

"I'll be okay. Don't try and stop me."

"I wasn't going to. I was trying to say that I'd better come with you. You can't go in alone."

Dan hesitated. From what he knew of Celine, she could look after herself, but someone had frightened her, made her sound panicky. If Celine was being held against her will, her captor had already crossed a line. He or she would be desperate, dangerous, and they may not be alone.

"We'll go in together," Dan said, "but I want you to wait in the lobby."

Alan was about to argue, so Dan added, "I need you to watch my back. I don't want anyone following me down, and I need to know that no one can get out of there without coming past you. Okay?"

Reluctantly, Alan nodded. "I can see the sense in that, but make sure you have your phone handy. If you call, I'll be right there."

Dan held up his phone, showing Alan that his number was already selected.

"Good," Alan said. "But, Dan, if you're not out in a few minutes, I'm coming down anyway."

"Fair enough. In the meantime, if the police arrive, you can tell them where I am."

"You mean *when* not *if*. The police *will* be here."

"Yes. Let's go." Dan led the way up the steps, and as promised, the glass door was unlocked. They slipped inside without speaking, both looking around nervously, but the lobby was quiet as a crypt and their footsteps seemed unnaturally loud.

Dan indicated the door to one side of the lobby. "I'll take the stairs."

"Okay." Alan checked his watch. "If I haven't heard from you in ten minutes, I'll come down the same way."

"Right." Dan headed for the door, striding with more confidence than he felt. He paused in the stairwell, listening, but there was nothing to hear.

Dan took the stairs slowly, staying close to the wall. At the bottom, a set of double doors looked as though they led to the main corridor. He hadn't been on this level before, but apart from the lift, there were no other doors to choose from.

There was a key card reader next to the door, but when Dan took hold of the door handle and pulled, the door swung open with a sigh. Beyond, the corridor stretched out to the left and to the right, but a helpful sign showed that the IT department was on the left.

Dan stepped into the corridor and prowled along it, alert and ready. Through a glass door he glimpsed what he took to be the IT department: workstations laid out neatly, each with three monitors. But where was the server room?

He tried the door to the IT department, but it was locked. Further along the corridor he found a plain wooden door without windows, and when he pressed his ear to it, he heard the faint murmur of rushing air.

Cooling fans, he thought. *This must be it*. Dan rapped on the door with his knuckles. A few seconds later it opened wide, and Dan stepped back in surprise.

He'd thought himself ready for anything, half expecting to see Celine's frightened face peering out at him, but here was Doug Petheridge, smiling broadly.

"Dan," Doug said as if greeting an old friend. "Good of you to come so quickly." He offered his hand for a shake, but Dan ignored it.

"Where's Celine? Is she all right?"

Doug sighed as if disappointed, then he lowered his hand. "Celine is absolutely fine. She's waiting inside, and I must say, we're both keen to see what you can do with this mysterious server."

"*Your* server, you mean."

"Well, they're *all* mine. It's my company, after all, but we're wasting time." Doug stood back, gesturing for Dan to come inside. "Come along, Dan. Best not to keep Celine waiting."

"All right." Dan squared his shoulders and marched inside, keeping his eyes on his erstwhile boss.

Doug slammed the door shut and pushed past Dan, marching away between the rows of server racks.

"Wait," Dan called out. "Where's Celine?"

"She's down here," Doug replied without looking back. "You'll see."

What the hell am I getting into? Dan asked himself, but he set off after Doug and soon caught up with him.

Ignoring Dan, Doug turned a corner at the end of the aisle, and there was Celine, standing beside the wall with her hands behind her back, her face pale. Doug moved next to her, and she flinched, drawing back but then coming to a sudden halt.

Dan went straight to her. "Celine, are you all right?"

Celine shook her head, her lips quivering as she spoke. "He's tied my hands to something."

"What?" Dan moved around her, his blood boiling at the sight of the cable twisted around Celine's wrists and leading to a battered steel door frame. He took hold of the cable, his fingers working at the knots, but Doug grabbed hold of Dan's arm and spun him around.

"I wouldn't do that if I were you," Doug growled. "Someone might get hurt."

Dan's fingers formed into fists, but then he saw the claw hammer in Doug's hand, the crazed look in his eye. Doug wasn't wielding that hammer for effect; he was ready to use it. He'd gone past the point of no return and he'd strike in a heartbeat, lashing out with all his might.

"Doug, you'd better put that down," Dan said. "The police are on their way. I called them before I came in."

"Nonsense! Why would you do that?"

"Because Celine asked me to. Three thirty-three, multiplied by three. Nine, nine, nine."

Doug sneered. "Very ingenious, but when the police get here, they'll find I've apprehended a couple of trespassers. My good friend, the chief constable, will shake my hand."

"Not when I tell him how you defrauded your insurers, and how you killed Seb Cooper to protect your secret."

"Is that what you think?" Doug let out a guffaw. "I'm the one uncovering the conspiracy here. You two have cooked up some elaborate cover story, but here you both are, clearly in league with each other, and hell-bent on stealing from my company. As for poor Seb, he died on Monday night, yes?"

Dan nodded, playing along. He had to untie Celine, but he wasn't sure he could tackle Doug on his own. Alan would arrive soon, and the police were on their way. If he could keep Doug talking, keep him away from Celine, there'd be a chance to deal with him soon enough.

"As I've just implied, I'm lucky enough to count a number of very influential people among my personal friends," Doug said. "On Monday night, I was attending a dinner with several of them, including the Police and Crime Commissioner for Devon and Cornwall, Stephen Cosgrove. The event went on rather late, and since it was out of town and in a rather nice hotel in the middle of Exmoor, several of us had booked rooms. I was there all night, as was my wife. Stephen and his spouse were in the room next to us. He snores; at least, I presume it was him. His wife doesn't seem the type."

"Which hotel?" Dan asked.

"The Old Manor House," Doug replied smoothly. "It's near Lynmouth Bay. My room had a view of the sea. I had eggs Benedict for breakfast, and they were a little overcooked for my taste. Is that good enough for you? It's what I told the police when they asked about my whereabouts, and they seemed satisfied. I'm sure they check these things."

"You might have an alibi, but you could still have had Seb killed," Dan said. "I'm not taken in by your story. You seem to think you can drop a name and you're in the clear."

"No. What I think is that you two have a great deal of explaining to do. I know somebody in this company has been stealing. I wasn't born yesterday, but neither am I the kind of man to wash his dirty linen in public. If there are rumours of thefts and fraud, our investors will run a mile, our plans will be left in tatters and I'll be left holding the baby. I wanted this to be dealt with in-house, and sadly I gave that task to Seb." Doug's face fell. "I had no way of knowing what might happen to him, but even so, I'll never forgive myself. All I can do is make amends, hence the strong-arm tactics, and now I have you."

"You can't be serious," Dan protested. "We've done nothing wrong."

"And yet young Celine broke into the building, and she knew about this server. What's more, she gave you up. She assures me that you have the password."

Doug waved the hammer in the direction of a storage cabinet. Celine stood beside it, unable to move away. She was shivering, her face so pale she might keel over at any moment. The cabinet had clearly been concealed behind the steel door that now hung limply from its hinges, but whether Celine or Doug had forced the door, Dan had no idea. An old server sat on a shelf, with an outdated console extending from beneath it. But surely, if the server was Doug's, he wouldn't have needed to damage the door. Did that imply that Celine had broken it down? Had she been involved all along?

Dan studied Celine's expression but could see nothing beyond the veil of fear clouding her eyes.

"Dan, please," Celine began. "Do something. He's lost it. We've got to get out of here."

"It'll be okay," Dan said. "Stay strong, Celine. I'll get you out of this. I won't let him hurt you."

"Ah, isn't that sweet?" Doug intoned. "But it won't last. Criminals always fall out in the end, don't they? But before you start heaping the blame on each other, there's a way out of this. Log on to that server, Dan, and show me what's there.

Depending on what I see, I may just let you go, give you a head start."

Dan narrowed his eyes. "Are you seriously trying to tell me that you don't know what's on that server?"

"Never seen it before in my life," Doug replied. "But if there's actionable information on there – for instance, if there are records that would allow me to recoup the company's losses – I might be inclined to let you go. The police will catch up with you sooner or later, but by then, the company will be out of the woods, and I really won't care what happens to you. All you have to do is put in the password, and this will all be over."

"Dan, do it," Celine urged. "Please."

"All right," Dan said. "I'll try, but that's not an admission of guilt. This server isn't anything to do with me. I'm not even one hundred percent sure I have the password. All I have is a hint that came indirectly from Seb. It's *Once more unto the breach dear friends once more*."

"Is it, by God?" Doug muttered. "But you needn't try to confuse matters with a cock and bull story about Seb. Just get on with it. Use your password."

Dan stepped up the console. Its screen was already showing a password prompt, and he typed in the initial letter of each word in the hint: *o, m, u, t, b, d, f, o, m, !*

Dan hit the return key, and a message flashed up on the screen: *Password incorrect*.

Dan tried again, changing the first *O* to upper case. Again, it was incorrect. He changed the first *O* to a zero, and when that didn't work, he changed both of them to zeroes.

Dan clenched his jaw, then he hit the return key.

This time, he was presented with a single flashing prompt. The console was ready to accept a command.

"I've logged in," Dan said. "What do I do now?"

"Don't pretend you don't know," Doug snapped. "Show me a directory. I want to see a list of all the folders and files."

Dan lifted his hands from the keyboard and let them fall at his sides. "I don't know how to do that. It's not my field. I'm sure Celine could help. Let me untie her."

"I'm not falling for that," Doug shot back. "Get out of the way. I'll do it."

Dan started to step back, but Doug barged in, shouldering him aside. Doug went to work, intent on his task, his fingers clattering the keys. Dan sidled over to Celine and reached behind her with one hand, pulling at a knot in the cable. He felt it loosen and he tugged at it, teasing the knot apart.

Leaning close to Celine's ear, Dan whispered, "Be ready to move."

Doug looked up. "What was that?"

"I'm checking Celine is all right," Dan replied. "She doesn't look well. She needs medical assistance."

"In a second." Doug beckoned Dan to come closer. "Here. What do you make of that?"

Dan studied the console's screen. There were long strings of letters and numbers, row after row of them, all the same length.

"I can't be sure," Dan said, "but they look like keys. Private keys, presumably."

"Keys for what?"

Dan ran his eyes over the screen, using the keyboard to scroll down the list. If these were private keys, there were hundreds of them. The server room faded from his consciousness, replaced by a pleasant park: Rougemont Gardens. Instead of Doug's repeated questions, Dan heard Neil Hawthorne, the man's voice veering close to the edge of hysteria: *What if there is no money, Dan? Nothing to follow. No way to prove a damned thing.*

Dan looked at Doug. "I understand. These are the private keys for accessing some kind of cryptocurrency. My guess is that someone has been using this server as a kind of cold storage, a way of storing the money they've defrauded from your insurers. They transfer the keys onto the server, then they switch it off so that no one can log in remotely and steal the keys. Whoever has the keys can access the funds."

"Excellent," Doug said. "I can reclaim what rightfully belongs to the company. You know, I really think I will let you go. You can finish untying your friend, Dan, and yes, I did see what you were up to. I'm not stupid."

Dan didn't hesitate. He released Celine as quickly as he could, and as soon as she was free, she backed away, rubbing her wrists.

"I have to get out of here," she murmured. "I feel... I feel like..."

"Take deep breaths," Dan said. "In through the nose, out through the mouth. Nice and slow."

Celine took one shaky breath after another, but her cheeks remained stubbornly pale, and she seemed unsteady on her feet. She staggered sideways, almost falling, but she saved herself, pressing one hand against the wall for support.

Dan put his arm around Celine's shoulders, felt her sway.

"Can't see properly," Celine mumbled. "Can't..." Her head lolled forward. She tried to say something else, but Dan couldn't make it out, and with a sickening sense of dread, he took her weight as she crumpled in his arms.

"Doug, Call an ambulance," Dan snapped. "Tell them she's collapsed. Get someone here now!"

Celine tried to speak, but again Dan couldn't make it out.

"Hold on," Dan said. "I'll help you to lie down." He put Celine in the recovery position as best as he could, then he pulled off his jacket, rolling it up and easing it under her head. From behind him, he heard Doug speaking into his phone, and for once, the man was putting his authoritarian manner to good use.

Celine said something, and this time Dan made out the word: "Migraine." Could a migraine do this to a person? Dan had no idea, but Celine was mumbling something. Dan leaned over so that his ear was close to her mouth, but he still couldn't make out what she was saying.

Celine reached down with her right hand and patted the pocket of her jeans.

"In there? Do you have medication?"

Celine nodded feebly, and Dan pushed his qualms aside and put his hand in her pocket. He found a slim plastic case and pulled it out. Opening it, he discovered a hypodermic syringe, and with a surge of relief he saw that there was a laminated instruction card inside the lid.

In the event of a severe migraine attack, the full dose was to be injected into the top of Celine's thigh. Dan removed the protective cap from the needle. He wasn't sure whether he was supposed to push the needle through her clothes, but Celine was wrestling one handed with the fastening of her jeans. She pushed the fabric down enough to expose a patch of bare skin, then she jabbed the place with her fingertip, pointing at her thigh muscle.

Dan checked the syringe didn't have any air bubbles in it, then he took a breath and slowly pressed the needle into Celine's flesh. Celine winced and Dan muttered an apology, then he depressed the plunger, delivering the dose.

Celine closed her eyes and let out a sigh, but her features were still pinched and pale.

Doug stood over them. "The ambulance will be a while, but there are first responders on the way. They should be here in minutes." He paused. "How is she?"

"I've no idea. I have to hope I've done the right thing."

Doug covered his eyes with his hand. "This is my fault. What have I done?"

Someone pounded on the door.

"That was quick," Doug said. "I'll go and let them in."

"It'll be Alan. My friend. You'd better open the door and then go upstairs and wait for the paramedics, make sure they know where to come."

Doug hurried away. The man might take the opportunity to escape, but Dan couldn't think about that. He couldn't tear his eyes from Celine. He'd failed her. He should've acted sooner, tried to rush Doug and knock him down. If he'd been fast enough, he could've got the upper hand, pried that damned hammer from Doug's fingers. Instead, he'd allowed himself to be drawn into Doug's madness. And there was something else; something worse.

I wanted answers, Dan reprimanded himself. *I played along because I thought I'd get to the truth*. He'd tried to be clever, and Celine had paid the price. He would never forgive himself for that.

Dan heard Alan's voice, and it raised his spirits a little. Alan would know what to do. In the meantime, Dan held Celine's hand and said, "Help is on the way. You're going to be okay."

Dan kept his voice calm, but he was by no means confident. He just had to hope that Celine was going to be all right.

CHAPTER 61

Dan and Alan stood on the steps of Corinthian House, and under the gimlet-eyed gaze of a pair of uniformed police officers, they watched the ambulance drive away. Dan let out a long breath.

"She'll be okay," Alan said. "The first responders were brilliant, weren't they?"

"Yes, thank God."

"Poor Celine. A severe migraine attack brought on by stress, so they said. They didn't like the look of those marks on her wrists. Your old boss has a lot of questions to answer."

Dan looked over his shoulder. Through the glass doors, he could see Doug sitting in the lobby with DI Spiller and DC Collins. The policemen had arrived before the first responders. Apparently, Spiller and Collins had been nearby when Kulkarni had relayed Alan's call. As soon as Spiller entered the room, he'd immediately taken charge, shooing Dan and Alan out of the server room. Dan had been reluctant to leave Celine, but she'd been looking better, the colour returning to her cheeks, and he'd had no choice.

Now Celine would get the care she needed. All that remained was to face the fallout.

Dan stared down at the pavement. "I should've kept Celine out of this. She wouldn't have been here if it hadn't been for me."

"I was thinking the same thing, blaming myself," Alan said. "We both talked to her, and we both played a part, but we certainly didn't make that damned man treat her like that."

"That's true. I'd no idea Doug could be so cruel."

"You can never really know what someone's capable of," Alan replied. "I've always thought that the worst kind of monster wears a suit and tie. He's a case in point."

Dan risked another glance through the glass door. Doug was sitting very still, but earlier he'd been in pieces. He'd practically fallen over himself in his rush to give himself up to Spiller.

Alan followed Dan's gaze. "It doesn't excuse what he did, but I wonder if that man needs help."

"That's for others to decide," Dan said. "He might claim he wasn't responsible for his actions, but I think he knew what he was doing."

"We'll see. I just wish I'd got to you sooner. I was trying to get in through the wrong door. I thought you'd be in the room with all the computer screens."

"I should've called you."

"Yes. That was the plan." Alan heaved a sigh. "You know, Dan, you don't have to tackle every problem on your own."

"I know. I've made a mess of it."

"Mr Corrigan."

Dan turned to see DC Collins standing in the doorway of Corinthian House. The policeman gestured for Dan to come inside.

"My turn to face the music," Dan said. "I'll see you in a bit."

Inside, Dan did as he was told and took a seat beside Doug, the two men eyeing each other warily.

"Thanks for waiting, Mr Corrigan," Spiller said. "Do you need a glass of water or anything?"

"No thanks, I'm fine. I'll help in any way I can."

"Right. Ordinarily I wouldn't talk to both of you at the same time, but I have to assume that today's events are linked to an ongoing murder inquiry, and I need to establish whether anyone else may be in danger, so I'm going to ask a few questions before we go to the station." Spiller nodded to Collins, who sat down beside his colleague and produced a notebook and pen.

Apparently satisfied, Spiller began. "Mr Corrigan, you are of the opinion that there is some form of cryptocurrency stored on a device in the room where we found you, yes?"

"That's right. At least, we found some private keys, and I think it's likely that they're for accessing a digital wallet."

"I see. What gave you that idea?"

"Well, I've used crypto in the past, and I recognised—"

Spiller raised his hand to interrupt. "No, I mean, what led you to the server downstairs? Or was that Ms Grayson's idea?"

"Celine had very little to do with it. I was given a set of numbers. They looked like dates, but Celine realised they represented an IP address. That's a way of locating a device on a network."

"I know what an IP address is," Spiller said. "But who gave you that information in the first place?"

"Neil. Neil Hawthorne. He used to work here. I was given his old office, and he told me that he'd left a photo of his wife hidden in his desk. The numbers were on the back of the photo along with a hint about the password."

"What are you blathering on about?" Doug blurted. "Neil isn't married, and he never has been."

"But he told me his wife died some time ago. He said her name was Felicity."

Doug bridled. "As I said, Neil was never married."

"Then who was in the photo?"

"I don't know," Doug stated pointedly. "But Felicity is *my* wife's name."

A memory came to Dan: the way Neil had gazed at the photo of the woman he'd said was his wife. There'd been an intensity in that moment that Dan had misunderstood. He'd thought the man was shaken by grief, but that look in Neil's eyes could've been something else; it could've been a desperate desire.

"Why would Neil have a photo of your wife?" Dan asked, but Doug pursed his lips, shook his head.

"Okay," Dan went on. "Why was Neil fired? What was the real reason?"

"Why do you think?" Doug muttered. "Neil was fired because, as you've discovered, he's unreliable. The board decided they could no longer trust him. I can see what you're thinking, but none of this has anything to do with my wife, and I'd like to point out that I've never seen this photograph you keep talking about. It could be a picture of the Queen Mother for all I know."

"Gentlemen, let's get back on track," Spiller said. "We'll talk to Mr Hawthorne later. He gave you the IP address, Mr Corrigan. As far as you know, where did he get it?"

Dan didn't reply. He was too busy wondering why Neil had lied to him about Felicity. Had he simply been trying to conceal an affair? Or was there another reason?

There's something I'm not seeing, Dan told himself. *I've made a mistake.*

Spiller looked as though he was losing patience. "Mr Corrigan, do you know where Neil got the information that you allege was on the photograph?"

"He told me that he'd seen those numbers on Seb's desk. Neil said that someone in the company had been committing insurance fraud on a huge scale, and I believed him."

"According to Mr Hawthorne, who was supposed to have been behind this fraud?" Spiller asked.

"He didn't tell me, but there were other factors that made me take him seriously. Everyone at the company was very cagey and secretive, and it occurred to me that they'd hired me, rather than a large firm of consultants, because they didn't want anyone looking too closely at all their accounts."

"Little did they know," Spiller said. "We've had several encounters, you and I, and I'd guess you poked into every nook and cranny of the books, am I right?"

"I would've done, but I'd hardly got started when a story appeared in the papers, making me out to be some sort of investigator. I was sacked."

"With good reason," Doug put in. "I went through all this with you at the time."

Spiller made a downward motion with his hands. "Let's stay calm, gentlemen. We'll have time to go through all the details when you make your statements. Right now, I need to see the lie of the land as quickly as possible. So, in a word, Mr Corrigan, your dismissal reinforced your belief that someone in the company was anxious that their crimes didn't come to light."

"Yes."

"Did you have any suspicions as to who might've been perpetrating the alleged fraud?"

Dan hesitated. "There's a man here who calls himself Joe Clayton, but I don't think that's his real name."

"Of course it is," Doug said. "Joe's going to marry my daughter. Did you think I didn't check his background?"

"But he didn't work at Microsoft," Dan argued. "He made that up."

Doug screwed up his mouth as if chewing something unpleasant. "I know about that. His name is not uncommon, and Joe has a tendency to exaggerate. When he found someone with the same name, he took it upon himself to borrow a piece from the other man's CV. I've warned Joe about it, and I thought he'd set the record straight, but he can be very headstrong. He feels as though he has something to prove."

"Because he's marrying the boss's daughter," Dan suggested.

"Yes. He doesn't like it when people assume he was given a leg up, but the truth is I've always given him an easy ride. I don't deny it. I gave him the kind of encouragement that was never given to me. What else can I say? I like Joe and I wanted to help him. I hoped that, in time, he'd grow into the role, and maybe, one day, he'd take the reins. What's wrong with that?"

"I'd say it's par for the course," Spiller said. "But how long has Joe been at the company?"

"A little under a month."

Spiller frowned at Dan. "That fact isn't consistent with the kind of fraud you were talking about, Mr Corrigan. In my experience, financial crimes are complex. Unless Mr Clayton is an extremely fast worker, I'd say you're on the wrong track."

"That much is obvious," Doug chipped in. "Joe wouldn't do anything to hurt the company. He has nothing to gain by it, and frankly, he hasn't got it in him. He might be a bit fanciful, and he lets his ego get the better of him now and then, but he hasn't got a devious bone in his body. I've no doubt that my daughter will be the one wearing the trousers in their marriage. She can already wrap him around her little finger."

Dan knew a dead end when he saw it, but he wasn't ready to give up. "Okay, I might've been wrong about Joe, but that leaves us with Seb Cooper. He had the IP address and password, he has a shady past, and as the CTO, he had the means and the experience to set up the server we found downstairs."

Spiller frowned. "I understand from DS Kulkarni that you think someone tried to run you down in the belief that you were Mr Cooper."

"Yes, presumably the same person who later killed Seb. Maybe Seb was working with someone and they fell out. His partner didn't want to share the proceeds, so they killed him."

"All I'm hearing is baseless speculation," Spiller said. "Let's concentrate on facts. *Verifiable* facts. Moving on, have either of you seen or heard of anyone in the company who used a painkiller called fentanyl? It may have been prescribed for severe pain, perhaps after an operation or a serious injury."

"I've never heard of it," Doug replied. "I don't recall anyone having an operation recently, but you could check with HR. They have all our sickness records."

Dan's reply to Spiller was one word: "No."

"Is that all you have to say, Mr Corrigan?"

"Yes."

"Well, well." Spiller sat back and turned to Collins, murmuring something Dan couldn't hear.

"I can do that," Collins said. "I'll have to nip out to the car." Collins stood and made for the door.

"If you could bear with us for a minute or two," Spiller said, "there's something I'd like you to see."

In the silence that followed, Dan studied Doug. The man was sitting bolt upright as if trying to maintain his dignity, but he must've known he'd be facing time behind bars. *I'm surprised he hasn't sent for a lawyer already*, Dan thought. *Maybe he's struck with remorse for what he's done.* Doug seemed to realise Dan was watching, and when he returned his gaze, Dan caught a fleeting glimpse of vulnerability. For all Doug's stiff upper lip, he was like a little boy who'd been caught carrying out some shameful act. His shell of bombast and bluster was paper thin, and now it had been torn away. Dan almost felt sorry for the man.

DC Collins marched inside carrying a tablet. He sat down beside Spiller and passed the tablet to him.

Spiller studied the tablet, tapping the screen, then he nodded to Collins. "Well done, Detective Constable." To Dan and Doug, he added, "By the miracle of modern technology, we have a short clip of CCTV which I'd like you both to look at. All right?"

"Fine," Doug said, but Dan had questions.

"Where is the footage from? And which case is this in relation to?"

"This concerns the investigation into Mr Cooper's death," Spiller replied. "It was taken from the car park where Mr Cooper was found, and it shows the minutes leading up to nine o'clock on the night he died. Good enough for you?"

Dan nodded.

Collins took the tablet and held the screen so Dan and Doug could both see it. He played the clip, and Dan watched the monochrome footage carefully. It showed the entrance to a car park. A figure passed through the halo of an overhead light; a man, walking with a swagger in his step, his shoulders back. Dan recognised him immediately, and from the sudden shift in Doug's posture, so did he.

"That's Seb Cooper," Dan said. "He looks confident."

"We won't presume as to his state of mind," Spiller replied. "But yes, we believe that to be Mr Cooper. Please pay special attention to the next person to arrive."

A moment later, a tall figure entered the edge of the frame, sticking to the shadows as if he was aware of the camera. The man had a small rucksack on his back, but that was the only detail Dan could make out. The man moved quickly. He was only in the frame for a second or two, and his features were hidden beneath a dark hoodie.

"Can we see it again?" Dan asked.

"No problem," Collins replied. He reset the clip and played it once more. Both policemen seemed on edge as if waiting for a revelation, but Doug shook his head, and Dan could do no better.

"I'm sorry," Dan said. "I'm positive the first man is Seb, but I don't recognise the second man."

"Nothing at all?" Spiller asked. "No idea who it might be?"

"None." Dan thought for a moment. When it came to recognition, context was everything. He'd never seen any of his acquaintances dashing around like thieves, but he knew someone who had.

"I've got an idea," Dan said. "Could we ask Alan to take a look at this?"

"I don't see why not. Collins, could you ask Mr Hargreaves to step inside?"

"Yes, sir."

Collins fetched Alan, who sat next to Dan and watched the footage with rapt attention. There was a moment's silence, then Alan looked up and said, "That's him. That's the man I saw in Dan's house."

"How certain are you?" Spiller asked.

"As sure as I can be. It looks to me as if he's wearing the same clothes. He's even got the same bag on his back."

"Interesting," Spiller said. "I believe DS Kulkarni is reviewing the break-in at your house, Mr Corrigan, so if there is a connection with Mr Cooper, we'll find it." Spiller nodded as if to draw a halt to the proceedings. "Right, it's about time we went back to the station and took statements. We'll take you with us in the car, Mr Petheridge. Mr Corrigan and Mr Hargreaves, I can arrange transport, or you can follow under your own steam."

"We'll drive," Dan said.

"Good. In that case, we'll get going." Spiller stood, and DC Collins helped Doug to his feet.

Dan and Alan followed them outside. The pair of uniformed officers were still stationed outside, but they seemed to know that Dan and Alan were free to leave.

"Hell of a day," Alan said.

"You can say that again," Dan replied. "And it isn't over yet."

FRIDAY

At home in his kitchen, Dan saw Alan passing the window. Dan made the necessary preparations, and when Alan knocked on the door, he called out, "Tea or coffee?"

Alan let himself in and said, "It's customary to say, 'Come in' or 'It's open'. Something like that."

"It's customary to do a lot of things," Dan said. "Are you trying to tell me you don't want a drink?"

"Coffee would be nice. Mind if I sit down?"

"Pull up a chair, make yourself at home." Dan fired up the espresso machine. "Your usual? Americano?"

"Can that thing do a flat white?"

"This machine can make any kind of coffee known to science. It'll be oat milk though. Okay?"

"Fine. I'm getting a taste for it." Alan sat down at the kitchen table. "Any news about Celine?"

"Yes." Dan forgot about the coffee for a moment, turning to face Alan. "She sent me a text. She's fine, but they're keeping her in while they run tests."

"You can't be too careful. Here's hoping they give her a clean bill of health."

"Absolutely." Dan went back to making the coffee. He couldn't bring himself to tell Alan about the last few words of Celine's text: *Thank you for everything you did*. Her gratitude seemed to let him off the hook, and he hadn't earned that privilege; it was too easy. He should never have dragged Celine into the mire at CEG, and for that, he'd have to make amends. It was hard to see what he could do to put things right, but he'd have to try.

"I wonder what's happening to Doug," Alan said. "Personally, I hope they throw the book at him."

"I haven't heard anything, but whatever happens, it'll be a long, drawn-out process." Dan started steaming the milk, concentrating on swirling the jug, and the hissing gurgle of the machine temporarily brought their conversation to a close.

Alan waited, tapping his fingers on the table, and as soon as Dan brought their drinks to the table, Alan said, "Thanks, but I didn't come around purely for the coffee. What's next? What can we do?"

"Hard to say." Dan sat and took a sip of coffee. "Not bad. Is yours okay?"

"It's fine, thanks, but is that all you can say? Don't you want to talk about the case?"

Dan took another drink of coffee before he replied. "Listen, Alan, this case, or whatever you want to call it, has been a disaster from start to finish, and I'm beginning to think Spiller was right."

"About what?"

"Yesterday at CEG, before you came in, he said that all I had was *baseless speculation*. He made me feel about three inches tall, but I have to admit, he had a point. We don't have anything to go on."

"So we give up? Is that what you're saying?"

"Maybe. I've said this before, but this time we're seriously out of our depth."

"What else is new? This isn't the first time we've been stuck, but we've always found a way to move forward. Perhaps this time we're up against a more sophisticated adversary, but whoever it is, we can beat them."

"*Adversary?*" Dan found himself smiling. "Perhaps it's Moriarty."

"You mean *Professor* Moriarty. I doubt we're dealing with such a criminal mastermind, but the person behind all this has been remarkably cunning. They set up a secret server in the company's head office, and they dealt ruthlessly with Seb when he got in the way. It's no wonder your friend Neil was so twitchy when you spoke to him. He must've been in fear for his life."

Dan didn't reply. He was staring at the window, his mind a whirl. *Alan's right,* he thought. *We're looking for someone extremely devious, someone who is not what they appear.*

"Are you all right?" Alan asked.

"Yes. You've never seen Neil, have you?"

"No, not as far as I know. Why?"

"Because he set this train of events in motion. He could be the one. He could be the man we're up against."

"Hold on a minute. He told you about the fraud in the first place. Why would he do that if he was behind it?"

"Because he's devious," Dan said. "He knows how to use people, how to press their buttons. When he was fired, he was probably escorted from the building, so he wouldn't have had time to access the server. Do you remember on my first day at CEG? There was that explosion, that bomb from the war."

"Of course I remember. But I don't see what—"

"I saw Neil near the office," Dan interrupted. "I heard the bomb, so I looked out of the window, and there he was, right outside. He was trying to get in through a fire exit. He admitted it when I saw him a couple of days later. He asked me to let him in, and when I refused, he came up with the story about the photograph."

"I've been thinking about that photo," Alan said. "I think Neil had a picture of Doug's wife because he was having an affair with her. He didn't want anyone to find the photo and work it out."

"That's incidental. Don't you see? Neil used me to get to the server. He fed me the photo. He knew I'd see what was written on the back, and he hoped I'd take the bait. You see, if it's his server, he wouldn't need the photo himself. He'll have a copy of the IP address and the password, but he couldn't get into the building, never mind the server room. He needed a proxy and he picked me."

"Then why didn't he just tell you what the numbers meant? We were stuck until Celine gave us the answer."

"That would've been risky. If he'd given me too much information, I might've simply reported it. Neil needed me to work in secret. He made me think there was a conspiracy at CEG, and he had me so rattled I didn't know who to trust. That was exactly what he wanted. Remember, I spoke to Neil on the phone before I was hired. He knows the kind of person I am, and he's probably heard about some of our cases."

"Not from that newspaper story," Alan said. "That didn't come out until later."

"True." Dan thought for a moment. "Neil knows Craig Ellington. I had a WhatsApp call with Neil when we first heard about Seb's death, and Neil admitted knowing Craig. He said Craig had described me as being like a dog with a bone. Craig could easily have told him about us."

Alan stared at Dan. "He didn't need the photo *at all*. The whole thing was purely a ruse to pique your curiosity."

"That's right. I mean, I'm sure the photo was already there, hidden in Neil's desk long before I arrived, but Neil realised he could use it. It was very clever of him not to explain the numbers on the back. If he'd told me about them, I'd have been suspicious of his motives, but he claimed he didn't know what any of it meant. I thought I'd stumbled onto a secret all by myself. It was a problem begging to be solved. Once I'd seen it, I was hooked."

"What about the hit and run? Was he aiming at you after all? Had you become a liability?"

"No, I really think he was after Seb." Dan clicked his fingers. "Remember that CCTV footage? Seb went into that car park feeling confident, without a care in the world. Doug had asked Seb to investigate the company's losses, but Seb was ambitious to the point of being greedy. What if he found evidence that Neil was behind a large-scale fraud? That would've given Seb a hold over Neil. Seb felt in control, so he marched into that car park, expecting a payoff. He didn't know what Neil was capable of. He didn't realise he was putting himself in danger."

"But when you saw that footage, you didn't say anything about Neil," Alan pointed out. "You'd have recognised him, wouldn't you?"

"Not necessarily. I've never seen Neil run, and I've never seen him in casual clothes."

"Okay, let's say you're right. Neil fed you some clues, then he waited to see what you came up with, but what was his endgame? He needed those private keys himself, didn't he? If you found them, you might've kept them, and then they'd have been no use to him."

"You're forgetting the break-in," Dan said. "Neil wanted to see what I'd discovered, so he broke into the house and took all my hard drives."

"But you hadn't found the keys – not at that point, anyway."

"Neil didn't know that. He must've been furious when he realised I hadn't got anywhere."

"You could be right," Alan said. "Maybe Neil's anger tipped him over the edge. Seb was killed later that day."

"No, I don't think Neil is a man who lets his anger get the better of him. This whole scenario is the work of someone cold and calculating. He was always going to kill Seb, and he expected to get away with it. First, he tried to make it look like an accident in the street, then he tried to make it look like an overdose. Seb's history of drug taking wasn't a well-kept secret, and I have a feeling he was still using. To Neil, that must've seemed like a gift. He arranged to meet Seb in the car park, and the scene was set."

"I've been doing some research on the drug angle," Alan said. "You said Spiller mentioned fentanyl. It's dangerous stuff. Very powerful. It can be prescribed for pain, but it's found its way onto the street, and it's sometimes mixed with other drugs. It causes a lot of deaths every year. Do you think Neil made up a lethal dose and offered it to Seb?"

"I doubt it. If he had, Seb might not have taken the drug there and then, and Neil couldn't afford that risk. I think it's more likely that Seb was given the drug against his will. Does it have to be injected?"

"Injected, absorbed through the skin, chewed, smoked or simply inhaled. If you can think of a way to take it, someone has probably tried it, and whatever form it takes, it's always incredibly dangerous. It can be a hundred times more powerful than heroin, and when it's made in an illegal lab, the users have no idea what dose they're taking. One sniff can be enough to kill someone."

A cold realisation settled on Dan's shoulders. Neil would be getting ready to make his next move. Doug's arrest had been reported in the local news, along with allegations of fraud. As a calculating strategist, Neil would assume one of two outcomes: either the police were on to him, and he'd have to hide, or Dan might've seen the private keys and decided to grab them for himself. Whichever held true, Neil would stop at nothing to retrieve the cryptocurrency he believed was his, and he wasn't going to turn up and ask nicely.

"We have to find him," Dan said. "We have to find Neil, before he finds me."

CHAPTER 63

Their coffee finished, Dan and Alan sat side by side at Dan's kitchen table. Alan had nipped home to fetch his laptop and he was tapping out one search query after another as they tried to find traces of Neil Hawthorne.

"We're not making much progress," Dan said. "Take a break for a minute."

Alan sat back with a sigh. "I've looked for Neil online before. I didn't find much then, and I'm faring no better now. We need another angle. I know he's taken part in some sailing events, and I remember you mentioning that he owned a boat. We could try looking for that."

"No good. He told me sold it."

Alan raised an eyebrow and sent Dan a reproving look.

"Point taken," Dan said. "He probably lied, but even if he still has the boat, I have no idea what it was called. Can we search for boat ownership records online?"

"I don't think so, but what about going back to the photo? I've a feeling it was taken by the sea. There may be a boat in the background."

"I'll check." Dan scooped up his phone and found the picture he'd taken of Neil's photo. It was easy to see why

Alan had guessed at a seaside setting. Behind the smiling woman, presumably Felicity Petheridge, an array of poles poked up at odd intervals: the masts of yachts berthed below the camera's field of view. And that wasn't all. At the very edge of the photo, the shot was framed by the corner of a building. Tall and obviously very old, the building boasted two wooden balconies, one above the other, and it looked as though the walls were white with an elaborate arrangement of black timbers.

Dan zoomed in on the building, then he showed it to Alan.

"It looks familiar," Alan said. "Let me compare it to a few local harbours and I'll see what I can find."

Alan resumed his searches, intent on the screen. "No, it's not Brixham," he muttered. "And not Exmouth either. The problem is, once you start to think about it, there are harbours and marinas all along the coast, and we mustn't forget North Devon." Alan looked up. "Really, it could be anywhere. He could've taken his boat to France for all we know. Since we assume he's with someone else's wife, he'd have wanted to be away from prying eyes."

"They'd have wanted a bolthole nearby so they could snatch moments together; somewhere Felicity could visit at the drop of a hat and be back home before anyone noticed she'd been away."

"Speaking from experience?" Alan asked.

"No. I'm just putting myself in their shoes."

"Fair enough. I'll keep looking. In fact, you've given me an idea. They'd want somewhere with a romantic atmosphere."

Alan tapped the keys once more, and then he looked at Dan, beaming. "Got it!"

He turned the laptop so Dan could have a better view, and Dan studied the image of a large timbered house, its impressive facade studded with black beams. And there, at the building's corner, were the railings of two balconies, just as in the photo. It was a perfect match; Alan had done it.

"It's in Dartmouth," Alan said. "It's called York House and it's right next to the marina. Dartmouth is an attractive little place, ideal for illicit meetings, or so I would imagine."

The two men shared a smile.

"How would you feel about lunch in Dartmouth?" Dan asked. "It's a change of scene, and you never know who we might bump into. It could be... interesting."

"That has to be the understatement of the year," Alan replied. "Will you drive, or shall I?"

"My car's still playing up. Besides, you probably know the best route, don't you?"

"Do you have to ask?"

"No, I don't," Dan said. "Let's go."

DAN HAD NEVER BEEN to Dartmouth before, and he could see why Alan had described it as attractive. The narrow, winding streets gave the place an old-world charm, and there were plenty of small shops and cafes tucked away in unlikely corners. They soon found York House, and they stood next to it, gazing out at the gaggle of boats bobbing in the harbour.

"We'll act like tourists and have a wander around," Dan said. "Keep your eyes peeled."

"Okay, but we still don't know the name of the boat, so what are we looking for?"

"I don't know, but that's all the more reason to get started. Come on." Dan led the way along the pavement beside the harbour, examining each boat as he passed. There were craft of all shapes and sizes, from rowing boats that looked as though they'd seen one too many winters, to sleek yachts with gleaming white hulls and a profusion of stainless steel fixtures and fittings.

Dan nodded toward one particularly luxurious vessel. "Look at that beauty."

"I can't see the attraction. They say you can achieve the same effect by standing in the pouring rain while throwing fifty-pound notes into the air."

"You're not a natural sailor, then?"

"It's not that I don't like being on the water, and I have no problem with the little fishing boats, but I don't think much of these hulking great pleasure yachts. They're just status symbols, aren't they?"

"You might be right." Dan let his gaze wander from the luxury yacht to its more modest neighbour. It was a nice-looking boat and well looked after, but then he saw the boat's name and he tapped Alan's arm.

"What is it?" Alan asked.

"Look at that one. Look at its name."

"*The Felicitante*," Alan read from the boat's hull. "It could be a reference to Felicity, I suppose, but it might be a coincidence. It looks an Italian word, and I've no idea what it means."

"It's no coincidence. This must be Neil's boat. He likes to play games, to thumb his nose at everyone. He used CEG to commit fraud, then he hid the money inside their head office and he based his password on one of Doug's sayings. This is similar. He's having an affair with Felicity, so he's named his boat after her, but not in a way that's immediately obvious."

Dan looked around and spotted a bar with outdoor seating. "I think the photo of Felicity could've been taken over there. Let's grab a table. We can watch the boat and see if Neil turns up."

"You're not going to charge up to the boat and try to catch him by surprise?"

"Not this time," Dan said. "We're going to wait and see."

"Well, there's a first time for everything. Let's go."

They crossed the road and Dan chose a table with a good

view of the harbour while Alan went inside to order them some lunch and a drink. *We could be in for a long wait*, Dan thought, but as Alan returned with a couple of glasses of something pale and fizzy, there were signs of movement on *The Felicitante*, a dark figure flitting past the cabin windows.

"They only had bottled beer, and nothing decent," Alan grumbled as he sat down opposite Dan and plonked the glasses onto the table. "I got you this. It claims to be IPA, but it looks suspiciously like lager to me. It's—"

Alan stopped talking abruptly and followed Dan's gaze. "Ah, there's someone on board. Is it him?"

"I don't know," Dan said. "Someone might come out in a minute. Keep an eye on the cabin."

They waited, motionless, and when the cabin door opened, Dan held his breath, because there, sauntering onto the deck, taking his time and looking relaxed, was Neil Hawthorne.

"My God," Alan murmured. "I can't be sure, not from this distance, but that looks like the man who broke into your house." Alan sat up straighter. "If I go over there now, I'll be able to tell if he recognises me."

"I don't know, Alan. I don't think you should face him on your own, and if we go together, he might cut and run."

As they watched, Neil busied himself with the ropes on the deck, then he paced back and forth along the boat, bending down from time to time as though checking everything was in order.

"He's getting ready to leave." Dan jumped to his feet. "We have to stop him. I'll go and talk to him, see if I can persuade him to get off the boat."

"That's no good. I'll come with you."

"No. I made a mistake not taking you with me before, but this is different. We're in control, but we mustn't frighten him away or we'll never find him again. I want you to hang back, but just for a few minutes. I need you as backup. Be ready."

"All right," Alan said. "I don't like staying back here, but at least I'll be able to see what's going on. You can rely on me."

"I know. Wish me luck."

Without waiting for a reply, Dan set off across the road, striding purposefully. A narrow wooden boardwalk led down the side of *The Felicitante*, and Dan made for it. His first interaction with Neil would be critical, and Dan did his best to focus, to harness his adrenaline, heighten his senses. There was no way to predict what Neil would do next. So far, he'd confounded everyone.

Whatever happened in the next few seconds, Dan would have to think fast and act swiftly. In a battle of wits, they were evenly matched, but if Neil turned this into a fight, things would be very different. Neil might well have killed a man already, and if he had a weapon, Dan could be heading ever closer to a fatal confrontation. Dan breathed deep, the sea air filling his lungs, and he savoured the salty scent of the sea as if each breath might be his last.

CHAPTER 64

Hoping to grab some lunch, DI Spiller was heading across the CID office when a young woman hurried toward him, a slip of paper in her hand. What was her name? Sharon? She was a civilian employee who spent a lot of time answering the phone and collating data. She hadn't been with them long, but even so, he ought to remember her name. Whatever she was called, the young woman stopped in front of him, breathless.

"Are you all right?" Spiller asked, glancing at her lanyard. Her name was printed in a typeface too small for him to read from that distance, so he trawled his memory one last time and hazarded a guess. "Cheryl, isn't it?"

"That's right, Detective Inspector." Cheryl caught her breath. "Message for you. Urgent." She thrust the slip of paper toward him and Spiller took it.

"Thank you. By the way, 'guv'nor' will do. We're all on the same team, but if you feel the need to be more formal, you can call me DI Spiller." Spiller scanned the neat, handwritten message, then he read it again. He looked up to see Cheryl watching him expectantly.

"The caller was very insistent. This had to be passed on to you and no one else."

Spiller nodded slowly. "Some people seem to think I'm at their beck and call, as if I can be summoned at a moment's notice, like a plumber."

Cheryl's expression clouded. "Should I not have brought it to you? I field a lot of calls, but this one sounded legit."

"It's okay. You did the right thing. I'll follow it up. Thanks, Cheryl."

Cheryl exhaled as if relieved, then she bustled across the office, no doubt hurrying to her next task. *What I wouldn't give to have that much energy*, Spiller thought. Thinking of youth and energy, he looked for Collins and spied him working at his desk. A few strides took him there.

Collins sat up straight, arching his back. "All right, guv'nor? If it's about that report—"

"Never mind about paperwork," Spiller interrupted. "Did anyone ever manage to get hold of Neil Hawthorne?"

"No. I checked his address and went round there myself, but there was no one home. Semi-detached. Neat. The garden all tidy. I knocked on a few doors. It's a quiet street, but the neighbours said they rarely saw him. Kept himself to himself, so they said. It's always the way, isn't it?"

"How did the place look? Any sign that he might've done a runner?"

Collins thought for a moment. "Nothing out of the ordinary. The house looked lived in, but I couldn't see his car anywhere nearby. Not his regular car, anyway."

"What do you mean?"

"His next-door neighbour took the chance to have a moan. She reckons Hawthorne is a bit of a car nut. He owns a couple of motors, but he usually drives an old MG, and it makes a racket, apparently." Collins smirked as if privately amused.

"What's so funny?"

"Nothing really, but the lady wasn't bothered by the car

engine so much as the noise of the garage doors. She said she could hardly hear *Crossing Continents* the other day, whatever that is."

"It's on Radio Four," Spiller said. "I listen to it all the time, but you still haven't told me about Hawthorne's other car. I take it you checked the garage."

"Yes, guv. I looked through the window and there was a vehicle in there. It was covered in a tarpaulin but it was something fairly big, like an SUV. And before you ask, the garage door is one of those big steel shutters. Heavy duty. I guess it makes a noise when you open and close it."

"I'm interested in this hidden car. Did you run a check on it?"

"It's on my list, but to be honest, I've been swamped."

"Do it now, Collins."

"Yes guv." Collins set to work, hammering out the query to search the database of vehicles and their registered keepers. When he was done, Collins' face fell. "I should've got around to this before. As well as a 1968 MG MGB Roadster, Hawthorne owns a Porsche Cayenne Turbo, and he bought it brand new. Between them, they must've cost him a packet."

"No doubt. It makes you wonder where he got the money, but the important point is this: *Crossing Continents* is broadcast on Monday nights and Thursday mornings. I know you can play anything at any time these days, but if the neighbour was streaming her programme, she could've skipped back a bit and no harm done. So, she listens live. Put a pin in that thought, Collins."

"Yes, guv."

"Now, the neighbour thought the noise of the garage doors was worth complaining about, and to a police officer no less. She wouldn't have done that if she'd heard the doors during the morning. You expect a bit of noise in the daytime, but in the evenings, it's a different matter. Put the two observations together, and what do we see?"

"Hawthorne might've been using his Porsche on Monday night. The night Cooper was killed."

"Exactly. And afterwards, he hides his car away, covering it up to keep it from prying eyes. Run the Porsche's number through ANPR, and let's see if we get any hits."

"Right." It only took Collins a few minutes to complete the search, then he cursed under his breath. "On Monday night, the Porsche was caught coming off the roundabout onto Frog Street just after quarter to nine."

"My God. Nip along Western Way and you're at the quayside car park in no time." Spiller took out his phone and began making a call. On its own, the ANPR evidence meant little, but taken with the message he'd just received, it formed part of a picture. Spiller knew what he had to do. Neil Hawthorne must be apprehended. There was not a second to lose.

CHAPTER 65

Dan drew nearer to *The Felicitante*, keeping a watchful eye on Neil, ready to react. But Dan's approach went unnoticed. Neil was busy on the boat's deck, rushing from task to task, making preparations as if for departure.

Dan was almost level with the boat when Neil scuttled to the other side of the cabin and out of sight. Dan stopped walking. Had he been spotted? No. Neil re-emerged, bustling to the stern where he bent down and began coiling a rope.

"Ahoy there," Dan called out. "I'm looking to take a trip around the harbour. Can you point me in the right direction?"

Without looking up, Neil said, "No, not really. Try Google."

"That's a shame. I was hoping you might be able to help, Neil."

With a start, Neil stood bolt upright. "Dan. What are you doing here?" Neil's gaze flitted past Dan as he scanned the harbour. "Are you here on your own?"

"Yes. I came over for lunch. I've been wanting to see Dartmouth for a while, and it's a nice day, so I thought, why not? Anyway, I saw a familiar face, so I came over to say hello."

"Right."

"Is this your boat?"

"Yeah," Neil replied absently, still looking past Dan.

"You told me you'd sold it."

"Ah, yes." Neil focused on Dan, his eyes sharp. "I meant I'd sold my old boat. This one is fairly new."

"It's very smart. I thought you were short of money."

"I was, for a while, but I shifted a few assets around, cashed in my savings, and I was able to buy this one. She's my retirement plan." Neil's manner suddenly altered, and he beamed with pride. "Why don't you hop aboard? I'll show you around."

"Thanks, but I was going to have lunch. Why don't you join me? There's a place across the harbour."

"I'm afraid I haven't the time. I'm going to set sail soon. Just a little jaunt along the coast. You can come with me if you like, have lunch on board. I've got plenty of food."

"I don't think so." Dan paused, waiting to see what Neil's next move might be, but Neil wasn't going to be rushed. The man simply stood, looking down at Dan, his expression unreadable.

"It's a funny coincidence, seeing you here," Dan said. "Your name came up just yesterday. Have you heard what happened at CEG?"

Neil rubbed his chin. "I caught something on the local news. The police were called in for some reason, weren't they? I couldn't make much sense of it. They said something about Doug, and was someone taken ill?"

"That's right. It was Celine Grayson. She's okay now."

"I'm glad she's all right. What happened?"

"There was an incident," Dan said. "I was there, actually. In the server room."

"Oh? What were you doing down there? I thought you'd been let go."

"That's true, but I was following a lead, as you knew I would."

"Er, I'm not sure what you—"

"I found the private keys," Dan interrupted. "All of them."

Neil lowered his eyebrows as though Dan had just spoken in a foreign language.

"The police have them now," Dan went on. "I have to hand it to you, Neil. The way you got me to figure out the IP address, it was inspired. I suppose if the police hadn't been involved you'd have come calling on me by now, or maybe you would've broken into my house. Again."

Neil chuckled. "This is some pretty weird stuff you're coming out with, Dan. Are you feeling all right?"

"I'm fine. Never better."

"Are you sure? Only, from where I'm standing, you're beginning to sound like a man who's had a liquid lunch."

"Come on, Neil. You must've figured out that I didn't bump into you by chance today. We both know what I'm talking about. Come down here, and we'll see if we can come to an arrangement. Maybe we can both come out of this on top."

Neil's smile tightened. "Honestly, I have absolutely no idea what you're on about, Dan, but you're right, we should sit down and have a chat, catch up. Come aboard and we'll talk properly. We can have a beer."

"Not today. I must head back home. I've got a lot of things to arrange, but I thought I'd give you a chance to grab a slice of the action. It's the decent thing to do. After all, you must've worked hard to put away so much cryptocurrency." Dan took out his phone and pretended to study it. "It's a good job I took photos of the screen yesterday. I got most of the private keys. You can read them well enough if you zoom in, and as we both know, whoever has the keys has the currency."

Neil pulled a face as though swallowing something

indigestible. "You've lost me, mate. I don't know anything about these keys, but hang on and I'll come ashore, take a look. Maybe I can help."

"Sure. We can adjourn to a quiet corner somewhere."

"Give me a sec." Neil ducked into the cabin and returned a few seconds later, hastily donning a jacket and checking the pockets.

"There's no rush," Dan added, looking back along the boardwalk. This would be an ideal moment for Alan to appear, but where was he? He seemed to have vanished.

"I won't be long," Neil called out to someone on the boat, and Dan heard a woman's voice, a sing-song reply: "See you later. Take care."

"I didn't know you had company," Dan said. "Aren't you going to introduce me to your lady friend?"

"Not now," Neil replied. "Maybe later, if there's time."

"That's a pity. I've got a feeling I know who it is."

"I doubt it, Dan. I doubt that very much."

"Of course, you've always been so careful, haven't you?" Before Neil could respond, Dan raised his voice and said, "Hello, Felicity. Any chance of a chat?"

Neil half turned and called, "It's okay, darling. There's no need to trouble yourself. No need to come out."

Despite his entreaties, the cabin door opened and a woman stepped out. Dressed in pale linen trousers and a pink cotton shirt, the woman looked as though she'd done battle with middle age and emerged victorious. There were fine wrinkles at the corners of her eyes, but her hair was immaculate, her complexion had a healthy glow and her smile was warm. She was the woman in Neil's photograph, and Dan was sure that her name was Felicity Petheridge.

The woman smiled at Dan, but when she spoke, there was a hint of puzzlement in her tone. "Hello. I don't believe we've met."

"We haven't," Dan replied. "You must be Felicity. Neil's told me all about you. I'm Dan, by the way. How are you?"

"I'm fine, thank you, Dan. You're a friend of Neil's, are you?"

"That's right," Neil said quickly. "We're nipping out for a chat. Why don't you go back inside?"

Felicity's lips formed a disapproving pout. "I don't want to go back in. I can talk to your friend, can't I? Anyway, I could do with stretching my legs. I could come with you."

"Not this time," Neil replied. "It's all going to be very boring, very dull. We're going to talk about work, and you know how you hate all that."

"That's true. You men and your shop talk. It drives me mad." Sending Dan a smile, she added, "Do you work with Neil? Are you part of his new enterprise?"

"No. Actually, I know Neil from his old workplace. CEG. I worked there for a while. With Doug."

Felicity's face froze.

"I suppose you must know what's happened to Doug," Dan went on. "Frankly, I'm worried about him. At his age, I'm not sure how well he'll cope."

"What's happened? Is he all right?"

"Darling, don't—" Neil started, but Felicity cut him off.

"Is Doug all right? It's not his heart again, is it?"

"He wasn't taken ill," Dan said. "He's in police custody. Did you really not know? Surely he must've contacted you."

"I… I've been away for a few days. On holiday." Felicity shot Neil an angry look. "I told you, I needed to keep my phone on. Where is it? What have you done with it?"

"Don't worry, darling, we'll sort all this out," Neil said. He tried to touch her arm, but she snatched it away.

"Where is my phone?" Felicity demanded, her voice wavering.

Neil turned on Dan. "Why did you have to go and say that about Doug? Can't you see she's upset?"

"That wasn't my intention, but Felicity has a right to know. Her husband has been arrested, and he's facing serious charges."

"No. He can't be," Felicity said. "What's he supposed to have done?"

"There's no doubt about it, I'm afraid," Dan replied. "Doug unlawfully detained a young woman who works in the office. He threatened her and tied her up. He doesn't deny it."

Felicity's hand flew to her mouth. "No. Not my Doug. He wouldn't hurt a fly. He likes to boss people about, but he's never laid a hand on anyone. Never."

"You'd better tell that to the police," Dan suggested. "It might help at his trial."

"Yes. I'll do whatever I can. Of course I will. I'll go now. Give me a moment."

Felicity hurried back inside. Neil called after her, but she didn't reply.

"This is your bloody fault," Neil snapped, pointing a finger at Dan. "You've screwed everything up, you bloody idiot!"

Felicity returned, a silk scarf wrapped around her throat, and a determined expression on her face. Slinging the straps of her handbag over her shoulder, she made for the side of the boat.

"Felicity, no," Neil protested. "Stay here. I'll go and sort everything out. Let me deal with it."

"I'm leaving right this second," Felicity said. "Don't even think about trying to stop me."

Neil followed her to the side of the boat, wringing his hands. "But darling, he doesn't deserve you. He doesn't even love you, not like I do."

"Huh!" With practised ease, Felicity hooked a boarding ladder onto the side of the boat and climbed down to the boardwalk. Turning back to face Neil, she said, "You're so controlling. We used to have fun, but not anymore. I can't do the slightest thing without you watching me, telling me what to do, and it's unbearable. I can't stand it. This is the last straw."

"Please, darling, let me make this right," Neil called after her, but she took no notice.

Felicity hurried to Dan and said, "Where's my husband? Which police station did they take him to?"

"I believe he's being held at police headquarters in Exeter. I have the number if you want to call."

"Right. Thank you, but I have to get there. I'll need to figure out a taxi or something. Neil drove me here."

"I'll be going that way soon," Dan said. "I can give you a lift. If you like, I can drop you at home first, in case you want to change."

Felicity glanced down at her summery outfit. "Yes. That's very thoughtful of you. When are you planning to set off? I'm ready now, but I don't want to presume."

"Now is fine," Dan replied. "It'll be my pleasure."

"No!" Neil barked from the boat. "This isn't happening. I won't allow it."

Felicity turned to face Neil, her glare simmering with repressed rage. "I beg your pardon. What did you say to me?"

"I didn't mean it like that," Neil said. "It's just that I can't bear to see you go like this. What about our plans? Our future?"

"Cancelled," Felicity replied. "I don't know what I was thinking. I must've been mad, but I see it all now. You never wanted me. You wanted to beat Doug, to pay him back for the way he talked down to you all the time."

"That's not true."

"Yes, it is. Doug never trusted you, and now I know why." Felicity dismissed Neil with a wave of her hand. "You can send my things back to the house. Use a courier or something, because I never want to see you again. It's over."

Neil's expression changed in an instant, his show of servility vanishing, replaced by the cold, ruthless stare of a predator.

The hairs on the back of Dan's neck prickled. He reached out to Felicity, urging her to step back, to get behind him, and Felicity complied, just in time.

Neil swung himself over the side of the boat and swarmed down the ladder. More agile than Dan had given him credit for, Neil wasted no time in squaring up to Dan. "Give me your phone," Neil growled. "Give it to me now, and I'll let you leave. You can take her with you."

"You're not in a position to dictate terms," Dan said, keeping his voice level. He started to put his phone away, but Neil tried to snatch it, his left hand latching onto Dan's wrist. Dan managed to keep hold of his phone, and with his free hand, he grasped a fistful of Neil's shirt, pulling him close until the two men were nose to nose.

"Give it up," Dan warned. "You've lost."

Neil didn't reply, but his eyes glinted with malice, and his right hand was at work, scrabbling in his pocket. Did he have a weapon? Letting go of Neil's shirt, Dan fastened his fingers around Neil's forearm, but he was too late. Neil had found what he was looking for, and he pulled his hand from his pocket, something small and white protruding from his fist.

Dan didn't wait to find out what it was. He tossed his phone aside, sending it clattering to the boardwalk. Neil followed the phone with his gaze, and that lapse in concentration was all Dan needed. Freeing his left hand, Dan grabbed Neil's right arm with both hands. Whatever Neil was holding, he couldn't be allowed to use it. But Neil lashed out with his free hand, landing a punch on Dan's cheek, and then another that connected with his eye. Hot pain arced across Dan's skull, but he blinked it away. He held onto Neil's arm for grim death, because now he saw what was in Neil's hand. It was a small plastic bottle, and Neil's finger was laid across its top, ready to press down. It looked like some kind of spray pump, and if it contained fentanyl, one squeeze from Neil's finger would be enough.

Neil pulled back his fist, ready to strike again, but Dan saw a dark blur from the corner of his eye, and then someone was pushing past him. Alan was there, clutching Neil's left arm and forcing it down, twisting it behind Neil's back. Neil cried out, and Dan seized the moment. He kept hold of Neil's right arm with one hand, while with the other, he grasped Neil's little finger and bent it back, prying the plastic bottle from his grip. Grunting in pain, Neil let the bottle fall. He tried to kick it into the water, but Dan shoved him hard, and with his leg extended for a kick, Neil lost his balance and went down on his back. He fell from Dan's grip, but Alan was like a terrier with a rat, and he clung to Neil's arm, pinning him to the boardwalk.

Breathing hard, Dan squatted beside Neil and grabbed his other arm. Neil struggled for a second, but then he glanced to one side, and the fight went out of him. He lay on his back, staring up into the clouds. He'd admitted defeat.

Neil had looked at Felicity, and she was standing alone, sobbing like a frightened child, her hands covering her face and her shoulders shaking. She'd seen the man for what he was, glimpsed the ruthless monster within, and she was terrified.

There's no way back for him now, Dan thought. *And he knows it.* He stared down at Neil, but the man refused to look him in the eye. Dan had no words, which was a damned shame. It would've felt good to tell Neil what he thought of him, but Dan let it go. Instead, he looked to Alan and said, "Thanks."

"No problem," Alan replied. "I cut that a bit fine. Sorry. I decided to call the police, but I couldn't get through to Spiller. I had to leave a message, and then Spiller called me back. You might like to know what he said."

"Go on."

"He said that on no account were we to approach Mr Hawthorne. He said we were to keep out of it, for our own safety."

Dan almost laughed. There might come a time when he would listen to Spiller's well-meant advice, but not today. Today, with Alan's help, he had come out on top, and that was all that mattered.

"The cavalry are on their way," Alan added, and when Dan cocked an ear, he heard the wail of sirens, at least two of them, growing closer all the while.

~

When Neil and Felicity had been whisked away in a pair of patrol cars, Alan and Dan strolled back along the boardwalk, heading toward the town. They had strict instructions to report to the nearest police station, but they both needed a minute to recover from their encounter.

"Did you hear what the police said about that little bottle of fentanyl?" Alan asked.

"Yes. I presume Neil used it to kill Seb. I wonder where he got it from."

"That's not the point, Dan. It could've killed you in a second."

"Then it's a damned good job you turned up when you did. I was taking a beating. I think Neil must've been going to the gym."

Alan stopped walking, and Dan followed suit.

"What's up?" Dan asked.

"You could've died, but I was late, and not for the first time. Yesterday it took me too long to find you, and I was slow at Haytor. I feel terrible. I'm not up to this, Dan. I'm not brave like you."

"Actually, you might be the bravest man I've ever known," Dan said.

"Don't make fun of me, please."

"I mean it, Alan. I can be a bit impulsive, but you're not. You stop and think, and you understand the risks, but you dive in anyway."

Alan shook his head, unconvinced.

"Listen," Dan went on, "if you hadn't stayed back and called Spiller, today could've ended very differently. If anyone's to blame, it's me for constantly jumping in with my size nines when a sensible man would wait."

"Even so—"

"Whatever else you may think, do not blame yourself," Dan interrupted. "You saved my life today, and nobody ever had a better friend. But I'll tell you what, next time I go to confront a murder suspect, I'm taking you with me."

"Next time?"

"Yes. You wouldn't want to miss out on all this kind of thing, would you?"

Alan tilted his head to one side, looking doubtful, but then he cracked a smile. "No, I really don't think life would be the same without it. I wouldn't miss it for the world."

"Me neither," Dan replied. "Shall we go and give our statements?"

"We'd better."

They started walking again, and when they reached the road, Alan looked over at the bar. "You know, I think I can see our lunch still sitting on that table. Do you think they might wrap it up for us? I'm starving."

"No harm in asking," Dan said. "But whatever happens, let's go to the pub tonight and have a huge dinner."

"It's a deal. By the way, it's your round."

"I thought it might be," Dan said. "I'd better bring my credit card. I have a feeling it's going to be quite a night."

MONDAY

CHAPTER 66

E arly evening in Exeter, and the end of a warm
summer's day. A few enterprising bars had placed
tables on the pavement and they were doing a brisk trade in
cold beer, but Dan and Sam breezed past them, noticing little
but each other. Besides, they were in a hurry. Dan had
reserved a table at Artie's, and they were late, having lingered
over their meal longer than they should've, enjoying each
other's company.

They arrived just in time to claim their table, and as they
finished ordering their drinks, a jazz band started playing,
and the conversation in the room died down to a murmur.

Dan listened carefully, trying to decide if the band were
any good. They seemed to be feeling their way through the
tune, but every time Dan recognised the melody, it slipped
away as if determined to be free. Still, as their drinks arrived,
Dan found himself tapping his toes to the rhythm, and Sam
looked happy, so the evening was going well, wasn't it?

Sam noticed him studying her, and said, "Are you okay?"

"Yes. I am if you are."

"I'm having a lovely time. It's nice in here, isn't it? A bit of
a change from the Boar."

"I like the Boar better," Dan said. "It's more down to earth."

"Blimey, I never thought you'd prefer a country pub to a fancy city bar. Mind you, we've seen you in the Boar a fair bit over the weekend. You and Alan have hardly been away from the place."

"We've been celebrating; the end of a case and the start of something new."

"Oh? And what might that be?"

"I've decided to turn professional," Dan said. "I'm going to try my hand at investigating cases for paying clients. DI Spiller gave me the idea. He seemed to think I've found something I'm good at, and now I've had time to think about it properly, I agree."

"If that's what you want, you should do it."

"You're not going to try and talk me out of it?"

"No, I'm not. When you get stuck into something, you generally rub a few folks up the wrong way, but in the end you help people, and you put things right. I say, go for it. You've been looking for something since you came here. This might be it or it might not, but you'll never know unless you try."

Dan had no idea what to say, and before he could frame a reply, Sam added, "But sometimes, I wonder... never mind."

"Wonder what?"

"It's nothing really, but I sometimes wonder, with you always being so keen to pick things apart, what you see when you look at me." Finishing her sentence in a rush, Sam hurriedly took a sip of her gin and tonic, lifting her balloon-shaped glass as if trying to hide behind it.

Dan took a breath and let it out slowly. "When I first saw you—"

"When you came in the shop," Sam interrupted. "You were in your running gear."

"That's right. I noticed your smile, and the light in your

eyes. I liked that smile very much, and I wanted to see it again, as often as possible."

"Not bad," Sam said. "But there must be more to it than that. I know you, and you're always trying to figure out what makes people tick."

"Not with you. With you, it's different. With you, I don't know what to think from one minute to the next. I only know what I feel."

"And what's that?" Sam asked, her eyes wide.

Dan searched for the right words but could scarcely put a sentence together. "I don't know how to explain. How about if I show you?"

"All right then." Sam leaned closer, and Dan went in for a kiss, his heart pounding in time to the band's double bass. But then Sam was pulling away, leaving him hanging.

Dan sat back. "Sorry. I thought…"

"It's all right, but look who's here." Sam nodded at someone over his shoulder, and Dan turned to see Joe Clayton and Teri Petheridge sitting at a corner table, intent on watching the band.

"Oh dear," Dan said. "This could be awkward."

"You're not kidding."

"Maybe we should try somewhere else. Unless you'd like to stay and listen to the music, that is."

Sam wrinkled her nose. "Do you know what? Jazz isn't really my thing. I can take it or leave it."

"Me too. Shall we look for another bar?"

"No. We've had a nice meal, and I've had a lovely time. Why don't we head home?"

"Oh, sure, if that's what you want." Dan tried to hide his disappointment. "I can leave this drink – it's only fizzy water with a fancy label – but what about yours. Do you want to wait until you've finished it?"

Sam lifted her drink and drained it in one go before

plonking the empty glass on the table. "Problem solved." She began collecting her bag and coat.

They stood at the same time, and as they headed for the door, Sam took his arm.

"I was thinking," Sam said, "about what we were saying before."

"Oh yes?"

"Yeah." Sam paused while they exited the bar. Outside, in the fresh air of the warm summer evening, she turned to him, standing close and said, "You reckon that you don't try and work out my personality and all that, but I wonder what you'd think if you saw my flat."

"I..." Dan swallowed. "Sam, are you inviting me back to your place?"

"Might be. If I was, what would you say?"

"I'd say, that would be very nice."

"*Very nice?* Is that the best you can do?"

"No, I'm sure I can think of something better," Dan said. "I'll see what I can come up with on the way home."

"You'd better," Sam replied, and arm in arm, they strolled through the quiet streets of Exeter.

EPILOGUE

D S Kulkarni was hard at work when she took the call from DI Blakey of Plymouth CID.

"Detective Sergeant Kulkarni," Blakey began, "I thought you might like to know, Jeremy Parker told us where they've been processing the stolen motors. A lock-up garage on the edge of Stonehouse. We've done a search, and we've turned up enough forensic evidence to arrest Aaron and Lee Parker."

"That's great."

"It wasn't hard," Blakey said. "They were careless. They stripped off the number plates and chucked them in somebody else's skip, but the guy who'd hired the skip saw them do it, and he pulled the plates out. Like a good citizen, he was going to report it to the police, but he hadn't got around to it. Anyway, the guy identified both Aaron and Lee from their mugshots, and it turned out that the number plates had fingerprints from both brothers. Plus, we've got gloves and masks from the site, all with DNA inside, and needless to say, we have their DNA on file from their previous arrests. We've got a solid match for each brother. They've got a lot of questions to answer."

"When are you taking them in?"

"Later today. That's why I'm calling. I wondered if you'd like to be in on the arrest."

Kulkarni hesitated. It would be good to see the case through, but she had so much work on, she couldn't afford the time, could she?

"It's tempting," Kulkarni said, "but I'm up to my neck in it at the moment."

"That's a shame. It would've been nice to have you along."

"I'm happy to leave it to you and your team, sir," Kulkarni said carefully. There'd been a hint of warmth in Blakey's voice, a suggestion of overfamiliarity that put her instantly on her guard. Even so, she couldn't afford to seem disinterested in a case that had started on her desk, so she added, "Maybe, if you can spare the time, you could let me know how it goes."

"No problem. I'll give you a call. Nice talking to you. Hope we can work together again sometime." A pause, and then he added, "You can drop the *sir*. We're not so formal over here. It's Russ. You're Anisha, aren't you?"

"Yes, that's right."

"What do you go by? Neesh?"

"Er, not really. Anisha is fine." Kulkarni pressed a hand against her temple. It was time to steer the conversation back to work. "Actually, Russ, I do have an idea."

"Oh yeah?"

"Yes, do you remember DC Collins?"

"I do. Seemed like a good bloke."

"He is, but he could use some more experience. He's aiming to make DS, and if he came over to help out on the arrests, it would be good for him."

"Okay. If you can clear it with your guv'nor, send Collins along. Always glad of another pair of hands."

"Especially when they're not being paid from your budget?"

"No comment," Blakey intoned. "Tell your DC to give me a shout."

"Will do," Kulkarni said, and she ended the call. Rising from her seat, she made for the DI's office.

The guv'nor wouldn't object to Collins taking a trip to Plymouth. Since Hawthorne had confessed to Seb's murder, along with a string of other offences, Spiller had been Mr Cheerful. Right now, she could probably get him to sign off on just about anything, but this temporary reassignment for Ben Collins would be enough of a win. As for Ben, he'd be pleased for the chance of some action, and he'd owe her a favour. *It's a win-win situation*, Kulkarni thought. *And that doesn't happen every day.*

CELINE OPENED HER EYES. She must've dropped off again. The hospital room was warm, and the stuffy air kept sending her to sleep.

She turned her head. Patrick was still sitting there. He must've been there for hours.

Patrick leaned forward and took her hand gently. "How are you doing? Do you need anything?"

"A glass of water maybe." Celine shifted into a more upright position and took the cup Patrick offered.

"It's mineral water," he said. "I fetched it from the shop while you were asleep. There was a jug of tap water on the table, but it wasn't cold."

"Thanks." Celine sipped from the cup and placed it on the table. "You don't have to stay, you know. I'll be fine."

"I want to stay for as long as I can. I..." Patrick's lip twitched as though he was having a hard time finding the right words. "I keep thinking about what might've happened, and I'm so sorry. I should never have got rid of your old meds."

"It's all right. I refilled the prescription. I'd picked it up that day."

"But if you hadn't…" Patrick cradled her hand between his. "Celine, I don't know what to say. I've been a jerk recently. I was so wrapped up in my exams and everything, I got so…"

"Uptight?" Celine suggested. "A control freak? Impossible to live with?"

"All those things and more. I'll never forgive myself."

"Well, you've apologised, and I know you mean it. You could carry all this guilt around with you forever, but what good would that do? Wouldn't it be better to put it behind us, to move on?"

"Can you do that? Can you forgive me?"

Celine offered a shy smile. "What do you think?"

"I think…" Patrick sniffed. "I think you're the most wonderful person in the whole world, and if you'll let me, I'll spend the rest of my life working hard every day to be the partner you deserve."

Later, when Celine looked back on their kiss, she'd place it firmly in her top ten kisses of all time. Maybe even the top five. But then, in her life with Patrick, there were so many to choose from.

≈

Thank you for reading Accomplice to Murder.
I hope that you enjoyed it.
You can get the series prequel free at:
michaelcampling.com / freebooks

MICHAEL CAMPLING

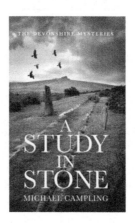

AUTHOR NOTES

IS EMBERVALE A REAL PLACE?

The village of Embervale is entirely fictional, but I imagine it to be somewhere in the Teign Valley in Devon which is where I have lived for over 25 years. The Teign (pronounced 'teen') is our local river. The other villages, towns and cities mentioned are inspired by their real-life counterparts, but they are used in a fictionalised way. In the descriptions of Exeter and Plymouth, real street names are used to give a sense of those places, but again, they are painted with the brush strokes of fiction.

Rougemont Gardens, the ruins of St Catherine's Almshouses, the quay, the Old Custom House, the beautiful cathedral and Cathedral Green are all real locations in Exeter but are used in a fictionalised way.

Similarly, York House is a real and rather impressive building in Dartmouth, but is used in fictional context.

Throughout this book, businesses, shops, cafes, pubs and hotels are all fictional, except for when Alan reels off a list of pubs near Hound Tor. The establishments he mentions are real. I didn't change those names because, although they plan to visit the Rugglestone Inn, their time at the pub is only referred to in passing. Also, I don't think I could come up with a better name for a country pub than the Rugglestone Inn.

WAS THE BAEDEKER BLITZ REAL?

Yes. Also known as the Baedeker Raids, these Luftwaffe bombing raids took place in the UK during April and May in 1942. Rather than attacking military or industrial targets, the raids focused on cultural and historic sites in the hope of denting British morale. Like many cities, Exeter was badly damaged, and this explains the odd mix of old and modern buildings found in its centre. Exeter Cathedral was one of the main targets for the raids, but it escaped serious damage.

WAS AN UNEXPLODED BOMB FOUND IN EXETER?

There certainly was, and it provided one of the initial inspirations for this story. In March 2021, a German World War II bomb containing 1,000kg (2,200lb) of explosive was discovered in a residential area of Exeter. The bomb was deemed too unstable to move, so it was detonated in a controlled explosion. The bomb was covered with a 400 tonne box of sand, and a ditch was dug around the site to reduce ground shock. If you search online you can watch footage of the explosion and see the plume of smoke. There was significant damage to nearby buildings but, as far as I know, when the dust settled nothing suspicious was revealed.

DID YOU MAKE UP THE LEGEND OF JAY'S GRAVE?

No. The legend is very much as Alan describes it. The grave is near Hound Tor, and there are always fresh flowers beside the headstone, although no one is ever seen putting them there.

There are also the remains of a medieval village near Hound Tor, and the car park is free, so why not come and visit? There used to be a mobile cafe in the car park, selling mugs of tea and hot snacks in little plastic baskets. It was called The Hound of the Basket Meals. Sadly, it isn't there anymore.

MORE BEER?

As usual in the Devonshire Mysteries, the drinks imbibed are all real brands, even the fancy gin and tonic enjoyed by Nicola. I do not receive any reward for doing this, but I do try to encourage local businesses, and there are many enterprising people setting up food and drink businesses in Devon.

IS THERE REALLY A CLIMBING ROUTE ON HAYTOR CALLED ACCOMPLICE TO MURDER?

Yes, there is, and I couldn't resist using it for the title of this book. Although Haytor is by no means a mountain, I wouldn't want to fall off it. People do climb the tor to practise their skills, and I tried to describe the route reasonably accurately. That said, the geography is there to support the story, not the other way around.

ARE THE POLICE PROCEDURES ACCURATE?

The Devon and Cornwall Police play quite a large part in this book, and I did a fair bit of research in an effort not to stray too wildly from real life. However, the Devonshire Mysteries are not police procedurals, nor are they gritty detective thrillers. These stories have a certain tone and it's important that I don't alter that too much. I tried to use only as much detail as was necessary for the story.

ARE THE MEDICAL DETAILS ACCURATE?

As with the police procedure, the medical details are based on research, but this book is a mystery, not a medical thriller. I'm sure a pharmacist could pick holes in my references to drugs and medicines, but I hope I've used these details in a way that isn't beyond the bounds of reason.

WHERE DID THE FENTANYL COME FROM?

I didn't think it was necessary to go into this in detail. Fentanyl is a highly dangerous drug that has found its way onto the streets, and it is available in various forms, including a spray pump. At one point we are party to the murderer's thoughts as he decides that it will take time to source and prepare his materials. This had to be an oblique reference or it would've spoiled the plot. I considered writing the details into the confrontation between Dan and Neil, but it would've felt forced and contrived, so I steered clear of it. Too often we see a villain pause in the middle of the action to explain his dastardly plans, and I didn't want to go there.

WILL YOU TALK TO MY BOOK GROUP?

Let's see what we can do. Please get in touch at: michaelcampling.com/contact

ANYTHING ELSE?

I hope I've covered your questions, but if there's something you'd like to know, please join my website at michaelcampling.com. Members can post comments on any article, and that's a good way to get an answer from me. Membership of the site will always be free and gives access to snippets of upcoming work and my regular photographs of Devon.

SIGNING OFF

I'll say goodbye for now. Thank you for joining Dan, Alan and the other Devonians on this mysterious journey. This book was a little different in that it involved the police a lot more than in the earlier stories, but I hope it remained true to the main characters and gave you something extra to enjoy. The Devonshire Mysteries aren't done yet, and I hope to bring you more stories soon.

The best way to find out about upcoming books is via my readers' group, The Awkward Squad, where you can also claim the series prequel, *A Study in Stone*, for free, and you'll also get an exclusive, not-for-sale Devonshire Mystery story, *Mystery at the Hall*, plus you'll get access to a specially written serialised Devonshire Mystery, *Death at Blackingstone Rock*.

Here's the place to learn more:
michaelcampling.com/freebooks

I hope to hear from you soon. Until then, happy reading and take care,

Mikey Campling
July 2022
Teign Valley,
Devon

ACKNOWLEDGMENTS

As always, my first thanks must go to Sue for keeping the faith.

Thank you to these regular supporters who send me mugs of tea via ko-fi.com/mikeyc: Lara, Cynthia, Lynn, Kathleen, Michele.

Thanks also to keen-eyed advance readers, Alan, Bridgit Davis, Dave Evans, Doreen Fernandes, Laura Johnson, Bev Scammel, Jean Soderquist, Helen Valenzuela, Rosalie Williams, Saundra Wright and Pauline.

The epigraph was taken from *I Ain't Much, Baby–But I'm All I've Got*, in which the author, Jess Lair, Ph.D, attributes the quote to an unnamed student.

ABOUT THE AUTHOR

Michael (Mikey to friends) is a full-time writer living and working on the edge of Dartmoor in Devon. He writes stories with characters you can believe in, and plots you can sink your teeth into. His style is vivid but never flowery; every word packs a punch. His stories are complex, thought-provoking, atmospheric and grounded in real life.

You can start reading his work for free with a complimentary mystery book plus a starter library which you'll receive when you join Michael's readers' group, which is called The Awkward Squad. You'll receive free books and stories, plus a newsletter that's actually worth reading. Learn more and start reading today at: michaelcampling.com/freebooks

[f] facebook.com/authormichaelcampling

[twitter] twitter.com/mikeycampling

[instagram] instagram.com/mikeycampling

[a] amazon.com/Michael-Campling/e/B00EUVA0GE

[BB] bookbub.com/authors/michael-campling

ALSO BY MICHAEL CAMPLING

One Link to Rule Them All:

michaelcampling.com / find-my-books

THE DEVONSHIRE MYSTERIES

A Study in Stone (an Awkward Squad bonus)

Valley of Lies

Mystery at the Hall (an Awkward Squad bonus)

Murder Between the Tides

Mystery in May

Death at Blackingstone Rock (an Awkward Squad bonus)

Accomplice to Murder

THE DARKENINGSTONE SERIES:

Breaking Ground - A Darkeningstone Prequel

Trespass: The Darkeningstone Book I

Outcast — The Darkeningstone Book II

Scaderstone — The Darkeningstone Book III

Darkeningstone Trilogy Box Set

© 2022 Michael Campling All rights reserved.
No portion of this book may be reproduced in any form without permission
from the copyright holder, except as permitted by copyright law.
This is a work of fiction. Names, characters, places, and incidents either are the
products of the author's imagination or are used fictitiously. Any resemblance
to actual persons, living or dead, businesses, companies, events, or locales is
entirely coincidental.

Made in the USA
Monee, IL
12 September 2023

42618538R00333